PRAISE FOR *BITTERBLOOM*

"Beautifully grotesque, hauntingly romantic, and as twisty as a woodland path—I loved every minute of *Bitterbloom*."

—**Hannah Whitten**, *New York Times* bestselling author of *For the Wolf*

"An eerie narrative bound skillfully together by luscious, biting prose, *Bitterbloom* wears the trappings of gothic romance like a crimson lace cloak—familiar yet enticing, with plenty of secrets lurking in the dark."

—**Maggie Rapier**, *USA Today* bestselling author of *Soulgazer*

"Brimming with emotion and told in fairytale prose, *Bitterbloom* perfectly captures the ache of female rage, and the lengths we will go to in order to escape disempowerment."

—**Lyndall Clipstone**, critically acclaimed author of *Tenderly, I am Devoured*

"Ethereal and gothic, *Bitterbloom* drips haunting imagery from every page. A beautiful exploration of the blood-soaked sins of religion, the power of women allowed to be their own, and the difference between never dying and truly living. I couldn't put it down!"

—**Alexandra Kennington**, author of *Blood Beneath the Snow*

"Dark, visceral, and ultimately redemptive, *Bitterbloom* is a mesmerizing journey. Readers will find themselves both lost and found in this riveting tale of reckoning."

—**Autumn Krause**, critically acclaimed author of *Grave Flowers*

"King's prose rings with the haunting timbre of a Reaper's bell and charts the necessary pains and joys of being alive. Decadently rotten and tightly plotted, *Bitterbloom* is for anyone who yearns for a side of horror with their fantasy romance."

—**Allison Saft**, *New York Times* bestselling author of *A Far Wilder Magic*

"A wickedly sharp and sumptuous tale, *Bitterbloom* rings with heartache, delicious prose, and spine-chilling twists and turns. The gruesome world that King has created will grip you by the throat and keep you turning pages late into the night."

—**Ruth McKell**, author of *Honey in Her Veins*

"*Bitterbloom* is a beautiful, macabre thing. A sharp-edged, dark fairytale of a book that will lure readers in and then haunt them."

—**Amanda Linsmeier**, author of *A Dance With Death*

PRAISE FOR *SPIT BACK THE BONES*

"Gruesomely romantic, *Spit Back the Bones* pulls you in as surely as the bog does. Gripping, ethereal, and ultimately hopeful."

—**Hannah Whitten**, *New York Times* bestselling author of *For the Wolf*

"Gorgeous and unsettling in the best of ways, *Spit Back the Bones* is an eerie, passionate meditation on grief, loss, and family, anchored by fierce protagonist Mila, whose voice simmers with longing and righteous rage. The unforgettable, beautifully crafted atmosphere of the bog coupled with King's lyrical prose makes this a story you won't soon forget."

—**Claire Legrand**, *New York Times* bestselling author of *Sawkill Girls*

"Emotional and atmospheric, *Spit Back the Bones* is dripping in heady bog water. You'll never look at black flies the same way again."

—**Saratoga Schaefer**, author of *Serial Killer Support Group* and *Trad Wife*

"*Spit Back the Bones* will consume you. King's world is nightmarishly beautiful; her setting will claw beneath your skin and settle deep in your bones. Beyond its delectably dark prose, this debut offers a deeper exploration of love and loss and the monstrous form one's grief can take in the dark."

—**Skyla Arndt**, author of *Together We Rot* and *House of Hearts*

"Beautiful and impossibly filled with the stench of stagnant water and loamy earth, *Spit Back the Bones* is a slurry of pain, rage, and hope. In her haunting debut, King exposes the horrors of coming home to the ghosts we never really bury and the pervasive rot of regret."

—**Tanya Pell**, author of *Her Wicked Roots* and *Cicada*

"Teagan Olivia King's debut tears through you like a scream and shows how home can be a place that holds you and haunts you all at once. Mila's dedication to her family will speak to anyone who has a sordid past they just can't shake—but can't bear to let go. Small-town religious corruption, a rekindled romance, and a bloodthirsty bog culminate in a story that will creep you out as much as it will lovingly embrace you."

—**Isa Agajanian**, author of *Modern Divination*

"Lush with dread and steeped in folklore, *Spit Back the Bones* is a spellbinding fever dream of grief, rage, and the monsters we inherit."

—**Lindy Ryan**, author of *Bless Your Heart*

"*Spit Back the Bones* is at once grotesque and hauntingly beautiful, exploring grief, rage, love, and of course, power—those who take it, and those who reclaim it. A monstrous debut that yanks at the heartstrings so well it hurts."

—**Amanda Linsmeier**, author of *Starlings* and *Six of Sorrow*

"Grief, family legacy, and religious trauma make for a truly authentic American gothic, this one possessed by the grasping hands of a living bog. *Spit Back the Bones* is equally gruesome as it is beautiful."

—**Dawn Kurtagich**, bestselling author of *The Thorns*

BITTERBLOOM

ALSO BY

TEAGAN OLIVIA KING

Spit Back the Bones

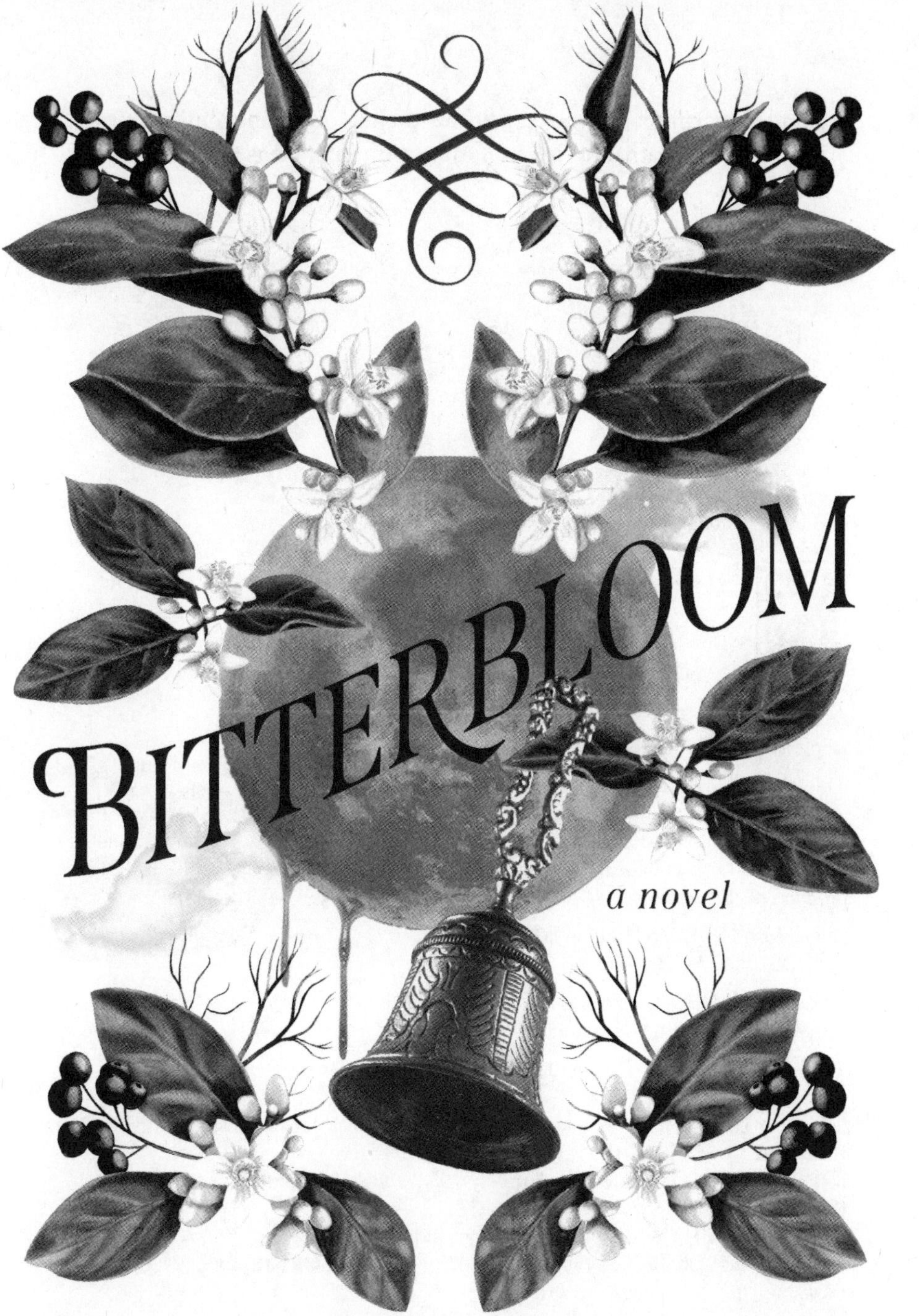

BITTERBLOOM

a novel

TEAGAN OLIVIA KING

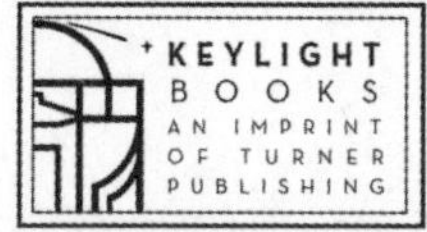

Content warning: This novel features themes including abuse, murder, gore, animal death, and religious abuse/trauma. Please read with care.

KEYLIGHT BOOKS
AN IMPRINT OF TURNER PUBLISHING COMPANY
Nashville, Tennessee
www.turnerpublishing.com

Cover design by Faceout Studio, Molly von Borstel
Book design by Ashlyn Inman

Library of Congress Cataloging-in-Publication Data
Names: King, Teagan Olivia author

Title: Bitterbloom / by Teagan Olivia King.
Description: Nashville, Tennessee : Keylight Books, an imprint of Turner Publishing Company, 2026. | "TW: abuse, murder, gore, animal death, religious abuse/trauma."
Identifiers: LCCN 2025019654 (print) | LCCN 2025019655 (ebook) |
ISBN 9798887981253 hardcover | ISBN 9798887981260 paperback |
ISBN 9798887981277 epub
Subjects: LCGFT: Gothic fiction | Fantasy fiction | Novels
Classification: LCC PS3611.I58624 B58 2026 (print) | LCC PS3611.I58624 (ebook) |
DDC 813/.6—dc23/eng/20250616
LC record available at https://lccn.loc.gov/2025019654
LC ebook record available at https://lccn.loc.gov/2025019655

Printed in the United States of America

To all those who suffer in silence,
who walk through every day knowing pain.
You are not alone.

In the narrow streets of the big town, toward evening when the sun was setting and the clouds shone like gold on the chimney tops, people would hear a strange sound like that of a church bell.

—*The Bell*, Hans Christian Andersen

Village of
Rixton
LYSDIN
Blackbourne Castle
Avery Manor
THE Queen's Road
River Thine
Farmer Whitley's House & Barn
Bakery
Rowan Wood
Village Path
Vicarage
Church
IDLEWILD

one

Nine days before I enter the rowan wood, I wear fabric in shades of bruised slate, the woolen swathes reeking of death and my mother's perfume. Notes of citrus and asphodel assail my senses while the villagers gather around the grave site, each handful of earth tossed down a solemn prayer to the gods.

Lilith Corley lies in satin beneath the oaken lid of her casket, a face so pale she is like the first shock of winter. Across the visage of freshly dug earth, her parents hold each other, their eyes dry. Lilith's death is only the latest in the long line our village has witnessed over many years, and there simply aren't enough tears to go around anymore.

Three days past, from my bedchamber window, I watched when they dragged her from the banks of the river, limp and wilting…

A chill breeze brushes up from the River Thine down in the valley, catching Father's black robes and throwing them about his towering frame like wisps of shadow. He holds fraying Blessed Scriptures in one hand, reciting the final rites. A church bell tolls—a lone, somber note.

In Rixton, villagers claim bells are for protection, rung to keep evil at bay, but I sometimes think it is the opposite. They welcome the darkness and death—open doors for it to slip in, curl its talons around our necks, and choke us.

The cold bites at my pallid cheeks, the color there long-since faded. Silver-white curls tumble down my back, and twists of lace cover the blackened bruises on my wrists. No need for the villagers to see what they already believe. That I am cursed. Touched by the Devil, by Erybrus himself.

They whisper he came to me one night, licked a silver-slitted tongue across my bones, and made me pale and sickly, like a corpse left to rot. The villagers don't know the truth of it, though.

The way the pain creaks along my bones and chest. The way I press my finger against Mother's old sewing needles and bleed black. They know nothing of the monsters that haunt my waking hours.

These visions are my most hidden, horrible secret. I have kept them from everyone I know: Father, even the woman I used to call my most beloved friend, Clara. And they despise me for it, this illness that quickens my veins. Call it a curse. It is easier to blame the gods when the minds of men cannot make sense of the truth. Or would rather turn a blind and hateful eye to the things they do not understand.

While the villagers raise their voices in a prayer of mourning, my pulse beats wildly in my throat, and I hurry a finger to the skin, if only to feel the beating.

A-live, a-live, a-live.

The strange *wrongness* to my heartbeat appeared in the months after my mother's death, with the blush of girlhood still on my cheeks. On a spring morning sometime after we buried her in the old churchyard, I ran along the riverbanks, picking forget-me-nots and daisies to twist into a knot for my mother's headstone. To my left, Clara stood ankle-deep in mud, weeds in her hair, trying her best to make me laugh.

But it did not work.

My little legs froze.

To my right, the rowan wood reached toward the heavens, casting darkness to the grass at my booted feet. I heard something that day—the brittle ringing of a bell.

My chest squeezed so tightly I thought I would die. Stars of brilliant white pain shot through my arms and legs, and my stomach clenched when I fell to my knees.

Clara called my name. Once, twice…My heart slipped, tugged like a fish on a string. My vision clouded with black, and I was lost to the world.

I rose the next morning, tied to a chair by my father's hand. The ropes that held me there left my skin broken, shadowed blood like ink drops in water. The only explanation my father ever provided was that I was simply cursed by the gods.

Now, staring across the graveyard to where the trees bite away the landscape, the same pain I experienced that day by the river blossoms at the root of my skull. It takes my breath away, and I turn my gaze to Lilith's burial plot. Blood pounds in my ears, hot with fear.

Lilith was a summer child, Mother always said. My opposite, with her dark hair and a smile that brightened any room she walked into. My heart is simply another thing that makes us different. It might not work the way the gods designed, but at least it pumps. At least it harbors the shadowed blood in my veins.

Lilith's heart is as still as stone now.

I still remember the body found one peaceful morning before Mother died: pale lips crusted in flaxen vomit, limbs stiff as tree trunks, and violet stains ringing an open mouth, as though the woman had been freshly kissed. My throat dries when I picture Lilith in a similar state, buried beneath my feet.

Even Mother's death, with her twisted tongue and eyes as wholly black as midnight, was *wrong*. Unnatural.

And I wonder, sometimes, if she was cursed too.

Finally, the last handful of earth is tossed onto the mound, and the villagers make their way back up the hill toward the church. Their black skirts and coattails follow them like so many raven feathers. They will eat now—Lilith's corpse still half-warm while they feast above her bones.

I wait until the churchyard is empty. Father foregoes the funeral feast and disappears into a black carriage, a banner embroidered with a silver rose hanging from the driver's box. Death does not wait long in Rixton. It is a hungry, vicious thing, and there is another deathbed to attend to. Though, for once, it is not a woman with poison stained on her lips.

Beyond the village, past the wheat fields and meadows of Avery Manor,

stands Blackbourne Castle. When the brother-gods still walked the earth, before the Rending, the structure was freshly birthed. Now, it rots and its lineage of men along with it.

For weeks, rumors have circled of the Lord Black's condition. Some in Rixton say he is simply too old for this world. Others speak of evil rife in his castle, the corrupt worship of Erybrus. His son, Ransom, will not say what it is his father is dying of. He hardly comes into the village at all. But my father has been visiting the castle every day for the last week.

Death is an unforgiving master. He comes for us all in the end.

I crouch in the dirt, running gritty crumbles of it between my fingers. This is the third Sunday in a row we have buried bodies in the churchyard. They are appearing on the riverbank faster than they used to. All of them women. All from Rixton, skin wan and lips bruised purple.

Villagers whisper to themselves of a curse enacted during the Rending—when the god Ithrandril, father of light and life, separated and cast his brother, Erybrus, father of lies and deceit, into shadow. But I do not think these deaths are the work of our brother-gods.

Mother used to tell me there were monsters in the rowan wood. I have seen them. Prowling at the edges of the graveyard, wisps of smoke that smell of rot. Who else could be killing the girls of Rixton? Better monsters than an ill woman with blood on her hands.

I wipe my palm along the wool of my skirt and turn on my heel, casting my gaze to the surrounding landscape. This churchyard I know like my own bedchamber. The faded grass my quilt, the stones my own grotesque playthings. One headstone stands out from the rest, a mere slab, the carved words already licked with lichen.

Mother's.

She was so afraid of death. I still hear her cries sometimes.

Please don't let him take me, Addie. Please don't let me die.

My knees go weak, as if someone has sliced the thin skin behind them. Nausea widens in my gut, presses up my throat. A thousand curses spring to my tongue, but I swallow them as the sickness sinks into every inch of me. Sweat blooms on my skin, and the world goes spinning. I reach out for the nearest thing.

Another grave. Another tangle of bones and old cloth beneath me.

I do not want to see Mother's, not today. So instead, I focus my swirling vision on the stone in front of me. *Bram Avery, Aged 24.* I swill the name in my mouth. It tastes familiar. Another strange death. Alive one day, gone the next. But before I can sink my teeth into it, there are footsteps swishing in the wet earth behind me. I do not look up.

"Adelaide?"

The voice tethers me to some semblance of reality, pulling me from my haze of sickness. I turn, finding Clara limned in the mist of the graveyard, her calfskin boots shushing in mud. Fear hooks in the corners of her eyes.

This is how all the villagers look at me. Like I am an old heirloom high atop a shelf, covered in dust and ready to fall. Her throat bobs, golden skin flushed with cold.

"Shouldn't you be inside with the rest of them?" I try to sound strong and sure of myself, but the result is something hoarse and desperate.

Clara wilts. "I saw you out here all alone and thought—"

"I don't need your pity." My grip tightens on the headstone. "Whatever you have come here to preach, I have already heard it a thousand times."

Clara hesitates, then reaches for something in the folds of her russet cloak. "I'm sorry," she says and holds out a half-drunk wine bottle, sloshing red liquid. "A peace offering."

I stare at the bottle, my tongue suddenly dry. How long has it been since I drank of communion wine? Father forbade me a long time ago, said my wickedness was too thick in my throat for a sip of forgiveness from Ithrandril. But I take it from Clara's outstretched hand and press my lips to the verdant glass.

The wine tastes like sin. Rotten berries and sweet mint from the hedges hemming the lanes through Rixton.

I give the bottle back and wipe my mouth on my hand, black blood streaking from where the skin is chapped. If Clara notices, she says nothing. Only tucks the bottle into her cloak.

Behind her, through the mist and up the hill, the stained-glass windows of the church wink in hues of vermillion and goldenrod. Bloody swords and jewel-rich crowns of two brothers who forgot what it meant to love one another. Who allowed their differences to morph into bitterness.

My eyes comb over Clara. Her chestnut curls flutter loose from their ribbons, frayed with rain and wind. Her eyes are sunken, and there are shadows in the hollows of her cheeks that were not there the last time I saw her. The previous funeral, only days ago.

I should say something, a polite *thank you*. Prove I am not the wicked thing the village has come to loathe—the woman whose father keeps her under lock and key, so sick she is only allowed out for death.

Just to stare it closer in the face.

"I'm sorry you've been so ill." The claggy morning softens Clara's features, but worry still etches lines above her dark eyes.

Ill. The word is bitter, lemons and wormwood. I twist a finger through the foliage growing on Bram Avery's grave. *Ill.* As if I were laid up in bed with a fever, a cough rattling my lungs, or angry pustules bursting a meaty pink on my skin. But it is something more than that, isn't it? The thing that keeps me inside…

I pull the lace cuffs of Mother's dress closer around my wrists so Clara cannot see the marks made by a father ashamed of his own child.

I wish I *was* ill.

Emptying my guts into a pot instead of having the ashen welts on my body from where my father ties me down, the aching bones of my chest when my heart beats like an untethered beast. A natural illness instead of the darkness swallowing me whole. Then, at least, I would have an explanation. A reason why I am this way, why I see the things I do.

I turn away from Clara, returning my attention to the tiny plants trailing Bram Avery's headstone.

Bitterbloom.

Their white petals velvet soft, yellow centers like an egg drop. They were Mother's favorite. But they shouldn't be blooming. Not now, with winter so near at hand.

"Please, Adelaide." Clara reaches toward me. "You are so missed. Hester, Liza, Finn…we would all love to see you."

The names are knife blades in my back. Hester Samuels, the mayor's daughter. Liza Thatcher, the woman who stole Clara's heart when we were all of thirteen. And Finn Adler, the blacksmith's apprentice who, until only days ago, was promised to wed Lilith Corley in the spring.

"They do not wish to see me," I say, ashamed of the pity the words seem to seek before they even leave my mouth.

"Of course they do! Many of us wish to see you, Adelaide." Clara takes a step closer. "You do not deserve to be locked away like you are. You're no longer a child."

I grit my teeth. While I may no longer be a child, I am still tethered to this patch of earth. Still searching for the one thing that might cure whatever makes me ill. Which might compel me to be right and whole again.

The love of the only parent I have left.

I turn to the line of rowan trees on the far side of the graveyard, intent on establishing that I am done speaking. Somewhere behind the clouds, the sun tips above the silver-barked wood. Mist claws at my back, drips idly down my cheeks.

"Adelaide." Clara's voice trills, but my eyes stay focused on the shifting trees, the shadows undulating between the trunks. "Addie, there is something I wish to tell you, something I—"

But her words are swallowed by the drumming of my own heartbeat in my ears. It comes on swift, rocking me backward, sending me crashing to my knees in the mire. Clara is by my side at once, but it is no use.

The monster has come.

Pain breaks out along my skin, a roaring forest fire of sparks. It shoots through me, peeling my mouth open in a scream, piercing the mist around us.

"How can I help you?" Clara shakes my shoulders. "Addie, you're scaring me!"

Bones near breaking, I lift my gaze to the tree line. The sight laid bare before me chills my blood.

White smoke billows out from between the trunks, morphing in ways my mind can barely comprehend. My body seizes, and I drop to my side. The mud slips cold against my arm, soaking in through my bodice.

Clara is screaming, but I can no longer make sense of her words. The smoke draws closer.

Agony rips through my body. I reel to my back, arching against the pain. My arms curl like fern fronds at my side. I gasp for air, and my muscles wrench with a curdling scream.

I am going to die.

The smoke ebbs and flows, drawn to my screams, which only grow louder. Torment floods my body. My heart stops in my chest, pitches against its cage of bones, beats again. Hard. Like it's made of iron.

There are voices in the mist somewhere above. Only fractions of sound while the smoke advances and the scent of sulfur assaults my senses.

Clara is calling for help. The ground shakes with the rush of running feet.

No. They cannot see me like this.

I try to rise but find my legs utterly spent, and I crash against Clara, screaming. *Always* screaming.

The smoke is so near now. So hungry. I do not know what will happen if it touches my body, but something tells me I would sooner taste death than know what it is feels like to be caressed by my monsters.

I scramble backward, mud and bitterbloom petals grinding into my palms. More hands are at my shoulders, and I release another scream.

"Do not touch me!"

Please, gods above and below, *do not touch me*. I cannot hurt anyone else. The fear rips down my sternum, making me sick all over again. I cannot be the one killing these girls. The edges of my vision feather black while the smoke coalesces before my eyes. Reaches, reaches…

Adelaide.

My name, whispered by a voice human but not. I look around, yet the features of the villagers' blur together. Clara becoming Liza becoming Hester becoming a hundred people whose names I forgot long ago.

Adelaide.

A gentle arm reaches down and brushes my shoulder. I balk.

No, no, you cannot touch me. You mustn't touch—

But it is too late. I smell her. Clara. Gingerbread and soft lilac. Her hand grips my forearm, guiding me up, away from the smoke. Smoke, which is forming, taking shape into something I cannot, *cannot*—

"Adelaide! Adelaide, look at me!" Clara's voice, filled with tears.

But my vision has tunneled, pitched toward midnight, and all I see before my world tips into shadow is the smoke. And it seems to be wearing a face.

two

Mother smiles at me, but there are too many teeth in her mouth. She braids together sprigs of lavender, rosemary, and mint and intertwines them with pale pink lace. I pull away when she crosses the bedroom to fit the crown to my scalp. There is something wrong with her face.

"Mother?" My voice is tiny and meek. I glance down to my hands and notice how small they are, how soft. A child's hands. "Mother, what is happening?"

She fits the herbs and lace on my brow. The plants scrape my skin, drawing blood. It drips black into my eye. I blink.

This isn't real.

Mother sinks into the mattress beside me, brushes a thatch of white hair from my cheek. "My Addie, as beautiful as a spring morning."

I slide my eyes from her to the foot of my bed, wrapped in quilts, and then to my window, where the sunlight spills like honey through the glass. Beyond this, birds sing, and the tinny laughter of children splashing in the river echoes from down in the valley. Dread closes around my heart. Thick and choking. I know this day. But it can't—

"You will make a beautiful May Queen, Adelaide."

I turn to Mother, her lips stained a muted pink. She wears flowers in her hair and a dress in shades of orchid. Mother is young, healthy, her skin flushed with vibrance, and for a little while, I allow myself to sink into this moment. Live it over and over, like I have a thousand times before. No longer frightened now that I know where I am, what this is.

A memory in the form of a dream.

Mother helps me out of bed and into a soft satin dress with enough layers that, when she turns me to gaze upon my reflection in the mirror, I decide I look rather like a daffodil. She presses a kiss to the top of my head, gathering my curls in a fist and breathing in my scent.

"My baby is no longer a baby."

Gripped by the wistful tone in her voice, I take her hand in mine. She is warm. Almost feverishly so.

"I'm barely twelve, Mother. Clara says we do not have to get married until we are at least twenty. And even then, she says that some girls choose not to marry." I press my palms to her face, and her eyes flood with tears. "Maybe I will never grow up. Maybe I will stay right here with you and Father, always."

"Oh, my Morning Glory." She wraps her arms around me, holding me to her breast, and I breathe in her citrus scent tinged with green and growing things. "I would love that more than you will ever know."

Before I can form a reply, the door to my room bursts open. Father stands tall in the doorframe. Fear imbues my chest, but then I remember what this is. Merely a dream. A memory.

He is a different man than in the present. His face splits with a grin, dark stubble shadowing his jaw. Here, he is younger too. Lighter. Like the weight of the world has not yet burdened his shoulders.

"Well, would you look at this? My little Addie, as yellow as a lemon drop." He scoops me into his arms, spinning around until laughter tumbles from my lips.

"I am *not* a lemon drop, Father! I'm supposed to be a daffodil." It is very important to me that he understands my costume. If not, the entire pageant Clara and I have planned for the villagers for Beltane will be ruined.

Father raises his eyebrows and exchanges a knowing look with Mother. "Oh, forgive me. What a beautiful daffodil you make. Tell me, are you and Clara ready to enrapture all of Rixton?"

Another giggle bursts from my lips, and I clap a hand over my mouth. "It's not *just* Clara and me. We simply wrote the pageant. Hester has a part too. And Liza and even Finn and Viktor." I lean in close to whisper in his ear, his stubble stinging my cheeks. "They're playing wasps."

Father erupts in a hearty chuckle, the sound rich and deep, like drinking chocolate. He sets me back on my feet before planting a kiss on my brow and reaching for Mother's hand. "Shall we go then and see this spectacle our daughter has cooked up?"

Mother smiles—a rose unfurling in the June-time sun. "Anywhere with you, husband-mine." They share a kiss, soft and slow and infused with yearning. I pull a face, making a mockery of their expression, but deep down inside, my twelve-year-old heart burns for the same thing one day. A love so strong, so pure, nothing but death could separate it. When they break apart, Mother strokes my cheek before following Father out the door.

"Ithrandril be with you," she says, the age-old adage smooth on her tongue.

"And also with you," I repeat.

Out on the hill, below the church and vicarage, the entirety of Rixton has gathered. The River Thine glitters like a jewel at their backs, and the rowan wood dances in the spring-kissed breeze. From the stage, which Clara and I have hobbled together from wooden crates and crimson velvet borrowed from her mother's sewing closet, I spy my parents eagerly awaiting from their blanket spread on the grass.

My chest aches with the love I have for them. From the moment I first bled black, when my mother kissed my brow and told me she would do everything to keep me safe, that not another soul would know, I believed her.

A hush falls over the crowd when Clara steps out from behind the curtain, swathed in cerulean silk. Our bluebell. She repeats every line perfectly, and the pageant begins. Viktor and Finn take their roles quite seriously, chasing

the flowers around the stage and drawing laughter from every throat. As it comes to an end, the six of us join hands, and I catch Clara's eye. She squeezes them in my direction, our secret sign of endearment. Unending friendship.

Father is the first to stand, the rest of the village joining in, clapping so loudly that we don't hear the screams at first. The cries of laughter from children still playing in the river edging, sharp and bloody.

My stomach drops to the soles of my feet, and Clara's hand goes sweaty in mine. Fear blooms a thicket of brambles in my chest.

I find Mother and Father in the crowd, their faces pale, drawn tight.

We know these screams. We have heard them before.

They are the sound the village makes when they drag another body up from the riverbanks.

I surge from my pillow, sweat drenching my skin. My chest heaves and crashes. I pinch the webbing between my fingers, centering, grounding myself to the present. A memory. It was just a dream.

I peel back my blankets and slip into a sturdy wool dress and boots. My stomach swims sick. The mind is a cruel master, bringing back remnants of happier times. These reminders only make my illness worse. After tying my laces, I cross to the door and fling it open.

The vicarage is empty, hollow. The wooden steps protest when I make my descent, and the hearth in the kitchen has long been left cold. But it is no matter. Seeing Father now would be too much against the vision I just experienced. A sour taste to steal away the sweetness.

I am sick of the memories, sick of the pain and blackouts and the monsters, which seem now to be growing faces. When the cold air of the outside chaps my nose and cheeks, it all comes flooding back. Lilith Corley, Clara, the smoke curling from the trees, features stringing together like puzzle pieces…

I dig my fingernails into my palm. My illness could shoulder all the blame, but I am more than this jumble of bones and blood, more than the visions that rock me and make the world turn black.

I need answers, need to know what is wrong with me so I can fix it before it is too late. Before the monsters turn to things with hands and teeth and devour me whole.

Ahead, on the lane, the church rises from the gloom, the windows fogged with mist. I do not know why I am drawn to it. Is it not just a relic of all I have lost? But if my curse comes from the gods, then maybe the gods have the answers I crave.

I slip between the creaking, wooden doors and into the nave. Dark buttresses loom over a stone floor, leading me to the stained-glass window high above Ithrandril's altar. It is set with enough gold to buy my mother's soul back from Death. The colorful glass depicts a scene from the Rending, when Ithrandril threw his brother down to the shadow.

Ithrandril stands tall, golden hair streaming behind him while he holds a flaming sword above his head. Erybrus, beneath him, grips a human heart in his hands, his mouth ringed with blood. The brother-gods ruled over our world for thousands of years, splitting power, sharing glory. Until Erybrus got too hungry, wanted humans all to himself.

"So, his brother cursed him," I whisper, my voice echoing off the walls of the empty nave. I drop to my knees before the altar, tears clouding my vision. "Cursed him and sent him to shadow, where he could only have the souls of those who chose him." I lift a hand and suck in chilled air as the ruby light catches the blackened welts on my wrists. "I am not for Erybrus. I am more than this shadow."

"Then what are you for, daughter-mine?"

I am up on my feet and spinning around faster than a flame.

Father stands in the aisle between the worn pews, cloaked in black robes. It takes me a moment to recognize him, older than he was in my dream. Sharper. No longer bearing kisses for my brow.

"Stay back." The fear in my voice might be taken for gentleness, concern, but the truth is, I cannot have him come any closer. It will shatter me.

"Have you come to atone for your sins?" he asks, staying put but gazing up at the visage of our brother-gods. "It is wise to confess before the darkness comes. Before death claims your soul and you are faced with a choice."

For the light or for the shadow. For Ithrandril or his hungry brother. I swallow a lump in my throat, following Father's gaze to the gods.

"Do you think me soon to die?"

Silence. Only the steady drip of mist on the windows, wind whistling through the steeple high above.

"Reapers come for all of us, Adelaide. No matter the consistency of our souls."

The fear in my gut carves deeper. Every child born into this world hears tales of Reapers. Agents of the gods, serving to ferry souls across into a realm waiting beyond. One where souls decide which god they are for. Which god claims their spirit for eternity.

I turn back to Father, mouth a tight line. There is a question ghosting my lips, scented of sulfur and white smoke. "And what is the consistency of my soul?"

He draws closer. The hem of his robes dust the stones at our feet. His face is a contortion of bitterness, like I am a sour lemon on his tongue. Gone is the father who embraced me, spun me around in circles, pressed his lips to my curls and called me his.

I lost both my parents the day my mother died, and I have stayed this long only to get one back. To remind Father I am still worth loving despite my illness, despite my shadowed blood.

"You're a curse, Adelaide." His face twists into something I don't recognize. "Sometimes, I wish you had died in place of your mother."

I draw a sharp breath, skin flushing hot-cold. My head rings with his words, as if someone has shoved a needle through my ear. My chest caves, and pain breaks out along my brow. My lips part, but I have nothing to say. Not now, not when—

I flee, tearing down the aisle, out the door, and into the mist clouding the village. My boots slip in the wet grass of the hill, and when I reach the churning water of the River Thine, I open my jaw wider until I am sure I will swallow myself…and scream.

It's a silent thing. The village cannot hear me, mustn't know I am out here alone. It will only give them more reason to believe I am the one with

blood on my hands. The cords in my neck strain and creak, the delicate skin of my lips splitting, when I press the quiet stronger.

Sometimes, I wish you had died in place of your mother.

Tears stream down my face, and only when I taste the blood on my lips do I close my mouth. I drop to my knees in the mud, eyes hot, blinking at the gray sky while I collect my thoughts. Every soul in Rixton knows what I am. *Cursed*. I fist my hands in the mud.

I cannot stay here anymore.

I could run.

Run and never look back. Just across the river, past the fields and the curving lane. To cities where cursed girls are nothing more than another face on another street.

There are places beyond Rixton. Lysdin, the Queen's city. Riddington, Eliexier, and Vrinhowe. I've read about them in books my mother used to keep on high shelves, away from Father's prying eyes. Places where the Scriptures aren't bent to break women. Places where the monsters cannot follow me.

Instead, I cast my gaze to the water, the sky reflecting from it like a sheen of molten silver. Before I can stop myself, I am up on my feet. I abandon my stockings and boots in the mud, shucking off my rough wool overskirt until I stand in hardly a stitch. The cold bites at my bare skin, and it grounds me.

Alive.

Not dead.

Alive.

I rush toward the water, the waves reaching greedily for the hem of my slip. It runs clear as crystal, frigid as ice exhumed from the bowels of the earth. I close my eyes, tipping my chin toward the gathering clouds. The cold is a respite, a gentling, a reminder that being alive is *feeling*. Even when that feeling is pain. I take a step deeper.

Something slices the delicate skin of my right foot.

I plunge into a panic, and my muscles falter, one hand dipping into the chilled water when I lose balance. A hiss sears my lips. Pain ricochets up my skin, like a knife has pierced my flesh.

I scramble out of the water, fighting back a cry. Heat sparks and my breath hitches. I collapse on the muddy bank, tugging at my petticoats, and uncover the wound. My lungs cave with a gasp. It doesn't take long for the warmth of sticky blood to inch along my heel.

This is no cut made by a river rock, but something keen-edged. My eyes burn with tears when I peel the cut apart. Something is there. Something embedded in my skin. Baring my teeth, I fish between the layers of tissue and pull a sliver of metal from the cut, its surface smeared with blood and river silt.

Another wave of pain radiates from my heel, and I try desperately to catch my breath. Now that the strange little splinter is free, the blood rushes to mix like paint with the icy mud at my feet. My skirts are soaked through with it. I must look a right state.

The small cut of metal, held up for closer inspection, seems like nothing more than a piece of forgotten rubbish. A nail from a carriage wheel, perhaps, or a chip from a worn horseshoe. My stomach constricts, and all I can think about is the way the rust might already be entering my bloodstream, carrying poison to my lungs, my heart, and my jaw. Freezing the bones in place.

I open my mouth, gasping in the air. What if this is the last of it? Whatever breath is trapped between my two lungs will shrivel to dust. My heart skips, and I clench my fist around the chipped metal.

No, no, no.

One finger on my muddy wrist, I count the beats. *A-live, a-live, a—*

"I must say, when I decided on my walk this morning, I did not expect to find the vicar's daughter covered in river dirt and blood—a sight to scare off half the population of Rixton."

The voice is like buttered bread. Thick and rich.

Nausea rises from my empty stomach. I turn, the metal shard still locked in my fist, and lay eyes upon the last person I would have expected to see on this blustery morning along the River Thine.

Ransom Black.

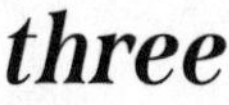

three

The blood between my fingers runs like shadow. Ransom Black towers over me, broad as an oak tree, his hair glinting honey-blond in the warming sun. His coat hangs in heavy folds about his frame, brass buttons reflecting the light on the water. His face reminds me of delicate porcelain: high cheekbones, an angled jaw, and full lips like a budding rose. Beneath bold, dark brows, his expression lies somewhere between haughty amusement and self-importance.

My mouth gapes like a shored fish. There is specific etiquette one is supposed to follow in the presence of a lord, but I find my mind completely and utterly empty.

Damn the etiquette.

I shove the metal shard into the pocket of my sweater and stand shakily.

"You are Adelaide Thorn, are you not?" His voice drops softer, curling around the edges of my body like fog. There is a glint in his eye, something akin to hunger, while he studies the exposed ankles beneath my skirts.

I wince and adjust the ruined fabric over the toes of my boots. "I'm not sure it matters who I am, my lord," I say, gritting the last words like iron between my teeth.

There is something on his hand, something like dirt, only darker. He wipes it on his trousers, smirks. "Oh, I think it does."

We stand there in silence for a moment, no sound but the river whistling through ice, the wind in the trees, and dry grasses susurrating on the banks. Wheels and hooves clack along the bridge—Farmer Whitley's wagon loaded with straw. He waves a hand to us, merely smudges in his poor eyesight, and Ransom gestures back.

I whet my lips. "Is there a reason you are walking alone along the river?"

He raises his brow and bends to collect a blade of tall grass, splitting the stem with a thumbnail. A small leather pouch swings from a belt around his waist. I wonder at its contents. Herbs, perhaps? A pencil and a small scrap of paper?

What does a lord do with his time?

"That's rather an intimate question for someone to ask if they are not Adelaide Thorn, the vicar's infamous daughter."

I almost laugh at this. *Infamous*. But another shock of pain sears up my leg, and my knee buckles. Like a willow switch across my skin.

"Would it even matter if I were?" I clench my jaw and sit heavily on a fallen log, lifting my heel over one knee and inspecting the fresh black blood gathering at the edges of the cut.

Ransom steps closer, and annoyance sparks in my stomach. Doesn't he have other places to be? Dying father and all that?

And then I freeze.

He'll see my blood. The color all wrong. And there is so much of it. Yet, I dig at the cut with muddied fingers, wincing when the delicate layers of skin rip like lace. I need to stop the bleeding.

"Are you hurt?" Ransom drops beside me, reaching out his hand, but I pull away.

"I'm fine, thanks." The words are taut on my lips.

He retreats, straightening the lapels on his coat, brushing hair from his eyes. "You remind me of your father."

My skin flares white-hot, chin jerking up, and I peer at him. I should feel pity, but there is only anger between my lips. "How do you know what my father is like?" I spit.

His smirk sparkles when it widens, teeth so white they might be carved from ivory. He laughs, triumph in his throat. "I knew it! The vicar's daughter, hardly seen outside her tower anymore these days, locked away—"

"It's hardly a tower," I grumble, turning back to my heel, the blood still beading midnight.

"I haven't seen your father since the day my mother died. He's at the castle now, you know. I always leave when I find he's coming." There is a sadness in his voice, and for a moment, I recognize myself in him. In the way he holds his fists. Always ready for a fight, always ready to lose. But I push it away. Just another soul with dead and dying parents.

"I assumed." My fingers dig into the crevice on my skin, searching for more metal.

"If you would just let me help—" He extends his hand toward me, but I pull away, hissing like a cat.

"I said I was fine."

His eyes connect with the color of my blood, and I steel myself for what is coming. A shriek. A sharp inhale. A stumbling backward while he stares at my cursed and gory skin.

But there's nothing.

His gaze simply glides across the cut and up to meet my own. Something stirs in my chest. A knowing. I push it away.

There is more silence while I fish around in my foot, only finding more ichor. My hands are slick with mud, and my mind slips from the sight of shadow staining my fingertips. My heart clenches, but I take my own pumping viscera as a sign.

A-live, a-live, a-live.

Wrong. But alive. I swallow, throat raw and reedy.

"You're going to make it worse." Before I can stop him, Ransom is down on one knee in the mud beside me, pulling a silk handkerchief from a pocket and dabbing at the cut.

I grind my jaw, sucking air between my teeth. "What the hell are you doing?"

"Saving your damned life. You don't want the blood fever, do you?"

Can't he see it? The gods' curse in my veins? But he only wipes away more of the syrupy liquid.

I catch the urge to scratch his eyes out if he gets even another inch closer to me, but all I picture are dark lines crawling up my skin, caged lungs, and death. Just another body buried beneath the bitterbloom. He drags the cloth over my skin, each movement sparking agony up my shin, and hurries to the river to rinse the staining blood.

Not a single word spoken over the unholiness of whatever lingers inside me. It sends shivers down my spine and heats my core in a way I cannot explain.

I loose a sigh when icy water passes along the cut and tilt my head up to the sky while the pain subsides. A flock of geese make an arrowhead shape against the clouds. Something sharp stings the sole of my foot. I flash my eyes to Ransom.

There is a needle between his fingers, black thread.

"Stop!" I scrabble at his hand and push him away, rising to unsteady feet. For a moment, it strikes me odd that someone privileged would know his way around a needle and thread.

His brows wrinkle, eyes glinting like polished steel. "What is it?"

"What the hell do you think you're doing?" I demand, a near echo of before.

He raises the needle, the sliver of metal catching the sun. "If you don't close that cut, it could get infected."

My knees shake, and I take a step deeper in the mud to steady myself, wincing when pain radiates up my leg. "Are you a healer, Lord Black?" My words drip with mockery.

His eyes go cold. "I'm trying to help you, Adelaide. I don't understand what is so wrong with that."

"This!" I grab the bloodied cloth from his hand and shake it. "Are you insane? I have already been caught out-of-doors with hardly a stitch on—"

Ransom flicks his eyes across the skin of my shoulder, where my sweater has slipped. "Yes, it's rather nice, isn't it?"

"Shut up." I pull at the fabric, working to cover my exposed flesh. "Shut up. I'm not going to let you sew my foot back together. Do you even know what this town would do to me if they found us out here? The vicar's wicked daughter and the lord of Blackbourne Castle?"

Ransom flicks grime out from beneath a fingernail. "I'm not the lord. Not yet anyway."

I breathe a sigh, chest constricting. "That's beside the point. You know—"

Another streak of pain flares up my leg, and I lower my gaze to the ruined cloth in my hand. "Get up. Get. Up."

His eyes widen, and for a moment, I wonder if this is the first time anyone has told Ransom Black what to do. He moves, slowly, and I sit, swinging my injured foot up onto the log, decorum tossed to the wind. I ball the soiled handkerchief and whip it at him.

With my fingers, I rip a stretch from my petticoat's hem and bend to inspect my skin. It is cleaner than it was, I will give him that, and I work quickly to wrap the ripped cloth around the wound, trying to stem the bleeding.

"What did you step on anyway?" he asks, returning the needle and thread to the pouch at his side.

"Nothing." I wrench a knot tightly across my foot. "Just a piece of rubbish."

He turns to look at my discarded skirts, boots, and socks. There is no rubbish on the shoreline.

"Do you want your things?" He steps forward.

"Leave them. I can do it myself."

Ransom holds up black-gloved palms. "You're as stubborn as my horse."

"And you," I say, grinding a fist into my knees while I stand, "are as arrogant as Farmer Whitley's barn cat." I press past him toward my clothes, slipping back into them and welcoming the warmth of the wool.

Ransom wrinkles his nose. "Tell me, please, how am I either of those two things? From where I'm standing, that cut would have been—*will* be—a whole lot worse if I weren't—"

"If you weren't what, Lord Black? My knight in shining armor? Please, do us both the favor of leaving me alone." I balance on my good foot, slip one sock over my injured heel, and plant it in my boot.

Ransom sniffs. "I take back what I said before, Ms. Thorn. You're not as stubborn as my horse; you're as bullheaded as my mule."

He is lucky he is standing several feet away from me and my left leg is suffering from a bleeding wound. My knuckles sting with the need to sink into the taut flesh of his jaw.

I suck in air while I balance and fix him with the coldest glare I can muster.

"Thank you for your assistance, Lord Black, but I think you best be on your way." I tilt my chin up toward the clouds. "Wouldn't want the rain to ruin your expensive coat."

His eyes bore holes into my chest, turning my bones to ash. He snaps his gloves tighter on his wrists and shakes his head.

"Have it your way then. Good day, Ms. Thorn."

He moves up the bank quickly, black boots slurrying in mud and grass, becoming little more than dusky shadow when he reaches the edges of the trees. Their yellow-feathered leaves dust his coat, and then he disappears. Like a wisp of smoke.

I drop my arms to my sides, eyes back on the clouds, and shake. The movement is healing, air moving like water over my skin. The knots at the back of my skull slacken, crackling like brush underfoot. My chest relaxes, heart returning to a familiar rhythm. Breath comes in steady waves, and I release the tension, slipping my hands in the pocket of my sweater. My fingers brush up against the sharp, cold metal, and my chest thrills once more.

I empty it out into my palm, the little shard now glowing a dull yellow in the darkening sun. It is a strange thing pounded from brass, lines etched jagged across its surface. It does not appear to be a chip from a horseshoe or a nail from a carriage wheel. Instead, it looks like—

I fall to my knees where my boot prints are still pressed in the mud. Throwing caution to the wind, I search the mucky shoreline for more glinting brass. The breeze whips my hair, carrying with it the scent of copper, but I do not stop; I only want to find the rest of the thing that bit my flesh.

My fingernails cake with mud, rotting leaves tangling in my palms, but still I dig. Only when the first raindrop falls from the sky, when my nose has filled with so much heat and the scent of freshly forged steel, do I stop. And when I do, my shaking, dirt-covered hands are filled with hammered metal.

I fit the pieces together, their edges sticking with river mud and the remnants of my blackened gore, and ignore the disappearing sun, the humming village, and the ringing in my ears while I stare at the object in the crux of my palms.

A little brass bell.

I hold it up, fear quickening in my veins. What if everything I have heard about bells is wrong? What if they *do* conjure evil? Free demons from the deep?

Those in Father's congregation speak of bells as something holy, but this one suggests other things. Claims a nature against Ithrandril. Whispers memories of the same notes I sense before the monsters take shape. A dark, twisted calling that starts deep between my ribs and scatters throughout my bones.

I bite my tongue, hoping it will keep the illness from making meat of all my muscle, keep back the encroaching darkness. But I am too late. My chest slips, heart skimming along my breastbone, while the tiny object shakes in one hand. I shove it into my pocket and let it rest silent. Slowly, I turn my chin toward the wood.

My breath catches when the mist gathers, then solidifies.

It flickers, a specter at the edge of my vision. I stand frozen on the riverbank, my chest contracting like a thing apart from my body. When I try to move, to turn back toward the vicarage, the safety of the garden wall, it takes all my strength just to breathe. The river rushes past, a scent like metal filling my nose, while the monster gathers at the tree line. Coalesces. My lips peel back to scream, but there is nothing.

Hollow air leaves me in gasps. My fingernails sink into the fabric at my side, and I try to cry out again, but the fear is a hand over my mouth. I blink when a body takes shape—a head, two arms, two legs, fingers reaching, reaching… Its joints crack like a marionette on invisible strings. Sinew on bone, teeth and tongue, mist rippling down a spine like hair.

I scramble back. The thing wavers at the edge of the trees like a guttering candle flame. The smoke collects, and a hand extends. The scent of citrus hits me in waves. My stomach curdles.

No, no, this is all wrong.

Wrong, wrong, wrong, wrong, wrong.

I do not know which god will claim my soul, but death is rife in Rixton. Dinah Bo passed when I was not much older than four, and years went by where her mother could be found at the edge of the wood, leaving lemon cakes wrapped in lace for her daughter. Most molded or were washed away by rain, but I remember the scent of them. Like all the creeping bitterbloom.

People say the trees that swallow the river are haunted, and if I have learned anything in my twenty-one years of life in this wretched place, it is that some people have a right to be afraid.

I try to push the lump at the back of my throat down, down, down, desperately searching for my voice, but the smoke—no, the *body*—only draws closer.

A sound: something faint, far away, yet drawing closer. Like a wind kicked up through branches, the cracking of frost on a pond. I stare at the monster, the silhouette that smells of someone I buried five years ago.

When I hurry to my feet, a sharp pain sparks up my leg, and I wince. The monster stills, a catch of white fabric so real I can almost touch it. Agony rips through the back of my skull, sending me to my knees, before I name the thing I see before me. The mist knits together more firmly, a mosaic of pieces I recognize as human but not. A hand, its fingers too long, a cheek with bones too sharp. It becomes feral, unnatural, and fear bleeds across my belly.

Mother. My throat aches with the name. *Mother*.

I blink and it is gone. Just a line of rowans, dry grasses swaying in the breeze.

Cool relief rushes from the center of my chest, and I heave a sigh. But the breath catches in my throat, snagging on the skin like wool on a rusty nail. A cough rattles from my lungs, trying to clear the space, and my body tightens. I scrabble for my neck, my wrist, behind my ear, anything to remind me I am alive, but my pulse is silent. No steady beat to guide me.

My legs buckle, knees almost crashing to the bloodied river.

And that's when I spot it, rocking, lapped by icy waves, before the blackness takes me.

Hester Samuel's cold body.

four

I am locked in the garden shed when they bring the body up the hill, a single window open to let in air. Neck craned as high as I can, I watch four men—village elders—slip their way down to the riverbank and roll her onto a rough cut of burlap. Dark hair sticks to her white face like leeches, and her dress is soaked through, half-frozen, hem ripped and stained with mud. I cannot see much more. But the men whisper.

A tear across her throat, a clutch of wilted bitterbloom in her hands, blood smeared across her lips.

I push to my feet using a pile of rough-hewn boards as leverage against my trembling legs. Father likes for the garden shed to serve as extra punishment for the moments when I black out, as if I have any control over it. Those in the village who know of this turn their eyes the other way, whispering that I deserve the treatment. Better to commune with Erybrus in private than out where Ithrandril can bear witness to my wickedness.

The bell in my pocket rubs against my thigh, and I fish it out. The metal catches the light streaming in through the small window. Designs are etched across the surface: twining veins, thorns, the empty sockets and toothy grin of a skull. The sight fills my stomach with vinegar, but I only tighten my grip on the wooden handle.

I kept the bell quiet when Father brought me up from the river and locked me in the shed, covered in river mud and blood he knew could only be mine. It was missing a piece—the tiny wire that held the bead to the dome. I tied it up with a lavender ribbon from my hair and wrapped the whole thing in a shred of my skirt hem to keep it silent before stuffing it back in my pocket.

Now, abandoned to the cold and dirt of the garden shed, I want to ring it and hear the clear cut of its note. But fear sinks hooks into my flesh. I wrap it back in cloth, returning it to my pocket. Only in my greatest need will I ring it.

I drop to the ground and release a breath trapped between my lungs. My fingers worry the edge of my sleeve where it is cut and stained with dirt. I already know what the villagers are whispering amongst themselves, that I am the one who killed Hester. And truthfully, how am I to know I didn't?

When my world turned black the day of Lilith's burial, where did I go? Did I call the monsters forth, just to watch them settle their teeth into the flesh of Hester's throat?

I glance around the darkened space of my prison. Every inch of it makes me ache with the remembrance of what I have lost. My mother who loved her garden beds. Upended rusty trowels, seed packets with faded print, crooked mountains of old terra-cotta pots, a pair of kidskin gloves gathering dust. I cross to the gloves and run a finger along their soft surface, blemished with dirt and the yellowing age of disuse.

Mother loved her flowers. Me most of all.

Oh, my Morning Glory.

I lift one of the gloves and fit my hand inside. The grit of old soil rubs into my palms. They are rather small, even on my own wiry fingers. I can barely remember her in full—Mother. Nine years is so much longer than it feels sometimes. But I do remember how small she was.

Father always told me it was her own sickness that kept her that way, burrowing into her bones and shrinking her from the inside out. But I didn't pay attention to that bit—not until the end. When I close my eyes, I picture her as she was. Lovely and whip-smart, always smelling of fresh citrus and lavender soap, her laugh like church bells. Before they learned to only ring the funeral songs.

For a moment, I allow memories to wash over me. Just a sweet sting until the bitterness clouds the air once more.

I am on the edge of thirteen, my body quickly becoming something I no longer recognize. Angles where the skin has tightened and the baby fat has trimmed itself away. Fuller lips, wider eyes, and a slimming waist. I sit at the small table tucked in a corner beside the hearth in the kitchen, braiding a crown of rosemary and hyssop.

Only days before, they pulled another body from the riverbanks. Rosalyn Eckers, the butcher's daughter. Skin sloughed from her bone, and Father shielded my eyes. But I saw enough. Enough to know Erybrus was at work in Rixton.

I braid the crown for Rosalyn, to toss it on her casket and pray that Ithrandril claims her soul. Pray I am not taken next.

Out the open window, the wind shushes in the trees, and the sparrows sing their night songs in the lilac bushes. Despite the death and fear running like the plague through the village, there is a peace to be found. I twist off the end of the braid, securing it with a mauve ribbon.

And that's when the shouting starts.

I leap from my chair, rushing to the kitchen door leading down to the valley. Shadows gather at the edge of the river, voices of my parents. Mother's coughing fits started months ago, small at first, then tinged with blood. I narrow my eyes, searching the darkness for their forms.

Stars glitter above, but they are the only lights shining when Father appears on the crest of the hill. He holds something in his arms.

Some*one*.

"Mother!" My feet are bare on the dusk-dew grass.

Father drops to a knee, chest heaving with effort. The light from the kitchen catches the shadows on his face. Something is wrong. Tears stream wetly down his cheeks and into the grizzled salt and pepper of his unkempt beard.

"What happened?" My voice is small.

I glance down at Mother. Her skin is paler than snow, eyes closed, lids limned in shades of indigo and mulberry.

He does not answer at first, labored breathing, his chest a rugged cadence against the slow rise and fall of my mother's lungs. She is still alive.

"Father. Tell me."

He glances at me then, eyes haunted, rimmed red. When his lips part, saliva strings between them, like the veins of a gutted rabbit. "Your mother is sick, Adelaide. She has been for a long time. You should prepare yourself for the worst."

He says nothing more, simply stands and sweeps Mother up to their bedchamber.

Over the next few days, I see hardly a thing of them, abandoned to my own devices. When Father finally does appear in the doorway of the kitchen, dressed in funeral blacks to lay Rosalyn Eckers in the ground, he takes one look at the crown of herbs in my hand and tears it from my grasp, throwing the braid in the fire.

My chest cracks with an unnamed emotion. Something I have never felt before. It aches, burns up the back of my throat. Tears well in my eyes when the ribbon catches flame, then the hyssop, the lavender I picked with my own fingers.

"Save your prayers and weeds, Adelaide. The gods do not listen to our supplications."

He leaves me there, tears budding at the corners of my eyes, my mother gasping for breath in her bed while he goes to bury more bodies.

I suppose I lost my father even before Mother took her final breath.

The feel of Mother's glove centers me back to the present. I peel it off and drop it beside the other. I don't need any more reminders of what I have lost or what I have become. My eyes drop to my own hands, now stained with dirt.

Wind buffets the garden shed, rattling the broken window. My gaze snags on a collection of stiff pages, scribbles in ink. I reach for them, and a plume of dust rises to greet me. On the other side of it, a leather-bound journal. *Mother's* journal. My chest caves with heartache as my fingers brush the soft cover. I open the pages, wipe the grime and the dark stains, like blots of ink. Sketches, diagrams, lists. Names I know and names I do not. Larkspur, foxglove, belladonna, oleander, bitterbloom.

I trail a finger over the looping script.

A bell rings, low and somber, from the church. A death knell. I tuck the journal into my waistband. Just another dead girl to bury. And this time, I know the face all too well.

Closing my eyes, I picture Hester. When we were children, she used to bring me herbs from her own mother's garden to braid into crowns.

Part of me knows I should pray, repent of my wickedness and beg forgiveness from Ithrandril above. And another fragment of me, the one that sees the monsters, recognizes the wrongness of my own heart, wonders if Hester Samuels suffered when she died.

If she cried and begged the monsters to stop while they peeled her flesh from her bones.

Father lets me out the next morning, my skirts stained from sweat, stomach rumbling. He leads me back into the vicarage and up to my room, where he points at my darkest frock and then at my boots, a jerk of his chin toward the door. I know these movements well, what they mean. Time to stare death in the face once more, see what awaits those who stray from the path of light.

Because that is what Father truly thinks, isn't it? That the girls of Rixton are dying of their own accord? Perhaps not by their own hands, but surely—to his twisted mind—their sins play a part of it. Their own wickedness.

I fight the burn to smash my fist against his jaw. Instead, I do nothing. Instead, I will stare into the face of death today, and I will ask why it hasn't yet taken me.

We make our way to the churchyard, and I ignore the sideways glances from villagers, the words I pretend not to hear.

Cursed, she is. Didn't you hear? She was caught out at the river, summoning Erybrus, calling for the death of Hester.

My heart freezes in my chest, skips a beat, rumbles back to life. The breath whooshes from my lungs while I hurry past the gossipers, quick on Father's heels. Perhaps they are right to fear me—*I* fear me—but I am not a murderer. I look down at my trembling hands.

At least, I don't think I am.

Father bows his head. "We call to Ithrandril. We ask him to greet us with holy warmth, to expel the shadow that our sin welcomes in and the

sins of his brother, Erybrus. We ask that he shine his face on our departed, welcoming her into the brilliance of life eternal."

Those attending lower their gazes against the drizzle streaming from the gray sky, fingers tracing the shape of flame over their chests. I keep my eyes open, study the trees veiled in mist. The wood is still. Too still. As if even the trees are holding their breath, waiting. For what, I do not know, but the thought chills me to the bone.

Hester's father—the mayor—tosses dirt to her casket, his pouched face clotted with tears. Her mother goes next, and then we all take a turn. When it comes time for mine, I stoop under the weight of a hundred thousand eyes. My throat runs raw, heart thudding—a mad thing in my chest.

I stand and catch the mayor's stare. His tears remain, but there is something else there too. Something I know all too well.

Hatred.

I toss the earth, the smack of it against the casket reverberating through the churchyard. Let them hate me. What does it matter?

"Ithrandril above, welcome Hester into your divine brilliance, where the shadow can no longer find her."

The villagers echo the pronouncement, and the bell tolls while Father concludes the rites. Unlike Lilith's service, no one files into the church. The village has gorged itself on death for long enough. I catch Clara's eye from across the tombstones, her arm hooked through Liza's. When she sees me, she turns away, and the rejection burns hot across my skin.

Merely strangers. No longer the friends we might have once been. She has seen my hard edges and knows there is no way to soften them now.

I am once more left alone amidst the graves. The rain pours down in steady streams, but I don't mind. This is what they expect of me now, I suppose. Naked and dripping wet. Dancing with the shadow. At the bottom of the hill, the silver-barked rowans stand like sentinels. There is hardly a leaf left on their haggard branches.

Something shifts in the corner of my eye.

White smoke.

A slight ringing of tinny sound echoes in my ears.

I choke. Back away. *No, not now.* But my ankle twists in something, and I am sprawling beside a tomb. I turn toward the white petals of flowers that shouldn't be blooming this time of year and a familiar name etched in stone.

Bram Avery.

Bitterbloom vines catch my boot, their fibrous fingers a hare trap at my heel. I scramble, tearing at them, while their deep scarlet sap leaks across my hand. And I wipe it hurriedly on a gloss of wet leaves, knowing even a drop could kill me stone dead. Just another grave to be dug amongst hundreds.

When I glance upward, the smoke is closer. Panic rises in my chest, fingers scrabbling at the damp earth to get up, up, up.

My heart races, throws beats so hard against my spindled bones I think they might crack. I crouch at the crest of Bram Avery's tombstone, tucking my head to my elbows and hurrying a finger to my throat. The answer that awaits me sends my blood boiling.

Doom-ed, doom-ed, doom-ed.

My chest seizes when the pain comes, the agony washing over me in nauseating waves. I try to rise, but I can't. My legs are useless, tethered to the dirt. Nothing more than a prisoner. And this time, the bars are of my own making. My own flesh.

I dip my head to my elbow and draw a steadying breath, then reach into my pocket and feel for the bell. While I can't explain it, the cold brass brings me comfort. A sense of grounding.

Get up. Just get up. It cannot hurt you.

But when I look back, the trees beyond the graveyard stand empty.

I breathe a sigh of relief, my sinew softening, heart slowing to a steady rhythm. My sweat-slick palm slides along the headstone when I rise shakily to my feet. Whatever was there is gone now, and even though my heart feels like it's slipping wetly in my chest, it maintains course. I take another breath.

"Adelaide!"

Father. His voice clawing at my ears through the fog of fear. I peer at him through the undulating mist enveloping the graveyard. He stands beside Mayor Samuels on the hill toward the church, his lips a thin line. Father bows his hat to the mayor, mumbles words I do not hear, and turns toward me. His cloak whips about his knees like dusky shadows.

"What are you still doing out here?" he demands, trailing down the hill, dirt smeared on his gloves.

I say nothing, focus on the returning calm of my heart.

"Come here."

I hold his gaze, challenge him, but I fail. His gloves tighten around his flexed hands.

He nods grimly while the ground squishes beneath my boots. Up close, he smells of tallow wax and stale wine. "What are you doing out here? It's not safe."

"Not safe for me?" I think of Mayor Samuels, the hatred in his eyes. "Or are others unsafe *because* of me, Father?"

His smile contracts, a stitch pulled tight and painful somewhere high on his cheek. "Do not play games with me, child. I do not deal in idle words."

I cannot hide my irritation. Idle words are all he knows. Blessed Scriptures from Ithrandril are nothing but a waste of time.

"What were the words you dealt?" I ask. "Just now, with Mayor Samuels?"

It is not the question I should be asking. In fact, I should ask no questions at all. Stay quiet, bide my time until I figure out what the hell I'm doing, lessen the chances of being tied to the chair tonight. My fingers curl at my sides.

His mouth twists, yet he offers an arm. "Let's take a walk."

I blink, try to swallow, but the muscles in my throat snag. I loop my arm through his and follow where he leads, the soft ground of the graveyard giving beneath my feet.

"Mayor Samuels has brought some…concerns to my attention."

Of course he has. I grind the inside of my cheek between hardened teeth.

"The villagers are growing worried about all the deaths, about the girls still left in Rixton. Many folks are thinking of sending their daughters away—their wives, even—to places deeper in the countryside, even to Lysdin, perhaps. The Samuels were just discussing it before…before…well…" His voice trails off.

Nerves tie knots in my stomach. I lave my tongue across my lips, but they remain as dry as sand.

"I have decided to contact one such place. For you. A house of healing near the border of Idlewild. The mayor assures me it is the safest option."

Dread prickles at the back of my neck, his words searing my skin like a brand.

A house of healing. I've heard of such places. Buildings made from iron and stone, filled with cells for those society no longer wants. Women who question their husbands and daughters who carry curses in their veins. Just another prison. Another place to be molded and formed to Ithrandril, when all that runs in my veins is shadow.

Dread curdles to anger in my stomach.

"Am I allowed no say in this?" The question cracks between my lips.

Father's eyes harden. "Your sickness runs deep, child. Who is to say your mind can even make the right decisions anymore?"

I swallow another jolt of anger. "There is nothing wrong with my mind."

"No?" It is not so much a question as it is a challenge. "Then tell me, where do you go when your sickness takes over? What do you do when everything around is devoured by shadow?" He reaches toward my cheek, then hesitates, as if a single touch might poison him.

His countenance shatters, and there is a flicker there of the man I used to know. The father who used to sing while he washed the dishes and lit candles in the windows of the vicarage every Yuletide. But then his face tightens, and he presses forward.

"The next coach arrives in Rixton within the week."

My boots slip in the muddy grass. His sharpened words cut my throat.

"I wonder, Father, if you say any of this for my comfort or only to make yourself feel better for sending me away. These houses of healing, they're mad. Filled with—"

His gaze snags on something beyond us, and then he grips my shoulder, fingernails digging into my flesh. "They think it's *you*, Adelaide. That your gods-cursed blood has made you a monster."

"I have done nothing!" Rain runs down my face, but I do not reach to wipe it away. It is a truth I already know, what the villagers believe me capable of simply because I am different. Sickly.

Father clenches his jaw. "Do you have something to confess, Adelaide? Otherwise, you have left me no other choice."

"You have *every* choice." Saliva pools at the back of my tongue, sweet as nightshade. I blink hard against tears. "You could choose to love me, to keep *me* safe, believe that I am not this…this *monster*, but you lock me in a room when my sickness—"

"Enough, child!" My father stretches tall, his fists clenched.

My eyes latch onto the pin of his cloak. In the hazy light, his eyes teem with hellfire, jaw so rigid every line, every bone, juts out like broken porcelain. I grit my teeth, and my pulse flutters in my throat.

"I am not a child."

"You will harken to me!" Father's voice is sharp as thorns, lips peeled back in a snarl. "You are a fool, Adelaide. A sickly fool. And you will do as I say. If you—" He takes a breath to steady himself. "If you ever loved your mother, you will listen and do as I say."

His rage turns to shadows on his face, and I can barely draw a breath. He stands there a moment longer, erect, the anger steaming off him in waves. And then he sighs, a ragged thing, lifts his hat from his head to wipe at the sweaty, graying locks.

"The decision has been made, Adelaide. I have been assured you will be well taken care of, that your illness will be *cured*. The men who run the house of healing are men of the church, blessed by Ithrandril. They say that when you return home, you will be every inch the woman your mother wished you could be. And you will be *safe*."

A hiss of hot air escapes my teeth when all the restraints binding my tongue snap. "Does it feel good? Saying the words you've practiced, over and over again, to yourself, in the bitter darkness of night, with perfect ease? Does it make you feel strong to send me away, to do what is *best*? Are you so scared of"—I glance down at my shaking hands, pressing them toward him—"of this that you spend so much time away, so frightened of the darkness you see in me? Maybe, Father, you should be afraid of yourself. Because if anything, *you* are the darkness."

I do not waste time watching my words hit their mark. Instead, I turn my back and trudge up the hill away from the graveyard. I wait for him to call me, to drag me to the garden shed by my hair and burn the whole thing to the ground with me inside. But I hear only silence and the steady scratch of willow branches against the vicarage.

I make my way through the kitchen door and to my room, the church bell clanging out a funeral dirge.

five

Hester's headstone is erected the next morning. I watch from my window, the latticed glass warping with rain. Father stands guard, a smudged shadow near the church. The same men who pulled her body up from the river now struggle in the dirt above her grave, straightening the stone as best they can.

It is futile work. In a few years' time, the stone will be like every other. Wilting to the side like a forgotten flower, covered in white petals that have no business blooming in the darker months.

I turn away from the window to where two objects sit on my bed. Mother's journal lies open to a page with more scribblings I do not understand. Scratched designs of patchwork, drawings of veiny root systems. I pored over them late into the night. Still my brain cannot make sense of the smudged ink. I wish she were here to help me understand. To tell me the places her mind went as the illness stripped her life away, while the madness and blood took over her body.

Maybe then, I could make sense of my own.

Beside the journal is Ransom's handkerchief. I lift the fabric in my hand and grit my teeth, remembering the gentle touch of the lordling, his fingers grazing my now-healing skin. The cloth is crusted with my dark blood, three letters looped in one corner in onyx thread.

RVB.

I rub my thumb over the stitches, barely a whisper-touch, and come up with a million things the *V* could stand for.

Vincent, Valentine, Virgil…

I shake my head. *Stupid.* There are more pressing matters at hand than the middle name of some high and mighty lordling. Namely, Father's desire to pack me on the next coach out of Rixton. I cannot leave my home, the one thing I still have tethering me to Mother. The last place she pressed a kiss to my forehead and whispered those three little words.

My Morning Glory.

An ache cuts across my chest. I cannot leave this place. My fingers trail the edges of my quilt while I take an inventory of my chambers. The bed pressed into the corner near the window, a jar of dried roses on the table beside that. Wallpaper printed with vines and ivory. In the center of the room, a wooden chair looped with ropes stained dark by blood.

A cold breeze whispers through the cracked window and sends the sheets of paper tacked on the walls rustling. My belly boils, anger and rage swirling there like a maelstrom.

Every one is a reminder. A witness to my wickedness. Father's handwriting is crystalline on each browning page. Words of Ithrandril, reminders of how he has forsaken me.

How dare my father even think about sending me away? I am no longer a child; I am a person. Whole and my own, am I not? If Mother were here—

I ball my hands into fists at my sides. But she isn't here, is she? She's dead.

My nails are dagger points in my flesh, digging until I have pierced through and drawn blood. It drips like ink along my palms. The tears come hot and heavy, rushing down my cheeks. Without a moment's thought, I tear across the floor, ripping each fluttering piece of paper from the plaster, until I am left with my forehead against the far wall, fistfuls of the Blessed Scriptures in my hands.

What good has any of it done me? Just a bunch of empty words meant to heal but only harm. My heart trips on the anger spilling up from my lungs, and I heave, shoulders shaking.

I will not be sent away.

It would be better to die than to board a coach for someplace Mayor

Samuels deems best. I bring to memory the hatred in his eyes, the accusation. His daughter's body half-warm in her grave and already placing blame.

Your illness will be cured.

The last word sits heavy and thick in my belly. Nausea hovers at the back of my throat, and before I can stop myself, I lean forward and vomit waxen sick on the floor. *Cured.* As if this illness, this *wrongness* about me, is something I can take medicine for. Merely a bout of chill, a share of ague. I lean heavy on the wall, the damp plaster giving way beneath my weight.

If only it were so simple. If only I knew the cure, I would do it myself. I do not wish to feel this way. If I could bring warmth to my cheeks or turn my blood to rubies, I would. But I will not be stolen away from the one place I have ever known love.

My heart tugs against sinew, and I breathe shallow while I glance at the ripped paper in my hands.

Cure.

It snaps a thread inside me.

I rush to my bedside table, hands shaking, throw open the small drawer, and dig through the contents to find a matchbook. Without a second thought, I flick a match along the red strip, and the sting of phosphorus rends the air. Beside the door, the hearth stands empty.

I toss the papers and then the flickering match against the coals, staring in stunned horror at my own actions. The flames lick the paper like autumn at the edge of oak leaves. Tears slip down my face, the firelight reflecting in the moisture while it leaves tiny tracks down my cheeks. I watch until the Blessed Scriptures are ashen, and my heart hollows out space in my chest.

When I sink my fingers into my pockets, the cold brush of metal breaks me from my stupor.

The bell.

A part of me wants to throw it out the window, crack it against the earth of Mother's garden beds to be buried with the snows, forgotten until some other poor unfortunate digs it up between their fingers and lays it bare. Leave it to the mud, where it can be swallowed once more.

Maybe, if I cannot hear it, the creatures of mist and teeth will not come for me.

Another piece, the one that sparked at the sight of a corporeal monster—a face—the part still picturing Ransom Black's eyes, still feels his fingers on my bare and bloody skin when he didn't shrink away, wants to hold the bell and keep it with me always. A tribute to the one inkling of freedom I have had in years. The one glimmer of *acceptance*.

Something scritches at my door.

Not Father.

My eyes dart to the window, down the hill toward the graveyard, where he still stands, cloak dripping wet. I cross and snap the window shut.

It comes again, the sound. A slow, stuttering thing, as though whatever awaits on the other side isn't fully there. As if their finger isn't made from bone or blood, but dust. My heart spasms, breath coming hot. I unravel the bell from its wrappings.

The sound comes once more, dry and thin as a barren twig.

I do not want to look. What if it is simply another monster come to lure me to the reaching branches of the hungry forest? Come to show me faces that no longer belong to the living?

My skin aches with nerves, a knot firmly set in the center of my chest. I try to refine my breaths. My lungs squeeze, heart fisting against my ribs.

My stomach turns, and my skin flares. Pain grows roots at the base of my skull. I toss my head back toward the ceiling, gurgling a scream at the back of my throat.

A soft scratch.

Why? Why *now*?

There is a telltale feather touch on my chest, the moment before my heart squeezes and stops, and I am sent head over heels, just trying to breathe. I stagger, head thick, the air around me stodgy, and I try to straighten just as my spine cracks like a twig.

No. Not now. Not today.

My finger itches for my throat. I want nothing more than to feel the anxious tremor of the vein beneath my skin, but I hold it firm at my side and bend my knuckles until the creases turn white as hoarfrost. My vision blossoms black. I blink.

No.

This fear is a wretched, wicked thing, and I don't want it anymore. Before I can stop myself, before I can think another thought, allow some other slip of my heart to guide my mind, I turn toward the door and hold out the bell.

It is strangely heavy for how small it is, like lead shot careening through my fingers. A wind blows up from the fields beyond the vicarage, rattling the glass panes of my window, sending rain against it like bullets. I focus on the bell, fisting my empty hand at my hip and wiping sweat along the wool of my skirt.

Bells are for protection, are they not? To be used as a warning against death and danger approaching? To keen against the ever-growing dark?

I give it no second thought. My wrist snaps, and the note that rings out is as clear and true as snow on fallen leaves. My breath catches at the sound, hooking in the wet, pink folds of my throat. But it isn't fear this time. My stomach bubbles, skin spreading with heat, and I realize, for the first time in so very long, it is *wonder*.

A cold wind stirs at the back of my neck, bringing with it the scent of salt and old bones. The sharp tang of lemons. I stare at the closed door, the warped wood. The heat of the paper still smoldering in the fireplace is a comfort on my skin. The chill breezes again, closer this time, frosting my eyelashes. My skin stiffens, heart thumping wildly.

No, no, no.

But I cannot stop it. Nothing can. I am powerless in the face of my own body. This cage of bones and flesh. My fingers fumble the bell, knees scraping the wooden floor, one palm run through with slivers. I release a small shudder of breath when the blood there pricks black.

And that's when I see it floating through the door of my bedroom. White as smoke.

The monster.

It wavers, light on water, coming in and out of focus while the bell rolls in my hand. The metal, so cold now, gnaws at the top layer of my skin. I cry out, teeth sinking into the soft flesh of my cheek, drawing more blood.

The monster begins to solidify. Colors warping from white to gray and from gray to black. My stomach swims, nothing left inside but my own sour bile. I clench my fists and scramble back, away from the monster, my breath leaving me in short, hollow puffs.

But it isn't a monster anymore.

A scream sharpens in my throat when it materializes a face, dark hair spooling over the cut jaw, amber eyes. I peel back my lips. The only sound filling the room is the spit of dying fire in the hearth. I push back toward the bed, away, away, away, but the monster—no, the *face*—turns to me, and I see it for what it is.

It's not a monster at all, not anymore.

It's a ghost.

six

I am damned.

That is the only explanation for the thing now standing in front of me. A monster of shadow and smoke, boasting a face. But not just *any* face. One I know.

My knees give out, betraying me. I crash against the bedpost, fingers scraping the wood for any sense of support.

"You." The word is stupid on my tongue. "How is it *you*?"

Silence.

It crashes in my ears like ocean waves, and I heave against the bed, my palm shaking on the cotton check of my quilt, smearing blood against the fabric. I stare at the ghost—the man—and my jaw locks, words crumbling to ash.

Father used to say ghosts were demons masquerading as flesh to drag us off to the shadow of Hell with them. To steal us away from Ithrandril. That in the Rending, Erybrus took his souls and Ithrandril ascended, allowed his brother to abduct who he wished. But this is no stranger, not a thing with horns and claws.

The figure steps closer, the mist around him undulating. I shake my head and press a finger to my throat. My heart beats a quickening step, my breath short and raspy. The room shrinks, and the man steps forward, fear dancing in his eyes like winking stars.

"You're Bram Avery." I wait for a reply, but none comes. Acting on instinct alone, I open my mouth and say the first thing that comes to mind. "You're supposed to be dead."

"How very astute." His nose flares in annoyance. Beneath a strong brow, his eyes are embedded with hints of something like grief and longing. His lips turn down at the corners, as though he is waiting for the whole world to come crashing around him.

For a moment, silence lays roots in my mouth, my throat, rolling down to tighten my lungs. This should not be real. And yet, Bram Avery—a man who should be dead, whose grave I knelt against only days ago—is standing in my bedroom. He winces and falls to his knees, as if kicked. Locks of hickory hair swirl around his head, like weeds caught in water.

This is no monster. I *know* him. Watched him walk with his little sisters to church, followed his coattails when he got lost in the orchards behind Avery Manor. I always thought him handsome, even as a child, but here he is, something else altogether.

When I drop in front of him, I reach out a shaking hand. My fingers pass through the lines of his body. I hiss and pull away from the cold.

"I don't understand how you're here," I say breathlessly.

His expression softens. He drops back against the wall, one leg outstretched, boot caked in reddish mud.

"If I knew, I would explain it. But all I know is that"—he points to the bell still in my hand—"finally let you see me."

Sweat breaks out along my forehead while his words settle around me. I slump to the floor, head against the side of my bed frame, skirt tucked around my knees.

"Have you been…in here?" I swallow, throat sharp.

"Don't worry. I've always been decent." He cracks a satisfied smile and drops his head back to the wall. "And no. It may come as a surprise, but even as a living man, I would rather be out amidst the trees than caught in the bedchamber of a woman I barely know." His eyes find me again, glinting like polished copper. "I've been trying to speak with you for years, though."

His confession twists my stomach. Bram Avery is my monster.

I release a breath. "What I need to know is why Bram Avery, who died ten years ago, is sitting in my bedroom after I rang"—I hold up the bell—"whatever the hell this is."

He shrugs, gaze licking the curve of brass in my hand. His own breath comes short and fast, as though he has been running for a very long time and has only now found rest.

"Where exactly are you?" I ask. "If you're dead?"

His eyes dart up to the ceiling, but it is not the plaster he is studying; it is something else. Something I cannot see.

"What is it?"

He is on his feet faster than I can stop him, breath rushing like winter gales on a pond. Bram reaches out to me, his hands passing like frozen teeth through the wool at my shoulders.

"Get away from the window!"

A gust of cold air knocks me to my hands and knees. Bram dives below the windowsill. When I look up, the truth is like a punch to the throat. There is nothing out there.

"Bram—"

He brushes a hand through his dark hair. "Look, we don't have much time. I need—"

"I don't understand how you're here."

The air hardens to ice. He slides beside me next to the bed, so close I smell a hint of woodsmoke on his tattered clothes. His eyes darken.

"Adelaide, listen to me. I need you to bring me back."

I stumble against the frame, the bell breaking free from my hands to spill across the checked quilt. His eyes narrow when it rolls to rest near Mother's journal, Ransom's handkerchief.

"I don't—"

"The bell." Panic beats in his eyes. "You can use it to bring me back. I don't know how you found it, but that is a death bell. A Reaper's bell. You know what this is, don't you?"

My mind is a jumble of words that make no sense, but I weed through it, reaching for Blessed Scriptures.

"In the Rending." My vision ripples. "Certain souls taken by Erybrus were cursed. Turned to Reapers. Tasked with harboring the dead to whatever awaited them. But you don't—" My gaze flinches to the bell.

"Yes. And each Reaper was given a bell to travel between the planes of life and death, remember?"

I nod. Yes, I remember. I have sat in church and heard the stories. But they were always just that: stories. Meant to scare us into submission, into a yearning to grow closer to Ithrandril.

"Look, Adelaide, if you don't—" Bram darts his eyes wildly around us, seeing things I cannot but sending my heart racing all the same. "I'm going to die here. I need your help. You have to use it."

I blink and shake my head. Maybe Idlewild is the right place for me to go. I am no Reaper. And if I am…then Mayor Samuels, my father, and the entire village is right.

I am touched by darkness. By Erybrus himself.

I stumble backward. "Bram, you're already dead. I don't see what this little thing is going to do."

He ducks, hands clutching aimlessly at the bed skirt. Still, there is nothing in the room besides us. He stays still for a moment, and when he finally looks up at me, his eyes could melt diamonds.

"I'm not fully dead, you know."

There's a catch of something in his voice, something like fear, and it liquefies my bones.

"Bram, I don't understand. My father spoke your funeral rites. I threw earth on your casket after your three sisters. I—" The words hitch in my throat. "Why are you here? Why are you not watching your family? If your sisters knew, your mother—"

"They cannot help me!" He spits the words like gravel. "They cannot see me like you can. Adelaide, you're the only one who can use the bell. I know it, deep down inside. I know you are my only path to salvation."

There's a desperation in his eyes, and it breaks me, shreds my heart to threads. But this can't be real. It isn't—

I glance once more at the bell, overwhelmed with my own desperate confusion. And yet, it all makes sense.

In my mind, it begins to slot into place, like pieces to a puzzle. My blackened blood. My wan complexion. The illness tremoring through my veins. Shadow-touched. Cursed. Which means I am something this town *should* be afraid of. A monster.

Tears hem my eyes. "This isn't—you have to help me understand. You died so long ago. I remember..." My voice trails off while I study Bram's face.

The first time I saw him, angling down Bantlers Close, his nose was stuck between the pages of a book. I thought him the strangest man I had ever seen. When all the other young men in Rixton were off foxhunting or stringing Farmer Whitley's cows into trees, Bram Avery could be found wandering the streets, sipping gingerbread tea at the bakery, or nestled under apple trees in the Avery orchards. Always, always with a book in hand.

I thought him marvelous, and as I study him now, I still do. The curve of his jaw, the mussed hair, the way his eyes flash like molten gold... My heart stutters, breath rushing from between my two lips when he catches my eye.

"What do you remember?" His voice edges near a gentler tone.

"It's just. It's *you*." My brow crinkles, and my mouth runs dry as sand. "You haven't aged a day."

He reaches for my hand, and when his fingers only pass through mine, I crouch down beside him. Like the closer we become, the more hidden he will be from whatever it is I cannot make out.

His jaw clenches, eyes weary. "I said I wasn't fully dead. Doesn't mean I'm not partially dead."

"You don't age? Wherever you are, I mean." The words feel impossible on my tongue, the very sound of them ridiculous.

I am talking to a ghost. A dead man in similar age to me now than he was ten years ago. My fingers itch to peel the skin from my own throat, just to feel the slick wetness of my veins beating against them. Just to know how alive I truly am. Because right now...I take a shuddering breath. Right now, I feel as empty as a corpse.

"The rowan wood." Bram draws a knee to his chest and leans heavy on a dirt-caked palm. His hair drifts like seaweed. The mist swirls so cold around him it is a wonder he doesn't shatter like river ice.

"I'm sorry?"

He gestures at the space around us. "Where I am. Where all the dead go to await their choice. Trapped between the living and whatever waits for us after."

My brain jitters with the information while I rationalize every possibility.

"Purgatory. You are still waiting to make your choice between the gods—"

"Adelaide, listen to me." Bram turns, eyes shining. "Call it whatever you like. I don't care. I just need you to get me out, bring me home. I can't let..." He turns back to the empty window, gritting his teeth.

I push myself off the floor, pacing. Outside, the world drifts toward night, nothing beyond the window except a village cloaked in shadow and the glow of lamplight. Chaos niggles at the back of my mind, eating away at my gray matter, like a worm on dead flesh.

This shouldn't be possible, *isn't* possible. I try to blame my heart, the pain growing like a thick-barked tree at the base of my skull.

A monster, just a monster.

But he's not.

All these years, I haven't been seeing monsters. I've been seeing *souls*.

And I am frightened of what it might mean.

My stomach twists into knots, and when I turn back, there he is—Bram Avery—the man who mysteriously died ten years ago. The only betrayal of passing age are the creases along his eyes, the look of hungry panic spilling from his irises like shadow.

"This shouldn't be happening." I retrieve the bell from off the bed. "It's just a bell. Rubbish I found down by the river."

Bram scrambles to his feet, backing me up against the bedpost, chest heaving beneath the tattered linen of his shirt. My eyes drift to his throat, the skin there taut and covered in scars. I suck in air, my flesh growing hot. I breathe in the chill of him, the distant scent of woodsmoke and something else...something so familiar my heart cracks along its own fissures.

Lemons.

"Do you remember the orchard?" he asks, voice low. "The day you caught me hiding up in the trees? I didn't have a book that day. I was just up there, hoping the branches would be thick enough to hide me from my father's fists."

I close my eyes, traveling back to my younger self, the girl who still had a mother and didn't know the cruelty of a father who had forgotten how to love her. A girl who wore a dress the color of daffodils and laughed at the sun. A girl who didn't know true fear until she found a young man tangled amongst leaves and ruby red apples and saw it there, pulsing in his eyes and just below his skin. A girl who was too little to help.

"I remember."

I watch as relief washes over him in steady streams, and he shoots a look skyward. Whatever he sees sends him ducking, scuttling across the floor like an injured beast, until his back is to the corner.

My stomach hollows. All this time, he has been here, just outside, trying to speak, to get me to pay attention, and I called him a monster.

"Bram." I hold out a shaking hand, tracing his hurried path across the room until I am crouched beside him, wishing he was solid so I could feel the warmth of his skin. Make up for so much lost time. "Bram, I don't think—"

He lifts a shaking finger to his lips. "Use the bell," he whispers. "Use the bell and come to the wood. Find the river."

Nerves like claws sink deep into my flesh, to peel it back and spill the shadowed blood.

Cursed.

I drop my gaze to the cool brass in my hand. Such a small, insignificant thing. I wrap my palm around it until its sharp edges carve grooves into my palms. Pain shimmers above my body, and for a moment, I shut my eyes, thinking when I open them this will all disappear—Bram, the bell, Father's sentence of the house of healing in Idlewild—and I will be here, alone. Nothing that has happened will be true. It will have been a dream. Even Clara and Hester and Ransom Black.

But I feel the crooked sting of the cut on my foot, the wrappings tight around the shredded flesh. Ransom's hand on my skin, warm and real, his breath on my face while he spoke to me with such anchoring surety.

I snap my eyes back open, and there Bram remains, huddled in the corner, arms now up around his head. My heart slips against my ribs. The bell vibrates in my hand. Brief, but enough to draw my attention back to it.

Fear coils in my chest. This isn't real. *None* of it is real. It is simply an illness. *My* illness. The wrongness of my heartbeat, the pain soaking my limbs like salt water. I press to my feet, cross to the table beside my bed, and open the drawer.

"What are you doing?" Bram's words are rushed and quick, a waterfall with sharpened rocks at the bottom.

I don't turn back, but keep my eyes fixed on the pearl-white glow of the moon above the fruited rye fields. "I can't help you. This—it's not right." The fist around my heart loosens, crawls up the back of my throat while I choke back tears.

"Adelaide." His voice is as hard and cold as shattered porcelain.

I squeeze my eyes shut, tears eking out to dampen my cheeks. My fingers fumble with the drawer when I shove the bell away, back between all the papers, the dusty bottles of ink.

"I'm so sorry, Bram."

Perhaps girls like me, girls without someone to love them right, maybe we are broken things. China dolls left on mantles, laden with dust, waiting for the day the ground shakes, gives way beneath us, and we tip head over heels to shatter on the floor.

I sink my fingernails into the soft wood grain of the table and open my eyes to darkness. All I know is that I am resolute. Mind firm in places it was pliable only moments before. Whatever it means—this Reaper's bell—it does not concern me. I turn back around to face Bram, barely registering the heartbreak etched on his face.

"You have to go back," I say. "Back to the—wherever you came from."

There is so much pain on his face I think it might break me. His eyes harden, and it takes all my strength not to crash toward him and wrap my arms around whatever fog and cloud forms his body.

"Adelaide, please. I'll die here."

"You're already dead." The words fall from my lips harsher than I mean them. "Bram Avery died ten years ago in the springtime. I remember because the cold earth was soft when they buried the casket and the flowers grew." My fingers flex at my side. I remember the way we all tossed the dark kernels of dirt over the wooden box. "You will only be my damnation."

Ghosts drag souls to Erybrus.

There is silence, the only sound the echoing *scritch* of a naked willow branch against my window. I cannot tear my eyes from Bram, sunk deeper into the corner of my room, shadows glistening on his face like oil. It is a familiar feeling, the helplessness leaking from his very skin. It pools at the hollow of my throat, threatens to sever the veins there, to crush my skull until I am nothing more than a pile of bone dust to be caught and carried away by the winter wind.

I am about to turn away, to curl up on my bed and watch the stars lick across the black sky until Father's cane is heard along the paving stones, when Bram turns his face up to mine.

"What if I told you there was a way to save someone else? Bring someone else back?"

His words set my heart racing, an ache spreading out against my chest and up my throat. "Who—what are you talking about?"

His lips quirk, a bitter, wretched twist of a smile. "You bring me back, and we rescue another in the process." His gaze snaps up. "Two faces beneath one hood. A deal."

My body goes as chill and stiff as a shaft of wheat in an ice storm. "I don't understand."

Bram peels himself from the floor, mist hounding at his heels. "You bring me back, and I'll make sure someone else comes with us. Someone I'm sure you'd very much like to see."

The cold licks around my spine and settles between my shoulder blades. I open my mouth, but the words shrivel into nothing. My lungs constrict, pulse quickening, a stunted laugh bursting from my lips.

"You mean my mother, don't you?" I half believe I have gone mad. That this is all a dream and soon I'll wake to Father splashing cold water on my face, calling me to obey him, even as I spit dirt and ice to the floor of the garden shed.

Bram takes another step closer, hands fisting at his sides. "Everyone with unfinished business is left behind in the wood by Ithrandril and Erybrus, waiting. That is our choice, Adelaide."

A coal kindles in my chest. "Waiting for what?"

Bram's smile widens, stretches like a snake bathing in the sun. "Their own deals. Their own decisions. The Rending made us this way, Adelaide. We must choose, and it is a terrible choice to make."

He ducks low when something invisible swoops overhead, and my heart crashes into my breastbone. I drop beside him, fingers groping at the shadow. At once, nothing and everything makes sense.

In the Rending, we were torn from Ithrandril. Tossed so near Erybrus, we spend every minute of our waking hours scrambling back toward the god of life's warmth. And when we die? Father preaches that with each good deed, our souls are brought back into the glow of Ithrandril. But what if we die while we are still deciding?

Choosing between the god we will serve for eternity hereafter. A place where light and darkness are still at war. A place where we must make one final deal just to find the rest we have so long hoped for.

My heart thrums in my ears. "How do I bring my mother back?"

Bram's eyes are untamed fire while they dart about my bedroom. My hands sink into the cold mist swirling around him like a maelstrom. It kicks up, bringing with it the scent of frozen leaves, ground licked by frost. I try to scream his name, to calm him as the shadows spin, but the rush of the wind swallows my voice, and I am blinking up from the floor, knees aching from where I have fallen.

Bram's hair whips violently around his face. His skin begins to stretch, peel back. My chest constricts.

"The bell, Adelaide!" he cries above the tumult. "You must use the bell!"

Between the rips of wind and tendrils of my own hair, my gaze snags on my table. So far, so very far. And now the wind smells of blood, growing hotter while it spills through my room.

"Bram!" The word dies as soon as it leaves my mouth, and I am up on my knees, tearing aimlessly through the empty air.

Bram is swallowed up by the coppery wind, the eking shadow, and I am left all alone.

I fall forward, palms slapping the cold floorboards. My breath comes in short gasps between sobs. I drag myself up, heaving toward the window, the little table beside my bed. My shaking fingers fumble the drawer, and the bell rolls to greet me. I reach toward it and then pull back as if bitten.

No.

If I do this, I will have to face the truth. That what the village, what my *father*, believes of me is true. That I am touched by shadow. Abandoned by Ithrandril.

Bram Avery is a ghost. A devil wanting to drag my soul to eternal damnation. I slam the drawer shut and look out into the night. My father's silhouette creeps down the garden wall, his shadow licking up the side of the church. I stare into the darkness, copper still coating my tongue, and whisper all that comes to mind.

"I'm sorry, Mother. I'm so sorry."

 *seven*

The next coach departs Rixton in less than a week, and already, I have worried my palms raw, flesh pink and peeling. I cannot go to Idlewild, where I am sure to be strapped to a chair, my brain pricked and prodded until I am empty. Men blessed of Ithrandril, my father said. And what are men blessed by gods other than tools of destruction?

I tell myself Father will change his mind, that I will awake to find him waiting outside my door, tea in hand and an apology written on his face. But the truth is, I have not seen my father since Bram appeared, scared of his own shadows and smelling of acrid citrus. I have not met with *anyone*, and I think it is better this way.

So, I stand in front of my window, the edges of my body reflecting in the dim light of morning. My face is drawn and tired, skin creased around my eyes like damp paper, lips bitten and dry. The sky outside is a blanket of gray, the trees like candlelight against its darkening visage. A murmuration of starlings kicks up from the fields beyond the silver river, reminding me of the way Bram wore the shadows, as if they were his very skin.

Faces beneath a hood. A deal to be made.

Two birds with one stone. Not one soul brought back, but two.

Yet death is not a power to be trifled with. Erybrus is a hungry god. I have seen death take too many, whisper across a soul and turn it into nothing more than a casing of flesh and coagulated blood. Young women left frozen along the riverbank.

Making a deal with a devil for one soul is a foolish mistake. But two souls? That would make me a thief.

Beyond the garden wall and down past the hill, the River Thine rushes beneath the bridge and through the village like a tongue of molten glass. I trace it until it disappears between the trees beyond the graveyard.

On the day of the Rending, when the world was torn in half between Ithrandril and Erybrus, it was said that rivers were the only openings back to the two gods. That they left some of their magic in the waters, which is why the waves are always at war between the darkness and the light. If Bram is right and his soul is held somewhere in the rowan wood, then there is some truth to the teaching.

I cross to the small table beside my bed and peel open the desk drawer. The bell lolls on its dome.

I should bring it back.

Grind it beneath my boot and send the pieces back to the river. It can curse the next unfortunate soul who finds it, make *them* see visions of the dead. For a moment, I wonder at how its original owner—a Reaper—lost it. But does it matter? With my white hair and blackened blood, I am not too far from Erybrus myself.

I bite down on my bottom lip until a coppery taste floods my mouth, reminding me of the scent of the room when Bram appeared or the tang in the air that sweeps up from the wood when the monsters—or the souls, as I now have come to know—show themselves.

There are monsters in the wood. Maybe not the things I have seen. But Erybrus harbors many a monster, hellhounds, Reapers.

I trail a finger along the cool metal.

Perhaps, this bell is the making of another.

Before I can think, I gather it into my fist, grab my coat from its hook, and set my hand against the door.

I will not live in this in-between place. This wishing and hoping for a life that was never meant to be mine, stolen from me while Mother took her last, ragged breath. Closing my eyes, I rest my head on the rough-hewn wood. I am more than this endless ache of something I will never have again. Whatever I am.

Father may wish to send me away. But if I go, if I let the healers in Idlewild attend me, will he love me again as he once did?

Perhaps that is the wish of a child.

I throw the door open and rush down the stairs. The kitchen is empty and cold. No fire in the hearth, no kettle on the stove. There is no warmth in this house. It is merely a cage of old bones.

My palm falls open, revealing the bell, and I watch the delicate brass catch the thin light.

"I'm so sorry, Mother," I whisper, voice wet. "I'm so sorry I couldn't save you. But now I've—I've—" My throat clogs, and it takes every bit of strength I have to stay on my feet, spine straight. "I have to save myself."

Without another look back to the kitchen, I wrench open the small door and spill out into the frosty morning, the taste of copper and lemons on my tongue.

The wind is a cold bite at my back, a shriveled palm pulling at the folds of my cloak. A shiver runs through me while my feet tramp down the long expanse of frosted grass, the lilt of snow on the air. Down in the valley, the river runs like a mad beast, spitting up between chunks of hardened ice, red leaves gathered and stuck in the crevices between solid and liquid. My stomach swills, boots squelching in the curdled muck, when I step down to the riverbank and pull the bell from my pocket, then hold it up against the dim sun.

A Reaper's bell. Bram's voice niggles at the back of my mind.

I almost laugh at the thought. A halting, messy sort of noise spilling from the back of my throat like sandpaper. I swallow, mouth the words over and over.

A Reaper. Death.

The very things hounding all the girls of Rixton. It sinks into my bones

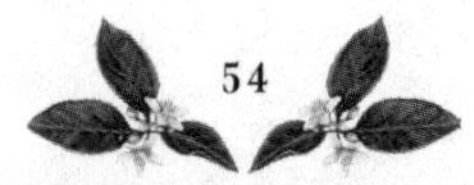

and flesh, that word, and sees me for all I am. Mother used to speak of death and the fear she carried finally catching her. I often wondered if she would ever find a way to keep herself from dying. She would stroke my hair by firelight, whispering things in my ear.

Chase Death, Addie, my darling. That way, he will never catch you.

Fine. *Come and find me. Show your face.* Tell me if it's mine.

But it's a fool's errand to tell Death how and when to act. And I am no fool. I am merely a broken-pieces woman who feels her own doom approaching with the grinding wheels of a rickety coach. And though they are one and the same, the Reapers and Death, why would they own something as trivial as shards of brass washed up on the banks of the River Thine?

And I am not Death, am no minion of Ithrandril or his greedy brother.

I am just a woman.

My knuckles shift white when I tighten my grasp on the bell, every thought now bent on destroying it. Saying goodbye. If I am to be sent away to Idlewild, there is one thing I know for sure. The healers there can poke and prod me all they like, but they will not heal me like my father expects.

I must heal myself.

"Adelaide?"

I drop my hand and spin on my heel. Mud sprays my hem. Clara stands behind me, brown hair wisping about her face, a basket hung from the crook of her elbow. Her skin is pale, cheeks bitten with the cold, and her eyes look as though she hasn't slept in days.

I swallow, my body hot with nerves, and nestle the bell deep into my pocket, hoping Clara didn't see it. Won't be able to tell a story about how she found the vicar's daughter down on the banks of the River Thine, with a crazed look on her face and a Reaper's bell clenched in her hand.

Clara smiles. A reanimated thing pulled from some distant form of life. I do not smile back.

"What are you doing out here?" she asks. "We aren't safe anymore."

Her eyes catch on the thin wool of my dress, the tangle of my white hair, the violet stains clutching high on my cheekbones, and I flinch. I find I cannot look at her while I answer, so instead, I throw my gaze to the village at her back.

"I could be saying the same to you. What business is it of yours what I do with my time?"

The sting of my words is a snapped band in the air. We say nothing, the rush of the water beyond the only thing making a sound. That and the ravens nesting in the creaking trees.

When I look at Clara, her eyes are clogged with tears, turning the whites bloodshot, rimmed in red. My stomach swims, tying itself into a knot that settles low and clings to me like a sickness.

"Clara, I'm—"

"No." Clara holds up a hand. "No, you're right. It is no business of mine. I'll leave you to whatever it was you were doing."

She goes to turn, the edges of her skirt making curls in the icy mud. A crack echoes from the forest, and I whip toward the line of trees on the far bank.

The monsters. *No*. The souls.

All the waiting dead things.

"Adelaide?"

I blink and turn back to Clara, her eyes sparking with curiosity. She's hardly a breath away from me now, so close I smell her father's bakery wafting from the folds of her rust-colored coat. Marble rye bread and apple scones.

"Adelaide, you look as though you've seen a ghost."

The irony of her words curdles a bitter laugh at the base of my tongue. "What do you know of ghosts, Clara?"

Her brow crinkles, lips forming a crescent moon over her chin. "Adelaide, *don't*."

It is not what I was expecting her to say, and it leaves me standing there, breathless, any witty comebacks left dry and shriveled.

Clara's eyes glaze with tears, her gaze darting from me to the river and back again. "Don't pretend as if I know nothing. As if I haven't watched you waste away, get all tucked up inside yourself. You were my best friend, Adelaide, and now…now it's like I don't even recognize you. You've turned so sharp."

I don't reply. What is there to say when every word she speaks is a truth so hard it lands like a stone in my gut?

"This isn't you," she says. "The girl I saw hardened in the churchyard, the girl right now, words like needles…that's not you." She steps closer, and there is pain in the lines between her brows, eddying there like a storm at sea. "What happened to you, Adelaide? After your mother died, I was here. I have *always* been right here."

My face heats under her words. Do I show her the scars on my palms from where my father hits me? Do I open my mouth and let every verse of Blessed Scripture he has made me memorize in the dark and the cold of my room spill out? Do I empty the bell onto my raw and bleeding palm and tell her the story of Bram Avery, the man who died, hiding in the shadows of my bedroom, begging me to bring him back from the dead? Do I tell her of the way my own heart betrays me, pulls me down until I see black and forget the things I might have done?

I cast my gaze to my feet, my toe scooping troughs in the muck. "There is so much you don't know, Clara. So much that you would never believe me if I told you."

Her boots come into my line of vision, shiny black leather dulled with frozen mud. Her finger curls beneath my chin, drawing my eyes to meet hers.

"You can tell me, Adelaide. And I will tell you my secrets. Sisters in silence."

A strange emotion grabs a hold of my heart and squeezes. For a moment, I brace myself for the pain, the slippage of arteries and chambers in the wrong moments, the wrong time. But they do not come. I am like a bud caught in spring frost, tossed about by bitter wind. There is so much to say, but all of my words taste of poison.

"I'm so very different from you, Clara," I say finally. "So very different from any of the women in Rixton."

Because my father beats me? Because I see dead people? Because I am known by the souls trapped in the rowan wood?

Because, perhaps, it is I who is the true monster? The girl who steals souls.

Mayor Samuels certainly believes it. And do I truly know where I go in the blackness of my fits? For the first time in my life, I allow my mind to truly drift to places I have only entertained. My black blood, my white hair, the way death seems to limn my body like a second skin. The Reaper's bell like a stone in my pocket.

Maybe I am in the shadows because Erybrus is all I have ever known. Perhaps my soul belongs to the darkness.

Clara clucks her tongue. "Even though I doubt that is true, I know what it's like to be different." Her eyes lower to the basket she is holding, and curiosity overwhelms me.

I study her sunken cheeks, the way she has almost seemed to age years since I last glimpsed her.

She frowns. "There are things you don't know either, Adelaide. When you lost your mother, I lost someone too." She reaches out, faster than fire, and grips my hand before I can pull away. "I lost *you*. I lost the person I told everything to. Every secret, every joke, every pain or hurt or joy."

Her eyes light at the last word. *Joy*. It's a funny one. So few letters for so big a thing.

"There's something I've been wanting to tell you. For years, really. But once your father pulled you from church, kept you locked up, I couldn't get to you. And now—" Her head swivels back toward the village, and I am left with an aching in my gut.

"What is it you've been wanting to tell me?"

When she turns, Clara's eyes are as large as hazelnuts. A smile brightens the tired hollows of her cheeks. She squeezes my hand tighter.

"Liza and I are getting married. Our parents know, and everyone is thrilled, but—"

I cannot help the smile—a real, true, alive sort of thing—breaking across my lips. In this moment, I am twelve years old again, running through fields with Clara, drinking gingerbread tea and reading contraband romance novels before the fire while we giggle into our too-pink palms.

"Clara, I—"

She rushes a finger to my lips. "There's trouble."

And I see it there, in the crushed petal stains around her eyes, in the way her fingers twitch on the handle of her basket.

"What do you mean?"

Clara sighs, dropping her hand to fuss with the lace napkin concealing whatever is inside her basket. "It's my father. He's… Well, Liza and I are planning on running away, and I know he doesn't want us to leave."

I blink. "The bakery."

It's a trivial thing to be concerned over, when there are monsters in the woods and ghosts in the house, with the coach only days away. But for Clara, it is her life. And life is never trivial.

She shakes her head. "I do not want it. Liza and I, we want to start our own. In the Queen's city. In Lysdin." She takes my hand again, her eyes welling with tears. A smile takes root in the corners of her mouth. "Think of it, Adelaide. We've all heard tales of it, simply bursting with opportunity. It's where Erybrus broke away from Ithrandril, where we can be closest to the warmth of all that is good and righteous. Where *we* may become good and righteous. Besides, Rixton is too small. And I want to see life out there, beyond Farmer Whitley's fields, past the graveyard walls and the Avery Manor orchards. Places even grander than Blackbourne Castle."

Breath hisses from my lungs at her last words. Ransom Black still sits at the edges of my mind, drifting there like a phantom. I can feel his soft hands on my ankle, pressing cotton against the cut on my heel.

"Adelaide."

Clara's kind voice draws me back, and I feel so small, wretched, and utterly insignificant. I pull my hands away, tucking a strand of hair behind my ear.

"I am happy for you."

A silence settles over us, and Clara steps back. It isn't entirely uncomfortable. I am used to the quiet, the way it fills the space between my bones like paste.

If I turn my chin over my shoulder, I dread the soul will still be there, waiting for me. Waiting for whatever it wants *of* me. I whisper a silent thank you to whatever is listening that Clara does not seem to be able to see it.

She unfolds the cloth from inside the basket, revealing a smattering of browned scones, each one dusted with sugar and orange zest. Clara holds one out to me, and for a moment, all I seem to be able to do is stare stupidly at it. She nudges it closer.

"Take it, for me. It's orange and rosemary."

My cold fingers wrap around the pastry, and I tuck it into my pocket beside the bell. "I will save it for later."

Clara nods. "Thank you for listening. I know it might seem silly—"

"It's not silly," I say before I can stop myself. "Love is quite a serious thing, I think. And I am happy you have found it with Liza. I wish you all the best."

Her smile cracks like a robin's egg, and before I can stop her, she is throwing her arms around me, and all I smell is yeast and sugar and something like lavender soap.

"Thank you, Adelaide," she whispers into my hair. "I've wanted to tell you for so long. Just, thank you."

When she pulls away, her cheeks are stained rose, and her eyes are shiny and wet. The knot in my stomach tightens, and I curl my hands in, letting the pain of nails in my flesh ground me. Hold me steady. Give me space to breathe. I clear my throat, bob my head, stretch a weary smile.

"You're welcome."

Behind us, the church bell rings the hour, and Clara nearly jumps from her clutch of scarves and shawls and coat. "I've got to go. Liza will be waiting for me. We're packing. The next coach from Rixton leaves soon."

How could I forget?

I wring my smile until all the joy is dripping down my chin. "Ithrandril go with you."

"Thank you." She turns to leave, then stops, a ghost of a grin still haunting her lips. "And, Adelaide, you deserve happiness too."

I nod, but I don't believe her. Ithrandril abandoned me a long time ago, and soon, so will everyone else. I watch Clara disappear back up the bank, across the bridge, and down the lane of thatched houses, taking all the happiness in the world with her.

I blow breath out from between my lips and pull the bell out of my pocket. The line of rowans is deserted. No white mist, no teeth damp with saliva, no words worming their way into the thoughts.

Only silence.

I roll the bell in my palm, watching it catch the dim light.

A Reaper's bell. Death's bell.

I barely know a thing about Bram Avery. Whether he is a liar or one who speaks truth. All I can be sure of is the way he huddled in a corner, afraid of things I could not see, and offered me the devil's deal.

Once, a fool. Twice, a thief.

I close my fingers around the bell, looking out at the rushing river warring against the ice.

Happiness. A word that should taste of honey but slips down my throat like fermented wine. The wheat fields beyond the water waver in the wind, gold against all the gray, all the dead and dying things. A wind dances through the rowans, and the leaves whisper words in my ears.

Love is quite a serious thing.

My words.

I swallow, fingering the bell, setting to memory the pattern impressed upon the brass. There has only ever been one person who loved me: Mother. I hear Bram's voice in my head.

Two faces beneath one hood.

Two souls to steal from Erybrus.

Three days. I have *three* days.

Three days to bring my mother home. With her here, Father will forget all thoughts of Idlewild, and I can move beyond this wretched semblance of a life. I can find joy once more.

If Mother is alive, maybe, just maybe, my father will become the man he once was. The man who smiled and brought me on his walks about the village. I close my eyes, picture the meadows in summer, Father's warm hand in mine, the way he used to laugh when I chased rabbits from the blackberry thicket. That is the Father I want. Not the fragile monster with scales for skin, scared of what the world will think, who ties me to chairs and threatens to send me away. I want him to be more than bitter memories. Resurrect the man who laughed and sang and read bedtime stories.

I imagine my mother. Her honey-gold hair, the light reflecting off the River Thine matching the blue in her eyes. The way she taught me to sink my fingers into the earth, tend the growing shoots of foxglove, oleander, larkspur.

I hold the bell up against the sun. Rays of light catch the metal's decorative swirls. It takes all my strength not to ring it right now, out in the open. But I do not want Ithrandril to see. To damn me when I cross into the dark. I clench my fist and turn back to the vicarage.

Once, a fool. Twice, a thief.

Well, then. Thief it is.

eight

The night gathers quickly outside my window. Shadows ghost in the garden, turning the mangled bushes to lurking ghouls. One wrong move and I am swallowed up, taken down to whatever awaits the dead.

Bram said he lingers in some liminal space of the wood. A part I cannot see. Not fully. A place neither dead nor alive. Ithrandril saving the souls who strived for goodness in their life and the rest rotting away until Erybrus claims them. Where restless souls—those claimed neither by Ithrandril or Erybrus—bide their time, their unfinished business, like worms trapped beneath skin.

My stomach buckles with the thought. Of Mother wrapped in the darkness of the deepening wood, hiding from whatever things Bram was so afraid of. Each breath painful, each moment agony while she waits…

Waits for what?

What could possibly keep her from peace? Her choice should be easy.

I dredge up every option, every moment of my life and hers that might be the reason she is trapped there, in some wood beyond. The realization cracks across my surface like shattered porcelain, and I find myself on the floor, head in my hands, tears running down my cheeks.

You deserve to be happy. Clara's voice filters through my mind.

And maybe that is all Mother wants for me. Happiness. Maybe it is the thing keeping her trapped between life and death. Mortality and eternity. Holding her back from making her final choice.

I reach for the bell where it sits on my desk, my teeth grinding. The handle is worn, the wood smooth, like it was made to fit my palm. I push to my feet, holding it aloft.

Two faces beneath one hood.

Two souls stolen.

I will make this devil deal if it will bring Mother back. If it will rescue her from a fate worse than rotting bones. One flick of my wrist—that is all it will take. Such a simple movement for so great a thing. I pull in lungfuls of air, swallowing until my belly is bursting.

Once, a fool. Twice, a thief.

I push the thought away and—

Hooves clatter on the lane outside the vicarage. I drop the bell into my pocket, hurrying to the window just in time to notice a streak of black rush over the bridge. Wheels screech in front of the vicarage, sending my heart pounding in my ears. There is only one carriage like that in town, only one that comes from the north.

It is, no doubt, from Blackbourne Castle.

Gently, I reach for my sweater and slip my feet into sturdy boots. The pages of Mother's journal rustle in my waistband. I pull it out and lay it on the bed. While I do not understand the scribblings, I doubt anyone can. It doesn't serve me to keep it.

I am careful not to allow the door to swing shut behind me as I slip out into the hall, easing it closed. Each step sends a flutter against my ribs, my heart nothing more than a starling caught inside a chimney. Downstairs, my father moves along the hall. His footsteps are heavy, each one a noose around my throat. Why has the carriage come?

The news of Lord Black's death swept the village the day after Bram appeared in my bedroom. Father is writing the eulogy, locked up in his study, pacing before the leaden glass windows. The bodies to bury, it seems, never run dry.

My guts swim, turning inside out on themselves while I tiptoe to the edge of the stairs. Father is in the foyer now, cane scratching the slate tile. There is a rap on the door. Three sharp knocks. My breath stills when the door opens. I catch the scent of woodsmoke and frost.

Low voices, words I cannot make out, shimmer in the air, and I wind down the stairs until I am standing in the kitchen.

"You cannot possibly mean that. I demand I accompany her."

It is Father's voice, cold and sharp as mint leaves.

"Apologies, Vicar, but it is what he requested."

I do not know the other voice. Then again, the servants at the castle rarely make their way into town, their every need already met within the great gray stones.

"I'm afraid I can't allow it." Hinges creak while Father tries to close the door, but a palm slaps against the wood, stopping him.

"The young lord was very specific, Vicar Thorn. She is to come alone, and she is to come now." The voice clears its throat. "Otherwise, he will be forced to take unfortunate actions. You know where the power in this town lies, Vicar, and as much as you'd like to believe otherwise, it isn't the church, Ithrandril save me."

Bile churns at the hollow of my throat. My fingers worry at my sides, nails piercing flesh. I swallow as much air as I possibly can. It is no use. My heart is already slipping out of tune.

A-live, a-live, a-a—

Father's cane makes an arc on the floor. "Very well."

My breath shudders when he comes around the corner. I have not seen my father in days, not up close. Shadow dusts his jaw in unkempt tangles, his shirt is wrinkled and stained by what I can only presume are tea and ink. His eyes are ringed in violet, and his shoulders slump while he makes his way into the kitchen. There is a cruel smile on his lips when he sees me.

"You've been summoned," he says.

She. Whoever waits on the other side of the door said *she*. But surely, they did not…They must not mean *me*. What could anyone at Blackbourne Castle want with me? And then the ghost of *his* hands brush my skin, Ransom's hands while they cleaned the cut, wrapped the silk around my heel, and told me…told me what? I push the memory away, squaring my jaw.

"What do you mean?" I ask, trying to ignore the anxiety tying knots in my stomach.

He comes closer, each scratch of his cane a shovel of dirt on my coffin. Father comes so close I can smell the stench of him—burnt black tea, iron, and sweat. I almost gag when he leans in. A candle gutters on the table.

"It appears our new patron would like to have words with you. And yet"—his breath is hot and moist on my cheek—"if anyone finds out, you are surely ruined."

Ruined.

I roll the word around on my tongue until it is sharp, bitter, and hot before projecting it back in his face.

"In your eyes, Father, I already am."

I go to move past, but his hand strikes like a viper, fingers burying into my upper arm. "What Erybrus has conceived with lust only births sin. Whatever you do, daughter-mine, do not let him touch you. The Lord Blacks are tricky gods."

My lips wrinkle a sneer, and I take in my father for all he truly is. Broken, battered, a shell of a man. I bare my teeth in the low light of evening. "There is only one trickster god, Father. The one who looks back at you from the mirror every morning, whispering words of deceit and decency alike, while you keep your daughter tied to a chair." I spit the words like belladonna berries and sweep past him, leaving behind nothing more than a trail of bitterness.

He does not move to stop me while I curl around the wall and into the foyer. A man stands on the threshold, his face pinched as though he has bitten something sour.

"Are you Ms. Adelaide Thorn?" he asks.

I bob my head. "I am."

He angles out into the night, pointing a gloved hand toward the carriage, where wax-wick lamps glisten like will-o'-the-wisps. To lead me into darkness, take me down, swallow me whole, and spit out the bones. I gulp air, one finger pressing the vein bleating in my neck. The response is strong and steadying.

A-live, a-live, a-live.

"Do I need to bring anything?" I look back toward Father.

He still stands in the kitchen, one hand white-knuckling the back of a chair.

"Just yourself, Ms. Thorn."

The words cut sharp. So, I will not be staying. Ransom will take what he needs, and I will be left powerless and—if Father has his way—boarded onto a coach and sent away.

Ruined. Cured. This is all I am to my father. Spoiled, in need of healing. I reach for my wool cloak, where it hangs by the door, and sweep it over my shoulders.

I slip my hands into my pocket, once more curling fingers around the bell.

Bells for protection.

I twist to look at Father, but he is gone. All the better. No one left to say goodbye to. I button my cloak against the cold and turn toward the man with the pinched, sour face.

"To Blackbourne Castle, then?" I step out into the darkening night, breath frosting on my lips.

"Aye, Ms. Thorn." He nods. "To Blackbourne Castle."

nine

There is a bitter smell in the air when the driver angles the carriage beneath a gate crowned in brown ivy and the skeletal remains of rhododendron blossoms. The stench creeps in through the open window, hollowing out the bones in my face and setting roots on my tongue. I bury my nose beneath the blue wool of my coat, taking small breaths as the world rushes by. It is an acidic smell, something like rotting pine and alcohol.

On the outskirts of Rixton, past the wheat fields and orchards around Avery Manor, the trees grow tall and dark before sweeping up into the mountains. The moon shines high above, silver rays tipping molten through the branches. I readjust in my seat, my fingers worrying in my lap, nails peeling at skin while my stomach boils like black-pine pitch.

Why has Ransom asked for me?

The young lord, that is what the driver said. Hiram Black is dead. Set to be buried in two days' time. So, what does Ransom want with the vicar's *infamous* daughter? The girl locked in a tower. I bite the inside of my cheek. Night leaks in through the window, and the driver whips the horses into a frenzy. I jerk backward in the seat, my head smacking the brocade-hung wall, pain exploding like hot coals.

"Damn Ithrandril," I whisper, cradling the back of my skull.

Father would have my tongue for such language, but he is not here, and so I say it again. Again and again and again until the words are etched into my skin like firebrands.

I am not the *vicar's* infamous daughter. No, I am the infamous daughter of wind and sky and river. The infamous daughter of outcast women too strong for the men who caged them. I am the infamous daughter of the wood and the river, who sees the souls of the dead and conjures their ghosts with the ring of a bell.

Whatever Ransom Black wants, *that* will be who he deals with. Not the woman locked in her room, tied to a chair, chanting Blessed Scripture until her tongue turns black with ink.

The carriage lurches to a halt, and my palm flies out to catch the opposite seat. I curse again, the words sharp between my teeth, and straighten, smoothing out the wrinkles in my woolen plaid. The driver jangles down from his post with the latch of a footstep, the stamp of hooves. I grind my teeth, slipping one hand in my pocket to feel the curvature of the brass in its wrappings.

Soon.

I will enter the trees, rescue my mother and Bram alike, and come home without even Erybrus knowing what it is I have done. But first, I must face the arrogant smirk of *Lord* Ransom Black. My stomach twinges.

The door swings open, and the driver's gloved hand appears, leather shining in the moonlight. I take it and drop from the carriage. A cold wind wraps hands around my throat when I look up at the mouth of the beast awaiting me. A bogeyman few have seen. The seat of House Black.

There are tales of gargoyles clinging to stone, coming alive in the light of a full moon. Whispers of blood dripping from broken-glass windows, ravens perched amongst the buttresses. A line of crazed men hidden amid their old books and stone and pages of symbols no human should read. Knowledge that was lost during the Rending.

But I see none of that here. Blackbourne Castle rises from the earth like some peaked tumor.

It crawls with shadow, the mist undulating around a high tower that pierces the clouds above. Light slips like molten wax from a single window. The bitter smell curls around my shoulders like rope, and I heave a breath.

Air coats my tongue, sweet and free. I turn toward the driver, but he is already heading for a small door cut into the gray stone, one hand on his hat.

"You must follow me, miss!" he calls above the gale, cloak billowing around him like waves.

My skin gooses with cold. I collect myself enough to put one foot in front of the other until I enter a chamber licked black with darkness. The scent on the air is damp, thick and riddled with the slash of mold. A lump forms at the base of my tongue.

Then comes the snap of wood and wick, the sting of red phosphorus, and the shadows retreat, cowering against the wall where the dark wood paneling appears wet. All thought flees my mind. Where awe should be, disgust sinks fingers into my flesh.

The walls drip with moisture, peeling back the delicate golden-brown wallpaper, weeping the paint down the portraits lining the hall. Every face, every jaw, every rouged cheek slips along canvas like melting wax. My heart flutters, and a shaky breath escapes my lips.

The driver holds a small lantern over his head, illuminating more of the distorted portraits. Some are in a worse state than others. Frames crawling with black mold, brushstroked faces chewed away by mildew, leaving behind only the remnants of painted flesh.

Behind these, where the wallpaper has shaved away, strange symbols are carved into damp plaster. A snake eating its own tail. Over and over again, they mar the wall, some neat and perfectly circular. Others rushed, ink dripping.

I stifle a gasp with a fist. It is the sign of Erybrus. Unchanging. Unbreakable. Ever-present. It reminds us how we must always strive to be closer to Ithrandril. Closer to righteousness. For if we do not, we will be caught in Erybrus's snare forever. Our suffering unending.

"It's been getting worse lately, the damp." The driver's voice cuts through the fog of my fearful thoughts. "Started back when I was just a boy, a stable groom for old Lord Cyrus Black. Appeared in the cellars, they say, where the light don't reach. That's where they used to—you know." He looks at me with expectant eyes, but I only shake my head. The driver clears his throat. "Well, don't be needing to talk about that. Anyway, only a matter of time before the mold began to grow."

My throat swells with bile. I want to press but am too afraid to. Beneath his pocked jaw, the driver's candle gutters. I fist my hands, sweat leaking out to slither along my wrists. I was a fool for coming here. An utter fool.

"Where is Ransom?" I ask before I can stop myself. Red shame roils up my cheeks, the cold air on them now arctic. "The Lord Black, I mean."

The driver, not seeming to notice the white tallow wax dripping lines down his fingerless gloves, nods to the shadows high above.

"Up in his tower, I'd wager. Spends most his days up there, up to Ithrandril knows what. There or the gardens. Not much to do 'round the castle anymore. Used to be, I reckon. Foxhunting, pool in the billiard room, seances when the guests would come…"

His voice trails off, listing more activities deemed gentlemanly by society standards and ridiculous to my own. I drive the symbols on the wall from my mind, replacing them with conjurations of Ransom in the gardens of Blackbourne, dirt beneath his fingernails, roots like lace between his hands.

Within the darkness, I search for any inkling of another living soul, but all I am greeted with are the melting and molding faces of those who came before. The hundreds of snakes gleaming wetly from the walls. Unending pain. Unyielding suffering.

Bram—trapped in some place in between—catches my thoughts, but I push it away.

"Does the castle not keep staff?" I ask, interrupting the driver on his distaste for the occult, something it seems the late Lord Black was fond of. Clearly.

He shuts his mouth, itches the corner of his bulbous nose.

"Just me now. And the husband. He does the cooking—if the young lord decides to eat, mind you—and I take care of the horses. Used to mind the gardens, willing the plants would ever grow, but the young lord has taken up that task now. Loves his green and growing things, he does. Most everyone else was let go years ago. Nasty business, says I. Nasty business."

My fingers thrill at the idea of Ransom bent over in the grass, doing the same thing my mother loved. The same thing she taught me. "What is it Lord Black grows in his gardens? If you don't mind me asking."

He shakes his head. "The lord loves to experiment with his plants. Breeds together poisons and—"

"I don't think our guest has come all this way to hear the inner workings of Blackbourne Castle, Bertram. Least of all my strange practices. I presume the horses are hungry after their journey."

The voice drips like honey from the shadow. I peer into the blackness above, yet it yields nothing. Ransom Black is merely a ghost. A kind of irony that tastes of steel on my tongue. I can see the dead, but the living, it seems, are more evasive.

Bertram, the driver, nods, a knuckle pressed to the brim of his cap.

"Right you are, milord. Right you are." He turns to me. "The carriage will be waiting in the courtyard for your return to the vicarage, Ms. Thorn. Whenever that might be."

His words leave something sour in my mouth, and I watch the flickering bob of his candle grow smaller until a door slams somewhere beyond. I am left in total darkness.

What Erybrus has conceived with lust only births sin. My father's words coat my lips like a film, and I wet them, hoping to wash the taste away.

"You must forgive Bertram, Ms. Thorn. Taken with idle gossip, that one. I am no gardener, like your mother was. Just someone who enjoys life, let's say." It's Ransom's voice. Descending.

"How do you know about my mother?" The words spill out before I can stop them. Silence follows, and so I open my mouth again. "I do not like being played with, Lord Black. Show your face."

It is a bold thing to say to someone above my station, but this man has already seen me bleed black, and did not flinch. There are few ways to be closer than that. Heat blooms in my belly and pushes the thoughts away.

Laughter ripples from the darkness like liquid silver.

"No one said anything of play, Adelaide Thorn."

There is a chill at my back, a slippery feeling that slicks the curve of my neck, drawing my skin to an edge.

"Though, if that is what you wish, I'm sure it could be arranged."

Hands press into my waist.

I jerk away, stumbling over my own feet in the darkness. "Get away from me."

Another slip of laughter, like ice water breaking over my skin. This is not the Ransom Black who met me on the banks of the River Thine. Here, in his own domain, he is another beast entirely.

I straighten my shoulders and grind my teeth down until I'm sure they'll break from their roots and pool bloody in my mouth.

"What is it you want from me?"

His footsteps fade on the marble tile, the click of black heeled boots. Saliva puddles at the base of my throat—the honeyed kind.

"Show your face." My voice trembles, and I clench my fists against the fear spreading wicked heat through my limbs.

Show me your damned face.

Then comes the sound of a match being struck, the pop of white light, smoke in the air. And I see him. He holds a candelabra, the light of it casting shadows along his cheekbones, hollowing out violet stains below his eyes. One eyebrow quirks, a distinct scar running through the fine hairs there I did not notice at our first meeting.

"You're staring, Ms. Thorn."

A blush heats my skin. "You materialized out of the darkness. What were you expecting of me?"

He flicks one finger through a flame. "Shock and awe."

Frustration collects in a moan at the back of my throat. I take a step closer. "Enough with the theatrics, Lord Black. You brought me here for a reason. Tell me why."

Ransom brushes past without so much as a glance, a scent rolling off him like drenched soil and distilled alcohol. Earthy and sharp. I follow the trace of flickering flame while he moves to the other end of the room and dips the candelabra toward something I cannot see. Within moments, the room floods with light, liquid hot and so bright my eyes sting.

Darkness vanishes. Replaced by the cloying chill of damp. The first thing I notice: a thick, dripping sound, like mud on reeds. The scent of tallow wax floods my nose, greasy and rank. I catch the flutter of cobwebs strung across a corner and try to ignore the continuing symbols on the wall. Some are drawn in a smooth and steady hand, while others seem the work of a madman, rushed and haphazard. Ransom sets the candelabra down on a table.

High above us, the ceiling weeps. A wound never fully healed. I fight the urge to gag, the scent of the place all rotten plaster, mold, and something like burnt hair. I bend, hands on my knees, trying to drag in some semblance of clean air. Above me, Ransom chuckles.

"Horrible, isn't it? This inheritance of mine."

I have no reply, the sick boiling in my belly answer enough.

"You get used to the smell," Ransom continues. "Though out in the gardens, the scent is more palatable."

"Gods below and above." I choke. "Then, why are we standing here?"

His laughter comes again when he moves across the room toward me. "Does your father know you have the mouth of a sailor?"

I look up at him through ringlets of white hair, loose from their ribbons. "You summoned me, as I recall. Not my father."

His brows quirk at this. "Rightly so, Ms. Thorn. Follow me."

We leave the ring of candles blistering behind, each drop from the ceiling causing them to spit and hiss like witches' cats. My eyes trace the darkening stone while we move into a corridor, the smell here turning to something like smoking herbs. Sage, thyme, the delicate bloom of rosemary. The boards creak beneath our weight, and I follow the flickering light of Ransom's candelabra, burying my nose in the folds of my cloak.

He stops before a dark door, a bundle of keys jangling from his pocket. My heart thuds. He flicks through them and fits one to the lock. The aged door swings out into the night with gentle ease.

Ransom was right to say the smell of the place was better outside. Soon, the stench of mold, must, and ruined paint gives way to wet soil, winter wind, and the hint of cracking ice. The storm has ceased, merely the light creaking of tree branches reaching my ears. I shiver and only notice our shoulders are brushing when he turns to me, offers me his arm.

A high lord caught with a vicar's daughter? Tongues will wag. I have no right to take it, so I study the creases in his wool coat, as though he has been bent over something, working for a long time. Part of me wants to reach out and touch them, ask him what keeps him up in his tower. Things of his own making? Or the sins of a father?

To hell with wagging tongues.

I slip my arm through his as easy as scooping water. We move silently through the gardens, the moonlight hounding our heels, until we finally stop in the middle of a desolate parterre.

There are many cold places in this world. Places where love has been sapped straight from the very bones, sucked out by brittle teeth like marrow. The gardens of Blackbourne Castle is one such place. The air swims with the smell of things better left buried.

Shrubs are cut to strange shapes. A raven, a skull, three-spiked stars, those swallowing-tail snakes—my breath catches—and a bell. Dead roses trail along stone boundary walls, and a faceless statue glows alabaster in the moonlight, cracks like lines of ink along its surface. It should be a cozy place, full of life, inviting and bright. Instead, I only feel hunger. It seeps up from the ground, trails from the darkened flower beds, to whisper across my skin and bore holes in the back of my skull. My lungs rattle with shaky breath.

"Impressive, is it not?" Ransom asks. He slips from my grasp, coming around one side of the statue, his hands moving along the figure's waist like those of a lover.

My stomach twitches. "Of course," I say, even though the words taste false.

He smiles. "I know when I'm being lied to, Ms. Thorn."

I don't trust myself to reply. Instead, I follow a thin stream of moonlight to a bed filled with nothing but the weedy remains of oleander hedges. I crouch to inspect the plants, their ashen stems smarmed with fungus. A faded bloom brushes against my sleeve, and I pull away, careful not to touch it with my bare hands. Even half dead, the thing is still capable of carrying a bite.

A cloud shifts above us, and moonlight catches on something white and half-buried in the soil. My guts scream at me to look away, but I reach forward, fingers wrapping around the solidity of the thing. I draw it from the earth like a sword, breath coming hot and fast.

It's a bone.

Long, lithe, and straight, smooth as carved marble. I dare a glance over my shoulder, but Ransom is busy with something in his pocket. My gaze drops back to the bone in my hands.

It must be an animal's. Surely, a large one. Perhaps a deer or even a wolf. My stomach churns, and I lay it back in its tomb. Press it from my mind.

When I turn back, curiosity flashes in Ransom's eyes and something akin to hunger. The same feeling flowing from the vines, the stones, the very soil itself. As if the whole place wants to swallow me in one gulp. Spit back my bones. I glance at the ruined oleander, trying to come up with something clever to say to distract myself.

"Do you grow many poisons?" It is a stupid question but the only one I can think of with his eyes on me.

The scar through Ransom's brow twitches in amusement, and he glances at the tangles of dead stems. "Is that plant poisonous?"

I stand. "You've brought me here for a reason. I'd like to hear it."

He leans against the empty fountain and sighs. "Very well. Take a seat, Thorn."

I would rather stand and put my back to a wall, where the stone runs solid beneath my palms and nothing can jump out and devour me. And then I remember the walls of Blackbourne Castle are rotting, are mouths themselves, and so I sit. The stone at the fountain's edge is cold despite my many layers, and I gather my skirts about me, shivering.

"Did you ever meet my father?" Ransom sits beside me and plants his feet to the white gravel path. Black sludge swills at the bottom of his boots.

"No, I did not."

Ransom's family hardly came into Rixton. I still remember his mother, Lady Miriam Black, always in shades of elderberry and wine. She was the one who brought Ransom to church until the news broke that she had fallen from her horse and died alone out on the moors.

The funeral had been a quick thing. No showing of the body, only a sleek black casket and violet roses crushed beneath dirt. The church bell hadn't even been rung.

All the better if less people know, Lord Black told my father.

I study Ransom in the moonlight and see myself reflected in the pain of his eyes, the cold outer shell. Just another soul who has lost so much and knows so little of love. My fingers release their grip on the folds of my skirt.

"Didn't leave the castle much during the day, I suppose." There is a far-away look in Ransom's eye, as if something across the gardens has caught his attention and the novelty of me sitting beside him has worn off. "He would have liked you, I think."

The words are strange things, curved and angled in a way. I don't think Ransom means them. But where pain is, love is choked out. The hangman's noose tightens around his throat while he tries to speak of a father who never knew how to care for his son.

My fingers itch to brush his. To wrap my arms around Ransom Black and show him just how deeply I understand. Instead, I think of the bone beneath the dirt.

"You seem distracted."

Ransom is staring at me when I lift my eyes to his.

I choose my words carefully. "Your driver interrupted me, and I would very much like to get back to—"

Ransom smirks. "To what, Thorn?"

"It doesn't matter. Please, tell me why you have brought me here and let me go. I know you have no intention of keeping me."

He leans closer. "Do you know why my father was never seen in Rixton, Adelaide? Why he never came to church?"

I shake my head.

Ransom tilts his head toward the dark sky. "Because Lord Hiram Black was obsessed with death."

The word catches like a bone in my throat. I picture Bram pressed against the wall of my bedroom, whispering of things beyond. A place where death isn't quite the end. I once more run a finger along the rim of the bell.

Whatever this meeting with Ransom is, it isn't a chance occurrence.

"I don't see what any of this has to do—"

"With you?" Ransom is up on his feet now, coming to stand in front of me.

I press myself against the stone, heart like cinnamon in my chest—hot and sharp. "I don't—"

"Do you know what burnt salt smells like? What blood does when it is mixed with melted wax? How to draw an Ouroboros, the everlasting snake, the sign of Erybrus?"

He drops to his knees before me, eyes burning like torches, leaving scorch marks on my skin. I shake my head again, tongue dry and swollen, like a stretch of desert in my mouth.

"Do you want to know how I know these things?" He's so close I smell the stale tea on his breath. "My father was hellbent on searching for a way to stop himself from dying. An endless return." He points to the shrub in the shape of the looping snake. "Used his own blood to try and achieve immortality. Served it to Erybrus in streams, hoping it would make him unbreakable. Immortal. But when that didn't work, he began to use my own."

There is pain in his eyes now. Something like gunpowder, just waiting for the right spark. He pulls back and studies the night sky. "Do you know, Adelaide Thorn, what waits for the dead? Surely, as the vicar's daughter, you must have some idea."

So, this is what he wanted? A theology lesson? Twigs crunch in the undergrowth behind us. My heart thrums. A sparrow against my ribcage. Ascension to Ithrandril—is that the answer he wants? Or being dragged into shadow? Reapers and bells and so much fire?

And then I remember Bram cowering in a corner of my room, frightened of phantoms. Bram, whole and real and almost alive. Trapped in a place where Ithrandril and Erybrus collide. Where I can rescue Mother. Heat courses from the center of my chest.

"I think only the dead can answer that question, Lord Black."

He crosses his arms, takes another step back, and spreads a smile. "Please, call me Ransom."

"Ransom," I repeat.

There is silence, thick and stifling as summer heat. Ransom glances toward a dying bed of flowers—one of many—its scraggled remains like bits of dry paper. I whisper a silent prayer he doesn't notice the bone sticking out of the earth.

His eyes trace to the stars, and his chest heaves a sigh.

"I know what it is you found, Adelaide. On the banks of the river."

My skin freezes, pulls, its surface licked through with spider cracks. I do not look up, keeping my eyes fixed on my feet. A strange kind of ache burrows into my palm, spreading to my fingers.

“I don’t know what you’re talking about.” I have always been a terrible liar, ever since the day my father caught me in a lie and made me drink vinegar by the spoonful.

Sour wine in the mouth of Ithrandril, he called me.

Ransom straightens and comes to sit beside me.

“I think we should make one thing clear.” His voice is almost soft now, rose petals on grass. “I only want to help you.”

I lift my eyes to him. The gunpowder is gone, replaced by something like spring rain. It melts away the ice. All the stars reflected in his face.

“How can you help me?”

He smiles again, and I think how beautiful he is—a broken, bloody man standing here in the light of a harvest moon, trying to be every inch the lord he is expected to be, and only wanting to do good. My edges soften.

“I told you my father was obsessed with death.” He lays a hand on mine.

My skin thrills with the touch. Father’s words once more permeate my brain. *Surely ruined.* I push them away. If sin was so wrong, why did the cosmos create Ithrandril and Erybrus alike?

“He would have done anything to get my mother back. He held seances, hired mystics, even spilled blood. *My* blood.”

I glance down at his hands, his wrists. And that’s when I see them.

The thin, pink scars threading up against the dark lace cuffs of his shirt. My stomach flips, a fish on a line. Is this why Ransom Black carries a sewing needle and thread? To stitch up his own wounds?

“Ransom, I—”

He holds out a finger. “Wait, let me finish. He was so close in the end, my father. Knew about the bells, those held by the Reapers. Knew that if he could only get his hands on one, he could—”

He could what?

I sit on every word, hanging onto them like the crumbling rocks of a cliff. Because Ransom is not the only one who wants to get his mother back.

One soul, a fool. Two, a thief.

What would three make me?

I don’t think I want to know.

“Everything you’re saying sounds like madness.” My hand now trembles against the brass in my pocket.

In one fluid motion, Ransom pulls me to face him, eyes glinting like green glass. My breath catches, a finger going to my throat to count the ragged beats. But to my surprise, they are even.

A-live, a-live, a-live.

I flex my palms.

"You know of what I speak, Adelaide Thorn."

His words are hungry things matching the muck and mold of the old house. The soil cries out beneath our feet with so much pain, and it feels like a living, breathing thing. So, I choose my own with equal bite.

"But do you, Ransom Black?"

A flicker of amusement lights his face, sends the freckles that dot his nose dancing like a constellation.

"There it is," he says. "I knew it. Show me the bell."

"And if I say no?"

He moves closer, hands dipping to my waist, breath hot on my ear. A shiver dances up my spine, so warm and delicious, and I can almost taste the spice of him on my lips.

"You won't say no, Thorn."

"Oh?" My breathing is short and hot, choked on the scent of him. "And why's that?"

"Because you need me."

ten

Sometimes, I wonder if men are made of reaching hands. Searching hands. Always hungry, never satisfied. But when Ransom presses closer, the smell of him cancels out the wet soil of the gardens. He is all I can think about. The bell is gone, and Bram is far away. Even the thoughts of Mother become nothing more than a buoy eddying at the back of my mind.

But there is something inside me, something that smells of lemons, peeled and festering in the sun, and it makes my fingers tighten around the brass. I pull away, standing to my feet. Ransom sits at the fountain's edge in front of me, gunpowder eyes ablaze.

"Don't fight it, Ade—"

"Why would I help you?"

His lips tense, tight against teeth. And then he stands, shoulders slack. When he looks back up, the fire is gone, and the bleeding man is back, dripping mildew and rot, just like the old house surrounding him.

"I thought we might help each other, Thorn. Get back what we both have lost."

His words play over and over in my ears, like an untuned piano.

Our mothers.

One, a fool. Two, a thief. Three—my heart whispers unholy hymns against my breastbone.

"I do not understand how you know about the bell."

His eyes widen at this, misty at the edges, like an autumn field thawing in morning sun. "So, it is true."

Betrayal washes over me in thick waves. "You said you knew! You lied to me?"

That mischievous grin spreads like butter on his lips. "I never lied; I only twisted the truth, and isn't it a delicious thing?"

I watch the curve of his mouth, then say flatly, "I don't trust liars, Ransom."

His smile wanes, and he steps closer. "Forgive me, Adelaide. I—" He takes my hand.

The air is brushed with sweetness, and I fight the simultaneous urge to both strike him and kiss him, neither being an unpleasant thought.

"You know how it is, don't you? Watching a loved one melt away into nothing. When my mother died, Father went into his study and never came out." His finger strokes my knuckles. "He was different after that, with his spells and seances and whispering. The house began to fall apart, the mold crept higher and higher, and then he died and left me to take it on."

I pull away. There are tears gathering at the corners of his eyes. The ghost of his fingers still kisses my skin, making my stomach swim. I can't remember the last time I was touched and didn't suddenly balk and gnash my teeth. It takes every inch of self-control not to reach up and wipe my tears away.

Between us, the dark air tightens, grows so hot I feel as though I'm breathing fire. I *do* know this pain, know it like I know the souls swirling at the edge of the forest. Like I know the way my heart beats uneven in my chest.

After pulling the bell from my pocket, I press it to Ransom's hand. "Tell me how to use it."

His expression changes, something akin to curiosity. His fingers curl at the edges of the bell. There is so much hunger, so much desire in his eyes. I will burn if he looks at me.

"You offer it to me freely?"

Our gazes catch, and my throat shuts tight. His hands against mine are like hellfire, brimstone, molten ash. A dull ache throbs through every inch of my body, the agony swelling in my chest. Ransom Black has turned into a dragon.

I withdraw the bell and slip it back into my pocket. My nose fills with basalt and brine. The smell of the river licking up through the soil at our feet. And something else too. A sucked-penny scent.

"Ransom—"

He steps forward, face twisted with shadow. "Let me show you how to use it, Thorn. We could rescue our mothers, together."

Together. The word is a boon to my lonely heart. To the woman trapped in her room, her only friends the illness thick in her veins, the scripture on the walls. There is a string connecting Ransom's heart to mine. Two wandering souls without the guide of a mother's loving hand, only the willow bark switch of a father's anger or grief taken out on the next best thing.

But the hunger in his eyes is molten gold, the heat of it already creeping up my bones, sinking teeth into the vein pulsing too fast just below my skin.

I press my lips into a bloodless line. "And if I do not?"

It is a gamble to play this game with a man who holds much more power than I do. But isn't that the way of things?

A man holds the world, and a woman scrambles toward it, only for it to bowl her over. Crush her time and time again. Perhaps the moment has arrived to change the game. The entire bloody narrative. To take the world into my fist and crush it until it runs green and blue between my fingers.

Ransom steps away from me, elegant fingers folding in front of him. A smile smears across his lips, this time like honey. Dripping saccharine sweetness.

"Oh, Thorn." He speaks my name with all the solemnity of a prayer. "I had rather wished it would not come to this."

Fear blossoms at the base of my skull, purple monkshood. A sting so cold it freezes the bones. My stomach ties itself into knots, but I shake my head, clearing the cobwebs.

"Are you threatening me?" Anger settles into the space between my ribcage, red-hot as cinnamon.

Men will never speak plain words. They like to twist them, shape them to form their own wills behind forked tongues.

I stalk closer to Ransom, the air between us souring with the scent of the gardens. The mold creeping along these old stone bones. His smile quirks, sparking something in my guts. Something so deep and primal it tastes of rich earth and blood.

"If you do not help me use the bell and find my mother, I will be forced to rescind my patronage of your father's good work, the vicar will fall to ruin, the money you rely on will turn to ash, and all you love will be devoured by Erybrus. You know how Ithrandril punishes those who cannot walk in His ways."

Above us, the clouds shift, moonlight throwing a darkening halo against Ransom, spreading darkness like wings.

A bitter laugh breaks on my lips. "Did you know my father ties me to a chair? Your threats are empty, Lord Black."

Ransom's face turns to sharp angles. Like if I struck him now, I would only hurt myself.

"Oh, but I know what it is you want, Thorn. You want to piece your family back together, soul by soul. Isn't that what every lonely child wants? A warm hearth, fireside reading, laughter?" He brushes a curl from my cheek, the touch once more lighting fire to my skin. "But there are other things I can do. I'm a lord now. There isn't much outside my grasp."

Anger curdles in my stomach. Not just at Ransom, but at this world of reaching men. "Your meaning?"

He picks at dirt beneath a fingernail. "Clara Weston and Liza Thatcher are planning to run away, are they not?"

"How do you—"

He presses a finger to my lips. "What matters is, they matter to you, and I could make life very difficult for all your…loved ones."

"Are you now threatening my friends?"

Moonlight drips down either side of his face. "I don't have to be, Thorn. If you help me, I could offer you means of fortune. I would not let you fall to ruin."

Ruin. My father's exact word. I clench my jaw.

"I do not need your salvation, Lord Black."

"Ah, but that isn't the full truth, is it?" His words slip around me like oil.

"I have heard talk of a house of healing in Idlewild for young women of your *condition*. Tell me, you are not much younger than me, are you not? One and twenty? Two and twenty?"

The hairs rise on the back of my neck. "One and twenty. But I do not see how—"

"Then you are old enough to tell your father no, to leave if you truly wished to." He paces around me. A cat stalking a mouse. "But you see, I believe I have stumbled upon the truth."

"And what truth is that?" I snarl. If he wants to cage me, to back me into a corner, then he will know the sharpness of my teeth.

A cold finger traces the line of my jaw, and my skin tenses with the touch.

"Adelaide Thorn, cursed by Erybrus and desperately clawing for Ithrandril. Your father promised Idlewild would make you better, didn't he? Told you the healers there could cure you." His breath is moist and hot on my ear, drawing a tiny, not wholly unpleasant shiver from me. "My father told my mother the same thing, you know. And when she came back, she was more broken than ever. Took to roaming the moors on horseback until the day she was thrown."

My heartbeat screams in my ears, chest heaving with ill-gained breath. Lady Miriam Black. Thrown from her horse only a week after not being seen for over a year. Whispers of her mind, how it had been broken a long time before her spine shattered on the rocks. Murmurs that she had sold her soul to Erybrus.

"I am not your mother."

"No, but you are going along with your father's plan for the same reason my mother did my father's. It's what keeps you tethered to Rixton when you have every ability to leave of your own accord."

Indignation causes me to tighten my fists, raise my chin. "And what reason is that?"

"You desire love from a man no longer capable of such a thing."

My stomach twists at this, blood pooling at the hollow of my throat. I want to hate him because he is right. While I have all the agency at my fingertips to run away from Rixton, to join Clara and Liza and flee to the Queen's city of Lysdin, where no one will ever find me, what I want, above all else, is a father's love.

"What do you propose I do, then?"

Ransom circles before me once more, blocking out the moonlight. His eyes glisten, and I do not hate the way it makes me feel. Like someone is spooning warm syrup into my veins.

"There is one more thing to sweeten the bargain. You help me, and in return, I offer you a way out of Idlewild while still maintaining the favor of your father." He closes the gap between us, reaching for my hand. "Take my name."

His words hit me like a blow to the gut.

"You're speaking of marriage?" The thought alone is enough to make me feel like a mad thing. Like this is all some elaborate dream my addled mind has conjured to make the pain of Idlewild all the more sour.

Ransom smiles wickedly in the starlight. "Would it be so bad? To be mistress of Blackbourne Castle?"

His boots shiver across the soil, and he wraps a hand around my waist, draws me in so tightly the buttons of his jacket press through my bodice. My breathing slips to something like ocean waves, crashing against my own lungs, my ribs. A ribbon of sweat licks down my back.

"If this is a marriage proposal, Lord Black, it is the worst in centuries."

He pulls back, silver light dancing in the green of his eyes. "That is not a no."

"It is also not a yes." The words are hot on my lips. "You cannot utter a threat to me and those I love and a means of rescue all in one breath. It is a devil's deal."

One more to add to the list ever-growing.

His teeth are alabaster in the low light. "Call it what you like. I'm not letting you leave without an answer."

So, this is it. This is why Ransom Black brought me from my house under the guise of damnation to my father. No belongings taken, only to be sent home. So that one night, when the moon is low and the souls in the wood are hidden behind their veil, he can meet me by the banks of the River Thine and watch me use the bell. But even that, I do not know how to do.

The need for Ransom's knowledge cracks across my chest like rippling thunder.

"You said you know how to use it."

His smile splits wider, hand tightening on my waist. "Is that a yes, Ms. Thorn?"

I spread my pink lips like oleander. To seize the bones. Even the ones trapped beneath the earth. "It is not a no."

His throat rumbles, nose inches from mine. My eyes drift to his mouth, blood-bitten and full, and back to his own. Still just as hungry. Maybe more so.

"The trees," he says.

"What?"

He takes a step back and drops his hand from my side. "That is how you get to whatever lies beyond—a copse of trees. In the Rending, Erybrus was cast away from Ithrandril. The power of that breaking created a place in between life and death, or do you not remember your father's teachings?" He grin is a pointed tease. "Trees are both living and dead, Adelaide. Alive and yet unmoving. They act as a passageway to this in-between." He moves back toward the fountain, boots slipping. "Father discovered the truth just before he died. During one of his seances."

The trees.

I roll the words around on my tongue until they taste of something familiar. Until they are worn down to something palatable. And when I swallow them, they light a fire in my belly.

The simplicity of it all. And yet, the truest things often are.

"The rowan wood."

"Doesn't matter which trees we pass through, as long as I know you will use the bell and help me bring my mother home. I can't—" He slumps to the fountain, the broken man again. "I cannot keep this castle by myself. You see it for what it is. Nothing more than a festering shell. And hell, I need *her*, Thorn." He looks at me again, the ghosts of pain in his eyes. "Please."

The brass in my pocket is heavier than it was moments ago. I pull it out. Oh, but it *does* matter. For the souls only come from the forest, tethered to the silver trunks like leashed dogs. The bell catches the moonlight, throwing gold stains on the twisted stems around us. I roll it on my palm.

One, a fool. Two, a thief. What would three make me? Death itself? A Reaper with my shadowed blood? I swallow, throat as sharp as needles.

"We meet tomorrow night by the banks of the river. Where the graveyard wall meets the trees," I say. "Tomorrow or no deal."

When I look up, Ransom's eyes are as red as the rowan leaves. My heart stutters, and I stumble, skirt catching on my heel. The bell leaps from my hand when I tumble back, rolling near the fountain. The world seems to slow while I watch Ransom's boots approach the tiny thing glistening in the light.

One, two, three, his steps strike hard and cold as steel. He bends, fingers brushing the brass. My breath hitches, snags in my throat like cotton thread on a nail.

"Ransom, please." The words escape me in puffs of air.

Spirits of hunger pinch the sallow of his cheeks. He holds the bell up to the light, watching in mummified awe while it casts liquid gold about the darkening garden.

"Ransom."

It takes him all of two steps to drop the bell back to my palm and lift me to my feet. His chest is solid against my hand, and the smell of him wafts toward me, like smoke from a candle.

"I will meet you tomorrow evening," he whispers. "And when we get back, you will become Lady Black, and all thoughts of Idlewild will be wiped from memory. This is your salvation, Adelaide."

And then he leaves me there, standing in the rot and dust, breathless against the night.

eleven

There is a stench of sulfur on the wind while the carriage traces the long drive of Blackbourne Castle and empties me back in front of the vicarage door. The shadows hound my heels, and my skin thrills at the idea of being caught by Father.

But the house is still when I enter. Not even the ghost of Vicar Thorn to be seen. The hearth is cold in the kitchen, the light beneath his study door gone out. Quickly, I take to the creaking stairs and enter my room, throwing myself down onto the bed and releasing all the breath I have kept trapped in my lungs since Ransom left me.

Already, I long to be back at Blackbourne Castle. I miss the slight touch of Ransom's fingers, his breath on my cheek. Even for all his threats, I miss his nearness. The way he does not shrink away from me but rather is drawn in closer. As though I am something desired. And I sink into that feeling—being wanted.

I study the water stains on the plaster, tracing the lines with my eyes. So familiar yet something out of a dream. Being stuck in this room forever. A reality that might have once been mine but will be mine no longer once I enter the wood. I have half a mind to draw out the bell and ring it, my eyes fixed on the corner, waiting with bated breath for Bram to appear like wisps of smoke.

But I don't and the bell settles between the folds of its wrappings like river silt as I wait.

Wait because I am a coward. I couldn't even make a promise to Bram. Two faces beneath one hood, he said. Two souls for one. But now I have said yes to Ransom, added another to the number. Two faces for what? Bloody sockets, a sucked-out soul, Death in the palm of my hands?

But Ransom has offered me a way out. A salvation of sorts. If I become Lady Black, Father will not be able to send me away, and instead, I will remain close enough to regain his love with the help of my mother.

I roll over in my bed, the scratch of the patchwork familiar on my cheek. It used to smell like Mother: garden dirt, fresh rain, and lemon blossoms in spring. But now it's nothing more than hollow air and the distant catch of old blood. I push myself up.

No more blood. No more death.

Tomorrow night, I will go through the wood.

The next day passes like custard through a sieve. The village lies silent, with chill wind. The bridge over the water is still; no one coming or going. Too many dead women. I know they think it is me, the killer amongst them. A wolf in sheep's clothing.

And who is to say they are wrong? Where do I truly go when my eyes swarm black? This ever-waking wrongness? If it is true, whatever everyone believes, that I am cursed by unholy shadow, then who is to say I am not the one with blood on my hands?

Erybrus only seeks to corrupt and steal, to draw souls away from Ithrandril. And maybe I *am* for Erybrus. Perhaps, when Mother died, a Reaper swept in for her soul and corroded mine in the process. Maybe I will finally learn the truth of the illness coursing through my veins.

I stretch my hands in my lap, the cuts softening from angry red to primrose pink.

There is only one way to find out, really.

Enter the wood. Make a devil's deal for Ransom's mother, for my own.

Find Bram and bring him home. He deserves as much after I turned my back on him.

I spend the day pacing my floor, swearing at each creak of the boards, and when night finally does come, the air smells of snow. From my window, I watch Farmer Whitley's wagon rumble across the bridge, lantern swinging, while he carries the last remaining crop for market in the morning.

I remember market days. The spritz of ripe orange flesh against my teeth, the comforting scent of roasting chestnuts, spiced rye cakes. Mother used to take me when she went to sell her flowers and tinctures. I remember seeing Bram there once, his little sisters trailing like goslings behind him, and I smile at the memory.

And then it is replaced by something else. A shadow approaches the tree line from across the river.

Ransom's voice is silk in my head, his hands on my waist like winter wind. I grind my teeth, jaw cracking. We enter the wood *tonight*. But I am not doing this for Ransom, for his father's obsession with death, for the wreckage and ruin that has become Blackbourne Castle. I am doing this for myself. For my family. For the mother I lost too soon and the father who has forgotten how to love me.

I look at a portrait above my small mantle. Mother's lips like rosebuds, a gold locket for Ithrandril hanging from her throat. Father's steel-gray eyes.

For them. Everything for them. To stitch my family back together, soul by soul, even if it means stealing two additional lives back from the gods.

The light of the moon is cool on my face, and I press the glass open, welcoming the night. It greets me with the cold scent of frost, the rot of apples down in the orchards, the leaves falling from the trees like flecks of gold in the moonlight. I take a deep breath of it all, letting it fill my lungs near bursting.

My door erupts, and my heart turns double in my chest.

Father stands in the frame, a candle wicking below his face, hollowing out the sallow shadows of his cheeks.

"Close your window." His voice is hard and cold.

I finger the bell, toying with the idea of ringing it right here and now, summoning Bram and showing Father the power I wield. This power of life and death. But I don't. I listen to the careful beats of my heart and smile.

"I'm sorry if the chill disturbed you. I was only—"

"I do not care for your excuses, Adelaide. I said, close the window." His words are sharp now, metal licked over by a whetstone.

But mine are the edge of beaten brass.

"Ithrandril is good to those who wait." The Blessed Scripture spins from my lips like mud from a wheel.

I watch in satisfaction while his lips part, shock veiling his eyes.

"And you have waited long enough, have you not, Father?"

"What are you talking about, child?"

"Ever since Mother died, you have wanted me gone. But you couldn't. The vicar, send away his own child? Heaven forbid it. So, you spoke of my evils, my weaknesses." My hand curls to my throat, just to feel my heart. "The town believes you now. *She's a monster, you know? The one responsible for all the killings.* That's what they say, isn't it? Down in the village? What the Mayor himself believes?"

Father flinches, steps closer, but my hand is already on the windowsill, reaching for the frame, the slate tiles.

"Adelaide, I know you are not—"

"You don't have to wait any longer, Father. The truth will set you free, will it not? And the truth is—" My words stick in my throat, turning to hot gobs of paste. I blink back tears. "The truth is, I'm going to fix us. I'm going to set this all to rights."

Before he can stop me, before I can turn away from this disastrous plan, I leap for the windowsill and crash out against the tiles. They crack beneath my boots, and the cold air rams into me like a thousand iron nails.

Father dashes across the room, my name on his lips, but he is too late. Already, I am hurtling toward my mother's forgotten garden beds. The wind blows at my skirts, and I hold tight to the bell while I slip into the night.

For family. To piece us back together.

Three souls will make me Death itself.

Ransom is standing near the tree line while Father's cries hound my heels. His stance is nonchalant, shoulders tipped back against the silver moonlight, but he straightens when he sees me. I fumble the bell from my pocket, sweat already freezing on my forehead, heart racing.

Ransom's brows lift. "Not the quiet escape you were hoping for?"

"Shut up."

I push him in front of me and glance behind us. Father is through the kitchen door now, the candle guttering in his hand. He bellows my name. In one fluid motion, I hold the bell aloft.

"What the hell am I supposed to do?"

"Ring it."

There is no time for arguing, even though the command seems foolish. Too simple. Father's footfalls are crisp on the frost outside. My mouth sours with panic.

Ransom's fingers sink into my arm, sharp as steel. In the corner of my eye, I see a wisp of smoke. Blinding white against the darkness. The souls are already here.

Father screams my name, over and over. A bloody, panicked cry. My fingers shake.

Let him wake the village. Let them all watch the miracle about to occur. The vicar's daughter, the woman who wields the power of life and death, all at the ring of a bell.

Ransom's fingers brush over mine, sending cinnamon sparking up my skin. My palms skim with sweat.

Father is near the riverbank now. So close, so close.

"Thorn." Ransom's voice is thin at my neck, pricking the little hairs.

"I know," I hiss. "I'm working on it."

There will be a price for this, I know it. And I'm terrified what that price will be. I can't think about what I will leave behind, who I might become if I ring the bell. Enter into this bargain of blood and bone and souls stolen. Damnation tastes bitter in my mouth. Images of tail-swallowing snakes drawn in blood come into my mind. Ransom's father holding communion with ghosts—demons. Erybrus laying claim to my own soul.

I am painfully aware that ringing the bell is a place I may never come back from. But it is too late for that now. The wood towers above us, seems to shiver with anticipation.

Come inside. Taste what it's like to feel death.

Father's boots squelch in the river muck, splash into the water. His silver eyes glint in the candlelight.

"Adelaide!" he roars, his face hardening to glass when he notices the bell in my hand.

Faces beneath a hood. One, a fool. Two, a thief. Three, a Reaper of Erybrus.

I turn back to the quivering trees, the white smoke, the dark nothingness of it all laughing in my face.

"Ring it." There is an urgency to Ransom's voice matching the untethered beating to my own heart.

But I do as I am told.

I lift the bell and give it one, gentle ring.

The note fills the air like honey. Like the first crisp call of birdsong in autumn. It cascades around my ears, filling and clearing them all at the same time. My father's cries fade to silence while the note swells.

And then the trees seem to grow. Reaching up, up, up, turning silver, sharp, and almost liquid in the moonlight. The two closest to us part, and a path appears. Gravel white as snow.

Ransom grabs my hand when red light pours against us, his mouth a grim line. "Come on."

My name is a scream on Father's lips, but I don't turn back. I move forward, skin swimming crimson when I leave the world of the living behind.

Into the rowan wood.

twelve

When I was little, my mother spoke of ravens taunting the skies with their crooked cries. But my mother is dead, and wherever it is I have come to find her lies silent. My boots crack against roots and leaves, and I blink twice before the world around me clears.

Trees stand dusted with crimson leaves, their trunks like polished iron. The sky too—if it can even be called that—drips like blood down black canvas. A white moon beats high above, its surface pocked with hollows.

I shiver, panic tightening my limbs, and pull myself up to my feet. When I turn around, I search the wood for signs of Father, but there is nothing.

I am alone.

"Adelaide."

For a moment, I completely forgot Ransom even existed. All I can remember is Bram, and I search the skies for whatever it was he hid from. The things that made him duck beneath my bed and tremble in the corner. But I see nothing. Nothing but crimson and black dripping against the branches.

"Thorn." Ransom's voice is at my back again, and I pivot.

He is framed in blood red, sweat slicking his brow in the sickly moonlight. His green eyes are not on me, not exactly. I look down to my hand and at the bell. It is humming in my palm.

"What's it doing?" he asks.

"I don't know. Shouldn't you? You knew where to find the bloody doorway."

Ransom hesitates, like he's afraid of giving up too much information. He shovels a hand through his hair. "My father—Look, I only learned bits and pieces before he died."

Right, of course. I want to slap him. *Of course*, he knows how to get us into this mess but not through it. Fine. I'll just figure it out myself.

I lift the bell, watching the metal vibrate in the cold air. The air that smells like… My stomach twists, and I shove the bell into my pocket amongst its wrappings. The air is scented of sulfur and iron. Like red-capped mushrooms freshly sprouting along the bank of the River Thine.

I *know* that smell. My eyes search the trees. Ransom scrambles in the leaves.

"What is it? What's wrong?"

The word buzzes in the back of my throat like a yellowjacket poised to sting. "Souls."

Ransom's hand snicks into mine, the creases of his skin damp and warm. He slips behind me, a wisp of smoke at my back. Fear ties knots in my belly while I wait for the dead thing to show its face.

"How do you know?" Ransom's breath is hot on my neck.

There are monsters in the wood. Souls. But I do not have time to speak the words aloud, to wrestle with how my mother *knew*.

Something snaps and I spin, dragging Ransom behind me.

There are two of them—the souls—bobbing at the trunks of trees. The smoke morphs and takes form. I close my eyes, unable to see another dead face. Another mouth opening to ask me to bring them home. I have already sold my soul to Erybrus without knowing the price. My heart should be flipping in my chest, but it isn't. If anything, it calms.

I straighten, open my eyes.

"Adelaide—"

"Be quiet." My words are quick, eyes faster.

The souls edge closer, wisping trails of smoke across the rot of the forest floor.

The miasma of eggs and blood turns to something sharper. Something familiar. The twist of lemon rind, the upturn of dank soil. I take in a great breath of the stuff. And then the ghosts come so close the scent rolls off them in waves. I choke, one thought bleeding from my mind. Is one of them Mother? I reach out a hand, but Ransom moves to stop me.

"Are you stupid?" he hisses between his teeth. "You don't know what those things *are*. They could kill you."

Anger blooms in my chest, my fist thrashing out and tightening around his collar. "If you ever call me stupid again, Ransom Black, I'll kill *you*."

I don't know where the boldness comes from, but it tastes like wine between my lips, and so I drink. My grip stays firm on him when I turn back to the forms of smoke.

"Are you the ones who came to me from the trees?"

I do not have to wait for an answer. They coalesce, then begin to take shape. Faces forming from mist, hair drifting around their cheeks as though I'm seeing them through water. Faces I know.

"Bloody hell." It is Ransom's voice behind me.

I turn, watch the color drain from his cheeks. "You can see them?"

"What are those things, Adelaide?"

I ignore him and focus back on the visage before me.

Lilith Corley and another girl from the village, Ethel Lawler, who died well before my mother. One of the first dead girls of Rixton.

Ransom's hand slicks hot with sweat, tries to drag me away, but I pull from his grip.

The ghosts draw near.

"Lilith? Ethel?" It comes out as a plea, a desire to have it all make sense. But the words land like stones. The time passing slow while they edge closer. Each second a pebble tossed into a pond, letting one ripple fade away before another can begin.

There is something wrong with them. Pieces missing.

The viscera in my chest tightens.

Ethel is harder to remember, was almost as old as I am now when she died. But Lilith…The air swims with bitterness. Her rouged cheeks are gone, cut away, one eye sloughing into nothing but emptiness. I open my mouth to scream, but there is no sound. She nears, and the scent settles in the folds of my stomach. I gag. Ransom's hand is damp at my waist.

Find our bones, Lilith whispers. *Find our bones and put us back.*

I drop to my knees, shrinking against Ransom's chest. Every breath a sob. If this is just another deal, another thing with an unnamed price, I have already lost.

"I cannot take you all with me," I whisper, shoulders slack.

Ethel holds out a hand. It is cold against my cheek. So very cold. She, too, is missing pieces. Darkness dusts from her right temple to jaw, a half-face lingering in the crimson light.

Find our bones, Adelaide. Her voice rattles in my head, distant as a spring breeze. *Find our bones.*

It must be a trick. The wrongness of my heart seeping to invade my mind. I blink through helpless tears, and then they are gone. Nothing but trees and the crimson sky. Ransom's arms wrap around me. My skin tightens at the touch.

No, no. I will not let him—but he only holds me closer. No one has held me like this in so very long, and my tears leave dark stains on his coat.

They are gone, the souls. The girls with missing faces. Girls I once knew. The smell still permeates the air when I unwrap from Ransom's embrace. The cloying stench of citrus peel makes my stomach turn, and when I peer down to the earth beside me, I see why. My knees buckle, vision swirling black.

There are bones. So many bones leaking up from the dirt, covered in the twisting vines of bitterbloom.

I only wake when Ransom's arm slips around my waist. My body courses with heat, and I hurry to my feet, brushing the dirt and twigs from my skirt. For a moment, I forget where I am. The trees stretch too tall, their trunks glinting like knife points in the vermilion light. Breath leaves me in great gasps, and I blink, trying desperately to make sense of my surroundings.

In a rush, it all comes back. Blurred colors, strangled voices, and the ringing of the bell.

We are in the rowan wood.

"You passed out." Ransom is in fine form, blond hair mussed, dirt smeared on his cheeks. He smiles faintly, blinking the sleep from his eyes in the dull, red light.

My heart flutters. "Did I hurt you?"

"Why would you have hurt me?"

"I…It doesn't matter." I loose a breath, thankful I didn't murder the only other living soul here. I hurry a hand to the pocket of my skirt and sigh in relief when the brass brushes cool against my fingertips.

Ransom props himself up on the earth.

"I have no intention of stealing the bell, Thorn."

Part of me feels this is a lie, the ghost of his fingers still trailing my waist, but I push the thought away. Below me, the ground is covered in leaves. No more bones, no more bitterbloom. The light is red as rotting meat when I plunge deeper between the leering trees.

Ransom is quick to his feet.

"Are you going to tell me what exactly is going on?" He paces after me. "What are you doing anyway?"

"Whatever I have to do," I snap.

Find our bones. Why would they ask this of me? My stomach roils with terror, with all the unknown. It doesn't matter. None of this is what I signed up for. None of it is going according to plan. But I'm here, and the dead are asking me to find their bones. I'm going to see it through.

Beneath my feet, the ground is velvet smooth with crushed leaves. I forge a path between the trees, the air around us reeking of sulfur and lemons. There is no birdsong, no wind causing the branches to creak and sway. All around us, the wood is still. As if it is waiting, watching, biding its time until it can open its gaping maw and swallow us whole.

My body aches to run. A restless energy spreads throughout my limbs, and we make our way deeper between the silver trunks.

A branch snaps, and my hair stands on end.

I hold my breath, crouching behind the nearest tree.

The air goes rank. Spilled guts, old blood, and nausea hollows out an ache in my stomach. I search the forest, looking for any hint of another presence, more waiting, watching dead things. But there is nothing, not even the slightest hint of a breeze or stirring.

And then movement.

But not from the woods, from my pocket.

I curl my hand around the cloth enveloping the bell, stilling it. Ransom's eyes catch my movement.

"What's it doing?"

I withdraw my hand and push deeper between the trees. "I don't know, but I'm not going to worry about it now."

A chill dampens the air, not so much a breeze, but a lack of everything. Like all the hollow spaces of the wood have expanded. Drawn closer. I stop in my tracks and turn my chin to the moon glowing down at us from between branches. How can time be told without a ray of sun?

This rowan wood is not *my* version. It is a land at war with itself. Between Ithrandril and Erybrus. Light and darkness.

My body chills.

"Do you think we'll find them here, our mothers?" I search the sea of silver-barked trees.

Ransom scuffs the ground with the toe of his boot. "I don't want to think about where they are if they're not here, Thorn." His face is soft, a sort of darkness harboring in the corners of his eyes.

I grit my teeth. If our mothers aren't in the wood, does that mean they have already made their choice between our brother-gods? I push the thought away and take Ransom's hand in mine.

"We will find them."

He smiles a cracked line, shadows playing in blotches on his face. "I believe you."

His words renew me, and I press forward, undergrowth shushing against my boots.

"If you were the brother-gods, where would you keep souls?"

I think of Lilith, of Ethel. We know where their bones are, don't we? Beneath the soil of the churchyard. Buried below headstones scratched with their names.

Ransom looks at me as though I have maggots crawling from my ears. "Do you think Erybrus is here, then?"

I shake my head. "In the Rending, Ithrandril separated himself from Erybrus, cast him into a place where Ithrandril could not reach. You called this place an in-between, but it's a purgatory." I bring to mind the shape of Bram's lips when he spoke the word. "It's a holding place, I think. The souls trapped here have neither claimed Ithrandril or Erybrus. They still have deals to make, a peace to find before they can make their decision." A shiver tenses my spine. "Though, I feel Erybrus here has a greater presence than any other god."

Ransom follows my hand, his eyes widening. "This is a hungry place."

Back home, the world is creeping slowly toward winter. But here, on the other side of living, there seems to be little sense to the earth. Heat smashes against chill, trees caught in stagnant autumn, a moon ever-hanging in the sky. And now, smoke. As though fire is burning along the horizon.

"Should we follow it?" I ask.

Ransom straightens his collar, runs fingers through his hair. "My concern, Adelaide, darling… What is causing it?"

What does it matter? We are here to slip three souls back from beneath Erybrus's nose. Ithrandril's too, if we are right.

Ransom's thinking the same thing I am, but he's not looking, not really. I see it in his eyes, a kind of glazed look. No focus. But to me, the trees are alive. They shimmer in hues of black, red, and ashen gray. Through their limbs, the sky is crimson, the moon a diamond lost to blood.

But beyond all of these, there is something else. Something that seems to hover just above the surface of my skin. I hold out an arm, inspecting the thin hairs prickling along its length. A shiver licks up my back but does not cause pain. Does not sink roots into the base of my skull.

It feels like…peace.

The bell vibrates in my pocket again. And it frightens me. I push it from my mind and sniff the air.

Something like wet mud wafts through the trees.

"We need to go that way," I say. "Find the river."

Ransom hunches his shoulders. "What makes you say that?"

"Because the air smells less like rotten eggs that way and more like rotten reeds."

Ransom scrunches his nose. "Not sure that's any better."

"Well, it can't be any worse."

He nods and slips his hands into his coat. I do the same, fingers wrapping around the humming bell. Whatever is making it do this, I hope it stops.

I look behind us again, searching the woods for Father, for anyone who might have followed us in. But there's nothing, only tall silver-black trees, shadows darting between them.

"We still have a deal, don't we?" Ransom asks. "Your mother and mine?"

"Of course we do," I snap, turning back.

But while I look at all that surrounds us, I know there is more to this deal than Ransom knows. Two families to piece back together, bones to unearth, and a man we all thought died so very long ago, here. Halfway to life. My stomach sours at the thought of Bram. Bram, who I haven't even mentioned to Ransom.

I fist the bell and step back on the path, listening for sounds of a river, but all I hear is the creaking of the trees.

There may be no living ravens in these woods, but while we make our way down the path, I feel eyes on my back and wonder what ravens look like when they're dead.

thirteen

The sounds in the wood slip like knife points through my ears. Gnashing teeth hidden behind tree trunks, the high-pitched laughter of children morphing into something like a blade on glass. The branches shush above us, reminding me of bare feet over floorboards and the susurration of river reeds.

We wander an endless stretch of needle-sharp trees, red sky, pale moon, and crumbling stone, searching for water. The scent of woodsmoke follows us, as does the constant thought of souls hiding, waiting to beg us for their bones.

A mile back, we passed the remains of some old structure—a house, perhaps.

A low wall crawls beside the meandering path. Moss, as bright and wet as blood, creeps along the stones, making them appear as living, breathing things. The smell can only be described as death: a catch of rot, meat left to slurry in the sun. It turns my stomach, and I sink my hand deeper into my pockets. We make our way through the towering silver trunks of rowan trees.

Ransom walks beside me, eyes darting nervously between the shadows. He is right to be afraid. Maybe the path will lead us to a long stone table, and the trees will open their sap-dripping jaws and devour us.

Dread blooms in my stomach. I steal a glance at Ransom, but he is as unreadable as freshly fallen snow.

The path winds down a hill. Rocky crags stick up from beneath the crimson carpet of leaves. The trees are so quiet they seem to be holding their breath. Every few steps, I peek up at the branches.

There is a catch of movement. Something like wings but made of shadow. I get the feeling we shouldn't be here. We don't belong. A switch of darkness passes overhead, and I snap my neck up.

A raven.

White eyes reel in hollow bone. I inhale sharply and catch my foot on a root. A smarting pain echoes against the healing cut still scarred on my flesh. Ransom's hand closes around my arm, steadying me. My breath comes hot and serrated, and when I turn to look at him, his face is woven with something more like malice than concern. I blink and the look is gone.

Imagination is a funny thing in the land of the dead. I pull my arm away and brush the hair from my face.

"Thank you."

"My pleasure." They are not happy words.

Gone is whatever petty amusement lingered in his eyes in the gardens of Blackbourne Castle. Is this all some terrible mistake? Bringing Ransom along? Coming here myself? Agreeing to marry him?

Worry etches out along my bones, replacing the world around me. We have no plan, no food, no real knowledge of where to go. I search the forest for answers, but there is nothing. Just endless rows of slender trees reaching for the bloody sky.

Ransom is strangely still. I cannot make out the expression on his face. Something between determination and fear, but beneath it lies an emotion I can't decipher. Like oil in a rain puddle.

I empty my mind of it and glance about the dead branches above us for the skeletal raven, but it is gone. Not even a trace of feathers left behind. Instead, a shadow catches in the corner of my vision. Like the hem of a coat. A wisp of something familiar, but only there in one moment and gone in the next.

I blink it away. The brightness of the moon stings my eyes.

Ahead of us, the woods are just as dead as they are behind. No sound. No change in the deep red light. Only the gentle swishing of the empty tree limbs.

I step forward, fallen boughs snapping beneath my boots. Ransom still does not move.

Then I hear it, a slight rustling, like cloth being dragged through underbrush. The air tightens.

Someone is here, watching us.

Ransom slips his hand into mine, tacky with sweat. His eyes fix on something behind us and blow as wide as harvest moons. My chest constricts, an uneven thrum to my heart, and I turn back.

Above us looms a woman. Or rather, what is left of one.

She seems to sprout right from the forest floor, her dress—if it can be called that—is all twisted shadow dusted with scarlet leaves. Her arms hang heavy at her sides, dragging along behind her, white fingers crusted with earth. The hollow of her throat is nothing but dry bone.

My eyes trail down the length of her. That is all she is beneath the shadows.

A tear in her dark shroud shows right through her ribcage to the forest beyond. Hair as white as a corpse slips around her face in wet strings, and her lips—stained like belladonna berries—part in a pale face.

I wait for her to speak, wait for her to do anything, while fear boils sour at the back of my tongue. But she says nothing, and in horror, I realize she is waiting for me to say the first word.

I open my mouth, searching for the right things to say, trying to string them together in a way that makes sense. But my brain feels like ash, my mouth as dry as dirt. Ransom's hand is tight in mine, the other snaking to my waist. He might break my bones if he doesn't release me.

I stare at the woman—the thing—before us. "Are you of Erybrus?"

In all our religious texts, the two warring gods have their servants, their minions. But never have I learned of something described as this. Our fear does not lie in their visages, but in what these creatures might do to our souls if we do not choose the right path.

The creature bends forward, casting murk, blocking out the sallow moon. Her body moves as if there are no bones, but they crack, catch like diamond dust in the dim light. Ransom pulls me flush against him, breath steaming at my neck.

The woman straightens, hair swinging like ropes, and then her lips peel back, exposing nothing but teeth. Rows and rows of teeth like hawthorns.

A *true* monster of the rowan wood. Not a thing of white smoke, a soul untethered. But something else. Something that reeks of copper and salt.

"Give me your name," I say, my voice no louder than a breath.

"Adelaide, what do you think you're—" But Ransom does not finish his question.

Instead, the air fills with the kind of silence that hollows the bones.

The shadow woman's skin stops stretching, her face stamped with a sort of broken grin.

"We do not have a name," she rasps in a chorus voice, metallic and bitter. "We have not had one in so very long. But you have one." A laugh like warped bells. "We know your name. Yes, we know your name, have heard it many times. But we don't like how it tastes. There is too much blood."

The woman clacks her teeth, hums a kind of hollow melody, and her tongue spills from her mouth like a long, black worm.

My heart—the gentlest tightening. I squeeze my fist in Ransom's, letting his warmth radiate up my arm to my chest. The fear at the back of my throat spreads like poison in my mouth. But this is the path I have chosen. This is the way to find Mother. To bring her back from this purgatory.

I take a small step forward, bringing Ransom with me.

"If you are not of Erybrus," I say, voice shaking, "what are you?"

She does not respond at first, not really. One of her hands slips through the leaves on the forest floor. She lifts it until I can count the boney fingers that rot there.

One, two, three, four, five. She wiggles them.

"She knew you were coming," the creature says. "But did not think there would be so many others."

So many others. The words are knives in my head, whittling out space between my bones.

The ghosts? No, they were already here.

Ransom?

My stomach caves. Did my father follow us in?

"Who are you talking about?" I demand. "Who is 'she'?"

The creature hisses. "So many questions. She did not say the nasty blood would have so many questions."

Nasty blood. Sickness tremors through my bones. As though my stomach is set to sea, my throat is thick with the need to empty my belly. But I shove it down, make myself ask the question I so desperately need answered.

"Do you know where to find my mother?"

The shadow woman drops her hand, lets it slosh in the leaves. She stares at me with unblinking, milky eyes. And then, her head cocks to the right, as if bent on a hinge. And her smile widens. There are too many teeth.

"Behind you!" she shrieks.

I whirl to search every trunk, every cut of stone, every stretch of crimson left in our wake. Ransom is breathing hot and fast, his palm sweating through the fabric of my dress.

But there is nothing, and when I turn back, the woman is gone.

I drop to my knees on the forest floor, the side of my skull aching, the bell like a weight in the folds of my skirt. Ransom lowers himself beside me, his hands tangled in my hair. I cling to him, the scent of dry gin, dark soil. The only thing holding me to this space of silver and red.

I reach into my pocket.

The bell is still.

I pull it out, running a finger along its brass surface. Why has it gone still? And why did it vibrate in the first place?

"Perhaps we should follow her?" Ransom's voice is gravelly.

I look to him. His eyes are lifted to the trees before us. Down the lane, past the place the shadow woman disappeared, the forest seems to thin, more milky light streaming in between them.

"Are you insane?" I get to my feet, replacing the bell to my pocket. "We need to find the river. There is no way in hell I am following that *thing*."

For a moment, I think Ransom might argue, but he just nods. "Fine. Let's move. The quicker we find our mothers, the quicker we can get out of the wood."

He moves ahead of me, boots crunching leaves, but I turn back.

The shadows seem thicker between the trees, like someone has taken a bite out of reality and left only blackened space.

Behind you, the shadow lady screams. *Behind you, behind you, behind you.*

We run. Run until our throats are dry and our tongues taste like iron. The delicate skin on my foot throbs where the metal embedded itself only days ago. But still I go, chest heaving. Footstep after footstep. Until the trees have thinned and the path is lined in opalescent pebbles.

I stop, lungs burning. A gentle quiet falls over us. Only the labored sound of our own breathing while Ransom's hand reaches for mine.

"I do not understand."

My eyes flick to him, to the sweat rolling down his face in beads. I cannot tell if his cheeks are flushed or if it is just the red light of the sky reflected upon his skin.

"What?" I ask.

He collapses to the ground beside me, peeling off his coat. His shirt sticks to his chest with moisture, and a dark stain spreads along the fine fabric.

"We have been running for who knows how long, and yet nothing has changed. I told you we should have followed the woman."

He is wrong. I straighten.

"She disappeared, Ransom. And anyway, the trees are different here, more spread apart. I can smell the river, and there's—" I swivel on a heel, taking in the rest of the landscape. "There's more of those stone things, the walls, like old buildings. There's three there, all in a row. And another..." My eyes fall on a cut of stone wall, more beyond it.

The shape is strange. Familiar, even. I move toward it, leaving Ransom hurrying to catch me.

"Thorn," he calls, but I have already reached the wall, am already moving through the space that might have once held a gate but now only plays host to rotten wood and crimson moss.

My boots crunch in the leaves. I weave up a familiar path and find myself at the threshold of a set of stone steps leading to nothing.

I close my eyes. Lift my hand. Imagine a brass knob, a wooden door. Beyond, a foyer, a kitchen cold as death, narrow stairs, a long-stretching hall, a room with a girl tied to a chair.

Me.

My eyes snap open, and I leap back, as though I've been stung. Ransom calls my name, and again, I ignore him. I lift my skirts and run the length of the tumble-down wall. It is home and yet not home. A shadowland. I dash around to the back of the ruins, and when I see what lies behind, my breath stops in my throat.

Bitterbloom.

The flowers are as thick as snow blazing up from the ground, reflecting the moonlight. I fall to the dirt, fingers clutching at the petals.

No, no, this is all wrong. Nothing can grow here. Nothing I have seen is truly alive. Even the trees, trapped in the death grip of autumn. Yet, these flowers almost seem to breathe.

I take a petal between my thumb and finger, the surface like alabaster velvet.

Ransom's boots crackle the leaves, and his shadow casts long and sallow over top of me.

"Flowers." He sounds less than amused.

"My mother's flowers. One of many."

But they cannot be growing here. There is no sunlight. No one to water them. To tend the blooms, to make sure no one digs them up, touches the roots…

A cold sweat breaks out on the back of my neck.

Mother.

I leap up, searching for any signs of life. Any signs my mother is here. My mother is…what? Alive? Between?

"Adelaide." Ransom's hand is on my arm now. "I don't understand. Why are the flowers so—"

"Don't you see?" I lift my skirts and leap onto the crumbling wall, coming down the other side, then sink fingers into the cold, red moss. "It's the vicarage. The ghost of it, at least. This is the kitchen, and this—" I run toward the front, pointing frantically. "This is the foyer, the front door, the path, and the gate in the wall beyond that."

I run for the lane, Ransom on my heels.

"That," I say, pointing back where we came from. "Those three structures? The Widow Foray's cottage, the Thatcher's, the bakery."

Clara.

My throat goes warm and sticky, and I try to swallow. Ransom is at my side, heaving. His hand slips into mine. The sudden warmth of his skin is startling, and I glance down at our joined fingers, the nearness of him spilling against me like mulled wine. My eyes trace to his face, his sharp jaw and piercing verdant eyes. We are little more than strangers still, yet here we stand, allies against the dark.

His gaze narrows. "I don't—I don't get it. Tell me where we are."

The knowledge strikes me like ice to the gut. A feeling touches the back of my neck, cold and slow and creeping.

"We're home. In Rixton. Just another version." I splay my fingers against the stone. "In the Rending, Erybrus was thrown down by Ithrandril, creating this place. An unholy realm where souls could remain trapped until their decision was made. For the shadow or for the light. The rowan wood—it's an upside-reflection of our own world."

And then we hear two things that strike hope and fear in my gut alike.

The first is a voice, warm like cinnamon and familiar.

Bram.

The second is more like a flock of ravens. And when I turn, I see why.

Bram is running toward us, his eyes wide, body firm and whole and *real.* He is flailing his arms wildly, screaming my name, terror streaking his eyes with shots of red. Beside him, a hound, jet-black with eyes like blood moons.

Behind Bram, I spot the cause of such terror.

Up from a bubbling, stinking version of the River Thine rise six of the shrouded shadow women. Though, here, I cannot tell if they are women at all. Their bodies are thick with darkness, hands dragging long and white behind them. Pale faces are broken with crooked smiles, tongues lolling like earthworms.

And I do the only thing I can think of.

I run.

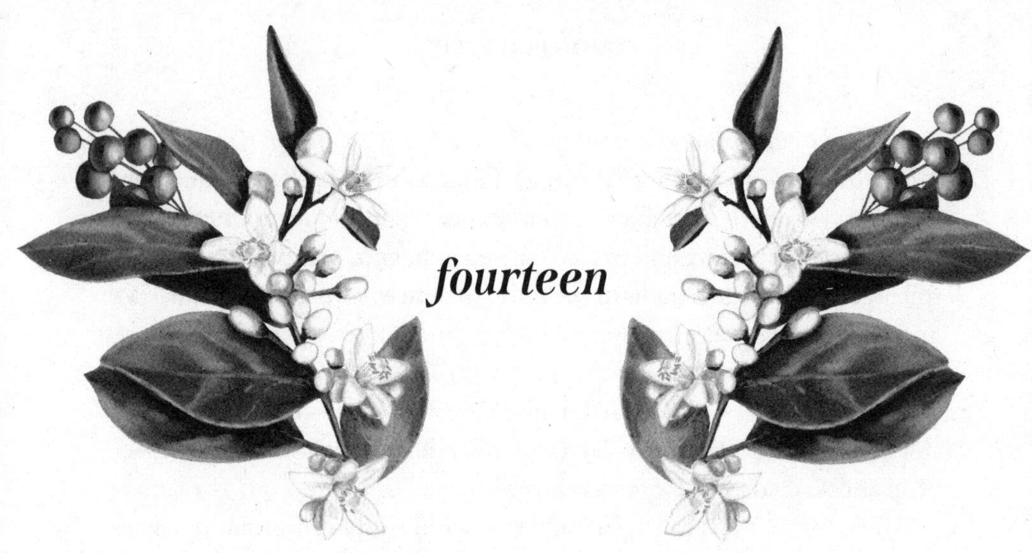

fourteen

Bram is screaming something I cannot hear over the pounding of my own heart. It is like drums in the deep. I am nothing but prey. Nothing but a corpse along the roadside, waiting for carrion birds to come and tear my wilting flesh.

But I do not have to wait. For the vultures are right behind me—the shadow figures. Demons. They shriek and shout, rounding us up, pressing us forward—toward what, I do not know. Tears sting my eyes, choke me. I veer left when something dark presses into the corner of my eye.

My heart buckles in my chest.

But it's only the hound. His paws beat the ground just behind me, eyes wild and wet. Ransom is ahead, coat slung across his shoulders and flinging behind him like wisps of smoke. Bram lifts his arm toward something. My lungs burn and my legs ache, and I am about to lie down, cover my head with my hands and hope for the best, when I catch sight of where Bram is pointing us toward.

The church.

It stands tall, unlike the rest of the shelters, its stone a testament to whatever rotten magic eats this place alive. Red ivy hangs down its sides, twisting vines cut away from the decaying wood door—so like the one I have watched my father walk through countless times and yet so very different.

My boot catches on a rock. I stumble forward, pain searing up my leg, and cry out, rolling onto my back. The sky overhead bleeds, and a shadow crosses over me.

I open my mouth to scream again, but no sound comes. Only hot breath. My fingers scramble in the earth, but I cannot get away. I am frozen to the ground.

A shrouded figure rears its ugly, pale head. Lips spreading wide, tongue twisting over sharpened teeth. The eyes bob in their sockets, as if they are barely holding on, might slip out any second and come rolling across the wet leaves to land at my feet. Fear blooms bright in my chest, spreading cold, like so many reaching fingers. I choke on it while the shadows close around me and the figure extends one of its long, white hands.

A smell turns sharp in the air. The emptied bowels of an animal, spoiled eggs. I gag.

This is how I will die. Devoured by minions of Erybrus, smelling of nothing but rotten meat. I lift my chin to the approaching monster, determined to not die a coward.

But then hands are on my shoulders, tugging at my arms. They lift me to my feet, and we are running. Bram and I, hand in hand, fleeing the serpentine creatures. It is only when we reach the safety behind the door of the church that I realize my heart has stayed calm the whole time.

"What the hell is going on?" It is Ransom's voice, ragged with heavy breaths. "And who"—he points a finger at Bram—"the hell are you?"

Bram ignores him and, instead, hurries to my side while I heave back against the door. I slip down the splintered wood until I am seated on the dusty stone of the floor. The familiar scent of home still clings to my skirts. Ink, stones, autumn wind. I take in deep breaths of it, try and push the dizziness from my mind, spread my knees, and hang my head. My finger shakes to my neck and waits for the beats I am sure are all wrong. Erratic and out of sync.

A-live, a-live, a-live, they greet me. Steady, strong, and so curious my skin prickles.

What is happening? There is comfort in the pain, in the wrongness to my heart, and not having it there is like ripping off the blankets. Exposed.

Something wet swipes at my cheek. The hound, eyes wide with concern, tail limp and tucked. My every muscle tenses at the sight of the creature, my breath coming stiff.

"That's Rascal," Bram says. "He won't hurt you."

I look into the red eyes, lift a finger to his pink nose. He licks it, and I laugh. A strange sort of sound. "What is he?"

"A hellhound."

My stomach drops, and I pull my hand away. Just another servant of Erybrus.

"He's harmless," Bram says between breaths.

Harmless is the last word I would use to describe a hellhound. I lave my tongue over my lips and gently lift a finger to the animal's throat. His heartbeat greets me, steady as my own. I sink against the sweat-dampness of his fur. There is nothing more comforting than the heartbeat of a hound.

"Will someone tell me what *the hell* is going on?"

Ransom stands near the altar, hair mussed, clothes torn and stained. His eyes are shot through with red. True terror echoes in the hollows of his face. It is the kind that breeds deep in the bones and makes the mind think impossible thoughts.

I open my mouth to come up with something, but it is Bram who fills the space.

"They're called Haunts."

Ransom crosses the aisle, boots clacking on the floor. "Those things out there, you mean? The shrouded dead things?"

Bram nods, shoving himself away from the wall. "Haunts are what remains of souls who haven't moved on for hundreds of years, never pushed forward into whichever path lays beyond. True death or the eternal life of Ithrandril. They are devoured by Erybrus."

"Bloody hell." Ransom's face goes pale. He drags a hand down his cheekbones, widening his red-shot eyes. "Who the devil are you anyway? Thorn, we can't just go trusting—"

"Quiet, Black," Bram snaps.

Ransom's mouth gapes like a fish, his face screwing up while he tries to place this dead man before us.

My gaze flicks between them, these two men of Rixton, warped by fathers who never loved them right. Where Ransom is all hard lines, white teeth, and smooth-shaven skin, Bram is a contrast. His brows are heavy and thick, and dark spools of hair tease the edges of his stubbled jaw.

Bram bends down beside me and puts a hand on my shoulder. It is strange to feel him—really *feel* him—like a solid, living being. When I glance up, his eyes are forest pools reflecting all the green and gold.

"Can you stand?" he asks. "I think it best if you come away from the door."

I nod and slowly get to my feet, leaning on his arm for support. He leads me to one of the few pews left standing. I take a deep breath when Rascal settles down beside me, turning in circles and laying his head in my lap. The monsters—the Haunts—slam their wet fingers against the stone outside, but the church holds steadfast against the darkness.

I place a hand on Rascal. "What do they want with us?"

Bram shrugs, leaning against the side of the opposite pew. "Your soul."

The way he says it is so casual, so simple, it nearly takes my breath away. Is this what he has been living? This life hiding away, here in this church? Are those the things he hid from the day in my bedroom?

I look around the church and see no signs of anything extraordinary. Just a tumble down of stones, leaves filtering in through cracks in the roof, broken tiles, and shattered glass.

"No, that can't… This is madness. This is all—" Ransom starts pacing again, running fingers through his blond hair.

Bram and I share a look, and he crosses his arms.

"I've been here for nearly ten years, Black. Trust me when I say it's very real."

Ransom stops, stares at Bram. "Ten years…" Recognition dawns on his face when he pieces together my deceit. "You're Bram Avery. Fuck, you're supposed to be dead."

A wry smile curves Bram's lips. "Thank you for reminding me."

"But you're… How are you here?" Ransom's voice is as thin as smoke.

"Because I still have a decision to make. But I've found a third option, and Adelaide is here to help me with it." He angles his eyes to me, like he's testing to ensure he is still a part of my plan.

My shoulders tense.

Ransom flicks his gaze to me and crosses his arms, a cocky snarl on his lips. "So, this your plan all along? To sneak in and save every dead person from Rixton?"

My head spins. Rascal nudges closer, nose wet through a tear in my sleeve.

"It was supposed to be just Bram and my mother, and then you came along and—"

"Yes, what part do you exactly play in all this, Black?" Bram narrows his eyes.

Ransom wrinkles his nose. "It's *Lord* Black to you."

"There are no lords in the land of the dead."

It is a simple enough statement, and it shuts Ransom up as soon as it is spoken. My gaze flicks between them, their edges going hazy.

"Ransom has lost someone too." I struggle to press the words from my mouth. "Isn't that enough?" I grit my teeth while the room tilts, my body feeling light as a feather. What is wrong? I try to reach a finger to my throat, but my muscles are weak.

Neither of them says a word, but Bram drops away from the pew and holds out his hand. "That cut on your leg looks nasty."

I blink in surprise, and only then do I notice the pain. My onyx blood stains a ripped shred of my skirt. My fingers hurry to pull up the fabric, and a gasp gets caught halfway to my throat.

A deep gash runs from ankle to mid-calf, raw and bleeding. Different from the cut on my heel. Jagged as broken glass. Sick suddenly swims in my belly, and at my side, Rascal whines.

"It must have happened when I fell." My fingers shake toward the wound, coming away sticky and hot. My skin shimmers in pain, roiling off me in waves. I lean heavy against the back of the pew, watching the blood drip, drip, drip.

"She's going to faint!" Ransom hurries to my side, but Bram brushes him out of the way.

"She's not going to bloody faint."

Bram's hand curls around my knee—such an intimate touch it startles me from the blackness encroaching the edges of my vision.

"Adelaide, I need you to keep looking at me, all right? Look in my eyes."

I try to do what I am told, leaning forward, but my stomach swills, and I heave. Bram's hands are at my shoulders now. Shouldn't he be panicking? Shouldn't he be asking Ithrandril why my blood beads black as midnight?

"Well, what are we going to do?" Ransom reaches for the pouch on his belt. "Ithrandril, we can't let her die."

Die? Part of me wants to punch Ransom for planting the thought in my head, but the walls seem to be melting, and I am barely able to keep my eyes open.

Bram growls. "We're going to keep our damned heads about us, Black. She's not going to die, not if I have anything to say about it." He turns back to me. "Listen to me, Adelaide. Wounds work differently here than back home. Especially if you're, well, still alive. You're going to have to trust me, all right?"

His words are murky when they spill between his lips, as though they're coming from deep beneath water. I nod and sink my fingers deeper into Rascal's warm fur. Feel for his steady heartbeat.

Bram shouts something to Ransom, something I cannot make out, and then Ransom is gone, deeper into the church, a flash of shredded black satin and lace.

Bram's grip tightens, his fingers so cold. So *desperately* cold. "Adelaide, I need you to look at me."

His hands are on my jaw, soft against my cheek. He turns me to look at him, but through my eyes, he is only mist and color. If I die here, will I die forever? Rascal whimpers, and Bram swears under his breath. His fingers go to my leg, and the pain sends shockwaves through me. I scream, and the world brightens.

"I'm so sorry," Bram says. "This is going to hurt."

I nod, though I don't know why. There is something swimming around inside me. Something that doesn't belong to me, and I want it out.

Out, out, out.

Ransom dashes back into the nave, a knife glinting in his hand. My brain goes sharp-edged. My fingers scrabble on the pew.

"What are you doing?"

Bram takes the blade from Ransom, bends back at my side. He looks me dead in the eye.

"When someone is wounded here, someone more alive than others, the wood latches on. I've seen it with animals that slip through by accident. It desires nothing more than to feed off that life. It sends pieces of itself inside you, and the only way to stop them from reaching your heart is to cut them out."

My throat goes dry, and my heart drops like a brick. But whatever it is—the thing in my leg—I feel it. *Inside* me. I pull up my skirt and sink my fingers so deep into Rascal's fur that he claws closer.

"Give me something to bite on." The sick feeling swims through me again.

Ransom picks something off the ground and sets it against my lips. I bite, the soft leather cover of a hymnal tasting of ash in my mouth. My vision swims. I look at Bram and nod.

Do it. Get it out.

I swear there are tears in his eyes.

The knife slips against my skin, cold as winter wind, and my body bursts. The pain erupts, and I scream, biting down so hard I think my teeth might crack. Bram's fingers, cold against the lifeblood leaving my body, wriggle into the cut.

I expect them to feel strange, wrong, but instead, they are unnervingly familiar while they grope, searching the tissue and bone for whatever piece of the rowan wood has made its way inside. Spittle soaks into the moldy binding of the hymnal, and all I want to do is rip the world in half. I bite down when the pain sears and makes my vision swim.

"Almost done," Bram says.

Ransom shouts something, but I am not listening.

I am only screaming. Screaming while the pain turns to shock, my body rushing hot, then cold. Something latches against my skin, *inside* my skin. Like barbed wire on tender flesh. I fight the urge to kick my foot away from Bram's grasp, spit out the hymnal, and cry until my throat runs red. But I bite harder, and the tears pour hot from my eyes.

"Take a deep breath, Adelaide." Bram's voice is calm in the chaos, and I cling to it, allowing it to pull me back from the brink.

I inhale through my nose, filling up all the empty space. Bram pulls. Something gives. I spit out the hymnal and reach for my leg. The blood gushes, and I press down, letting it eke out between my fingers.

In his hand, Bram holds something. Like a worm, but thicker and made of dark ether. It squirms there, flailing its serpentine body against him. He hurries to his feet, runs to the nearest window, and sets it free.

It curls against the glass and shatters it, colored shards raining down on Bram. And then it is gone, twisting into the crimson sky like smoke.

I shake in the pew. Bram walks back over, my blood dripping down his hands.

"Will she be all right?" Ransom's voice is more angry than worried.

Bram wipes his hands on the stained black of his trousers. "She'll be fine. Just watch her for a moment. I'll be right back."

He nods to me, and then he's gone, darting deeper into the church.

"Bloody hell." Ransom is down on his knees beside me now. He fishes in his pouch and pulls out the needle and black thread.

I want to run as far away from that glinting point as I can. But Ransom's hand is on my knee.

"You're going to let me sew you up this time, Thorn, or you'll bleed out."

I grit my teeth and nod, tears leaking hot from my eyes. The metal slips into my skin, and it takes every ounce of strength I have left not to scream. The thread pulls through, rough against my flesh. Rascal whines, nuzzles closer. Ransom sews quickly, with precision that still surprises me. He ties off a knot and bites at the excess thread.

"Stay still," he growls.

Quickly, he takes off the cravat tied around his neck and peels at my skirts. I let him. His touch is fire on the soft skin below my knee. There is no place for decency now. He wraps the fabric like a bandage and ties it tight.

Ransom drops back on his heels, brushes sweaty thatches of hair away from my face. "Ithrandril above, but you're in a fine state."

I manage a thin smile. "I'm not sure you're supposed to swear in a church, Lord Black."

His hand is tender on my cheek now, wiping the moisture still clinging to my skin. "A church in Erybrus's realm, in a place where dead things turn into monsters and a hellhound seems like nothing more than a common dog—I'll take my chances."

The pain slowly subsides. The pressure of the tied cravat stems the bleeding. I look at Ransom, past the fear that still seems to beat there, to the broken man standing in rot, wishing for his mother.

"I suppose you're right."

He smiles, thumb stroking my jaw. "We've got to stop doing this, you and I."

"What?" I ask.

He leans in so close I can smell the alcohol lingering on his shirt. Gin, now mixed with blood.

"You," he says, "hurt, in need of rescue."

I laugh weakly. "I am hardly in need of rescue."

Ransom opens his mouth to say something, but Bram is back in the room, holding a sloshing bottle in his hands. He kneels beside us, blinks twice at the cravat, the hint of black stitches in my skin, blood already leaking through the fabric.

"You did this?" he asks.

"I'm more than a fancy lord in a silk coat," Ransom replies.

Bram raises an eyebrow and opens the bottle. The scent of heady wine floods the air. "Well, we should still disinfect the wound. Just in case."

"With what?" Ransom snaps. "Dead man's wine?"

Bram bends down, shoving Ransom out of the way. "Communion wine is about as clean as it comes around here." He takes a swig, and the ghost of liquid travels down his throat. Bram catches my eyes, his own blazing. "This is probably going to hurt."

I reach for the hymnal but then let it rest. The pain, I can take. It reminds me I am alive. I pull my skirts higher and grit my teeth. "Do it."

Coolness rushes against my wound, then the stinging bite of alcohol against open flesh. I fist my hands and sink teeth into my lip until I taste pennies.

Beside me, Rascal groans. I shift uncomfortably when Bram pulls the bottle away and dabs at the running wine with the corner of his sleeve.

"How long will it take to heal?"

He shrugs. "Like I said, wounds work funny here. Could be a few hours or a few days. The good news is, the leech is out. You should heal right as rain."

I open my mouth to ask if there is even rain here, in this wood between life and death, and how am I supposed to rescue my mother if I can't even walk? But I shut my mouth.

Bram stands, and Rascal lifts his head, red eyes glowing at all three of us.

"Strange travel companion, a hellhound." Ransom glowers at the dog, arms folded.

I look at Rascal and ruffle his ears. He yelps in delight and throws his weight against my ribcage, earning a laugh.

"I think he's sweet."

"They tend to wander the wood. I was terrified of them at first, but when this guy came along—" Bram bends down and scrubs his fingers along Rascal's crown, sending the hellhound's tail beating on the pew. "Well, I guess I couldn't say no to that face. Plus, he's good at knowing when there are Haunts around. Keeps a sharp eye out."

Ransom harrumphs.

Bram straightens, the bottle sloshing in his grasp. "The Haunts should be gone by now, but we should stay here in the church a little longer. Holy ground and all that. Fancy taking first watch of the night?"

Ransom wrinkles his nose and straightens his jacket. "I hardly think—"

"I think the one who ran the fastest without looking back should be the one to take first watch." Bram's words are edged steel, and they cut across Ransom's face, bleeding anger.

"Fine," he says. "Where should I go for said watch?"

Bram points behind us, toward the doors. "Sit with your back against those, and if the Haunts come knocking, you'll feel it. I'll take Adelaide back to the vestry and relieve you in a few hours." He shoves the half-spent bottle of wine into Ransom's arms. "You seem like the kind of chap who'd need the stronger stuff."

Ransom glares and then wilts beneath Bram's words, reaching for the bottle. "Fine," he says. "But I get the hound."

Rascal whimpers and draws closer to me while I pet the curled fur at his neck.

"Go with Ransom, Rascal." I gently nudge the hound with my foot. "He promises he won't turn you into a coat."

Rascal trots to Ransom's side, his tail hanging loosely, and Bram offers me an arm. I slip my hand into the crook of his elbow, still half-surprised to feel the solidity of him beneath my skin. He is cold, and when I touch him, he flinches. Almost as if my warmth is something he hasn't experienced in a long time.

With each step toward the back of the church, my skin sears, and droplets of blood press out against the stitches. Through a small door, we enter a room with only a single window, half hung in shredded velvet, the walls stained almost black with age. There is a makeshift cot tucked in one corner, a piling of old hymnals and candles beside it. On the walls hang dusty candlesticks, milky wax dripping from the brass.

If we weren't in a place of half-dead souls, I would say it is almost cozy.

Bram leads me to the cot and peels back the velvet covering, which is nothing more than another curtain. I crawl beneath it, my bones stiff, and lay my head on the pillow of leaves tucked into a sack.

It smells like home, like the trees beyond the river. Not this one, this upside-down place of dead and dying, but the true, yellowing trees swallowing the river in Rixton.

Bram settles on the floor beside me, his back against the stone. "I can't believe you're really here."

"What do you mean?" I tuck a hand under the pillow, my gaze matching his own.

"I just...Well, I didn't think you would come, after seeing me in your room. Thought you'd think it was all a dream or something." There is a hitch in his throat, and he looks away. "Gods below and above, it's just been so long."

My stomach aches when I think about it. This dead man, trapped in this place of rotting souls. "Well, I'm glad I came."

He smiles at me, a soft kind of thing. "Me too."

We stay in silence for a moment, the wind outside the only sound. I stare at the ceiling, but it is so high above us I can barely make it out. Father never allowed me passage to the vestry, so everything is strange. Even here in the rowan wood.

"How do you know when it's night?" I ask, breaking the silence.

Bram looks up at me. "What do you mean?"

"Out there, in the church, you told Ransom to take the first watch of the night. But isn't the moon always out here?"

Bram nods, understanding. "It took me a while to figure it out after I died. There are moments when the Haunts are more dormant, retreating to shadows. I call it night, though for all I know it could be morning. When they stopped beating against the doors, I figured the evening must be drawing close." He nods to my leg. "We could move now if it weren't for that leg. You should rest."

I digest the information. Haunts, souls of the dead who have not yet crossed over. Skin morphing into shadow, eyes turning white as marble. The pain in my leg beats a dull thrum.

"Can I ask you a question?" The words leave my mouth in a breath.

Bram nods.

"Why didn't you flinch when you saw my blackened blood?"

Bram's eyes penetrate me. Like he can see every vein, every muscle, every bone. My breath catches.

"I have seen my fair share of Reapers these last ten years, Adelaide," he says. "Their blood is no cause for alarm."

The words strike hollows into my bones. *Reaper's blood?* So, it is true. The air turns hot in my lungs. I am cursed by Erybrus, already sold to his side. But what does it mean?

I bottle the thought and press it to the back of my mind. No sense in worrying about things I have no control over. Instead, I focus on something I *can* influence. Or at least explain.

"Are you angry I brought Ransom? He's harmless."

Bram curls his lip. "A better word, I think, would be useless. He ran from those Haunts."

"Anyone in their right mind would run from those things, Bram. Did you see them?"

He is silent, one arm thrown over a knee while he studies the nothingness of the wall in front of us. I look around the room.

What a stupid thing it was of me to say. Of course, he has seen them in his ten years of making the vestry of my father's church—whatever version this is—his home. Alone and running, always fleeing from those creatures. Those monsters in the wood.

I swallow. Have I been seeing Haunts all my life? My monsters of teeth and shadows? A shiver licks my spine, and I snuggle deeper against the rough cot at my back, my leg throbbing.

"I'm sorry. That was a careless thing for me to say."

Bram does not reply at first and curls up on the floor, the ground his pillow. I should reach out, offer at least the stretch of dusty velvet. But I don't.

"It's fine," he mumbles. "Just get some rest."

Guilt swarms my stomach. I roll toward the wall and study the black lines drawn in coal. Countless numbers of them trail the stone, and while I fall asleep, I realize what they are.

Bram has been marking each day since the moment he died.

fifteen

I wake in a cloud of red light. For a moment, I can't recall where I am, and the panic sets deep in my bones. My fingers claw the cot, and I gasp for air.

My eyes adjust to the dim.

Four walls, a break in the roof above, velvet curtain, tally marks on the wall. One for each day since Bram Avery died. The knowledge hits my gut anew. I cannot fathom how awful it must be for him, how long he has waited for someone to notice.

How long he waited for *me* to see him. Guilt weighs heavily on my shoulders, but I push it away.

My fingers slip down my sides and into the pocket where the bell rests. It is still a mystery to me—how I came across it. Fate has a funny way of dealing hands. I clamp my own around the bell.

Beside me, the floor is empty. Bram must have taken watch. I go to slip from beneath the velvet covering, but something weighs heavy at my feet. When I look down, Rascal is lying there, curled into a ball, the pale velvet of his belly rising and falling in a gentle rhythm.

A smile curves my lips, and I reach to scratch his ears. His eyes blink sleepily, but he only nuzzles his nose deeper into the makeshift blanket.

"As long as one of us can get some sleep." I shift my feet to the chilled stone floor. My boots topple over beside the wall, and I lace them tight, then stand gently. Pain slices hot up my leg before subsiding to a dull throb.

At least I can walk.

The church is cold and empty. The only sound is of my boots scraping the floor. I exit the vestry, spilling out into the nave. It is lit with so much red there might as well be a veil of blood over my eyes. The doors are shut, and for a moment, anxiousness swells inside me.

What if they have left without me, gone to rescue Ransom's mother, leaving me behind to fend for myself? To find Mother on my own?

My fingers go to the bell. No. They would have taken it with them if they were to betray me. I push the niggling thoughts from my brain. A pew creaks, and a current of ice rips up my spine, sending my heart racing.

Scattered and dead leaves crackle beneath my feet when I go to look, finding Ransom asleep on the hard, curved wood, his jacket acting as a blanket, one arm tossed over his eyes.

Here, in the murky red light streaming in through the stained glass, he looks like a saint. An oil painting of a martyr revered for all his spilled blood. The broken man. Something like awe overwhelms me, and all I can think about is sinking my hands into his hair and tasting the gin on his lips.

There is a splintering noise outside, and my spine straightens.

Haunts.

No, I would smell them. The sulfur and lick of red phosphorus. And the air hints at nothing but dry leaves. I inch toward the door and slip into the chill of morning. Or whatever time it truly is.

Bram holds a splintered maul, cracking the dull blade against blackened logs. He brings the blade down, and the wood tumbles over either side, making my ears throb. Bram looks up when he hears my boots scoring the damp ground.

"Good morning."

"Are you sure about that?" I squint up at the sky—nothing but the pale moon and swirls of black, red, and silver gray.

He follows my gaze, shrugs. "No, guess I'm not. But I had to figure out a way to survive. Told myself if there was day and night back home, there was day and night here too. Helped me keep track of time."

The tally marks on the wall. All at once, it strikes me how futile this

seems: the bell, rescuing Bram, my mother, Ransom's mother, stealing them from Death. I can't stop thinking about the fear I saw in Bram's eyes that first night in my bedroom, the same fear that matched my mother's when she held my hand limply and floated into nothingness.

What kind of daughter am I? Thinking I can enter the domain of Death and bring her back to what? Back to life? What if she is naught but bones? What if she crosses the line of rowan trees and crumbles to dust?

I study Bram in the bloody light,. For a moment, I picture him as he lies in his grave. Flesh dry and slack, teeth too wide for his mouth, eyes empty and black. Is that all he will be? All any of us will become?

I can't stop thinking about it, the death, the chaos. It is all-consuming. I want to deflate. Want to pool at the ground and cry to the skies. What is the point of it all?

But I am not that woman.

I am the woman bound to a chair, fighting.

"I'm sorry," I say. "That you died."

Bram leans on the maul. "It wasn't all so bad, you know. It almost felt like peace in the end, knowing that nothing could be worse than what the sickness was doing to my body." He gives a self-deprecating smirk and swings another log up to the block. "Little did I know, eh?"

My eyes watch the skies, and with each wisp of shadow, I feel the empty space inside me. The space the wood tried to fill.

"You were sick?"

Bram smiles, a bitter thing, and lifts another log to the block. "Mother noticed it first, blamed my father. Thought he'd been—" He cracks the maul down, shakes his head. "Doesn't matter what she thought in the end. I died anyway. The nausea was the worst of it, puking my guts up into a crock and watching helplessly as Matilda washed it out, only to replace it moments later."

Matilda. The eldest of his three younger sisters. I remember seeing her in the market, all copper curls and blue eyes. What it must have been like to watch her brother waste away before her.

A familiar sort of sadness settles in my gut before it turns ashen with fear and memory. Reaper's blood.

"Do you remember the face of the Reaper who took you?"

Bram blinks, like it is a strange question, and then his gaze darts to where my injured leg lies behind woolen skirts. "It wasn't you, if that's what you're wondering. I never saw his face."

His face. A man, then. A breath of relief shudders through me.

"Have you found peace here?"

Bram plants a cut of oak to the block. I want him to say yes, to reassure me that wherever Mother is, she is okay. She is safe. But his face tells me otherwise. He lifts the maul and sends it cracking down again.

"Nobody can prepare you for the rowan wood, Adelaide. It's like smashing through a wall, only to find a cliff on the other side, and you're just falling." He lifts another log. "And when you finally hit the bottom and realize you're dead, it's too late. You can't scramble back up, no matter how hard you try." *Crack.* The log splits open and tumbles down, splinters raining.

"That…that sounds awful."

Bram throws the kindling on the growing pile. "It is. But it's not the worst of it. The worst part is what comes next." He throws another log to the chopping block. "Shadows and a voice and three choices. Ascension to Ithrandril, a true hell with Erybrus in the place he resides, or here, staying put and futilely trying to climb your way back up the cliff."

I blink at him, dazed. "Who would choose Erybrus?"

"Many people choose darkness, Adelaide. Sometimes, pain tastes sweeter."

I march toward him, my feet moving without heed. My blood pressure rockets when he looks at me, the light catching his green and gold eyes. With Bram before me and Ransom behind, I feel vulnerable. Like my heart could choose either way and it will be my undoing.

I am doomed.

But this is not why I am here.

When he stoops to pick up the rest of the kindling, his dark hair sweeps from his face, and I notice a thin scar on his neck.

I am a thousand miles away, breath whooshing out of me.

"What is that?" I ask, pointing to his throat.

He tosses the wood. "What?"

"That mark on your skin."

His fingers brush the pale line. "It's nothing. Just a cut I got when I was little."

I glower, fist my hands. "I don't like being lied to, Bram."

"That's rich, coming from you."

I wince with guilt. "What's that supposed to mean?"

Bram throws the maul to the ground and gathers the kindling in his arms. His movements are pinched, like I have hit a nerve he is trying to pretend doesn't exist. "Look, I'm sure you have your own reasons for bringing Lord High-and-Mighty along on your little trip to the underworld here, but he wasn't part of our original deal. It surprised me, is all."

I stalk closer, until there is only breath between us and the scent of death and dying. "He wasn't part of my original plan either, all right? But if you have a problem with Ransom, take it up with him. I'm just here to find my mother."

Recognition dawns in his eyes. Betrayal. My stomach sinks to my toes.

"You didn't come for me at all, did you?"

The accusation in his voice breaks me. "Bram, I—"

He brushes past, the rough logs scraping my arm.

"Bram!"

He stops, turns back. "What?"

"I came for both of you. You *and* Mother. Please I—I just want your help in finding her first. Then we can all go home."

The golden light seeps from his eyes, leaving them almost empty. "You seem to have come to the wrong place then," he says. "I don't know where she is."

sixteen

I wander the church by myself. A mad woman. When Mother first got sick, she would stand at the foot of my bed, drenched in sweat and speaking nonsense. That is the first time I felt what it was like to be truly alone. To realize there was no one else to walk the weary world with me. And now, the feeling is only stronger.

The confessional box looms before me. It is nothing more than a warped relic in this dead world, varnish peeling away and leaving behind a sickly, darkened surface that only seems to absorb the red light leeching in through the high windows. I clench the bell in my fist and study the wood grain, the small carvings on the door of saints and sinners alike.

I could burn it. The bell. There are candles and matches in the vestry. I could hold it out over the flame, watch the handle turn to ash, the metal to liquid. Take it in my hand—never mind the heat—and throw it into some great, dead pool, where it would sink to the bottom and never be seen again.

I close my eyes and picture Mother. She stands at the edges of my vision like a ghost, and I go somewhere far away, somewhere no one can find me except her. Her fingers in my hair, her breath on my cheek.

Chase Death, my dearest. That way, he will never catch you.

I am *trying.*

Father's words cut sharp in my mind. *Do you have something to confess?* I bite the oily pink folds of my mouth, open my eyes to the dark wood of the confessional, and allow the anger to fill up all my sad and empty places. It is an emotion that makes sense. More sense than the grief, the fear, and uncertainty churning in my guts. I know what to do with my anger. Everything else just sits there like a stone at the pit of my stomach. Grief for Mother, for who Father used to be, for how they used to love me...

My eyes flood with tears, and I blink them back, tucking the bell into my pocket.

"Adelaide, are you all right?"

It is Ransom's voice. I have half forgotten about him. Wiping my eyes, I turn.

"I'm fine." The words come out in a rush, breathless and false.

Awareness brushes through his gaze—the knowledge I am lying. That I am far from anything fine. He stretches his long, broad arms and yawns, sleep gathering violet beneath his eyes.

"Bram relieved me sometime in the night, though who could tell with all the bloody red light." He stands to his feet, fisting his jacket.

His hair is tousled, shirt crumpled and stained. I sigh with something similar to exhaustion but also like need. It clings to the back of my throat. The desire to be wanted.

Here, in the church with Ransom, I can almost pretend we are back home, our interaction delightfully domestic. The garden at night, when he wrapped his hand about my waist and drew me in so close I could almost taste him on the air. Gin, mint, and scented geraniums. Heat flushes my cheeks. The gardens of Blackbourne are a reality so far removed from the one I stand in now. It never occurred to me that I could be happy. Ever really. Yet here I am, losing myself in the *aliveness* of Lord Ransom Black's eyes.

He catches my gaze and grins, eyes blurring toward something akin to hunger. "Did you sleep well?"

I stifle a laugh. The answer should be obvious by the bags beneath my eyes. "No, not really. Did you?"

He brushes past me, close enough that I catch the scent of him—all ink, roots beneath dirt, and the stale tang of alcohol. Gods below and above, I want to taste it. It is a foolish fancy, I know. But it is all I can focus on right now, in this dead place. All that makes any damned sense.

Ransom is the only thing alive here, other than me. *Truly* alive. And I need to remember how it feels to run my hands over something warm. Something beating.

"How's a bloke supposed to get any breakfast around here?" He takes a step toward me, only inches of red between us.

I keep my voice light. "I don't know. Bram's out back, though, chopping firewood. If anyone does know, it would be him."

Ransom gazes at me through hooded lashes, eyes like stones in a river. "Do you think the dead eat?"

It is a horrid thought, and the answer is, I don't know. I am sure I don't *want* to.

All I can smell is food. The imaginations of lemon scones, fresh butter, roasted venison… My stomach rumbles, and I place a hand on the fabric of my dress. Ithrandril be damned, I am hungry. I should have thought this through before we left. This and more.

"I'm sure we'll figure something out," I offer.

"I'm sure we will." He closes the distance between us yet again, lifts a brow. "Look, Adelaide, I was hoping we could talk."

"We're talking now."

"Right, well. I suppose I mean alone. *Alone*, alone." His fingers reach toward my waist, barely brushing me, but it is enough to send his pupils wide with desire.

Heat claws up my throat, my ears, and my eyes drop to his parted lips, soft as rosebuds in June. The confessional is hot at my back. A secret space, quiet, *alone*. And then loathing pulses through me, if only for a moment.

Whatever you do, daughter-mine, do not let him touch you. The Lord Blacks are tricky gods.

Father's words cloud my mind. Etch themselves into my skin until I am sure I will bleed black in this forest.

Ransom closes any semblance of a gap left between us and splays his hand against my navel, his touch so warm it burns. I shouldn't want this, *can't* want this. But Ithrandril above, I do. More than anything. Perhaps simply to spurn Father, maybe only to touch something alive, but I do not push away the feeling, the rapt desire to have his skin against my own.

Yes, I think. Yes, I do have something to confess. I have entered the realm of the dead, have used a Reaper's bell to steal souls back from the grave. Surely, damnation awaits me, so what is the sweet sting of a little lust on my tongue?

I rock forward, arching into Ransom's touch, and part my lips mere inches from his own. "Come with me."

Ransom's hand is hot in mine when I push him through the creaking door of the confessional and follow inside. The air is tight, and the weight of all the wool on my body makes me itch. A catch of sweat breaks out along my neck, and I think I might explode if I don't get a drop of normalcy soon. Just a little hint of what reality *could* be.

"How's this?" My mouth is a hair's breadth from Ransom's.

"Perfect."

I steady myself against one wall, and my heart beats an unruly pattern against my ribs. Ransom's hands smooth down my waist, over the curve of my bottom. He makes a sound low in his throat that lights a fire inside me.

"Ransom." My voice is a rasp, dry stalks of wheat against skin.

He presses a knee between my thighs, drawing a gasp from my throat.

"Yes?" His jaw is rough against my cheek. He dips his tongue to suck the sensitive skin behind my ear.

My stomach sharpens with a hot tug of desire. My hands go to his chest, his throat, up, up, up, into the soft golden curls at the nape of his neck.

Everything has been hell these past few days. Burying Lilith, then Hester, finding the bell, Bram, my father threatening to send me away…and I want it to all wash away. To be forgotten.

Back home, in Rixton, I picture our wedding day. Spring sunshine, blossoms bursting pink and white in the orchards. Home, where Ransom and I could live far away from the prying eyes of the village. Home…

And then I stumble upon the truth of it all.

We might not return home.

This might be the end of everything, here in this wood between.

With Ransom's lips so close I could reach out and bite them, take them, I don't have to think about the could-bes. His shoulders flex beneath my hands, and he lets out another groan. I suck in a breath, and then, for a second, I picture Bram.

He has been here in the wood for thousands of days, each one a scratched tally on his wall. Can I suppress whatever it is I feel for him for a few moments of bliss pressed against the side of the confessional?

Yes, I can.

"Kiss me."

Ransom catches my lips with his own, sliding his mouth against mine and darting his tongue between my teeth. I mold myself against him, but there is too much fabric between us. Too much space. I want to feel him. Touch him.

I reach for his rumpled shirt when he deepens the kiss, drawing out another gasp. His teeth nick the delicate skin of my lip. I trail a finger up the sculpted planes of his stomach. Every inch of him burns.

Ransom breaks the kiss, catches my fingers in his own, and presses them behind my back.

"So greedy, Thorn." His eyes are dark with lust and desire, and they stay trained on me while his fingers come to stroke my throat. They stay fixed on me when he pulls at my collar, exposing the pale skin, the salient bone. He leans closer, nips at the skin.

I suck in a breath, hips rocking forward.

"What if Bram comes back?" My voice is breathless.

Ransom growls into my throat. "What if he does? Are you going to stop me?"

I shiver. "No."

"Good."

When his mouth slides back over mine, desire replaces fear. Takes the place of guilt, anger, and my own deafening silence like an infection. Ransom tastes like every dark thought I have ever had. Deep and unholy. My fingers pull at his hair, his own trailing my collarbone, down along the small mounds of my breasts. I feel clumsy and yet wholly new. A freshly birthed calf blinking in the morning sunshine. Everything is bright and beautiful and mine for the taking. Not because I am kissing Ransom, but because there is danger dancing between us.

The true, sweet danger of having something finally worth losing.

And so, I do exactly that. I take it.

Hands outstretched, I push Ransom against the opposite wall, his hair falling messily into his eyes. He grins, a hungry thing, and there is a flash of something else there, a darkness humming just below his skin.

"Good girl." His eyes shadow with something like black hellebore. "I like a woman who knows what she wants."

And I know what *he* wants. Control, power. The need to *have* me.

I sink my lips into his, and he lets out a deep-throated groan. The gin on his breath is bitter but tastes like heaven. Nightshade berries and oleander.

Ransom's hands curl up my spine, where the laces of my bodice are tied tight. He works to loosen them, and *Ithrandril*, I want this, don't I? This aching, throbbing need to get lost in another living soul. But deep down, my heart hungers for something different. Something I cannot name. Solidity, where Ransom feels like a plume of smoke. Here one instant and gone another.

I freeze. The desire heating my core wars with quick-spreading resignation. I pull away, breath coming hot and wicked fast.

"Ransom, I can't."

His hands drop from my back, and he shovels hair from his sweaty face. "Why not?"

I rush to retie my laces, heat flushing my neck. "I got caught up. I—I can't. I'm sorry."

His face twists, hurt pooling in the color of his eyes. "You're sorry? Ithrandril above, Adelaide, I thought—"

"I know." Confusion courses through my veins. The sweat on my brow cools and sends a chill down my spine. "I just—I can't. Everything is happening so fast, and to add this—" I gesture to his chest, where I know his heart is beating. *Alive*. "I can't add this to all of it, not yet."

He nods, though the disappointment is rutted in the contours of his face. "Sure, that's fine." Ransom stoops and retrieves his jacket off the floor, straightening the collar of his shirt, rebuttoning buttons I don't even remember undoing.

My face flushes. "Ransom, I'm—"

He brushes past me. "I said it was fine."

I throw myself out of the confessional and nearly slam into Bram. His eyes widen, turn cold. His gaze catches on the wisps of hair matted to my forehead and slides to where Ransom is still wrestling with a button.

My throat tightens. "Bram, nothing—"

"The Haunts will be back." He cuts me off, refusing to meet my gaze. His words are a punch to my gut.

"But we're safe here. You said the church was hallowed ground."

Bram drops a pile of kindling on the floor beside a makeshift firepit. He shrugs off his coat and stacks the wood with practiced ease. Rascal tramps over to me, nuzzles his nose into my side, but my eyes are pinned on Bram. A muscle feathers in his jaw.

"Something has changed."

My stomach twists inside me. "What do you mean? What has changed?"

Bram crouches down beside the stacked kindling. He draws a flint from his pocket, the knuckles of his hands going white when he strikes a spark. "Did anyone else follow you through that door?"

His words are strange, sharp-edged in my mind, while I try to follow them.

"What do you mean? Nobody could have followed us. I alone used the bell."

Bram blows a thin stream of air, coaxing flames to life. Ransom, fisting the fabric of his jacket, sighs and drops into a pew.

"I was there with her. No one followed us through that damn door."

Bram stands, moves to one side of the room, and produces a small pot filled with water. "The night you came through...did the bell act strange?"

"It bloody opened a door to the world of the dead, Avery. What do you expect our answer to be?" The exhaustion is thick in Ransom's voice.

But that is not what I focus on. The tips of my fingers and toes twinge with dread. "It shook."

"What?" Bram looks back up from the fire.

"That night, after we woke in the wood, the bell was vibrating. I thought I caught a glimpse of movement, like something familiar, but—"

"Someone followed you through."

No, that's not possible. Who would have—

I reach into my pocket for the bell, and my blood runs cold. When I turn the fabric wrappings out, heart racing, I come up empty, save for a few tufts of lint and dry leaves.

"It's gone." Sickness surges in my stomach.

Bram is on his feet. "What do you mean?"

"The bell." The words crumble from my lips. I dig deeper into my pocket. "It was there a few minutes ago, and now…Bram, it's gone."

The fear in his eyes mirrors my own.

"How…that's not possible."

It shouldn't be, but it is.

I can't stop shivering. Not from cold, but from fear. I look to Ransom, watch his lips tilt in a smirk.

"Did you take it?"

He throws up his hands. "Are you joking? Adelaide, trust me. My thoughts were not on the bell when we were"—he clears his throat and points his chin toward the confessional—"in there."

"I don't want details," Bram cuts.

My cheeks go hot, and I look back to Bram, whose own face swims with unbridled panic. He pivots toward Ransom.

"Turn out your pockets."

"I'm sorry?"

Bram curls his lip. "I said, turn out your damned pockets."

Ransom looks to me, hoping I will step in, tell Bram to shove off. I can still feel the ghost of Ransom's hands on my waist, going lower, pulling at my skirts.

"Do what he says."

My stomach tightens while Ransom digs into the folds of his jacket, his eyes seething. Dry flowers fall from his pockets, a bit of black thread. He goes to empty his sewing pouch, and all that tumbles out is a pair of shears, more thread, and the needle he used to sew up my leg.

His eyes narrow to Bram. "There. Satisfied, Avery?"

I still myself for Bram to push farther, make Ransom strip down until he is nothing but skin and bone, but instead, he turns and ducks beneath a pew.

"Let's just keep looking."

We dart through the church, searching under and over things with no set pattern. I run toward the altar and throw back dusty velvet, toppling over tarnished goblets and candlesticks. But the bell is nowhere to be found. By the end, we are sweaty, and I feel sicker than I did before.

Bram scowls. "You're sure it didn't fall out of your pocket while you were sleeping, Adelaide?"

I shake my head. Stupid, *stupid*. "No, I held it this morning."

Bram's eyes slip up to Ransom. "And your lover didn't stash it away somewhere?"

"He's not my—"

"First of all, I already said my thoughts were *not* on the bell. And second, I sure as hell wouldn't leave without Adelaide."

My lips part, but Bram is already nose to nose with Ransom.

"Why do I have the sense that I shouldn't believe a word you say, Black?"

Ransom narrows his eyes. "I don't know. Why don't you just go fu—"

"Enough!" I shout, squeezing between them. "Look, I don't know what is going on between the two of you, and frankly, I don't give a damn. The bell is missing, which not only means we can't bring anyone back, but also, we are now truly stuck here. So, perhaps we should just have some breakfast and figure the rest out on full stomachs."

Ransom's mouth is a thin line. "Fine."

"Fine," Bram echoes.

They each stalk away, one back to the fire, the other outside, his lips still raw from where I kissed him. My fingers slip to the pocket of my skirt, and once again, cold emptiness greets me.

Someone followed you. Bram's words filter into my mind, and I blink the sting of them away.

Surely, not Father. He would have called it the portal of Erybrus, would have done everything in his power to close it up. All the better for him, ridding himself once and for all of such a wicked daughter. Better to bury an empty coffin than enter a demon realm.

I wonder what he is telling those back in Rixton. That I am dead? That I have gone to Idlewild and shall never return? Whatever lie is on his lips, I am sure he likes the way it tastes.

That is what breaks me, I think. Softens my anger to wretched grief.

I draw a thumb across my own mouth, remembering the feel of Ransom there, so bitter and delicate. His hands on my hips, my waist, higher and higher…

No, he wouldn't steal the bell, would he? What purpose would it serve? Taking what he wants and trapping me here? It wouldn't…

A shadow crosses in front of one of the windows, and I look out to the sea of red beyond. Ransom sits on the chopping block, jacket still swung over his shoulder. He rummages for something in his sewing pouch, and breath sticks like glue in my lungs.

But when he takes it out, it is only a golden chain that looks strangely familiar. Like the one my mother used to wear around her neck.

Not the bell.

He did not lie, then.

I close my eyes, biting down hard until blood coats my the tender skin of my mouth.

Sometimes, pain tastes sweeter.

And Lord Ransom Black knows nothing but pain.

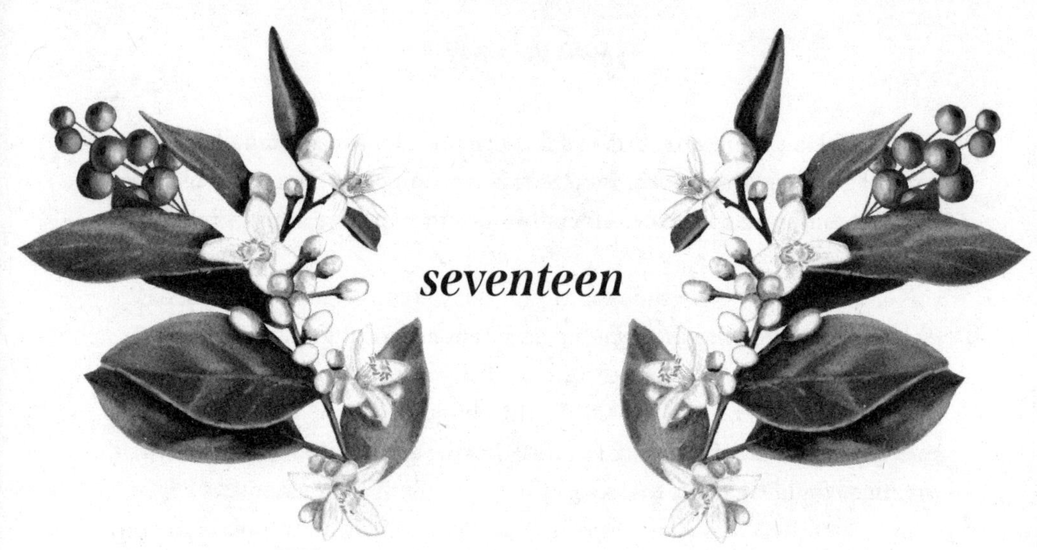

seventeen

A day passes, and the bell is nowhere to be found. Bram is insistent we do not leave the area surrounding the church. Ransom tries to argue, but we are in Bram's world now, and he will tell us when it is safe to leave.

I would smash their heads together and march out of this church myself if not for the blooming dread that I will be stuck here forever. A living soul amongst corpses. The thought freezes my bones.

The Haunts do not bother us, even though we hear them in the distance, their cackling like the baying of wolves.

Ransom and I do not speak of the kiss. He keeps mostly to himself, only bothering to move from his pew when it is his turn to take watch, slipping swigs of communion wine when he thinks no one is looking.

I steal glimpses at Bram sometimes. He is a strange creature. Someone so familiar yet so far away. Like something out of a dream, a mirror image of the world as it once was. A man who lived and laughed, but now, the only remembrance of that life are the gentle lines around his amber eyes.

He barely speaks to Ransom, stewing in his anger. It is rather beautiful, like that I see in myself. Angry at the world for what it did to him, what it took away. And the smell of him. Like lemons. It haunts me—a reminder of the mother we now might never find.

On the third morning, I wake to an empty vestry. Even Rascal has abandoned my side. My bones are stiff and heavy, the result of sleeping too many nights in all my skirts and bodice. To hell with decency, I want to say and rip the fabric from my body until I wear nothing but a shift. But I fear what Ransom might do if he saw me like that. And I shudder when I realize I don't think I would stop him.

I push the thoughts away and step clumsily from the cot, my hand instinctively going to the pocket I know to be empty. The open space greets me like icy wind, and I dig fingernails into the soft flesh of my palms.

In the nave, our fire from the night before dwindles, cores of half-gnawed apples rotting on the floor. Bram does not say where they come from—he does not need them—and sometimes, I wonder if it is safe to eat the food of the dead, drink their drink. But it seems, for now, I have no other choice.

My fingers curl around the edge of the door, and I peek outside, praying against any Haunts, against whoever—or whatever—Bram swears followed us that first night into the wood. There is nothing but red, dusty light and, beyond that, the crumbled walls of the vicarage. I have to approach it, to feel the somehow alive bitterbloom petals, soft and damp between my fingers.

Fear boils hot in my belly. I have stayed within sight of the church, hardly leaving the stones behind.

Outside, the air hangs with a chill, the scent of creeping hoarfrost on the wind. Ransom is nowhere to be seen, but Bram, his back turned to the church, kneels near the line of the forest.

My feet crunch on the frozen grass. He straightens when I approach. I stop just behind him, a metallic scent filling the air. My stomach turns. When Bram shifts to look at me, I notice his hands are covered in blood.

"Are you hurt?" I ask, falling to the cold ground beside him.

I do not need an answer, though, for the truth lies clear before me. A creature of fur and bone lies prostrate on the frozen earth, its blood warm and sticky on the grass.

"How..."

Bram gathers spilled guts into his hands, shoving them back inside the carcass. "I didn't mean for you to see this."

"What exactly is it that I'm even seeing?"

He does not answer at first and, instead, covers the dead beast with leaves and twigs. The mangled pile of bones and crimson blood holds my gaze.

"Sometimes," Bram begins, "humans aren't the only ones who get through."

I blink blearily at him. "You're saying this…whatever it was…is the thing that followed us into the wood? So, you killed it?"

He shakes his head. "No, it's not like that. It's hard to explain."

"Two nights ago, you told me I have Reaper's blood flowing through my veins. Try me."

He sighs and wipes ichor down his trousers. "Sometimes, things get through, even without the bell. Animals, mostly, just poking around in places they shouldn't be until they end up here. Sometimes a human, though that is rare enough. It's usually when they aren't looking for it. Just another lost soul."

I try to digest what he is telling me, but the words scramble in my mind. "So, you gut them?"

Bram grows frustrated. "You wouldn't understand if I told you."

I vomit laughter. "None of this is understandable, Bram. The bell, the Haunts, this damn place itself, whatever the hell I am. I think I can handle a little spilled blood."

"Fine." He leans back over to the pile of now-damp leaves and uncovers the body, which I see now to be a rabbit, fur glistening white beneath the blood. "I didn't kill it. Sometimes, they show up like that. Half-alive and gutted."

Bram slips fingers into the slit at its belly, and my body swims with sick. He pulls thin lines of intestine out, followed by what can only be its kidneys, its lungs, its heart.

The sight of the last organ alone is enough to send my pulse racing. I reach for it. How small it is compared to my palm. Is this how mine looks, pressing so hard against my lungs and chest some days it feels as though I will never breathe again?

"Interesting choice," Bram muses.

The heart is feather-light in my hand. The blood pools around it, slipping into the creases of my palm.

"Interesting how?"

Bram rocks back on his heels. "They say the heart is the core of our emotion. That is where we truly feel things. And you, Adelaide Thorn, felt enough for a perfect stranger to come rescue him from Erybrus itself."

My smile slides over to him. "So, you're not angry with me anymore?"

He winces. "No, and I shouldn't have been so upset with you the other day. We both hid things from one another in hopes for the outcome we wanted. I'm sorry I lied too."

My smile softens around the edges. "I forgive you." In the red light, his eyes are almost feverish, tinged with a haze, so lifelike it steals my breath away. "Besides, you are no stranger, Bram Avery."

He arches his eyebrows. "Oh?"

I shake my head and look back at the heart still warm against my skin. "That day, in the orchard, wasn't the first time I remember seeing you. I used to watch you when I was little. You and your sisters trudging down the lane from Avery Manor with your mother and father. I think I was jealous, really, of what you had and I didn't. I always thought you had a nice smile."

When I look back up at him, there is no smile. Instead, a shadow haunts the corners of his eyes. His shoulders shrink in, eyes flashing.

"There wasn't much to be jealous of, if I'm being honest."

There is silence for a time, and I watch the blood coagulate on the ground in front of me. Red liquid merging to form a jelly.

"You seemed happy enough," I say finally.

The skin above his eye twitches. He turns back to the trees. "Father didn't approve of my…well, my enjoyments. He thought it was better for me to learn to hunt, to keep the manor, to become worthy of the seat of Avery Manor than to stuff my nose in books. I told him I didn't want it. Why couldn't Matilda have it? She was next in line and smart as a whip. He didn't take too kindly to that." He fidgets with the collar of his shirt. "He used to beat me, Adelaide."

I nod. It is something I have long suspected, but that doesn't take the pain away. "I'm so sorry. No one deserves that, Bram."

He looks back to the dead beast at our knees. "Better if Rixton thought him the great man he seemed than the man he was at home."

I swallow, and the ridges of my throat press tight. *I'm sorry* doesn't seem like enough. Not when the men of Rixton beat their daughters, drain blood from their sons, force their children into spaces they have no desire to be in. Sometimes, the only real question I have is, what is the necessity of men?

"I know you didn't just come for me," Bram interrupts, nodding back to the heart. "I know you're here to find your mother, and I'm sorry I lied to you."

His eyes are so soft now in the light, a kind of sunset glow. The blood drips down my wrist while I stare at the tiny organ.

"I understand now, I think, why you did it. I want my mother back just as much as you want to be back with your sisters." My throat catches. "Just as much as Ransom wants his own mother back."

There is silence then, nothing but the wavering wind through the strange trees. Bram reaches forward, sinks his fingers between the folds of the rabbit's belly, and tugs. There is a soft pop.

When he draws his hand back out, his skin is sheened in carmine. He wipes the viscera away and holds up something pale and pocked in his hand. I steal a glance at his face, but his eyes have lost their softness.

"This rabbit was sick."

I drop the heart, wiping my hands with leaves, but Bram does not seem concerned. He holds the yellowed organ up to the light.

"Poisoned, I'd say. Ancient scholars used to believe the liver was the source of life and death." He drops his hand and stares directly at me. "Ransom is not to be trusted."

Before I can stop myself, a laugh cracks against my teeth. "You're getting that from the liver of a rabbit?"

I don't want to believe him, *can't*, but the way he looks at me—the hard-set line of his jaw—tells me that the words he speaks, his very existence in this dead world, is the only thing there is to believe.

He drops the liver beside the dead beast and cleans his hands off in the damp grass. "I don't make things up for sport, Adelaide. I only speak what the animals tell me."

I watch him, curious. "Are you a witch, Bram Avery?"

I mean it as a joke, something to lighten the air between us, but he doesn't smile.

"I don't know *what* I am, to be honest, but I've always been able to do that." He nods to the rabbit. "My mother caught me in the gardens with a dead sparrow in my palm, its intestines spilling out, telling of how my father would die, his own body poisoning him. All that damned wine he drank. That's when we stopped attending church. What was the point of trying to please Ithrandril when we were already struck through by Erybrus?"

I almost choke on his words. "That's horrible. I'm so sorry. I didn't mean—"

"There's a lot you don't mean, Adelaide, but things happen anyway." He gets to his feet, brushing the last of the blood away on his trousers. "We should get going, pack up after we eat, set out on our way."

I try to ignore his former words, the way they singe my skin like I'm standing too close to a fire. "On our way to where?" I ask.

"To find your mother, of course. Your leg seems healed up enough. Ransom isn't good for much, but he's adequate with a needle."

I blink stupidly and scramble to my feet. "Right, of course. Do you know where to start looking?"

Bram is already walking away from me, back toward the church. "Haven't the foggiest. Though, I do know where we can go for information."

Anticipation threads through my bones. "Where?"

He turns, a slick smile on his face. "Where everyone goes for a bit of gossip—a dead pub."

His words stop me in my tracks. Whatever this destination is, I don't like the sound of it.

I gnaw on the inside of my mouth. If I'm going to find Mother, there are probably many things I will not like. I go to follow him, but something rustles in the grass behind. My stomach folds.

Beside the torn rabbit, the heart lies in a pool of blood.

And it seems to be beating.

eighteen

We set out when the Haunts are least active, though the air kissing the nape of my neck tells me we are not alone. But how can one truly be alone in a wood of dead souls?

The moon shines so white it nearly blinds me. Around it, the sky swims red as blood, and the trees glisten, like the heart did in my hands. It is foolishness to think it was beating when I left it. In a land of dead things, life cannot just return, can it? And yet—

Ransom nudges me in the shoulder, and I look up. His hair is almost pink in the light. I still taste his bitter-gin lips on mine, though we have not spoken of the kiss since. Bram stalks the ground in front of us, Rascal at his heels.

What a strange party we are. A hellhound, a dead man, a high lord, and the daughter of a vicar, whose heart sometimes feels as though it is not her own. Yet, the odd thing is, I have not had a fit since the moment my foot touched down in this realm in between. No rush of untethered movement, no rapid pounding of my heart, no pain blossoming at the base of my skull.

I lift fingers up to the soft flesh of my throat and wait for the steady beats. It is almost a comfort, but in some ways, it is like waiting for the shoe to drop. For the rug to be pulled out from underneath me. For my heart to go skittering and my end to come.

"Penny for your thoughts?" Ransom asks.

"Father used to tell me my thoughts were wicked," I respond. Our feet crunch on the crimson leaves.

Ransom grins. "Wicked thoughts tend to be my favorite."

I whisper a silent *thank you* that the sky floods us with such scarlet light, or else I fear Ransom would see the blush washing down my cheeks.

"I'm simply thinking of the bell, I suppose." I turn my eyes back to the path ahead. "I have no idea where it went. I'm half terrified I won't be able to save any of us without it and half grateful I don't have it anymore. It was too powerful sometimes. Like a weight around my neck."

Ransom stops and grabs my arm. "Hold out your hand."

I blink. "What?"

"Your hand, give it to me."

When I do as he says, something cold presses against my skin. I peel back my fingers.

The bell lies there, just as it has always been. Brass shining in the moonlight, wooden handle, the ridged dome edge. I should be relieved, grateful even at Ransom for finding it. But I feel none of these things. Suspicion winds through my gut.

I stare up at him, mouth pinched. "Did you take it from me?"

A flash of something crosses his eyes, hot like flame. "Do you really think so low of me, Thorn?" He turns and starts walking away, the sight of his back filling my stomach with guilt.

I pocket the bell in its wrappings to keep it from ringing and run after him.

"No, I'm sorry. I just…Ransom, look at me." I spin him around.

"What?" His heartbeat flutters in the notch above his collarbone.

I take a deep breath, keeping my voice low while Bram walks on ahead of us. "I didn't mean to accuse you of anything, but where did you find it?"

He fingers the pouch at his hip. "In the confessional, just before we left. I thought it might have fallen out while we were in there. We must have overlooked it. I didn't give it to you right away because I didn't want Bram to accuse me of stealing it." He grins a roguish smile. "Consider it an early wedding present."

Relief and unease flood my mind. For a moment, both feelings tingle along my skin, like the brush of insect legs. When we return home, *if* we return, I will not be returning as Adelaide Thorn, the vicar's daughter, but as Lady Adelaide Black, the woman with secrets pulsing beneath her skin.

I try on a smile, but it only pulls at my skin painfully. Of course, he didn't steal it. There is no reason for it. I fold my hand around the bulge in my skirt.

"I'm sorry. I shouldn't have said what I said. Thank you for finding it."

He nods, a sharp and short thing, dropping his roguish smile.

"Are you two coming?"

"Oh, would you just ease off, Avery?" Ransom snaps.

Bram is turned to us, Rascal running circles around his heels. I would almost laugh if not for the look on Bram's face.

He is not to be trusted. I steal a glance at Ransom. The scars on his wrists mirror images of mine. But pain makes monsters of us all.

Bram hurries before us, the moonlight spilling on his back. Something catches there, pale where shadow should be. And if he knows of pain, who is to say he is not a monster? I picture the scars at his wrists and bite my lip.

"Yes, we're coming." I rush to catch up, the bell heavy in my pocket.

Bram only stops when we reach the outskirts of a village. The stone walls are in disarray, ruins of some place forgotten. The smell that permeates the air reminds me of Blackbourne Castle, all humidity and iron. I lift the cuff of one sleeve over my nose. The scent does not seem to bother Bram.

"The alehouse is just on the other side of that hill." He points through the darkness toward a small mound of dirt and charred trees. Beyond that is an echo of light, like the sun reflecting in a muddy pool.

"And remind me again what the purpose of our visit is, Avery?" Ransom hangs back, arms crossed in front of his chest.

Bram turns, eyes flashing. "Maybe you forget, Black, but the whole purpose of your visit to the wood is to get Adelaide's mother back."

Ransom grins and holds up his hands. "A man can ask questions. Just don't see how going to an alehouse full of dead folk is going to help us find Thorn's mother."

I sink my fingers into Rascal's fur, letting the warmth ground me. "Will you two please stop bickering like old ladies after church?"

They both look to me, faces downcast. Ransom smirks. One step, that's all it would take to close the space between us and smack him.

"We're here for your mother as well," I say.

Ransom flinches and pulls at his hair. "Right, that too. Though she was never one for the alehouse."

Bram grumbles something about Ransom's mother not being one for anyplace and starts back for the hill. Rascal bounds after him. I lock eyes with Ransom when I pass.

"Behave," I hiss.

He smiles and shrugs. "I'll try."

I have never seen so many dead people in my entire life. Even when the bodies piled high in Rixton, all the murdered girls, nothing could prepare me for this. Scattered amongst a lane of ruined buildings and red-leafed trees, the alehouse sticks out like a fungus on bark. The air smells sickly sweet, of slurried earth and decaying fruit. But also like roasting meat and golden, buttery potatoes.

"Bloody hell." Ransom sighs, his eyes feasting on the scene before us. "Is there food here?"

All we have had in the last few days are bottles of communion wine and the rotting apples we found in the church, our teeth careful not to ingest any of the ruined flesh. The notion of hot food and drink sloshing around in my belly makes me forget all thoughts of the dead women.

Bram winces. "It depends on what you call food. Nothing really grows here, and if it does, it grows wrong. The dead don't need to eat, but there are those who like the remembrance of taste. Even if that taste is poison. Just be careful. We're here for information more than anything else. Don't take anything you're offered, only what I say is okay to eat or drink."

"I don't care if it's made from old chicken liver and brambles. If it's hot, I'll eat it." Ransom huddles down deeper in his coat.

That word again, *liver*.

I look to Bram, but his eyes are on the alehouse. The moon scatters coins of silver light over us when we push through the doors and stumble inside. Before I can look around, Bram's hand is at my wrist, and he hisses in my ear.

"Don't go making deals with these people."

I nod, almost feeling as though I am back in Rixton. But our village never had an alehouse. The closest one was—

"This is Kinnington?" I whisper to Bram.

He nods. "Of a sort."

The ceiling slings low, like the hull of a ship, and cobwebs flutter like lace in every corner. A fire blazes merrily in the stone hearth, and there is a scent of cooking pots and yeast on the air. But beneath it all, I sense the rot. The decay.

Ransom, who does not seem to notice, sidles up to the bar and places down a silver coin.

"An ale, please. Strongest you got."

Silence sifts into the alehouse, and every eye turns to us. By my side, Rascal whimpers.

The bartender, a man in a black cap pulled low over sallow hair, turns slowly and flings a stained cloth over one shoulder. My breath catches in my throat when he makes eye contact with Ransom.

Half his left cheek is missing, flesh like a gourd chewed away by hungry mice.

"Your coin is no use here, boy." His words come out funny, the sound of them slurring through the space between blackened teeth and missing skin.

Ransom curls his lip. "Then what would you have in exchange?"

The bartender leans closer, and my skin prickles with unease. "How about your soul, lad?"

The silence sticks in my ears like knife points, and I struggle to swallow. Behind me, Bram stiffens, his hand coming to find mine.

And then the alehouse erupts in laughter.

For a moment, shock washes over me like cold water, and all I can do is stare. But then Ransom's face breaks with that wicked grin.

"You almost had me there, good sir."

Almost, I want to scream. Almost? I could strangle Ransom, who does seem to be the type to barter his mortal soul for a tankard of bitter ale. The bartender produces three chipped glasses and fills each one with a frothy, golden brine I want nothing to do with. He pushes them across the bar to Ransom.

"On the house, lad. Been a while since we had any live ones."

The way he says the last two words makes my skin crawl. I steal a glance at Bram, but his eyes are fixed on the bartender, that look of distrust in his eyes. As if he wants to slit the man from neck to navel and spill his guts on the floor to read his intentions.

Ransom swipes the glasses from the bar and sloshes toward us, his grin dripping on his face.

Bram grunts and leads us to a rough-hewn table tucked into a far corner. While we settle in, the alehouse returns to its heady noise, and I watch the patrons in awe-like horror.

Some are skeletal, ale sloshing out between their bones and staining meager scraps of clothing. Others appear more like Bram—whole, still mostly alive, the ashen sheen to their skin the only thing giving them away. Ransom passes us each a glass, but I shake my head.

"I think I'll pass, thanks."

Bram, who eyes the glasses with suspicion, grabs his and tips it back against his lips before I can stop him. When he places it back down on the table, a line of froth sticks to his upper lip.

"It's fine for you two to drink. Seems to be the real stuff."

Ransom does not need any more encouragement. He fists the glass and swallows the lot in four greedy gulps. "Glory be."

I roll my eyes and turn to Bram. "I don't understand. How can it be real ale if nothing grows here? You can't make ale from dead crops."

Bram shrugs, takes another drink. "You can and you can't, I suppose. That's what most of our food and drink is made from here—dead things. Okay for us to consume, deadly for someone still living. But things find their way into the wood. Sometimes, Reapers bring in more than just the dead."

I stare down at the bubbles in my glass. Reapers. I do not want to think about my blood, what it might mean. If I have Reaper's blood, which parent do I have to thank? Which parent has lied through their teeth?

"It's safe enough to drink, Adelaide," Bram says.

We spend the rest of the day holed up in the alehouse, talking to no one, explaining nothing. But there is food to eat—a sort of meat pie I hope is rabbit—and the ale reminds me of home, though we rarely ever had it at the vicarage. I snuck some when I was little to impress Clara. It hadn't worked, of course. After several sips, I found myself bent over in Mother's garden beds, emptying my guts out on the soil.

So, I am careful, nursing the honeyed liquid. The same can't be said for Ransom. By the time we are led up the stairs to the two rooms we will rest in, he is sloshing ahead of me, leaning heavily on Bram's shoulder.

Bram's face is pinched, and I hide a giggle in my hand at his irritation.

"You and Rascal can have the second room, Adelaide." Bram fumbles the key in the lock while Ransom begins singing the opening notes of an old Rixton drinking song. "Wake me up if you need anything."

"I don't think I'll be the one needing anything," I say, nodding to Ransom.

Bram turns to him, features traced delicately in the moonlight. "I'll make sure to tuck him in."

For a moment, we stare at each other. Ransom begins the next verse. I hear the voices of the mingling dead downstairs, the clinking of glasses, the clamping of exposed jaws, the clicking of dry bones. But it is only Bram and I for a split-second, standing in the hall, the scent of rot all around us.

"Well, goodnight," I whisper, breaking the tension. "Or good day. Who can say anymore?"

Bram readjusts his hold on Ransom. "Right, well, I hope you can get some sleep."

"You too." I open my door.

He does not respond, only nods, and I wonder if Bram Avery sleeps at all.

The room behind the door is as expected. A bed, a window boarded over, no pictures on the walls. The quilt is riddled with moth-chew, but the hues of powder blue and russet woven into the fabric remind me of home. Rascal makes short work of bounding across the floor in springy strides, then circling up in all the dust-kissed pillows.

I laugh, almost forgetfully, as though I am not surrounded by dead things, searching for my mother to bring her back to life. It sounds ridiculous when I think it so plainly.

I slip off my boots and unlace my stays, almost crying when they release and allow my ribs to stretch. How long has it been since I last took them off? Days now.

I scurry from my woolen skirts until I am wearing nothing but a thin cotton chemise. The chill air licks my ankles, and I climb into the bed quicker than a whip. The mattress is soft, and I nestle down amidst the warm wool and linen. Rascal curls next to me, and I weave my fingers through his fur.

My legs will hurt like hell come morning, from all the walking, but we are getting closer to Mother. We must be. I reach into my discarded skirts and lift the bell from my pocket, tucking it safely beneath my pillow. Whatever its role in bringing Mother back home, I must keep it safe and whole. I can risk no harm to it.

Just as I am drifting off to restless sleep, Rascal straightens, a low growl starting in his throat. My skin pricks with cold, and I sit up. Shadows pass beneath the door, back and forth. I hold my breath, counting the seconds, tasting bile at the back of my tongue when knuckles rap on the soft wood.

Rascal leaps from the bed, the hair on his back sharp as needlepoints. I wait for my heart to rocket into my throat, but it doesn't, so I curl my toes from the blankets and slip another over my shoulders.

The knock comes again, this time accompanied by a voice. "Thorn, it's me."

Ransom. Sounding less drunk than before but not by much.

I clutch the blanket tighter and move toward the door. On the other side, Ransom leans heavy against the frame. His hair is mussed, and there are wrinkles on his face from where he fell asleep on his pillow.

Here, in the reddish light streaming through the far windows, he almost looks like an avenging angel. His eyes go wide when he notices I'm not wearing my dress.

"Sorry, I should have—I can go back to bed."

"No, it's fine." I brush hair from my eyes. "Is there something you wanted to say?"

He hesitates for a moment, makes a pained expression. "I wanted to say that I am sorry for acting like an ass back there in the woods. When I gave you the bell. Of course, you would have thought I'd taken it. If I'd been you, I would have thought the same. I'm sorry I took my own feelings out on you."

"Your own feelings?" I step closer, so much so I can detect the lingering ale on his tongue.

He shrugs. "It is hard for me when people don't trust me. I get angry, closed up. It's not your problem, and I am sorry I tried to make it so."

Never in a million years would I think Lord Ransom Black would be standing in front of me, apologizing for being an ass. I smile. "No harm done, Ransom."

He sighs, like a weight has been lifted off his chest, and moves closer. His sweat is bitter and cold. I make a face and hope he doesn't notice it in the shadowy light.

"We should do something to remember this, you know?"

"Remember this? Ransom, what are you talking about? Where's Bram?" I peek around him, but the hall is empty. Perhaps we should not be alone.

"Went downstairs, I think. Listen, Adelaide. *Wife*." He presses nearer, and Rascal growls a protest from the bed.

I plant my hands firmly on his chest. "I am *not* your wife yet. And you're drunk. Perhaps you should—"

His finger goes to my mouth, flesh salty on my lips.

"*Shh*, listen to me. We should run away, you and I. Grab the bell, find a place here of our own. In the wood. Think of it. We could be the only living souls in this whole place. You saw how the dead downstairs treated us, like we were gods, Adelaide." He pushes into my room and pins me against the wall, his hand hot and tight on my thigh.

"Ransom—"

"With that bell, we could rule. We could command who came and who went. Reapers, think of it. No more lordly duties, no more fathers telling us what we can and cannot do. We'd hold all the power, Thorn. All of it."

His words run together like spring mud, and I blink, trying to slow their meaning down in my mind. Pick them apart until I understand them. But they are madness. Live here? Amongst all the rot and death? The idea creeps along my skin, leaving a feeling of damp in its wake.

"Ransom, you're not making any sense."

"I'm making perfect sense." His hand goes to my waist, and my skin flares.

Do not trust him.

"Ransom." My hands are back on his chest now, pushing. "Please."

"There's so much power here," he whispers against my neck. "And it could all be ours."

A knot of tension pulls taut in my stomach. His hands brush higher. Sweat breaks out on my neck.

"Ransom, get off."

And then his lips are on mine, and they *hurt.* They crush and bite, and all I want to do is claw and spit. Rascal jumps down from the bed, jaws peeling back in a throaty growl, but even this does not stop Ransom Black and his greedy hands. His entitlement to rule over those in these woods is sickening. He has never been told no—a lord's son, only told, *Yes, take more. It is all yours.*

My mouth tastes sour.

I think of the dead rabbit, the still-beating heart after I held it in my palm. Of my mother's bitterbloom vines pushing through the soil, growing in a dead land without sun. Of Bram—the one person who has ever seemed to *care*. And I fight.

My knee comes up between Ransom's legs, and my elbow connects with his jaw. He crumples, expression confused, pain leaking from his eyes.

"Adelaide, what the—"

I stare down at him while he wilts, eyes flashing, taste the ghost of blood in my mouth, the feeling of Father's words cutting my throat.

"I will not live in this wood, Ransom. I will not become some puppet of Erybrus. And I'm calling our bargain off. When we return home, I will not be your wife. I will be myself." The words come to me as easily as water from a pipe.

Ransom twists his features. "Do you even know what that is?"

Righteous anger floods my veins. "Get up and get out."

Ransom scrambles up from the floor, wiping at his mouth. At the open door, he turns back.

"Adelaide, I'm—"

"I said, get out. I'll see you in the morning, and there will be no more about it." My skin shakes, but I remain resolute, my expression set in stone.

Ransom's face hardens when the door creaks ajar and washes him in ruby light. He opens his mouth to say something more, but I do not give him the luxury. The sound of the resounding slam and the snick of the lock is a comfort to my ears.

Shaken, but strong, I make my way back to the bed and curl up against Rascal beneath the sheets. My fingers reach for the bell beneath the pillow, and I close my eyes, hot tears stinging my cheeks.

When I finally fall asleep, I dream of cutting Ransom open, spilling his guts out in the moonlight, and finding only rot and the wriggling shoots of bitterbloom flowers.

nineteen

There is a scream in my throat when I wake. I am lying in my bed, but the room is different, darker. There are no windows, only the musty smell of closed-up spaces. Rascal's warmth has vanished, and I shiver in the sheets.

I am alone. The ghost of Ransom still lingers against my lips, but I press the memory away.

"Rascal?" My voice is a hushed thing in the blackness. "Hello?"

I push myself against the headboard, bringing my knees in tight against me.

"Bram?" But even when I open my mouth, I know he will not answer.

The darkness presses down on me like some unseen force, a kind of monster ready to swallow and devour me with its slick, black tongue. I reach for the stammering of my heart I am sure is there, but it is gentle. This is who I am, this pain, this wrong beat. And if it is gone, who am I?

What am I?

I open my mouth to call Bram's name again, but there is a click of light in one corner, and my breath hitches, turns sharp.

"What a pretty living thing," a voice says. "Sure to catch a good price."

I gasp, choke on cold air. "Who's there?"

A shadow crosses the brightness. It happens so quickly.

A match is struck, a lantern lit. My suspicions were right. I am no longer in my room, and Rascal is gone. The ceiling here is lower, damp. The walls drip with condensation. I squint in the sudden light, wrinkling my nose at the smell of mildew and rot.

"Look at me, you pretty little thing."

I grind my teeth and turn to the voice, to the gnarled hand holding the lantern. "Show yourself."

There is laughter—thick and rotten, like a raven choking on peach pits—and then a face appears above the flickering light.

The innkeeper. He stands against the wall, jawbone sticking out like the ribcage of some shored fish.

My arms buckle, and I press myself back against the headboard, wood creaking. "Where am I?"

He chuckles, something wet gurgling in his half-exposed throat. "Let's just say I gave you our *special* room. Where we put all the livings when we get one, which is far and few between, mind you." He points to the darkness beyond the bed. "There's a door there. You can't see it now, but it's there."

I scratch at the sheets and say a quick prayer that the bell is still within reach. "Where are my friends?"

My body is ringing with terror. I could reach beneath my pillow, use the bell, and go home. But what if this man followed me? And what of Bram?

The innkeeper's jaw cracks with the force of his smile. "Let's talk about you first, my dear. Call this place a cage of sorts. A trap." He leans in against the light, shadows dancing across his corpse. "Tell me, would you like to make a deal?"

My stomach fizzes. Bram's words echo in my ear. *Don't make deals with these people.*

I lift my chin. "Tell me where my friends are."

The innkeeper drops to a chair. "You know, pretty little thing, I was told by someone very important to send all living souls to them if I ever ran across any. I would be paid in redemption, my own soul taken back home, where I could live forever. Doesn't that sound nice?"

I fight to spit a laugh. No one can live forever. "You aren't answering my question."

He raises a brow, his bones crackling beneath his skin. "One of your friends is already gone. Made his deal early this morning. I can tell you where he went, or I can sell you…but for the right price, I could tell you where your friend went *and* let you go." He slides his chair closer to the bed. A stink comes off him, like spoiled meat. "Want to make a deal?"

Before I can answer, before I can ask who has already left, something stirs in the corner.

"Ah," the innkeeper says, rising from his chair. "The dead one."

The lantern illuminates another corner, where Bram and Rascal are tied to the floor. Rascal's lips peel back, revealing sharp white teeth. I scramble in the sheets, my chest skimming with sweat. No.

The innkeeper laughs.

"Won't catch a price for these two, them being dead and all. But you—" He turns to me.

"Adelaide." Bram's voice is weak. "Don't do it."

In the shadows, I slip my hand below my pillow, fist the bell. But I can't bring myself to ring it, not without Mother. And not without Bram.

"Name your price."

The innkeeper smiles. "I will set you loose and tell you where your friend went, but you must do something for me in return."

"Anything."

"Addie—" Bram's voice is cut short with a growl from Rascal's throat.

The man laughs. "The girl seems to know what she wants, man. Let her make her deal." He inches closer to the bed. "I'll make this easy for you. I'll tell you what you want to know, and if you get back to the land of the living, you send someone here."

My heartbeat thuds in my ears when I realize the meaning behind his words. "You want me to kill someone?" Dread coils in my stomach, and I think I might get sick.

Bram's presence is steady in the corner.

"I'm asking exactly that, pretty little thing."

Cold seeps into my bones. What will this make of me? A murderer, just as everyone already believes? I steal a glimpse of Bram from the corner of my eye.

If I can't uphold my promise to him, that makes me something worse. A liar.

I concentrate on the bell in my hand, run my thumb along the brass. It is like a rifle in my hands, aimed at some target I cannot see. I draw a deep breath, hold it, steady my aim, no longer able to hear the sound of my own heart.

My mind goes blank, eyes training distantly on the man before me. The dead man.

He tips back and folds his arms, like someone who already knows he has won.

"I'll do it."

Bram groans, and the man's grin spreads so wide he might swallow his own bones.

"Sign."

Bram is quick as a whip, on his feet, straining against his bonds, but I ignore him, eyes still trained on my target. Rifle raised.

The man holds the knife out to me, produces a flask of wine from his pocket. "On my hand," he says, holding out a gnarled palm. "Sign."

I stare at the knife, the lantern light reflecting on the metal. Bram is stiff, fear rolling off him in waves. Rascal whines. I crawl to the foot of the bed and grab the knife, not giving myself time to think before bringing the blade down against my flesh. The skin sears, blood beading.

The man's eyes widen. "A Reaper. Well, this is fun." He offers me the flask of wine, pours it over the cut.

I grit my teeth.

"Addie."

Once more, I ignore Bram. We have to find Ransom. There's no telling what he will do.

The dead man's hand is rough and dry beneath my tender flesh, but I sign my name. The letters look strange in red, unfamiliar. As though they no longer belong to me. The man smiles, his teeth slipping in his jaw.

"You have yourself a deal, little Reaper."

"Tell me where our friend went."

He squeezes the blood between his brittle fingers. "There's a castle a short distance from here, back the way you came and a little to the west. Here it has no name, but back on the other side of the wood, back home, people called it Blackbourne."

Every bit of energy drains out the soles of my feet. "*Blackbourne Castle*?"

"Aye, that's the one. One of the few buildings left. Your friend seemed all too interested when I offered him his deal. When he heard who lived in the castle, he was quite eager."

Curiosity prickles at my neck. "What was his deal?"

The innkeeper clucks and shakes a blood-stained finger. "I wouldn't worry about that if I were you. You've enough troubles of your own."

Bram ignores him. "Who lives in the castle?"

The innkeeper turns. "I'm not making deals with the dead today."

"Then tell me, please." I scramble closer to the edge of the bed, the bell still hidden in my palm.

He faces me. "You'll kill anyone I ask you to?"

I will make myself the monster if it means getting my mother back. "Yes."

"They say a lady lives up in the castle. A Lady Black."

My eyes meet Bram's, fear and recognition alike on his face.

I glance back to the innkeeper. "And who is it you'd like me to kill?"

His mouth gapes open, letting out the thick scent of decay. "A man who lied to me. Told me I would see my daughter again when I died. But she isn't in this place."

"And who is that?"

"The vicar of Rixton parish, one Felix Thorn."

twenty

My skin rattles in sheer terror of it all, but I grind my teeth and straighten my spine. Kill my own father? I am here to seek his redemption, not to damn him—and myself in the process—to living death. But I could bring him back, couldn't I? Carry through these dead man's words and then bring him back? I fist the bell.

"You have a deal."

His fingers wrap around mine, cold and slimy as worms, a grin cracking along his face. I do not know much of the world outside Rixton, but I have been taught that murder is a cardinal sin, one punishable only by the fiery tongue of Erybrus, and I have just damned myself by promising to slit the neck of my own father. But I will bring all of us back. Stitch our family together.

The innkeeper crosses to Bram and Rascal, cuts their bonds. "Looking forward to my prize, little Reaper."

I hurry into my clothes and walk with Bram from the inn. His fingers are cold at my back through my blouse. When we reach the cover of trees, he grips my wrist and turns me around. I bite back a groan.

Every inch of his face reads fury. The fire in his eyes, the twist of his lips, the way the light catches the shadowed hollows of his cheekbones. I hate it. But it's the disappointment I hate the most. It ekes in the air like poison, covering him, suffocating me. I wrench my hand away, my mouth a severe line, nostrils flaring.

"What?"

"*What?* You know what. I warned you not to make a deal with these people, Adelaide. The dead are not forgiving. If you don't follow through with your end of the bargain, that man, he'll—"

"He'll what?"

I am so close to Bram's face. The delicate loosening of his skin is apparent, just below his eyes. A gentle decay. It hurts to imagine what he will become if I don't bring him home. If I don't *save* him too.

"He'll hunt you down and take your soul to Erybrus."

I try to ignore the dread pricking holes in my stomach and reach into my pocket, bringing out the bell. "You forget, I have this."

A crease deepens between Bram's brows. "How did you get it back?"

"I don't see how that's important."

His jaw juts from the papery skin of his cheek, teeth grinding. He is going to shout at me, leave me here in the dark. And for the first time, I realize how much I need him. *Want* him.

"Bram—"

In the hush of the forest, he pins me against a tree. His face is arresting. All hard lines, dark stubble. His hands are at my waist, anchoring me. Something warm slips along the center of my core.

Bram Avery is unlike anything I have ever seen. His focus, his surety, his conviction…it's striking. I fight the desire, the way he makes every inch of me tremble.

"You trust too easily, Adelaide Thorn," he whispers, and then he's walking away.

All I know how to do is breathe deeply and follow him. I can't let him out of my sight. His anger is grounding. It is real. Perhaps the only realness in this world of dead things.

"You act as if you know everything there is to know about this place," he spits. "Like you can just go making deals with dead people and suffer no consequences."

"Bram, I—"

He whirls on me. "There are so many things you don't know."

The shadows in his gaze send a chill through my bones. Here, in the dim light, he looks more dead than alive for the first time since he appeared in my bedroom. His skin seems sallow and thin, stretched tallow wax. The violet stains beneath his eyes are wan and deep, dripping down to his chin like spilled ink.

"I'm sorry," is all I manage, but Bram is already moving away through the trees.

"Don't bother," he clips back. "You've already made your deal."

He disappears amidst the crooked white and silver trunks, and I am here, and I am not. I am tied to a chair, my mouth stuffed with words that are not my own, verses scrawled in Father's hand.

"Are you coming or not?"

Bram's voice sends me crashing back into my own body, chest heaving. My skin is slick with cold sweat, and a shiver runs the course of my spine. Bram stands at the tree line, brow dark, but with more concern now than anger. Rascal waits at his side, tail wagging. I clench my fists and move toward him, though the memory niggles at the back of my mind.

I am wicked; I am weak. If I were stronger, I would take the bell in my hand, send Bram home, and face this weary world without him. But he is right. I know nothing of this place, and I need him.

The walk through the red wood is filled with sounds that send my skin crawling. Groans and screams, the laughter of young children morphing to the scraping of nails on stone. It turns my stomach, makes me cling fast to the bell. I hold it so tightly I fear it might come apart in my hand with each step.

Bram does not know of this, not now, not after everything I have put him through. When we reach the ruin of Rixton, I pause at the vicarage. Look up. Envision what it looks like back home.

Even there, it is a broken thing. Even there, so am I.

Little Reaper. I leave Bram's side and dive through the opening, spilling out on the other side where the bitterbloom weaves, rebellious in the light of a dead moon. Bram chases after me, his feet crunching the broken earth beneath us.

"Adelaide, what the hell are you doing? We need to reach the castle."

I shove hair from my face and stare down at the flowers. "I don't understand—"

He reaches for my wrist, his fingers like dagger points. "If we don't get to the castle soon, who knows what Ransom will wind up doing."

I spin, my cheeks racing hot. Ransom's greedy hands still linger on my skin, and I taste the bitter bite of his lips. I close my eyes for a beat, brushing away the memory and trying desperately to replace it with a daydream. Ransom running to the castle before us, finding our mothers, apologizing when we arrive. Saying he's sorry, but look, he found them! Doesn't that make up for it? But trying to make the thought real, force it to fit, is like shoving solid rock through cheesecloth.

Bram lifts his hand from mine. My skin tenses, but I continue to stare at the blooms, reach a finger to brush the velvet petals. Each one so vibrant. So alive. How can they grow in a world where the faces of people are sloughing off?

"How are these alive?"

Bram shifts beside me, his voice thin with irritation. "How would I know?"

"Because I know nothing, remember?"

The bitter bite of my words hit their mark. He rubs his eyes.

"I honestly have no idea, Adelaide. It doesn't make sense. There, is that the answer you wanted?"

A sort of blush rises in his cheeks. It is horribly distracting.

Ever since he spilled the rabbit blood and watched me hold the heart, I swear there is something more human about him. More pain, more joy, more fear set behind those amber eyes. Even when Ransom had me pressed against the wall, I couldn't stop thinking what if it was him—Bram—to make it better. Make it safe. Because that is what he makes me feel more than anyone else in this wretched world ever has.

Safe.

I could imagine it was Bram who had his hands at my waist, his fingers like knife points in my thigh—

The flowers. Back to the flowers.

"Touch one."

Bram lifts his brows. "I'm sorry?"

"I said, touch one."

"Adelaide, we don't have time for—"

I grab his hand and pull it toward a snowy bloom, the centers like drops of honey. Almost instantly, when his fingers brush against it, the bitterbloom shrivels. He gasps and pulls away.

"What the—"

I stare at the dead flower, each petal now a burial shroud. None of the others have been affected, only the one Bram touched. I reach out toward it, my finger like a butterfly kiss. And the petal unfurls. Turns white once more. Gray to cream to pure milky white. I pull away, my skin stinging.

"What the hell did you just do?" Bram brushes his hand along the bed of flowers. The blooms go dead at an alarming rate.

I do not look up, my eyes trained on the bitterbloom. It seems to waver, as if a breeze has come. And then, I reach for all the flowers. I gather them in fistfuls, careful not to pull them from the earth, and watch while each and every one turns a shade so bright they are almost blinding.

Bram goes slack-jawed. "This is impossible."

I touch every flower until the bed is bursting. Honey yellow, nacreous pearl, pops of almost unnatural green. They seem to grow right from my very fingers, kissing my flesh as though I am the sun. They take my breath away. Something sizzles in my veins, and I press my hand against Bram's arm.

"Are you seeing this? It isn't just me?"

"Perhaps we shouldn't have drunk that ale. Perhaps we're still at the alehouse, intoxicated. Or…" His voice trails off.

"You know that isn't true. Look at me." I reach for Bram's face, and he

flinches. As though my touch is painful. "When you gutted that rabbit and I chose the heart, you said it was an interesting choice. Why?"

His eyes dart like a caged beast. "Most souls here, we crave the things we have forgotten. The taste of fresh bread, the swill of wine on our tongue. I have seen people rip apart a deer, only to come away with the punctured stomach, the liver. Just to taste something that reminds them of home, even if that means tasting grass, the poison of river water. But you chose the heart. Which means the thing you desire most is life itself."

My body goes rigid. The memory of the heart in my hands is hazy, trapped on the other side of a frosted window. But I can still remember the way it felt in my hands.

"That's foolish, Bram. You've seen my blood. You heard what the innkeeper called me."

Little Reaper.

He shakes his head. "You don't get it, do you? Here, in the wood, we are neither Erybrus's nor Ithrandril's. We have a choice. The Reapers, they have a choice too. Ithrandril wants all souls to come to them, but it allows the Reapers to make their choice. Are they for Erybrus or for Ithrandril?"

"But the dead, Bram. The dead are brought *here*. And the dead belong to Erybrus." I am desperate, trying to make sense of all this against the teachings I have grown up with. Father telling me time and time again that I was cursed, death walking, touched by shadow.

"You've missed the entire point of this place, Adelaide. People aren't trapped here because they want to come back to life. We're trapped here because we're greedy. We don't know how to move on into true death. There's something we feel we've been cheated of. Something that holds us to home with fraying ropes."

Don't make deals with these people. Bram didn't tell me just as a warning. He told me because the inhabitants of this place are obsessed. With winning. With beating and *cheating* life.

"But don't...don't you want to be brought home, Bram? To be brought back to life? That was our deal...." My voice drops, and I feel punched in the gut. I twist on him, eyes hard. "You tricked me."

He raises his hands in surrender, a shy smile on his lips. "I did no such thing. I made a deal to be brought home. I bargained for life, not to cheat death. And I've upheld my side thus far, haven't I?"

What am I even doing here?

What could someone like Bram possibly need from me when I can't even find my own mother? I have signed away my own father's life. How can I uphold my end of this wretched deal with Bram?

"I just want to find my mother." I only realize I'm crying when I reach up to wipe at my cheeks, my hand coming away wet.

Bram looks at me like I am a portrait in a gold frame hung in some museum. Behind rope. Behind glass. Untouchable.

"Don't."

"What?" he asks, shrinking back.

"Don't look at me like I'm something broken."

"I'm not. I'm—" There, in his eyes, the recognition. "Sorry, let's…let's get moving."

He turns, takes one step, and freezes. The mud slurries around his boot, letting up an awful stink. Rascal whines and nuzzles my leg. I sink my fingers instinctively into his fur.

"Bram, what is it? What's wrong?"

He holds still, so motionless he might be made of marble. Breath turns to ice in my lungs. Slowly, he turns, one finger pressed against white lips. The sight of it is enough to turn my insides hollow.

"Haunts," he says. "They've found us."

twenty-one

They rise from the river, dripping shadow, their faces filled with gnashing teeth. In a frenzy, Bram pulls me behind his body, and I do not stop him. Rascal inches out ahead, his lips pulled back in a vicious snarl.

The Haunts move toward us, their arms dragging along, eyes white like the moon. My heart pulses in my fingertips. But it is steady, and I hold my ground, even when the air around us turns sick. I bury my nose against Bram's shoulder, and his hand slips reassuringly into mine.

One of the Haunts breaks away, traces lines in the mud when it comes toward us. The air grows cold, and I shudder, spine cracking like a twig. The shadow woman—full, gray lips; a prim nose; a face with bones like diamond edges—stops and smiles down at Rascal as if he is a toy. He growls.

"Quiet." The word drips from her slackened mouth like water.

Rascal obeys. He snaps his jaw shut and runs behind me, tail tucked. My eyes flash to the creature.

"What do you want from us?" Each word feels feral in my mouth. An uncontrolled beast of fear and fright.

She cocks her neck to look at me, bones peeking from dry flesh. One eye warbles in its socket, as though trying to focus on me.

"Little Reaper wants to know. Little Reaper wants to see." The voice is a singsong of slurred words that rattle in my ears.

I set my jaw. "What do I want to see?"

The shrouded creature on the left of the woman hovers closer. It smells of rot, even more than its companions. Wet soil turned up to cure in sunlight. It slides its lipless mouth open—nothing but a fleshy, pink gash.

"Little Reaper has a deal to make."

I cannot move my body for fear. Every muscle tense, every tendon a line of shrill ice.

"I am done making deals here," I say.

After a moment, the creature to the right sidles closer. This one almost appears like a child. Its skin is more intact than the others, smoother. Its eyes are milky, a line of film over what once might have been blue. When it opens its mouth to speak, a tongue flops out, pink as a newborn baby.

"Ask us a question, Little Reaper. Ask us a question, and we might set you free."

The voice is a child's lilt, the echo of tin bells. It sends my stomach swimming, and my fingers tighten against Bram's.

I open my mouth, trying to think of something to ask. Anything really. What does it matter? But it is Bram's voice that fills the space.

"Adelaide, don't. It's a trap."

The childlike creature frowns, lines deepening in its decaying flesh. "The dead man knows. The dead man will not let us play our games."

"Hush," says the one in the middle. "There is no time for games." Her listless gaze pierces me. "We must bring her to the Lady."

My eyes flash to Bram, whose own fill with recognition at the name. Lady Black. Hope begins to ease within the spaces inside me that the fear will not. Perhaps Ransom's mother will know where my own is.

The Haunts smile. In tandem. No lips, full lips, young lips cutting across their blank faces, like a finger in soil, ready to sow.

The center one reaches out one hand to me, the fingers limp like worms. "You will fly with us, Little Reaper. You will fly with us, as will the dead man and the hellhound. We must bring you to the Lady. We must do as she commands."

"We must do as she commands," the others echo, leaving me with a sinking feeling in the pit of my stomach.

But this is how we will locate Ransom, how we will hopefully find my mother. And a flight on the shadow of the Haunts is surely a quicker way to travel than our own two feet.

I glance at Bram, who seems like he would rather spend an eternity here than ride a Haunt, but I grab his hand. "We can do this. It's going to be fine."

The look on his face proves his thoughts do not match mine. He pulls me close, his lips hot on my ear. "I have not heard of Haunts acting this way, serving someone outside Erybrus. Whatever this is, it can't be good."

Anger cuts through me. "You promised to help me find my mother, and I promised Ransom to help him find his. I'm going with them. You're welcome to stay."

I turn back to the Haunts. The one in the middle widens her smile.

"Will the Little Reaper come?"

I swallow the lump at the back of my throat and lift my hand. "I will."

Her fingers slosh against mine, each one a wriggling, writhing thing. I weave my hand into hers. The breath whooshes from my body when I am sucked into the shadow. It swirls around me, midnight black. No light. I open my mouth to scream, but no sound comes out.

When I pound against the shadows, they only mold around my fist. There is a storm of noise, a crashing of cold wind in my ears. I crouch down—on what, I have no idea—but the shadows beneath me feel solid. There is a tearing sound, the scent of iron, and then nothing but the gentle shushing of wind in my ears.

I curl up against the shadow, shivering in the blackness and gloom. Even here—wherever *here* is—the light of the red sky and the sallow moon do not penetrate. Black, red, white. The only real colors I have known for days.

I miss the River Thine, the pink of Clara's smile, the honey brown of Liza's eyes. And I roll over onto my back, whispering a silent prayer that they boarded the coach to Lysdin. Escaped. Together and in love.

Love is a funny word. One I don't quite understand. It is what I thought I felt for Ransom, but that was something else. An insatiable hunger that dwelled somewhere too deep in my bones. It hurt to pull it out. And then there's Bram—

Before I can finish my thought, I slam against something cold. The air is forced from my lungs, and my throat goes raw from coughing. I blink. The darkness swirls, and from somewhere in the blackness comes rustling.

"Bram?"

"Adelaide?"

I could almost cry from the sound of his voice. On the other side of me, Rascal whimpers.

"You came."

Bram groans. "Of course we did. You think we'd just abandon you that easily?" His boots scuff the ground. "Shit, I can't see anything. Where are you?"

I reach out my hand, blink again. The shadows begin to move and weaken. There is bleary light coming from somewhere. It is not natural, but the white glow of candles. I stretch my hand farther, and it brushes against something soft.

"Is that you?" I ask.

"That's not my hand, if that's what you're asking."

I go red, thankful for the shadows, and rip my hand away. Bram chuckles and slips his hand into mine.

"Here, let me pull you up. I think whatever is below is solid."

The light grows stronger. Bram moves beside me. Rascal too. I reach down and pet the velvet of his nose. Then the shadows part.

We are surrounded by black stone walls. Above me is nothing but shadow, the ceiling so far overhead it is nearly invisible. I blink, unable to tell if my eyes are truly open for a moment, and focus on the light. Three candlesticks stuck into an iron candelabra.

The scene is eerily familiar. I grip Bram's hand tighter. The smell of dark and damp things ekes out from between the stones, and for half a moment, I wonder if I am back at Blackbourne Castle. The *real* one.

Though here, standing amongst all the rotting bones of the rowan wood, it does not seem much different. Rascal whines. I should be afraid, and yet, somehow none of this frightens me. Instead, I drop Bram's hand and move toward the light.

"Adelaide, where are you going?" His footfalls chase after me.

"There should be a door here, somewhere."

"How do you know that?"

I stop, turn around, and watch the shadows dance on his face. "Have you ever stood in the great hall of Blackbourne Castle?"

He shakes his head.

"Trust me, there should be a door."

The light grows dim while I move around the room, hands groping idly in the darkness. I have half a mind to give up, when my fingers brush against something rough and dry.

"It's here, Bram."

He comes up behind me, his breath on my neck. I search for a knob, a handle, anything to throw it open. But as soon as my hand presses against the surface, it gives way.

The door swings open, welcoming in so much light I blink in near blindness. Noise greets my ears, the chatter of voices, the slice of knives in wet meat. The smells too: cooking grease, wine, and…bitterbloom. I reach for Bram's hand. Feel him shudder behind me.

My eyes adjust. I lean against the doorframe, lungs suddenly weak in my chest. Ahead of us sits a great table. There are a handful of people, seated, forks half raised to mouths, lips slack and sloughing. These I do not recognize. Have no wish to know.

I tear my gaze away from them and up, up, up, toward the other end of the table.

For the first time since we entered this unholy place, my heart rebels. A sparrow caught in a cage. I gasp for breath, squeezing Bram's hand with all the strength I can muster.

At the head of the table, a lady sits, swathed in a gown so purple it might be black. Her brilliant gold hair is scooped at the nape of her neck, curls like spools of the finest thread. Her ruby lips part when she sees me. And then—

"Adelaide."

I fall to my knees at the sound of that voice.

Mother.

twenty-two

After a long moment of silence, my mother screams. It is a happy scream, but it shocks me to my core all the same. The idea of sound coming from her mouth. *That* mouth. The mouth I wiped blood from, that sang me lullabies and coughed until her lungs dried up. The mouth that pressed kisses to my fevered skin, taught me about flowers in the garden, laughed when I toddled haphazardly across the kitchen floor. The mouth that curled inward, turned red to black to gray.

The mouth that couldn't even say goodbye when all was done.

Making sound. It feels impossible. *Should* be impossible. All along, I have known finding her was my goal. Bringing her home, back to life. And yet here I stand, gazing into her eyes, like pools of deepest blue, itching to touch her golden hair. Her cheeks almost rosy in all the blistering candlelight. The pallor of sickness is gone, as if it never was. I want to believe it, and I wait for the sweet relief to course through my veins.

But all I feel is the cold.

"My Addie!" Mother shoves her seat back and runs at me with open arms.

When she enfolds me, she smells like lemons, lavender, and earth. Warm, good earth. But I keep myself from breathing it in fully, from believing this is real and happening. I reach through her hair and press a finger to her throat.

Nothing.

My mother is dead. I watched the men take away her body, lay her in a grave, and cover it with dirt and a stone cross. *Esme Thorn, Devoted Mother, Dutiful Wife. Died Age 36. Blessed be she by Ithrandril.* Those words always made me angry. Mother. Wife. She was so much more than that. More than what she gave to other people. An artist, a light, a place of warmth and growth.

My arms hang limp at my sides while she squeezes.

"My darling, how I've missed you." Her voice is soft and calm, sweet as river water. Her hand runs over my tangled hair, and I almost break at the touch. So gentle, so familiar, it hurts.

I push away. "How—"

Her face is full of tears. They glisten in the fire's glow, each one a diamond. I fight the urge to brush them away, to throw myself back into her arms. But I smell something else beneath the scent of earth and citrus.

Iron. Sulfur.

I step back, holding out a hand for Bram to catch. His fingers wrap solidly around mine, and I press my thumb to my throat.

A-live, a-live, a-live.

But my mother is not. There is a tug of unease in my belly. I should feel happy, relieved at finding her. But I don't. There is something wrong, a catch in the air. Not of lemons or ripe soil, but a sour tang. Mother's face is too perfect, too *new*.

She is supposed to be dead. Her eyes go soft as egg whites, and I brace myself against Bram.

"Adelaide, you have no idea how long I've waited for this. Please." She puts her arms out again, beckons me in.

But if I go, if I accept this reality, what do I do if it proves to be false? Can a ghost be trusted?

Bram is steady at my back. He is real and solid and there. And even if he *is* dead, he is the most alive person I have ever met. Violent and fierce and wildly unyielding. I knead my thumb against his hand.

"How do I know it's you?"

Mother's face twists at this, her lips curving down. "Oh, my Morning Glory. Of course it's me."

But it isn't. There is something wrong. Something in the way she smells. In the way she carries herself—as though she is the most important creature in all the world. Her dress is finer than anything she ever owned in life, and her ears and neck drip in pearls.

My mother wore linen and wool. Simple, hardy fabrics to get her through a day in the gardens, in the kitchen, tearing after me when I toddled down to the banks of the river. She wore her simple flame-shaped locket for Ithrandril about her neck, nothing else, and smelled of soil, flowers, and rainwater.

But the face is right. And that's what scares me the most.

"Do you remember what you said to me the day you died?"

Her face softens, and she sighs. "How could I forget?"

The air between us releases, like it is being pressed from trapped space. My ribs release a breath, and I step forward. There are tears in my eyes now, hot when they slip down my cheeks.

"Say it. Please."

Her hand wraps around me, and even though it is cold, it feels familiar. "Chase Death, my dearest. That way, he will never catch you."

I fall against her, every inch of my body loosening. We hold each other there, sinking to the floor while our chests rise and fall in sobs. I cry until my lungs burn, until the salt water clings to my cheeks. When I finally do pull away, Mother is smiling. Each tooth so white it shines like ivory.

"You must be exhausted after your travels." She tucks a strand of my hair behind my ear. "I can have someone take you up to a room, draw you a bath. Would you like that?"

All I can think about is warm water running over my body, thawing the frost, cleaning the muck from my ankles. I should ask after Ransom, but the pressure of his body against mine is still too raw and real, so I push him away and nod.

"I would give anything for a bath."

Mother throws her head back, a laugh like lilting birds filling the air. Behind us, at the table, the men and women mirror her, their heads tipping toward the ceiling, a symphony of glee. I smile and look to Bram.

But he is not grinning. His eyes are fixed on those seated, on each of their laughing, lolling tongues. I frown and turn back to Mother.

"Can a room be cleared for Bram as well? He is the one who helped me find you."

Mother flicks her gaze to him. For a moment, there is something behind her eyes, an emotion I cannot make out. A flash of something akin to recognition. But then she softens, turns to spun sugar.

"Of course he can," she says, voice butter smooth. "Your friend is welcome to stay as long as he needs."

I look to Bram, but he seems to stare right through me. His lips quirk in a forced smile, and he inclines his head.

"Thank you, my lady." His eyes slide back up to look at her. "You are, in fact, the lady of this castle, are you not? There is something oddly familiar about you."

Tension fills the air, a stone dropped into a glass of water. My mother's face tightens, skin stretching over bones, and I notice death there for the first time. A graying pallor to her cheeks, sunken hollows. A mask of sorts.

And then it is gone, replaced by a brilliant smile. "I am. And you are the Avery boy, are you not? Died of unknown causes, isn't that right?"

Bram squares his jaw. "I believe there is someone who knows the cause."

My skin prickles. The silence between them sits too long, thickening with each breath. Bram holds my mother's gaze, challenging her, looking for a fight. I reach for his hand and look between them. Wolves in the night. And then I think of Rascal.

"Where is my dog?"

Mother's blue eyes catch my own. "What, the hellhound? You've not made him your pet, have you?"

"He's Bram's, actually," I say. "But can he not stay in my rooms with me?"

There is silence, only the guttering of candle flame. My heart is a hammer and anvil. It clangs against my ribcage like a stuck bird. There is a giggle from one of the ladies at the table, and my stomach turns.

"That's enough." Mother's voice cuts the air like a knife. "I will see your pet is sent to your rooms, Adelaide." Her arm comes around me, heavy as a paperweight. "But you must rest now. I will come find you before the party, and we will talk." Her hand clamps around mine, spins me so I am facing her. "We have so much to catch up on."

I want to tell her to wait, to stop. What party? Aren't I supposed to find her and bring her back? Back home to Rixton with Father? Back home so I can know love once more? But she is already pushing me toward another door, already waving over a woman in black.

"Take these two to the rooms in the eastern wing, Istelle. And make sure the Haunts release the hellhound. Though, have care with the beast. We don't want him tracking in…refuse."

The voice is so unlike my mother's, I try to turn back, but Istelle's hand is steadily pressing between my shoulder blades, forcing me out the door. Bram says nothing, just grabs my wrist, pulling me behind him. We follow the woman in black from the room, out into dim light. The last thing I see of my mother is the door closing on her pale face.

In the sallow light, her skin looks like cracked porcelain.

When I pull myself from the bath water, I notice a slip of paper on the bed that was not there before. I reach for a towel, wrap it around my body, and cross to the bed. It seems wrong, this room. Out of place. The bed all delicately carved wood and white duvets. Lace pillowcases and a linen pouch of something that smells of lavender, tucked between the sheets.

Everything else about the castle is dead. Dark stone, rotting lichen, the steady *drip-drip* of condensation and mold.

I reach for the note, only for a knock to sound at the door.

My heart leaps into my throat. I pull back and glance around the room for something more substantial than a towel. My eyes land on a silk dressing gown in shades of ice and hoarfrost. I hurry to throw it over my shoulders and tie it tightly. In the tarnished mirror, my hair is dripping wet. A small groan of frustration echoes from my throat.

The last word I would ever use for the gauzy fabric is *substantial.*

The knock comes again. Harder this time.

"Come in!"

"I was just coming to say—I—Addie!"

I turn at the sound of Bram's voice, the catch of shock.

"Sorry, I didn't realize—" He ducks from the door, red creeping up his cheeks.

"It's fine. I have clothes on, Bram. You can come in."

Curls sweep across his face when he slips into the room, gently closing the door behind him. "Sorry, I just—" He clears his throat. "Did you get one of these?"

He waves a slip of paper. The edges scalloped and tinged with red. Its twin rests atop my pillow. Bram passes me the paper. It is cold in my hand.

"Read it," he says, voice like whiskey in my belly.

A midwinter masque. To be held when the moon has turned to blood.
Blackbourne Castle.

Rascal lifts his head from where he was sleeping on the duvet and groans his disapproval. But Bram is silent. He watches me, for what I don't know.

"We can't go," he says finally.

"What do you mean? Who did this come from anyway?" I flip it over, searching it for a name, *her* name, anything. But it is blank.

"Who do you think?"

There is a bitter edge to his voice, and it makes me angry. "You've been an absolute brute to my mother, do you know that? A brute. You're beginning to act a whole lot like Ransom."

His eyes sliver with shadow. Before I can take my next breath, he is across the room, pressing me against the wall. A dull ache starts deep in my chest, anger mixed with something else. Oil in water. His eyes are like a wolf before a hunter, hungry and afraid, all at the same time. The chill of him cools the water on my skin, a shiver cascading down to the small of my back.

"Say it again," he growls. "That I am just like that no-good, deceitful, arrogant son of a bitch. *Say* it."

My stomach flutters from the touch of his skin on mine, the softness of his breath against my throat. "I'm sorry."

"You should be." His hands leave the wall and smooth down the sides of my waist, my skin catching fire as they go.

I suck in air, lightheaded and desperately eager.

"Bram…" My voice is thick, choked with roots of desire and ache.

It is all the encouragement he needs.

He curls his arms around the swell of my bottom and swoops me onto the bed. Rascal protests loudly and jumps to the floor. Laughter ripples from my throat. Real, true laughter, before it is smothered by Bram's mouth, which is somehow as warm as brewed tea. He is far gentler than Ransom, reverent almost. As though I am something holy.

His hands blaze up my breasts and curl around my chin, and his tongue slides past my lips. He tastes exactly how I wished he would. Spring sunshine and dew, ink-stained pages, and something like lemons. Something I cannot place.

The ache inside me deepens, the one I have felt for days but never knew how to name. For Ransom, it came easier. I knew what to call that: contagion, infection, lust. But with Bram, it is somehow different. A slow kind of falling. His hands slide along me, as though they were meant to. Like whatever we were molded from is made of the same stuff and we are finally fitting together after so many years apart.

I yank at the collar of his shirt, and he rewards me with a low growl from the back of his throat, flipping me on top of him. His hands are cold through the fabric of my dressing gown, his hips pressed against me. I inhale—sharp and sweet. Feel his lips drag along my jaw, teeth snicking at my skin. His fingers brush against my knee, the soft skin of my thigh. I gasp, his teeth wicked against my neck.

And then Rascal bays.

I freeze, and Bram's body goes rigid. The knob clicks on the door to my chamber, the hinges creaking open.

Mother stands at the threshold, putrefaction in her eyes.

twenty-three

Mother cuts a sharp figure against the soft glow of the chamber. Her face pinches, and though she is a small thing, her anger swarms around us like oil. Bram rolls off the bed, hastening for his buttons and the slack buckle of his belt.

"I—gods below and above," he sputters, cheeks more alive and burning than I have ever seen them. Bram brushes fingers through his hair.

"Get out." Mother's voice is as sharp as cut steel. "Now."

Bram takes a step forward, mouth open, gathering courage. "Mistress Thorn, if I could just—"

"I don't give a damn about what you could or could not do, Mr. Avery. I said *get out*." She kicks the door open wider, and Rascal whines. "And take that mangy creature with you."

I open my mouth to protest, collect myself just enough to ask her to stop, but when I sit up higher on the bed, my voice squeaks. "Mother, please—"

"I don't enjoy being ignored," she snaps. The edge in her voice frightens me more than the darkness seeping into the chamber. "Take that dog, Mr. Avery, and get out of my daughter's room."

Bram's eyes dart to me, begging me to open my mouth, to tell her off, to beg for him to stay. But I can't come up with anything. My body tenses like a freshly strung bow.

"I'll see you at the party, Bram."

There is betrayal in his face when he hurries across the room and past Mother, Rascal behind him. My stomach folds, and once more, I am just a girl wilting in the presence of someone who thinks they know what is best for me. But when do *I* get to make that decision? When is it time for my voice to be loudest?

Tension swims thick as Bram leaves the room. My mother's eyes trail him and then back, hard on me. I push myself up more, but her gaze is piercing.

"Do you hate him?" I ask.

She blinks. "Don't be ridiculous, Morning Glory. You can't hate someone you don't know."

Saliva sticks hot in my throat. "But you *do* know him. You said—"

"I know him merely as the young man who died back home, nothing more."

Back home.

I scramble forward in the bed, sheets scratching my skin. "Mother, I was thinking, once we've attended this party and all, we could…" The words stop halfway up my throat. I swallow, force them past my teeth. "We could go home. Back to Father and the vicarage and Rixton."

Her face lights up like candle-glow, only to be blown out by a shadow leaking from her steely irises. "Why would we do that?"

I wait, listening for more, hoping her lips will break out in a laugh and she will reassure me she is only teasing. That, of course, we can go home. But she doesn't. Her face only twists into shapes I do not recognize. I do not answer her, too stunned for words.

Mother strides deeper into the room and throws a dress on the bed. "Istelle will be up shortly to help you dress." She turns to leave but sets her eyes on me. "Be careful, Adelaide. You'll be deciding where your allegiances lie before the end."

The door slams, and I am left with my skin burning. Both from the pain of Mother's words and from where Bram traced me with his lips. I try to blink away the thought of her not coming home, but it clings to me like houndstooth weed, sinking into my flesh.

She *will* come home. I will make sure of it. If not, what will there be to go home to? And what will remain here, tethering her to this place in between life and true death?

I push the edging dread away and reach for the dress, hold it out in front of me. It glistens blue, like ice beneath the candlelight. Beads like shards of glass trickle down the bodice, and the sleeves cut away to show off my shoulders. Istelle comes to lace me into it, and I shiver beneath her touch.

Everything is so desperately cold here. Like an unlit hearth in winter, a hollowness where warmth should be.

The invitation lies crumpled on the bed, where it was lost between Bram and I. Istelle ties a mask tight around the crown of my head and turns me back to the mirror. Breath sticks in my throat. The upper half of my face is swathed in silver, spindles of ice shooting from delicate white lace. A crown of winter.

Istelle sniffs. "The Lady picked it out herself."

My stomach boils at that. *Lady*.

My mother does not belong here. She needs to be at home. With me and Father. This stupid mask and dress and party is a waste of bloody time. But what do I know? The day before yesterday, I let Ransom almost have me in the confessional box, and mere moments ago, I found myself tangled up in Bram. Nothing makes any sense.

I close my eyes, fist my hands. One deep breath after another. I will do as Mother wants, attend this silly party of hers, and then we will all go home—even if I must force her. The bell will make her whole again.

We just have to find Ransom first. "Damn it."

Istelle raises a brow. "What was that?"

"Nothing." I shuffle toward my own homely dress and search its pockets for the bell.

When my fingers brush against the metal, Istelle's eyes pierce the back of my neck. I freeze. My skin flares hot, heat crawling up the back of my throat. I release the bell, instead slipping my fingers in its wrappings.

When I spin, there is a saccharine smile on my face. "Just looking for a hair ribbon." I hold it out to her, and her face pinches.

"You're to follow me," she grunts.

My boots skim the stones while I walk behind her through the door. The lock snicks into place, and my heart goes hard against whatever waits below—mothers and ghost boys and things that should not exist. I wrap my fingers around the bell in my pocket and hope that, whatever awaits me below, it will not be the end of me.

There is a moment when the world freezes. When autumn falls away into the white ether of winter and the breath fogs from your lips. It is not a gentle slipping. It is a rugged crash to the ground. A tangle of limbs and falling snow. This is how it feels when I enter the ballroom of Blackbourne Castle and see the dead dancing.

There are so many of them—men and women—skirts and coattails swirling in a storm of blues, golds, and purples, bits of bone showing between laced corsets and silk-lined waistcoats. One woman wears a dress the gentle shade of shushing water, her dancing hand devoid of flesh. Her bones dig into the shoulder of her partner, a woman with only one eye shining through her ebony mask. She catches my gaze.

I try on a smile, bob my head.

The room ghosts with cold. Ice crawls up the stones, slicks the floor. And so, it is strange when I catch the scent of the place—all soil and the sour pinch of lemons. It sends me reeling. Back to my mother's skirts, back to the way her hair smelled after hours spent in the garden. Scrubbing the ruby sap of bitterbloom off her fingertips.

My eyes burst with black, then white, and I am ten years old, standing in the rain outside the garden shed. I listen to Father's frantic whispers, footfalls in something wet, the squelch and pop of meat and bone.

Here, in the dead castle, my lungs pump, and yet the air does not come fast enough. I reach for something—*anything*—to steady myself on and brush against something cold.

Cold and moving.

"Adelaide, what's wrong? Tell me." It is Mother's voice, soft now at my ear.

My heart pulls in two directions, pain blooming at the center of my chest. One side wants nothing more than to turn around, sink against her softness, and cry. Beg for answers in the shadows. But the other side is hard. A locked chest. Terrified she might be angry at me for wanting to take her home, when she has so obviously made a place for herself here, amongst the dead. Worried she might not be the same Esme Thorn I lost on that bed, covered in blood and vomit all those years ago.

But what is life if not the flip of a coin? A shot in the dark? So, I take mine and turn.

Mother is breathtaking. She wears a gown the color of spilled blood. It seems to drip off her very skin. In her hair, hundreds of little white flowers flutter like living things.

Bitterbloom.

I take a step away, hardly able to believe what I am seeing. Esme Thorn, the vicar's wife. Esme Thorn, up to her elbows in the earth or hidden behind the garden shed door, the bitter scent of lemons spilling out to greet my inquisitive nose. Esme Thorn, like a queen in this underworld. My throat turns sharp, and I try to smile, but all I seem to manage is a thing like weak tea.

"Are you all right?" she asks, one lithe hand coming to rest on my cheek.

My pulse quickens. No, no, I am not. I can feel the bones beneath her skin. Count them as if they are my own. They seem so brittle here, like a bird's, and yet when I look up at her, *brittle* is the last word I would choose.

Here, she is something else. Transformed. A creature of red and white and gold. It is both haunting and beautiful, and I feel as though I am being tugged in by ropes on either wrist. I swallow, try on yet another smile.

"I'm fine. I just—I just want to go home."

She curls her hand around my jaw, cups my cheek. Mother towers over me, her face so much like my own it's like a shadow come to life.

"I'm sorry for how I responded earlier, my darling. I understand your feeling," she says, and hope kindles in my chest. "I understand the desire to go back home, feel the wet grass beneath your feet, the spring scent in the air." Her eyes flash behind me to the dancing figures. "But what if I told you there was something better?"

My breath drops to my stomach, my knees shaky. "Something better?"

Her smile glistens like glass. She takes me by the hand, leads me over to a darkened window, and draws aside the curtain. White glimmers outside. White and green and yellow alike. It takes me a moment to realize what I am seeing, but once I do, my mouth drops open.

Bitterbloom.

Hundreds of brilliant, bright white petals. They are a field, a moat, each bloom lifting a glossy head to the pale moon. My breath fogs up the glass.

"How are they growing here?"

She says nothing for a moment, as if sifting through words to try and find the right ones. "They grow where the ground tells them. Where there is a remembrance of life."

A remembrance of life. The words stick at the back of my throat like a film. Before I can ask her to explain herself, she is whisking me away from the window, her elbow hooked through mine.

The music swells, a haunting melody of strings not quite tuned. It grates on my ears and runs a single finger down my spine. Mother leads me to the center of the dance floor, the scent of citrus in her wake. She folds her fingers through mine, places a hand at my side, and begins to turn me through the melee of surrounding death.

It begins as a twist of her lips. Subtle, if not for the fact I have pictured her face every day since we laid her in the ground. Her teeth glint out—not a smile exactly, more like the face a fox makes before it pounces on prey.

Hot spikes pierce my belly, and I tear my gaze away, searching the room for Bram. But I do not see him. There are too many faces—dead ones—and none I know.

"You are afraid, Addie," she says. "Look at me."

I do not want to, do not want to peer upon the dead thing behind my mother's eyes. But what choice is there? Mother's lips have gathered into a sneer. Her skin is gray in this light, and each bone of her face is outlined against her flesh. Cracks in the skin like shadow. I swallow, throat tight.

"*Should* I be afraid, Mother?" I hope my voice sounds braver than I feel.

There is a shush of skirts when she spins me deeper into the crowd. My head feels light, my skin almost floating.

"I never thought I'd see you again," she says. "Did you know that? Never thought you'd be the one to finally piece it all back together."

My skin gooses with cold. "Piece what back together?"

"The bell, the rowan wood, the boy…"

A noise gathers at the back of my tongue. Something between a whimper and a growl. I can feel the heaviness of the brass in my pocket. "How do…"

Mother's sneer curls upward, a half-moon slash in her graying face. "Oh, my Morning Glory. There is so much you don't know."

"Then tell me." My fingers grasp her tightly.

She needs no encouragement.

Hand digging into my side, she whirls me to the opposite end of the ballroom, emptying us at the foot of a grand staircase, all crumbling stone hung with flowers. They are everywhere, now that I notice them, the same ones she wears in her hair. The bitterbloom. Trailing in the gardens, spilling from beneath the shed door, weeping across Bram's grave.

Across all the graves of all the dead girls back home…Mother's fingers come to my jaw, pull my eyes up to hers.

"He didn't want me to have it, you know? The bell. Kept it from me all those years, even as I grew more and more sick. Told me it was an unnatural way to do things—use it to keep me alive, keep me safe. But now I have you."

A sound like an earthquake, a roll of thunder cracking over my ribs, bleeding down to my wrist. Some vast shattering, a chasm deepening. And then I realize, it is my mother.

Or not my mother.

The woman who stands before me is hard as stone, eyes flashing like lightning in an autumn sky. Her fingers dig trenches in my skin.

My words die on my lips. "Mother, you're hurting me."

But she does not care; she holds faster. Stronger. A peal of danger rings out in my head, and Bram is nowhere in sight. What has she done with him? What has she done with herself?

“You must listen to me, Adelaide.” That unnatural strength pulls me tight against her chest. “Here, in this place, I live a half-life. I do not want to belong to Ithrandril *or* his brother. I want to remember what it was like to taste, to smell, to feel the ground *alive* beneath my feet. Don’t you understand? I have fought so long and hard for this, and now it is in my grasp. I will not let you take it from me.”

I hold back tears. “Take *what* from you, Mother?”

“Eternal life.”

twenty-four

I remember the flowers. Their acrid, lemon smell. It used to waft in through my bedroom window on a spring evening, dust against my nose.

Bitterbloom.

Mother never allowed me to touch them. But she has no sway over me now. Everything I have worked for is dead. I wrench from her grip and lift my hand to the petals in her hair.

"You were always so afraid of death," I say.

She snorts. "*Everyone* is afraid of death."

"But not like you." My gaze rises to meet hers. "You kept me from so many things. The river's edge, the poisonous plants, the forest… Not to keep me safe, but to keep me *alive*. And when you finally died, Father carried on your work as best he could. Alive. But not safe."

She tenses at the mention of Father, face pinching. "I'm giving you a choice, Addie. Let me use the bell and give us both the life I have wanted for us, the life I have dreamt of giving you."

"Or?"

The sneer hovers now, like something else inside her is fighting for a way out. "I believe there is someone who has been waiting to see you."

My eyebrows form a pair of matching arches. It is not the response I was expecting. I imagined a threat, words perfectly barbed, chosen to whip me into obedience.

There are footfalls on the steps behind us, dissonant against the music. Mother's lips widen, and I see, for the first time, one blackened tooth at the base of her tongue. It sits there like a carrion bird, reminding me of all the rot in this place. My heart quickens, and I turn toward the stairs.

Ransom Black descends. A phantom from the back of my mind. He is dressed in a suit of spring green so soft he reminds me of a snowdrop, pressing against the earth for new life. His honey-gold hair is sleek, pulled back in a velvet ribbon, his skin shorn and shining.

Lord Black.

He fiddles with the cuffs of one sleeve, grins wickedly when he catches my eye, and my stomach curls into delicate knots. I hate him for how he makes me feel despite everything.

Mother backs away, sways left, and is lost amongst the crowd. I open my mouth, but Ransom is already beside me. A gentle finger brushes on my lips and silences me.

"You look radiant."

I know what those words are meant to do. Meant to make my knees go weak, fall against him and realize how much I need him. But he doesn't get this power over me anymore. He is every man who operates under the impression that what swings between their legs gives them the ability to do whatever they want. *Take* whatever they want.

But I am not for the taking. Not anymore. I shove my fist into his shoulder.

"How dare you," I spit. "How dare you leave us without saying *anything*!"

He sweeps one hand over my bare shoulder, my skin pricking with cold to meet him. Ransom grins, self-satisfied. "Does it matter?"

Lips like pale apples come to brush against my cheek, his hand drawing slow circles up my back. I inhale, breath fogging the space around us. For a moment, I entertain how easily I could lose myself here, swept away beneath the charm. The promise.

Mother called it eternal life. It sounds lovely, the idea of living forever. Of never having to fear the quick cut of death. But that is not life. Not *true* life. Ransom pulls me flush against him, but my palms slam back into his chest. His gaze meets mine, and something deep down cracks inside me.

Life is horrible and terrifying and unpredictable—all the things my mother is afraid of. It can swallow you in one greedy gulp and spit you out as nothing but skin and bone. But it is also lovely. A kind of spring awakening. Green shoots pressing through the last of winter's snow. Without death, we do not crave the life. We do not watch the stars and moon in their orbits. Death is the last great healing. Without that pain, there is no love, no wonder, no living.

I shove Ransom away, wrists snapping back, and he stumbles against the steps. His eyes flash angrily, hot and almost red. He twists away, up on his feet.

"What the hell, Adelaide?"

"Do not touch me." The thought of him pressed against me makes me ill.

He curls his lip, the expression fermenting like dry wine. "You're acting ridiculous. Are you feeling well? You know how you can get in your *condition*."

His palm is a firebrand on my cheek before I knock it away.

"I said, do not fucking touch me." I rip the mask from my face, throwing it to the stone floor where the icicles shatter.

His grin widens when he steps closer, the wood of the banister digging into my spine. "You should join your mother, Adelaide. Let her use the bell. The things she offers." He looks down at his hand, spreads his fingers before looking at me with eyes that could be made of fire. "We could live forever. Your mother found a way, showed *me* the way—"

"What…what do you mean, showed you the way?" I pull away from him, stumbling.

His grin ekes out the corners of his lips, like someone has cut him. "Don't you get it? Don't you understand? Eternal life. *Vita aeterna*. An everlasting circle. Blessed by Erybrus. No more worries, no more rot, no more trouble. Here, he would make us kings."

An everlasting circle. I recall the snakes drawn on the molding walls of Blackbourne Castle, the sign of Erybrus, the Devil. I close my eyes and see only red. The red of natural blood, the red of the unnatural sky, the red sap of Mother's bitterbloom vines.

The remembrance of life. Bones half buried in dirt.

I should know what it means, but my mind is a fogged window. Ransom is so close now I smell the scent of him. *Lemons*. I choke.

Hands thrashing, I push him out of the way and scramble up the stairs. I take in the ballroom around me, all the dancing dead. Is this what we will all become, shades of our former selves, waiting in this purgatory until we align with the light or the shadow? I look at Ransom, and there, in the pits of his eyes, I see it.

The truth.

He has already sold his soul.

My chest cracks in half, hands grappling for the banister, anything to steady myself on. His eyes catch mine. He recognizes the knowing and smiles. All teeth and rotten tongue.

"What have you done?" The words are weak when they leave my mouth, fear shimmering on the surface of my skin like sweat.

The floor beneath me shudders with each step forward he takes, closing the space between us. "I have joined her, Adelaide. I have joined the side of eternal life. And don't you want it too? We could be king and queen of this place, you and me. What I would give to see you enthroned, wrapped in shadow."

I shake my head, claws hollowing out pits in my stomach. "This is a half-world, Ransom. You and I, we wouldn't be ourselves. We'd be bitter, broken, dead things bent on making deals and . . . and cheating death. We would belong to Erybrus."

There. Just there. Behind the darkened eyes, I find the man I met in the garden beneath the moon. The *true* moon. The man who was broken, who held pieces of his heart in his palm and asked me to fit him back together. I lunge for him, taking his hand in mine.

"Ransom, what about your mother? Don't you want to find her, bring her home?"

For a moment, a light dawns on his face, and then it vanishes. Something akin to greed—that *hunger*—swathes his face like moonshine. His hand crushes mine, and when I look at his lips, his teeth hang in cracked and bleeding gums.

This is no longer Ransom Black.

This is a monster. A *true* monster.

"My mother is already claimed. Ithrandril took her the day she was brought here. Righteous and pure and for the light. I watched my father kill her. After he pulled off her face, took the skin to build a body, I brewed poison from the bitterbloom in my garden, slipped it into his tea every day, and watched as it carved away his life until there was none of it left. And then, I did the same. Took his skin and the skin of others. Over and over and over again."

My breath shudders, stomach dropping to the soles of my feet. The scent of upturned soil. The catch of slurried fruit baking in the sun. My knees cave, and the floor rises to meet me. One hand slips to the bell, the cracks familiar, grounding.

"You're…you're not making any sense. You didn't—you couldn't. This isn't you talking, Ransom. It's something—"

"It has always been me, Adelaide Thorn." His face is inches from mine, the scent of his breath like apples rotting on the branch. "I only picked up where she left off."

Where *she* left off. Not his mother. But someone else. *Someone*.

My stomach swills, and I am sure I will empty whatever lies there out onto the stairs.

Another hand at my back.

Solid. Cold. Dependable.

Bram.

He lifts me to my feet, steadies a hand at my waist. The scent of ink-stained pages, dry leaves. I sag against him.

"Leave her alone, Ransom. She isn't yours."

"And that makes her yours, then?" Ransom's voice is thick with greed.

Bram positions himself in front of me, his face hard, determined. "She is her own, you fool."

Ransom's face cracks, the illusion of beauty weeping away, like the painted portraits in his home. Rivulets of something like ink spread across his cheeks, down his neck, along his hands. I open my mouth to scream, but Bram's hand covers the sound.

He moves an arm tight around my middle, drags me up a step with him.

"Ransom, I said—"

"Oh, I heard what you said, dead man. I heard *exactly* what you said."

The voice that breaks from Ransom's lips is not his own. It is, and yet, it isn't. It is the sound of a hundred, thousand voices, and when I lift my eyes from him, I see why.

The ballroom has gone still, every dancing dead thing now like stone. Their faces are turned to us, repeating the same words Ransom says, their features flooding with shadowed rot. And beyond them…

No, no, no.

I scramble with Bram's cuff, sobs ripping at the back of my throat. He drags us further up the steps. Up, up, up. Away.

Beyond the dead things, my mother stands at the far doors, her arms raised, blackened roots swarming her body like marionette strings. Except, she is not *being* controlled. She is the one *controlling.*

Every word is her own. Every movement the dead things perform, *she* is making. My head swims, becomes as light as air. Ransom's legs and arms jerk in swinging motions, and he takes to the stairs, his head cocked at a wrong angle, eyes lolling.

I open my mouth to cry out, to tell her to stop, to just let him go, but all I taste is the salty sweetness of Bram's hand.

"Adelaide, look." His voice is a hot whisper at my ear. "Look at your mother."

What is there to see but the rotten vines, the bleeding skin? But he whispers it again. Over and over until I do as he says.

And my stomach falls to the depths of my toes.

For Mother is not Mother. Not anymore. Her face—her body—is made up from things that are not hers. A patchwork of stolen features held together by black string. My knees buckle. Bram's hands come to catch me.

The pages of her journal sitting on my bed at home…The sketches of what I thought were merely catches of fabric, bits of thread. A body to live in forever. Made from…

The truth settles over my skin like a film. Sickly and bitter. The tang of lemons in my mouth. The bitterbloom. The dead girls buried in the churchyard. My mother coming in late from the garden shed, smelling of freshly scrubbed skin, the upturn of soil, red sap still dripping from beneath her fingernails.

The poison.

A murderer stitching together the skin of dead girls to make herself an immortal body. To become a god.

"We need to leave." Bram's voice is a rushed breath at my ear. "Now."

I nod, barely able to tear my eyes from my mother. But she isn't Mother anymore, is she? She is something else. A monster. Not Lady Black. She only used that name here to draw us in, like a fly to a spider's web. No. She is something else now.

Lady Death.

I find my feet, pulling out of Bram's arms while he pushes me toward the door. Rascal comes around a corner, mouth open, baying. The sound sends my hair on end, prickles my skin. His eyes are red as blood, and his snarl is wicked.

Everyone stills. Even Ransom, halting like a porcelain doll on the stairs.

I grapple with my skirts, searching for the bell—I must not lose it. It greets my hand with its cold brass sting, and my lungs find air again. Mother is screaming something, something that sounds of blood and anger. I stare at her open mouth, watch the shadows run from it, each one turning, morphing into…

Haunts.

Three of them. The ones who took us from the river. They rise from the tendrils of darkness eking from Mother's lips, arms dragging, teeth gnashing.

Bram's hand tightens at my waist again, the catch of fear in the air.

My fear.

"Adelaide, we must go! Now!" Bram's screams ring in my ears.

And then we are running. Through the doors and out into the blood-soaked night.

twenty-five

It is not the cold that stops us; it is the color. White, lemon yellow, glimpses of red seeping from roots. I sag against Bram, his hand firm at my side. The bitterbloom by the ruined wall of the vicarage wink their wicked faces at me, reminding me what I have lost.

What once was will never be again.

The remembrance of life.

I pull away from Bram, Rascal quick on my heels, and perch on the crumbling wall. "Have we lost them?"

Bram turns back, searches the sky beyond. "I don't think they were ever chasing us to begin with."

My feet burn, each spark of pain a blister. I gather my skirts and lift them to examine my skin. It flares a sickly orange-pink trimmed in the black of my blood, flesh slipping where my shoes have rubbed to the bone. I toss a boot to the ground, drag a finger along one heel. The pain swells, shoots up my leg like venom.

"Here," Bram says gently. "Let me help you with that."

"What are you going to do about it?" I snarl, all my sharp edges showing. While I should retract them, tell him I am sorry, Bram is the safest place I know, and so I bite. "Haven't you done enough already?"

Betrayal winks in his eyes, and a twisted laugh cracks from my lips.

"What do you mean?" His voice is soft. He crouches low, his hand reaching for my knee.

Anger boils inside me, seeping between my bones like black tea. "It's your fault I'm here! It's your fault Ransom is…is whatever the hell he is! It's your fault that—that—" My voice melts into tears, and I am on the ground beside him, weeping in the dead grass.

His hand comes to cup my jaw, brush my hair, and I do nothing to stop him. There on the ground, I am nothing more than a shell. A corpse of the girl I once was. The one who held her mother's hand and ran wild through the wheat and rye fields. Who watched her parents embrace when they walked through the village. The girl who used to laugh at the stars because they were so small and she was so big.

Now I am nothing but blackened blood.

Bram's hand is steady at my back, helping me sit up slowly. When I stare down at my hands, the bell lolls in my palms. I must have reached for it. Just to feel its solidity. My chest stings.

I study the engravings on the brass. The skull and crossbones. The wilting flowers. It is such a little thing to cause so much toil and pain. So much loss. And what can it really do? Open the doors to this purgatory?

It can restore someone to life, yes, but it also is held by hands who collect souls and morph them until they are nothing more than whatever it is Ransom has become.

Do not make deals with these people.

Bram leads me inside the crumbling walls of the vicarage and stops when we reach where the kitchen should be.

"What is it?" My eyes are still trained on the bell.

"Do you remember leaving a fire going in the church when we left?"

Tears roll down my cheeks when I look up. Smoke belches black from the cracking steeple.

"No."

My fingers itch with anxiety, and I wring them against the bell. But the darkness is beginning to swarm. I tuck it away between its wrappings. Hidden. Secret and safe. Bram's eyes are on the church, the curl of black smoke.

"Stay here," he says.

But I am not a dog, and even Rascal is giving him a look that says, "Over our dead bodies."

"I'm coming with you."

Bram turns, eyes flashing. "Like hell you are."

"If you haven't noticed, Hell is exactly where we are," I spit. "And I'm not being left alone. Especially not when…"

I think back to my mother—rather the thing beneath my mother's skin. Wearing faces that don't belong to her, half-smiles of dead girls in dirt. Flowers in her hair, like dying stars.

I move past Bram, my body still hazy from everything I have seen. He says nothing but follows.

His footfalls crunch in the icy snow. While we move toward the church, my courage subsides. It leaves me like steam from a teacup, and I am glad for Rascal at my side, glad for the warmth of his fur to rid my fingers of this wretched cold.

Behind the stained-glass windows, there is a soft, orange glow. Someone, or some*thing*, has indeed lit a fire in Bram's makeshift ring of stones. He is at my back, and I swallow the fear slipping up my throat.

"What should we do?" I ask.

"All that there is left to do." He presses past me and pushes on the door.

It does not budge.

Something scampers inside—the sound of feet on stone, the shushing of cloth. I bend low and fit my eye to the tarnished keyhole. Rascal growls in my ear.

Shadows shift inside the church. A fire crackles near the altar, a pile of blankets beside that. A pair of brown boots.

A strange sense of familiarity tangles through my bones. My sight goes black, and an eye matches my own. A hazel eye.

Breath whooshes from my lungs, and I fall backward, clambering up against Bram while I rattle the door.

"What? What is it?" Bram's voice is stringent.

I tear at the wood, not caring when splinters break off and sink into my skin. "Clara."

Bram blinks stupidly at me for a moment, and then his fingers are at the door, rattling the hinges. "Clara, it's Bram and Adelaide," he hisses. "Please let us in."

I wait for a reply, that voice I know and love so well.

"How do I know you aren't…aren't the dead things?"

A sob cracks against my ribs. "We aren't, Clara. We can explain everything."

There is silence. The wind stirs, bringing with it a scent of iron. My eyes flash to Bram.

Gods below and above, let us in.

There is the metallic shushing of a bar being drawn back, a latch clicking. The door swings open. Clara stands in the frame, the glow of the fire bright as morning sun behind her. Dark curls lie in tendrils over her face, dirt smudging her cheeks, tear stains streaking in lines.

It takes Clara all of a moment to throw herself into my arms, body shaking. I say nothing, only stroke her hair softly. Bram hurries us into the church and secures the door behind us.

"Clara," I whisper, reaching for her face. "Are you all right? How are you…how are you *here*?"

She presses a finger to her lips, eyes frantically glancing to the nearest window. "They can hear you. Every word. They listen for it, crack their hands against the walls until the very ground is quaking. Sometimes, they get in and I have to hide." Her face darkens, turns to me. "Prove you are not one of them, Adelaide."

I pull the bell from the fragmented folds of my gown. It catches gold in the fire glow. I run a finger along the rim of the sharp-edged dome. Pain stings through me, and the blood beads like licorice drops on my skin.

"There," I say, holding it up to the light. "Not dead. Not exactly."

Clara hesitates, takes a hold of my wrist, drags a finger through my blood, and rolls it on her thumb. I wait for her to balk, to spit curses at the sight of my illness. My Reaper's blood. But she doesn't. She only turns her eyes back to mine.

"Fine. Not exactly dead. But what about him?" She points to Bram, who is crouching over the fire, hurrying for something in his satchel.

For some reason unbeknownst to me, I smile. "Oh, he's very dead. But he will not hurt us."

Clara appears ready to knock Bram to the floor when she notices Rascal. She freezes. "Is that…that's a *hellhound*."

I whistle, and Rascal bounds across the room, burying his nose against my skirts. Clara gasps and backs away, but I am already down on my knees, scratching the hound behind his ears. He bays, licks my face, and gazes expectantly at Clara.

"His bark is worse than his bite," I say, standing. "He's really no harm at all, unless you're one of the Haunts or…" My voice trails off.

Or my mother. My murderous mother.

A thought rises inside me, and the wind howls around the steeple of the tumble-down church.

"Clara, how did you get here?"

She is still staring between Bram and Rascal, trying to piece it together. A puzzle with too many razor points. "I don't know, really. I'd been following Lord Black, I suppose. He'd been in Father's bakery the day before, acting strange. Asking after Liza, about our plans regarding the future, marriage." She hugs her arms around her chest, shivers in the chill of the room. "I didn't think much of it until the next day, when I saw him coming from the graveyard behind the church, carrying something—a bag, I think. He saw me and grinned."

She grabs my hand, pulls me so close I can smell the yeast and sugar still clinging to her clothes.

"It was awful, Addie. A thing of nightmares, really. All stretched and patched skin. And his teeth were so white they might have been made from glass." Her body shudders beneath me.

The description plunges me into a panic. "What do you mean, his skin was stretched and patched?"

There are tears in her eyes, glinting off the fire glow. Bram, behind us, mutters and cuts at something with a knife. The scent of iron slips past my nose, and I bite back a gag.

Clara's eyes shine. "Like he was a quilt. Made up from pieces all stitched together. But the stitching was crude, done with too big and dull a needle.

Blood had dried in the cracks between the pieces, and something was dripping from that bag. Something that smelled like…" She sniffs the air. "Like whatever it is I'm smelling now."

Blood.

I turn to the fire where Bram still crouches, the flames reflecting in something wet on his hands. "Stay here a moment," I say to Clara.

She nods, pulls her knees up to her chest.

Bram doesn't look up when I approach, but I see what it is he is holding. A rat, its tail long and fleshy pink. There is a slit in its belly, viscera spilling out in oily tangles.

"It was near the fire when we came in," he says, one finger slipping through the meat. "Took it as I sign, I suppose. Did the only thing I could think of."

My stomach swills, but I bend down anyway. The thick tang of fresh blood fills my nose.

"And what do you see in all the mess?"

For a moment, Bram doesn't look up. He sweeps a finger through the guts, making patterns and swirls in the red. I recognize the lungs, the pink lump of stomach, the stilled heart, and lean forward to take it in my hands. Maybe what happened with the rabbit heart was a fluke. A cruel trick of my eyes. Something that shouldn't have happened.

But the bitterbloom. The touch of my hand. *A remembrance of life.*

A hot pressure starts behind my eyes, a tightening in my chest that makes me want to drop the thing, go back to Clara, take her home.

And then—a gentle thud.

My breath quickens.

"Bram, are you seeing this?" I don't look up at him, just keep my gaze fixed on the beating organ.

"Gods below and above." His voice is a whisper at my ear.

The heart contracts in my palm, like organ bellows. And then the blood on the floor begins to move. It creeps like a creature, sucking up each drop spilled, each organ ripped from the cavity of the rat. It crawls between Bram's swift cut until all that is left is the heart in my hand.

With fingers shaking, I place the heart near the corpse. Still beating, it inches its way across the floor until it too disappears between the bones and sinew. Bram and I fall away, the bell clattering in my pocket.

Slowly, the slit in the rat's stomach sews itself back together, fur fusing. My stomach wretches. My hands burn when the thing moves to its feet, eyes glinting in the light of the fire. It bares wicked fangs at Bram, and Rascal bays.

"Adelaide, what's happening? What's wrong?"

I do not look up at Clara's voice, only hold out a hand. What even is there to say? My own pounding heart presses into my ears until I can barely form thoughts. My breathing comes short and quick, and panic seeps into my gut. Bram's hand folds around mine, still warm, but now bloodless.

"Adelaide, breathe. It's all going to be all right."

Nothing about this is all right, I want to scream. My mother is made up of pieces of all the dead women from home. Young women who have been missing for *years*. And *Ransom* is part of it. How or why, I don't know. I picture his face. His *real* face. The sharp line of his jaw, the hard blue of his eyes, the way his hands pressed against my hips that first night in the garden. The garden that smelled of…bitter lemons.

My eyes snap open. "It's him," I whisper. "It's been Ransom all this time."

"Doing what?" Bram seeks my face for an answer, but I push myself to my feet and run to Clara.

"Is Liza still alive? When you left, when you followed Ransom and me through the door, was Liza still alive?"

Clara's face twists, and tears leak down her cheeks. "Yes, she was. I kissed her before I left, told her I had to run an errand. It was a lie. I just wanted to figure out what Lord Bl—Ransom—was up to. And when I saw him with you, I didn't know what to think. I had to know what was going on, and then—" Her eyes go hazy, like steam on glass. She looks up at me and sweat breaks out at the base of my neck. "I didn't follow just you and Ransom through that door. I followed someone—some*thing*—else."

My skin stills, and I reach for the bell. It is so cold. Colder than it has ever been. It cuts a line against my palm. I crouch down beside the pew and place a hand on her knee. "Can you remember what this something looked like?"

The expression in her eye is like something out of a nightmare. The kind of thing that has you waking up in a pool of your own sweat, hot to the touch but shivering in a kiss of air. She blinks, nods slowly.

"Yes, I can remember what it looked like."

I wait for her to continue, but her eyes go blank, as though her soul has vanished and all that is left is a shell of bone and flesh.

"Clara?" Bram's voice is soft above us.

Her eyes lift to him, and a shadow crosses her face. "Wait. You said your name was Bram. Bram Avery." She scuttles back in the pew, realization echoing across her features. "How is it you? You're supposed to be dead. I watched them bury you."

I know that fear, the stuff that bubbles like tar in the pit of her stomach, and I hurry into the seat beside her, a hand steady on her knee, if just to keep her grounded.

"Clara, it's all right. He's not here to hurt you. If anything, he's been helping. I came here to bring him home."

Her eyes shift between us, a rabbit caught in a trap. She buries her head in her hands, rocks back and forth. Her ribs expand with crooked breaths. I stare at her, notice the rips on her bodice, the stains on her skirt.

For so long, I was alone. For too long, I washed my own wounds, bandaged the cuts and bruises left by my father's ropes. Afraid of how people would react when they saw my blood, already believing I was cursed by Erybrus. For the shadow. And then there was hope—just a glimmer, but enough to make me take the damned bell in my hand and ring it. Now, the truth is that my mother is gone, just a thing of death and darkness. I might no longer be able to save her, but I can save Bram. I can bring the three of us back home.

I press my hand harder around Clara's knee, slow her rocking. "Can you remember who you followed through the door?"

She stops moving. A moment passes, and the wind rattles the doors of the church. A low growl rumbles at the back of Rascal's throat, and Bram puts a hand on my back.

Haunts.

I move closer to Clara. "Whoever it was, you can tell me."

Silence. Stinging, blistering quiet. She lifts her head.

"He was normal at first, dressed like any other man in the village. But just as you and Ransom slipped through that door, something changed." Her face wanes. "It started in his hair, a twist of knots and tangles that quickly turned to shadow. They grew down from his shoulders like wings, a cape as dark as the night sky. He turned around then, didn't see me. But I saw him and…" Her fingers strike out, wrap tightly across my own. "I knew him, Addie."

My breath sticks hot, sweat skimming the surface of my skin. "Who was it, Clara? Who did you see?"

"It was your father, Adelaide. It was Vicar Thorn."

twenty-six

Red bleeds through the stained glass like an open wound. I lie on the cot, staring at the ceiling, while Rascal bays in the nave. One night has come and gone, and the Haunts have left us alone, though the church is no longer consecrated ground. I think of Ransom, his soul already sold to my mother before we even stepped foot into the rowan wood, and something inside me cracks. The part that thought I could fix him, piece him back together.

But maybe I only broke him a little bit more.

From the stained-glass windows, the Haunts are seen eddying at the edges of the blackened River Thine, like buoys awaiting a storm. The sight chills my bones.

Clara stays near the altar to Ithrandril at the front of the church, a makeshift bed of dusty blankets, with her cloak perched atop it like a nest. She says the closer to the father of light she is, the safer she will be from the Haunts. But I do not think the god is in this place.

Here, a different power is at work. Something that morphs my parents into monster and monster alike. One of shadows, one of stolen faces.

This might not be Hell itself, but Erybrus's presence is palpable here. A taste like rotten wine in my throat.

The patterns on the ceiling contort while I watch them. Knots in the wood becoming eyes of those I once knew. Frances Gordon, the girl Rixton buried when I was all but four. Dinah Bo, the postman's daughter, who Mother always said had the most beautiful, rosebud lips. And then Rosalyn Eckers. Hair like copper, eyes wide and weeping blood, screaming empty sound from an open mouth, a strangely stained tongue when they brought her body up from the banks of the river. The way her skin had been peeled and removed from her right arm. The patterns of freckles broken.

Bile bubbles in my mouth, and I sit up violently, swallowing as much of it as I can. I wince as the sourness slips back to my stomach and look down at my hands. The cut on my thumb is still raw and red. So much death, so much blood, and for what?

Eternal life, Mother said. But the words had come from the lips of another, a body made up from pieces she took. Pieces she had killed and stolen for. And somehow convinced Ransom to do the same.

My back itches, the stays of this tight gown still rigid against my skin. I miss my plaid wool, the softness, familiarity, and smell of home. Wheat fields, crisp leaves, and frost thawing in the autumn sun. There is a sudden heaviness in my pocket, and I reach for the bell, feel its harsh ridges against my thumb.

In the bloody light, it looks like such a little thing. Part of me wants to crush it. Place it beneath the heel of my boot and hear it shatter. Watch the metal snap. But then Clara and I would be trapped here forever. Bram too. Haunted by things of my mother's making.

My shoulders slacken at the thought. How long has she been the one poisoning the tongues of Rixton girls and wearing their flesh? My blood runs cold, and I feel the whisper of her soft hands on my hair when she tucked me into bed. Soft and lovely and smelling of lemons.

My stomach twists. Did I ever truly know her? Or is she just another part of me that is a lie?

I twist the bell. If I destroy it, I might never know the truth and put it to rest. I will be hunted by a man who is so broken he doesn't even recognize himself in a mirror. He has already stolen too many faces.

Lilith Corley.

Hester Samuels.

Liza would have been next—I am sure of it.

I slip the bell back into my pocket when the doors to the vestry creak. Bram's face peeks from the opposite side, a smudge of ash above his brow.

"Fire's finally lit. Took it a while, with the wood being wet and all." He shivers.

Outside the tiny window, snowflakes dance through the colored haze. Midwinter is upon us. Back home, the wheat and rye will be piled in Farmer Whitley's barns, the apples picked for pies at the bakery. I shudder against the thin fabric of my gown, wishing I could rip it off my body and replace it with something warm. Something sturdy.

"Are you cold?" Bram crosses the room in easy strides, shrugging out of his jacket.

"No." I raise a palm. "I'll just sit by the fire. Keep your coat." I try to move past him, but he doesn't budge.

Here in the dull light, he is so solid and real it almost hurts. Part of me is afraid that, if I reach out and touch him, he will vanish into a cloud of dust. Another part of me wants nothing more than to hold him, to feel him against me. The pattern my fingers would form against the splay of each and every bone and know they are his. That he is who he says he is. Not something with the face of one thing and the soul of someone sold to shadow.

Just himself. Bram Avery. The man who read books in the apple orchards and woke up dead in a place he didn't know, with a bitter taste in his mouth.

My hands snap to my sides. I sit back on the cot, heavy and placid. Bram comes beside me, placing a palm on my shoulder.

"Adelaide, what is it?"

The pieces are fitting together, and I plead with them to stop. I want their edges to turn sharp again so that no matter which way I turn them, they will only get messier. But they click perfectly.

Dead girls. A poisoned man. White flowers. The bitter taste.

Tears cloud my vision when I turn to him. His eyes are like sunlight through amber while I study his gentle face.

"You were ill before you died. Do you remember from what?"

His face darkens a moment, turns to stone. He drops his hand, flexes it in his lap. "That's not the question I thought you were going to ask."

"It's not the question I want to be asking, Bram." My fingers weave through his, drawing him closer. "But I need you to tell me the answer."

I am not sure if it is the desperation in my voice or the fact that things cannot get much worse than they already are that makes him sigh and turn to me, shoveling a hand through his disheveled dark curls. "It wasn't a natural illness. In the last day of it all, when my lungs filled with fluid and my skin turned ashen, I knew the truth."

"The truth of what?"

His throat bobs. "It was poison. My mother bought a tincture from down in the village market for my bruises. It took me a few days to realize what was happening, but by the time I did, it was too late." He grits his teeth. "I'd seen something, something I wasn't supposed to see."

"What did you see?" I cup his jaw in my palm, watching warmth begin to seep into his skin.

"A woman coming up from the churchyard, a body slung between her arms. I didn't see who it was, not really. But the next day, I went to church, and by the following day, I was here. Dead. Given my choice. But I chose not to choose. How could I when—" His eyes turn haunted, ghosts of his past masquerading there as memory. "I watched my own funeral, you know? What a terrible thing it was. No one told any good stories."

A smile cracks on my lips. I don't want to think about who the woman was. What she might have been doing with a body ripped from hallowed earth. I lift a hand to Bram's arm.

"The village mourned for you, Bram. Everyone felt your loss. Your mother didn't leave Avery Manor for months, and when she finally did, she was all skin and bone. She hardly comes into the village, even now—"

"I know." Bram's voice is soft as downy feathers. "I watch her and my sisters sometimes. They're all so old now. Isabel is set to be married in the spring, to a coppersmith from Kinnington." There is a catch to his voice, and I fight the urge to take him into my arms right here and now. He clears his throat. "Somedays, all I dream about is going back home, being a part of it all." He steps away, looks down at his hands. "But how can I, really? I'm a walking dead thing, Adelaide. They'll think I'm a monster."

I observe the man in front of me. The man with so much life it hurts. Who holds the dying in his hands and sees stars. Who stood afraid and broken before me and asked to be brought back home. There can be no monster in something so beautiful.

I take his hands in mine, pull him close until I smell the lifeblood rushing through his drying veins. Ink and strong tea and old books. I trace the lines of his palm, raise my eyes to his.

"You are not a monster, Bram Avery."

He dips his brow low, his voice deep and soft as crushed velvet. "Are you flirting with me or trying to start a fight?"

My smile widens. I lift a hand to his jaw. Once more, warmth is spreading. He makes a sound at the back of his throat that lights a fire in my belly.

"Why not both?"

He closes the gap between us in a single movement, lips coming to mine. My stomach flutters, a thousand bumblebees trapped against the viscera. Bram lifts me in his arms and spreads me out on the cot, as though I am as light as air. The red light streaming in through the window paints him in hues of caramel, his irises like fire.

Here, in this place, his armor is cast down. Destroyed. I can read every thought on his face, every desire and need. His hand comes to peel away my sleeve, lips tracing the line of my collarbone. I suck in air, fear boiling in my belly.

With Ransom, it was all heady and rushed and hot. There was no love in it. Only wicked, suffocating desire. An all-consuming forest fire. Control and power and the need to have me. To own me. To make me his so he could raise himself, become as strong as Mother.

But with Bram, his fingers gently rake my sides, and I shudder. He is nothing but frosty mornings. Hearthside with a wool blanket, a mug of tea, a tattered and well-worn book. Bram is winter on a window, ice like patterns of lace.

"Bram," I whisper, throat choked with an emotion I cannot name.

"Yes?" His voice is a breath at my throat.

Can he feel it against his lips, the rhythm of my heart?

A-live, a-live, a-live.

But there is something more now too. Something that, in one blisteringly lovely moment, is both wonderful and terrible at the same time.

Love-d, love-d, love-d.

I stop, push Bram off me, and sit up. My hands are shaking in my lap, birds with clipped wings.

"I'm sorry," comes Bram's voice. "I shouldn't—"

"It's not you," I say. My breath is coming in short puffs, chest heaving and crashing like a storm at sea. "It's me. There's…there's something wrong with me." I look down at my hands, the scars running silver at my wrists.

"What?" Bram's voice is gravelly, his face twisting. One hand reaches for mine, but I pull away.

When I look up at him, his face morphs through my tears.

"My father used to tie me to a chair. Used to make me memorize the Blessed Scripture because he thought it would make me better." My lips tremble. "You are not the monster, Bram. Because…because I am. A Reaper."

"Oh, Adelaide."

The sound of my name in his mouth is enough to send my heart racing. He cups my jaw, pulls me closer. One hand slips across my waist, settling at the small of my back. I press my hands against his chest, maintaining distance between us, something to lessen the pain.

"Bram, what happens when—"

"Stop," he murmurs again, lips against my hair.

"Stop what?"

"You're always worrying about the future. And right now, gods below and above. *Addie*." The sound is nothing more than a choked groan, thick and heady. "I need you here."

My knees go shaky, and part of me hates this man who turns my brittle bones to molten flame. And yet, at the same time, loves him for it. That's what frightens me the most. The loving. Something I have not felt in so many years.

"Why?" My own throat clogs with foolish tears.

"Must you make me explain it?" He rests his forehead against mine. "Because you *came*. You could have chosen to stay behind, where it was safe and warm and alive. And yet you risked it all to come here. To save me."

I open my mouth to protest, but he presses a finger to my lips.

"I know you came for your mother. But the fact you are still here after… after everything…Adelaide, don't you get it?"

My entire being screams at him not to say it. *Please don't say it.* And yet something so deep inside my bones—it might be the most original piece of me—wants nothing more than to watch the shape his lips make when those three little words spill from them.

"Don't say it, Bram," I whisper, wanting with each breath to take the words back. "I can't hear you say it, not yet."

"When?" His voice is a gentle groan in my ears.

"When we're safe. Only when we are safe."

He nods, knowingly, and tucks his fingers beneath my chin, pulling my eyes up to meet his. There, in the ruddy light, he is *alive.* Those eyes like twin flames, cheeks rugged and filled with warmth. My fingers brush his lips, and he shudders beneath my touch.

"Then, if anything, let me show you."

The air blazes, nothing but heat and caught breath between us. My stomach fizzes, but I don't care about that. Don't care about the Haunts watching us from outside or my mother's face made from the patchwork skin of all the dead women I have buried. Even Ransom, the man who I thought only wanted to be made whole, vanishes from my thoughts, taking his rot and sold soul with him.

And all I am left with is Bram. Beautiful, broken Bram. Who tasted poison one night and never woke up. Who, for years, waited. Waited for me to find the bell, to fit all the jagged pieces back together, and to bring him home.

It was never about Mother. Never about making my family whole. It was always about Bram. This beautiful man who only deserved to live.

I reach up to tangle my fingers in his shaggy hickory curls. "Yes," I say, voice thick with emotion. "Yes, you can do that."

Bram needs no more encouragement. In a single motion, he takes me by the hips and spins me, pulling my body down against him on the floor. His skin burns beneath mine, and for a single moment, I feel the steady thrum of his heart through his shirt. His mouth tastes of honey, of spilled coffee on old books. His fingers dance across my back to find the laces of my bodice. They are clumsy things, and I almost laugh when he struggles to gain purchase.

"Is this your first time undoing a lady's stays?" My lips tease his throat.

He pulls back, face red. "Actually, Addie, I should say this is my first— Well, I've actually never—"

A smile splits my lips. I nudge him gently with my nose, voice so low it barely makes sound. "Me too, Bram."

"Are you all right with it?" His hands regain their fortitude, trailing up my back. "With you and me, I mean?"

I lean my forehead against his, brush the twitch of his lip with my finger, and study the way his shirt is already sloughing off the hard muscle of one shoulder. In truth, I don't know if I will be all right with anything, really. But maybe this is the beginning. One gentle, brilliant falling into healing. Maybe this is how I learn how to love, even if now isn't the right time to hear those words.

I brush a thatch of hair from his face and sit back on my heels, pulling him up to meet me.

"With you, Bram Avery, everything is perfect."

He groans, the sound low in his throat, and it sends ripples warming me to my core. In a single, fluid motion, he rolls me over onto my back, and I am breathless there on the floor of the church. He straddles me, thighs pressed against my hips. My hands reach up, finding the brass buttons of his shirt. I undo them one at a time, the waiting sending heat to the space between my legs.

Bram maintains searing eye contact, his pupils blown wide and shadowed with a desire that damn near takes my breath away. I unclasp the last button of his shirt, laying the fabric wide, and run my hands over the hard plane of his chest, his stomach. My fingers trail down a dark line of hair disappearing beneath the waist of his breeches.

His entire body shudders. "Addie."

The ache in his voice is undeniable, and when I run my hands along the length of him, I know why. Even for our clothes, I feel every hard inch of him, and it sends my hips bucking forward.

He grins and dives toward my neck like a starved beast. I form my fingers around his hard ridge, and a growl echoes from his lips. He catches my hands with his, splaying them to the sides.

"You first."

His words send shivers along my legs, and faster than I can blink, he tugs the loose sides of my bodice down around my shoulders. Lips like velvet trail my throat, the jutting bones of my shoulder, landing on the soft mounds of my breasts. I moan at the gentlest touch while he runs his tongue over my skin and sucks my nipple between his teeth.

The sounds release something in him, animalistic and feral. His muscles tense, and he rips his breeches from his body, tears the silk of my bodice until I am exposed to the navel.

To hell with this dress. With its scent of bitter almonds and poison.

Another shiver ripples down my spine when Bram pulls back, studies every inch of me like I am some rich jewel. His length, now free of his breeches, is long and hard and so beautiful. My center aches with more need than I ever thought possible.

Bram trails his hand down between my breasts, pressing against my stomach. My back arches at the touch, and I reach for him, taking him in my palms. He groans, leans down, and buries his face in my hair.

"Addie, you're a work of art." Slowly, he presses my legs apart and pushes my skirts up around my hips.

I gasp when the cool air touches my heated flesh.

With hands on the ground at my sides, Bram stares at me, the eye contact threatening to tear me apart.

"What are you doing?"

His smile simmers with devilry, the light from the sky pooling red around his head. A holy icon from the depths of Hell.

"Do you want this?"

"Yes." I barely breathe before the word is spilling from my mouth. "Yes, Bram. I want this. I want *you*."

He braces his hand against the floor of the nave and slides his length into me, filling me up until I think I will burst. I edge so close to pleasure my heart races into my throat. Every inch of him burns, makes me ache beyond desire. It morphs to something like hunger. For him. For this.

I flex my fingers and reach up to twist them through his hair. He moves with slow, deliberate thrusts, drawing out the moment, keeping his eyes fixed on mine. I trail my hands down his shoulders, nails raking his back. He looses another groan from his throat, falling over me, drawing out and pressing in again.

I move with him, the slick ache drawing lower into my stomach. His tongue slices my throat, then up against the sensitive hollow behind my ear.

"Addie." His breath is hot on my skin.

"Don't stop," I gasp. "Please, gods below and above. Don't stop."

He doesn't. Instead, he thrusts harder and deeper until I am sure I will come apart there in all the bloody light. Bram sends me teetering toward the edge of oblivion with each press, each breath from his throat. My fingers flex and release, succumbing to the darkness, the truth. I am no vicar's daughter. No cursed creature, touched by Erybrus.

I am the daughter of both darkness and light. Of earth and Heaven and Hell. I am poison and healing in one. A Reaper. Neither for the light nor the shadow, but for something in between.

The taste of soil fills my mouth when Bram pushes me to the edge of climax, and I surrender. Bitterbloom breaks through the stone of the floor, petals unfurling in a blossoming of light. Bram increases his speed, and I stiffen. Every inch of me feels ready to explode. To come apart in this place until all that is left of me is dust.

He brushes his lips against the curve of my shoulder, moaning my name like a holy prayer. Like I am something he has come to worship.

I shatter. Sparks cascade through my core, my chest, my limbs, while I cry out in pleasure. My back arches and Bram follows, stifling his cry in the white curls gathering at my throat. Together, we crash and fall, bursting and then coming together through gasps and moans and delirious smiles.

The woman afraid of dying and the man who only wanted to live.

I do not know what time of day it is when I follow Bram from the vestry, wrapped in a dusty wool dress of winter white. It was tucked in an armoire, gathering desiccated insect shells and cobwebs. Something warm brews at the center of my chest, the fire Bram lit still roaring inside me.

Clara peeks her head over the back of a broken pew, a knowing look glinting in her eye.

"Haunts have been quiet."

Bram, his hand wrapped tight around mine, nods. "Good to know."

"A few mice scampered across the floorboards earlier. They seemed alive, not missing fur or teeth or eyes or anything. They were bleeding, though. Thought that was strange, but…" She shrugs. "Didn't want to disturb you."

Bram shoots me a strange look, but I read it perfectly. Things—*living* things—slip into the rowan wood every now and then, yes. But this many in so short a time? Something is wrong. Or more wrong than usual.

I drop his hand and slip into the pew beside Clara.

"Do you remember telling me who it was you followed here?" I ask.

She nods, though the look on Clara's face says she wishes she could remember anything but. "I swear that's who it was, Addie. And I'm sorry. You probably don't—"

"I believe you." My gaze shifts to Bram. "You know how my blood runs black, Reaper's blood?"

Bram nods, a rather pained expression on his face. Like he's trying to hold back the truth but it's like swallowing poison.

The realization spills across my skin like oil. Smothering me. A lump sticks in the back of my throat. "I think my father is a Reaper. The Reaper of Rixton."

When the words tumble from my mouth, something I have long wondered at, the truth, is apparent.

My father is a Reaper. Created by Erybrus and Ithrandril alike in the Rending. A servant to harbor souls to this under-land while they await their choice, their final judgment. Or seek a way to broker their peace. Their deals.

Something outside one of the windows catches Bram's attention. He puts a finger to his lips and crosses the room, each footfall barely a breath.

Clara closes her fingers over mine, and Rascal, from where he lies sleeping next to the cold coals, lifts his head and utters a low, mean growl from the back of his throat. My skin prickles.

"Addie?" Clara's fingers dig into my arm, but I keep my eyes on Bram, who sidles up to one window and peeks through the glass.

His face goes white, lips peeling back in a snarl. He turns to me, and that's when I know.

It was a good thing to keep him from saying those three words in the vestry because we will never be safe again.

"Addie, run!" His words echo off the church walls.

I grab Clara's hand, Rascal leaping to his feet beside me, and pull her off the pew. She is screaming something, but I can't make out the words. Can't hear her over the sudden wind, the sound of splitting wood, of Bram yelling at me to run, to get out of here, to go home, over and over and over.

Through the chaos, our eyes meet, and the spark in my chest goes out. Frost sharp. The ice I have been holding onto for so long cracks.

I run for the door, Clara tripping behind me, Rascal on our heels. For the world outside, the flood of iron and snow, all the dead and dying things. My nose fills with the wet scent of rot, thick and sickly sweet. I gag on it, my knees rocking.

No.

The door is knocked off its hinges, wood splintering. I shout, cover my eyes, bend myself over Clara. Rascal rushes forward, haunches raised.

Something crashes through the roof behind us, and Bram cries out. When I turn, dust blooms in great clouds, filling my lungs and forcing me to my knees in a fit of coughing. I still feel Clara at my side, Rascal a shadow now in front of us. And something else, *someone* else, comes through the shattered door.

"You know, I never thought you'd be the next woman I killed, Adelaide Thorn, but here we are."

The voice shoots through me like a holly spear, spreading poison between my ribs.

Ransom stands at the door. Ransom and yet not Ransom. Gone are his handsome features, replaced by a patchwork of skin that does not belong to him. One eye blue, the other brown, blink out at me from beneath a crooked brow. His hair is matted in shades of red, gold, white, and black.

My stomach swills, expands, presses into my throat. I reach to sink my hands into Rascal's warm fur, but he and Clara have scuttled into the shadows, too far away from me and the thing standing in Ransom's clothes.

"What have you done?" My voice is choked. Bram struggles behind me, but I do not turn. Not yet. I keep my eyes firm on Ransom. And the face that does not belong to him.

"What have *I* done?" he asks the question as though the words taste sour. His boots scuff the floor, and then he is bending down, a black-threaded nose coming equal to mine. The smell rolling off him is foul, blood and cold metal and the sting of winter wind. "The real question is, Thorn, what have *you* done?"

I match his gaze with stone, lips pressed into a line. My fingers itch to reach forward, to peel apart his skin, to reclaim it for the girls he stole it from. I search his eyes for any signs of remorse, but all I find is the truth: the boy who cried wolf is the monster in sheep's clothing.

"You murdered all those girls, Ransom," I say finally. "Lilith, Hester… Liza was next."

It is a relief to say it. To know I am not the killer. That never, in the darkness of my fits, did I lose control. That I was simply becoming what I am. Who I was always meant to be.

A Reaper.

For the first time in so very long, I feel no guilt.

Ransom smiles. A twisted thing that, I realize, is all that still belongs to him. "Your mother was a great teacher, you know." He pulls something from his pocket. "Even from beyond the grave. She taught my father first. He didn't mean to call on her. But once it was done, he couldn't turn down her offer. Eternal life. Neither claimed by shadow nor light. Neither for Ithrandril nor for Erybrus. But making our mark here. Ruling here."

His eyes glimmer, and he holds the thing from his pocket out in front of him. A flame-shaped locket. My knees go weak. My mother's locket.

"Where did you—"

"Ah, not important, Adelaide. What is important is that we learned how

to communicate with her. Father first, then me as Father grew…*ill*." He smiles. "It was easy, really, taking the power. Poison is so easy to distill undetected when you're learning from the right teacher."

"You're a monster," I spit.

His smile deepens, skin tearing at the seams. He hooks a finger under my jaw. "Oh, Adelaide. I am no monster. I am a miracle."

Something inside me snaps, something that remembers the rub of rugged ropes, the taste of vinegar on my tongue. I slash a hand across Ransom's face, my fingers exposing something wet. His hands are at my wrists, searing pain blooming in my shoulders, and he wrenches me around, pulls my back flush against him.

Bram stands in front of us, arms held by two Haunts, their graying, shadowed frames like empty holes where the light can't shine. Hot panic fills my chest. How have they gotten inside? And then I remember Ransom at my back. His presence has desecrated the place. Turned it unholy.

Bram's mouth is open wide, as if he is screaming, but there is no sound. He is frozen. The touch of the Haunts so cold, so bitterly unalive, they have sapped any semblance of life left in his bones.

"Now you see, Adelaide, there are two sides to this." Ransom's voice is ice in my ear. "The side of life eternal. Ruling this place—ruling all of it, really. Who comes, who goes, who is sent to the fires or light beyond. We would be greater than Reapers. Their kings and queens. Or…you can choose the side of living death." He grabs my jaw so hard my teeth crack. Points my gaze to Bram. "That is his side, by the way. Your dead man."

I twist, my muscles aching for release. "You killed girls, Ransom. You and Mother."

He chuckles, breath like hoarfrost. "Oh, Adelaide. To gain life, other life must be taken. It is a simple rule, and your mother perfected the technique. Passed it on to me through this." He lifts Mother's locket. "The dead can speak through objects, Thorn. And your mother was all too willing to carry on her work through another."

I fight against it, the idea that my mother—Esme Thorn, who kissed my brow at night and sang of gardens and sunlight—murdered women in Rixton. "You're a liar."

Ransom's laugh grows, morphs to something sick. "Adelaide Thorn, the daughter of a Reaper, of death, and a woman who refused to die."

His words are stones in my belly, ropes around my heart. I sag against him, breath whooshing like poison vapors from my lungs. In the shadows, Rascal's eyes glint like twin moons. Waiting.

"You know it's true, don't you?" Ransom's voice is a growl in my ear.

Yes, I know. My stomach roils, nausea like a thick film in my mouth.

"That's how I pieced it all together. The bell, your mother, this place. I followed your father home one night, when he thought he was alone. He walked into the graveyard, and when the shadows hounded him, when the trees curled and parted at his very touch, I knew *exactly* what he was. My father used to say the line between the living and the dead was thin in Rixton. But he didn't know it was because he had a Reaper preaching holy words to him from the pulpit each Sunday."

The truth spills along every inch of my bones. It makes sense. My blackened blood. My father hiding me, afraid of what I was becoming. What if that meant I would become as powerful as him? But I push away those thoughts. It does not matter that I am what I am. All my mind focuses on are the dead of Rixton parish. Of life stolen.

"How did you do it?" I ask. "Murder all those girls? Steal their life, their faces?"

"That was the simplest task of all. Just as your mother taught me." The curve of Ransom's lips brushes my ear, and his voice drops. "Bitterbloom."

My chest seizes. A twinge of pain at the base of my skull. No, no. My stomach churns.

And then the souls appear. The first in so many days I can't remember. There are twelve. Twelve shimmers of cloudy white. The dead women. And they have come to help.

"Rascal!" I scream. "Now!"

The dog pounces before Ransom has a chance to register my words. He sinks his teeth deep into Ransom's thigh, and I wrench away, reaching for Clara, who has balled herself up on the floor.

The souls—the dead women—brush their wisping hands across the shadows of the Haunts, and those poisoned mouths gape open. The

Haunts scream. My eyes feel as though they are about to pop. Their lips break open, and the muscle and teeth begin to clatter down to the floor.

Bram drops to his hands and knees, life slowly filling him back up. Behind me now, Ransom is screaming. The voices are not his own. They are the girls: Lilith, Dinah, Frances, even Hester. And they have come for vengeance.

I pull Clara to her feet and run for the door. Rascal follows, a chunk of black silk hanging from his mouth.

"Bram!" I scream, turning when the snow outside lashes my face.

He is there, at the door, the dead women holding back the Haunts. Ransom is on his hands and knees, black slime slurrying down his face. Bram is almost past him.

And then Ransom's hand snaps out, a knife glinting in the moonlight.

He slices Bram throat to navel, and I watch in stunned horror while the dried and dead viscera spills out like ash.

Bram's face twists, turns gray, and he falls to his knees.

"Bram!" I scream again, going to run, to hold my hands against his skin.

Clara's fingers hold me fast, pulling at me.

"Addie, we must go!"

Ransom stands, smiles with too many teeth, while Bram kneels before him. He turns, makes sure I am watching—*knowing*—and sinks his fingers between the cut in Bram's chest, pulling out his heart.

It is still beating. Just barely. A shrunken, wilting flower of pale pink. A remembrance of life.

A cry curdles at the back of my throat. Clara's arms come to wrap around my waist. Rascal's teeth are at my heels.

Ransom holds up the heart, squeezes it. Bram buckles and gasps for air. Ransom's brow peaks, eyes glinting like wicked coals. His lips part, and he speaks a single word.

"Run."

And so, I do.

twenty-seven

Through the trees, the sky drips like blood. This world smells of it too, and my throat closes in on itself. I push up from the damp leaves, leaning back against the nearest tree, sharp-edged twigs scraping my palms. My gown is stained with mud. The skin on my wrists, where Ransom held me, molts purple.

I catch my breath, shivering in the cold, my arms goosing. Clara lies beside me, bundled in her wool cloak. Bits of red leaves catch in her oak-brown hair, and she turns to face me, blinking in the sullen light.

"What time is it?"

I stare blankly ahead. "There's no way to tell. I think we've been asleep for a few hours."

It is a lie. I have not slept at all. How can I?

I close my eyes, conjuring the image of Bram slit open, gray guts spilling to the mud at his feet. My own ache from running, blisters rubbing raw on my heels, boots puddling with my own blood. We stopped only when Clara could go no further. I told her to sleep, and she did. Though judging by the charcoal circles beneath her eyes, she has not gotten much.

"Any sign of them?" She rubs the dirt from her cheeks.

I assume she means the Haunts, and I shake my head. We ran as though they had whips at our backs, but we never saw them. Rascal stirs in the leaves at my side, sits and sniffs the air. I ruffle his ears.

"Do you smell something, boy?" I bury my nose in his fur, taking deep breaths of his smoky musk.

He prickles, skin pulling taut. My eyes dart to the trees surrounding us, each gray and white trunk a corpse. A forest of living death.

A branch snaps in the undergrowth behind us, and I push to my feet. Clara and Rascal are alert at my sides. She takes a hold of my hand, her skin chilled.

A shape grows amongst the trees. A shadow of a black so deep the space it takes almost seems empty. More a void than a solid thing.

A growl starts at the back of Rascal's throat. I place a hand on his head to settle him, to calm myself. Fear grows in my gut like mold while the thing before us blossoms, stretches tall, and turns a face toward us in the red light.

My stomach drops to the soles of my feet.

My father stands before us, drenched in inky shadows. Father and yet not Father. His face is the same: stone-set and heavy-browed. But there is something else, something that clings to the hollows of his cheekbones, the citrine irises of his eyes. When he meets my gaze, a smile spills along the line of his lips, dripping a cloying sweetness I have never seen him use. The shadows form a cloak at his back, embracing him like raven wings.

Here, he is Father—Vicar Thorn—but he is someone else too.

He is Death incarnate.

A Reaper.

"Daughter of mine," he muses, voice like cracking ice. "I have been looking for you."

My body tenses, goes rigid. Everything I have ever known seems a lie. Our home near the river, the flower beds beneath the window, Mother and Father dancing in the kitchen before the world turned gray. Before Mother wasted to ash in their marriage bed. And if that is all a lie, what does it make me?

Father takes a step closer, the pin on his cloak glittering in the moonlight. "So, you have discovered my secret?"

Clara trembles beside me. I tighten my grip on her hand.

"You lied to me."

Amusement glistens on his face. "I never lied, Adelaide. If you would have only asked me."

"Asked my father if he was Death? A Reaper? If he was the thing that killed my mother?"

He scowls, the shadows deepening around him. Rascal whines and paws at the dirt.

"I did not kill your mother," Death growls. "I have killed no one, in fact. I only harvest souls once they have died. A faceless blur on the wind. Your mother was responsible for the actions that led to her loss."

Anger boils hot in my veins, tearing down my arms like cinnamon. "You watched her die. You allowed it to happen, and in the end, it was me who lost. *Me*!"

The darkness grows, closing in around us, but I do not care. I only shake. My heart pounds while Clara's hand loosens in mine. Father steps closer.

"Your mother was sick, Adelaide. Her mind had grown weak. Her obsession with life eternal grew like a weed in her gardens. She did not *want* to be human. She wanted to be a *god*. I did my best to pluck it out, to show her that death was only a beginning, that no matter what we could always be together, but that was not what she wanted." His shadows swirl and brush my cheek with the scent of pine needles and sage. "In the end, I had to let her go."

His words are a punch to my gut, lungs collapsing, and the breath rushes from me.

Let her go.

"You let her die?"

Father takes a step forward, one hand outstretched to cup my cheek. I do not pull away, though his touch is ice.

"I could not save her, Adelaide. So instead, I tried to save you. To keep you from your true nature. I thought, if I hid the truth from you, you could live some semblance of a normal life. But you were bred from light and shadow. Your mother was special, touched with a hunger for life that inspired me, drew me to her. But after we wed, she discovered my secret, caught me ferrying souls in the rowan wood, and stole the bell."

My fingers go to my pocket, where the brass greets me, cool and clear. "She knew about the bell?"

Father nods. "She told me she only wanted to use it once, to bring her own mother back from the dead. But I told her it didn't always work that way. Most times, souls made their choice quickly. For Ithrandril or Erybrus. Light or shadow. But she was desperate for power and took it. I chased her down to the river, struggled with her to gain it back. She fell and cracked her spine along the stones."

My mind goes dark, fills with memories. Mother and Father *not* in the kitchen, their voices rattling from the riverbank, my face pressed against frosty glass while he brought her up the hill, slung like a rag doll in his arms. She was never the same after that.

My father continues. "With her body so broken, she could no longer carry on with her work and, eventually, gave herself the bitterbloom poison so she could continue on from the other side, through the soul of another."

Ransom.

My stomach swills sick.

"But what happened to the bell?" I ask, one finger still tracing the sharp edges.

"I abandoned it. I knew it was only a matter of time before Esme found it. She had been killing those girls for so long, burying them in her flower beds, and I knew—"

Breath hardens in my chest, turns to iron rock. "What do you mean, she buried them in her flower beds?"

The shadows around us darken, swirl until all I see is Father. No Clara, no Rascal. We are alone. I wrap my hand around the bell.

"You must know now what your mother was doing all those years. Frances, Dinah, Rosalyn …they were all stolen by her hand, and now, beneath her façade, she wears their faces as trophies. The lives she stole to live forever. She even taught the little Lord Black when she sensed his hunger. And I was…I was so scared, Addie. When he called you up to the castle, I thought for sure he would kill you too."

His hand sweeps through the darkness, reaching for my face. But I pull away, loathe to let him touch me.

"Why didn't you stop him?"

Father drops his hand, face morphing to grief. "Because I do not have that kind of power. I cannot stop sin, Addie. I can only carry out the results."

My stomach turns, one hand groping in the darkness for Rascal's calming warmth. But all I find is empty cold.

"It doesn't make sense."

"Chaos is not meant to make sense. And that is what your mother has become. She almost died once, before we wed. And the fear of it morphed her into what she is now. I didn't know it was her at first, killing the girls in Rixton. They don't speak to me when I bring them over, the souls. But I caught her. Katherine Wright—do you remember her?"

The name brings a ghost to my eyes. Hair like sand, eyes as pale as the winter sky. She was the innkeeper's daughter, nearer Bram's age than mine, though that would make us the same age now. I swallow the bile creeping up the back of my throat.

The day they buried Katherine beside her own mother in the church graveyard, her father placed a stone angel in the upturned earth and cried tears I thought were made of diamonds. Ransom mentioned that the line between the living and the dead was thin in Rixton, but I think it is something different. It is a town touched with grief. Perhaps that is why Father was drawn to it. My eyes flash to him.

"You should have stopped her."

A sort of sadness collects on his face, sinks into the hollows of his cheeks. "There was no stopping her, Adelaide. By then, she'd perfected her technique, and she was so close to gaining what she wanted. In the end, it was her own mind that ruined her plan. But then the Lord Black learned of her work, kept it going. And by then the bell was gone. I did my best to help those girls to peace as Ransom stole their bodies and buried them beneath the castle."

The castle.

Mother's bitterbloom beds.

A remembrance of life.

"They have been here the whole time," I say, more to myself than anyone else.

The bones.

"What?" Father's face twists.

I picture the bitterbloom behind the vicarage, the petals like a moat around this twisted version of Blackbourne Castle. The way they bloomed brighter at my touch, seemed to grow.

"But now that she's here, she doesn't want to go back," I say. "She asked me to join her."

Father nods, scratches his jaw, the ring on his finger glinting. I can still feel the heat of the metal when it cut my lip.

"She learned that with death she could have more power and control. Become as close to Ithrandril and Erybrus as is possible for a human soul. And without me here, without access to the bell, she took rule of my dominion." His shadows undulate. "But I intend to take it back."

His eyes flash to my pocket.

"I need you to give it to me, Adelaide. Give me the bell."

My fingers tighten, the sharp brass slitting lines in my skin, and my blood drips hot. Somewhere, outside the bleating darkness, Rascal growls.

"Why do you want it?" I ask.

A flicker of irritation crosses Father's face. "So I can stop her. Don't you understand? If she gets her hands on it, if she and Ransom take the power, they will be able to hold dominion over both the wood and our world. Esme will take my place, *become* a Reaper, and take any soul she wants. The bell bends to the Reaper, Adelaide."

The answer I was looking for. I fist the bell; blood leaks along its cracks like veins.

My parents are Death and death alike. One, a shepherd of souls. The other, a thief. I thought the bell would make me a thief too. The lines of my name signed over in red ink to Erybrus. But I am so much more than a thief. Once, a fool. Twice, a thief. The power of death in my hand, deals made in blood.

I am the very power of the bell itself.

"*If* I use it, if I ring the bell and bring Bram back home, I will become a Reaper, and you'll what…die?"

Father stiffens. "I thought I was keeping you safe. When I abandoned the bell at the bank of the river, I thought that was the end. But then your mother…I heard every girl screaming, begging for me to help them cross over." His visage twists, pain growing in his eyes. "That is what a Reaper does, Addie. And it is the last thing I want for you. If you give me the bell, I can convince your mother to let it go. We can stay a family. Here, in the rowan wood."

Family. My heart aches, pinches in my chest. I bite my tongue and shake my head.

No. I will not belong to a dead family. And we have been dead for so very long.

"I am not giving it to you." I set my jaw, hard and firm.

Father's face clouds, the shadows around deepening until all I can make out are the citrine glow of his eyes. A monster in the wood.

"Do not defy your father, Adelaide."

I grit my teeth, clasp the bell. "I should have defied you from the beginning. I should have climbed from that window in the garden shed years ago. You're a monster."

He stretches tall, growing like a silhouette in a broken mirror. His face turns gray, handsome and terrifying at the same time. As if he can see to my very soul and know what it is made of. But I hold my ground.

"That's where she did it, you know." His voice is poison sap dripping from a tree. A weeping wound. "That's where she cut the girls to pieces, chose their best parts to build herself an everlasting body."

I almost choke on his words when they slip around my throat like a noose. A brick covered in blood, black thread amongst bitterbloom and oleander seeds, goatskin gloves stained, smelling of earth and iron. Mother's journal speaking of ways to create an everlasting body. My stomach turns sick, claws sinking into my flesh and peeling back the folds. I clutch the bell so tight the brass starts slipping.

"You locked me in there on purpose, to face the sins of my mother, even though I knew nothing of them."

A smile slips against the darkness. Each tooth polished and sharp. Father's laugh ripples through the swirling shadow. "We are all the sins of our parents, Adelaide. Some just have more than others."

The sins of our parents. My knees knock together, and I almost yearn for the taste of dirt in my mouth. The release of death. But then something breaks through the cloud in my mind.

Bram's soft hands, caring for living and dead alike. The way he held me in the vestry, worshiped me like wine on an altar. I take the bell from my pocket, and shock spreads hot fingers across my chest.

It is glowing. Like fire without the burn. It lights the space between me and Death, and I see him here for what he is.

Nothing but a corpse. Gray and rotted skin hanging in dry folds. Broken horns curve from his head, and his smile is made from lips like burst pustules.

"There you are," I whisper.

Death steps toward me, the scent of him no longer pine needles and sage, but turbid fruit, a carcass left over from the hunt. Sick rises in my throat, but I swallow it down. Hold the bell aloft.

"You cannot use it for what you want." His voice is like metal in my ears. "The bell is broken."

In the near-blinding light, veins crack along the brass. I clutch it to my breast, some sort of absurd self-preservation.

"You're a liar," I hiss, holding it tighter. "I will never give you the bell."

"I am so sorry, but you have already lost." Death steps closer, the moon like a halo behind his crooked horns, as if it has been pinned there. When I concentrate on him, on the shifting blackness, white bones seem to throb beneath his skin. Beat an unsteady rhythm.

My arm tenses. Something akin to pain. I grind my jaw, take a step back until Clara's warmth blossoms at my spine.

"You could have stopped them both. Mother and Ransom. You knew what they were doing, what they were trying to accomplish, and you just sat by and let them."

All the faces flash before my eyes. So many dead girls. And Bram, the man who saw what he shouldn't.

"She wasn't mine to stop." Death's voice is a shadow now, a mere leaking of words between dry lips.

My arm trembles with pain, and I clutch the bell fiercely. "She was *only* yours to stop."

Death opens his mouth to speak, but it is Clara's voice that filters through the trees. "Addie, your arm. Look at your arm."

My hands are suddenly numb and shaking, a keening sound whistling in

my ears. Something sizzles hot in my veins, the same heat that shook me when I touched the bitterbloom behind the ruined vicarage.

I lower the bell, my jaw going slack at the sight of my bare skin. The delicate bones of my wrists are smeared in dark liquid. I hold up an arm, the light from the sky glowing red in the wetness.

Blood.

And yet, not blood. It runs warm, but the smell is something else. I gag, retching dryly, while the scent floods my nose. Bitter. Lemons and wormwood. Wet soil. Farther up my flesh, past the freckles dotting my forearm, something like coiled rope spills and curves.

Vines.

My lungs squeeze.

"What is this?" Father's voice—the one I know—filters through the glade. When I look up at him, he is all flashing eyes and pointed teeth. And I see it, there in the black pits above his hollow nose.

Fear. For the first time, Vicar Thorn, Death himself, is afraid.

Beneath me, the ground sways, and Clara falls to her knees behind me. But I cannot turn around. Something holds me tight. I lift my skirts and find the cause.

All the creeping vines of bitterbloom.

They twist up from the ground, wrapping about my ankles, skimming the soft skin of my stomach, looping around my chest to spill along my arms. Sap drips ruby-red down my wrists, and my stomach roils. Sap that kills. One taste and the heart will spasm and still forever.

I raise a shaking hand toward my father, and a hundred blooms burst on my skin. Each one as delicate as a snowflake and as hot as fire.

He steps closer, the shadows pouring out behind him like raven feathers. "I asked you a question."

The sap seeps into the creasing of my palms. I should be afraid. An odd feeling coats me like a waterfall. Peace, calm, surety. A smile slithers across my lips. "I made a deal, Father. He asked me to kill you. Didn't give me a reason. I've learned not to ask questions in the wood."

I lift a palm, and vines thread out between my fingers, reaching toward Death, each one so green the air smells of spring. They wrap through his shadows, bursting with white blossoms.

The bitterbloom.

What Mother used for death, I now use for life. My life.

Father opens his mouth, his teeth like crooked tombstones, and a root spins flaxen from my fingers. It stretches out, long and lithe, before it takes hold and flowers bud on my father's tongue, slip down his throat.

He screams. It is an unholy and spine-cracking sound, bubbling from him while my knees hit the ground.

Something splinters along my bones, my heart bursting against bone when the vines crumble from my skin and turn to dust. I scramble back, not meaning, not wishing, to hurt him, but there is no strength left in me. All I smell is the leftover remains of lemons.

The bitterbloom.

"Adelaide." My name is sharp in the Reaper's mouth. "Give me the bell."

Something inside me hardens to ice, and somewhere, in the darkness, Rascal gives a low growl. The sound alone gives me courage, and I step forward, the bell once again outstretched.

"I will not give it to you."

The scent of iron fills my nose, chokes my throat. I fall to my knees, sick with the stench, and darkness swirls around me. Agony, like nothing I have felt before, ripples through my body. The shadow grows teeth, sinks them into my flesh, and I open my mouth to scream, but the sounds turn to decay on my lips. I stagger but keep a hold of the bell.

"I will not give it to you."

Every word is forced between my teeth while I gasp for breath. Father's magic whirls stronger, quicker, until I am completely cut off from the light. It descends, pressing me to the forest floor until my hands are etched in dirt. A great weight blooms along my shoulders, my spine, the back of my skull.

Through the black mist, Clara shouts my name, but Death is descending. White petals rain on me, kissing my brow like snow while the darkness grows.

Twigs cut lines into my cheek, and my chest seizes like cords around my heart. Is this how it ends? Devoured by the thing I once called Father?

And then a horrible shriek floods the air.

Rascal howls, gnashes his teeth. The sounds shatter the mist, distort the air around me. But when I unfold myself from the ground, I smell the blood. Thick and tainted.

Father is prostrate before us, shadow gushing from the meat of his leg, trousers shredded. Roots and leaves and petals sprout from his skin.

Rascal hurries to my side, dark fabric and pale muscle threading his teeth.

"You are a fool." Father struggles to his feet, darkness still dripping from his shoulders like torn wings. "That bell is broken, Adelaide. You'll need me before the end."

With grit between my teeth, I stagger backward. He disappears in a cloud of dark mist.

Clara is beside me, clearing the dirt from my cheeks, but I hardly make out her face. My vision swims, lines and colors turning to haze.

"Addie?" Her voice is soft, fingers now on my shoulders, shaking me. "Addie, can you hear me? Are you all right?"

Nausea roils in my gut, and my body wrenches back to the earth, emptying my stomach into the wet leaves. Clara strokes my hair.

"Is he gone?" I ask, my voice like sandpaper in my throat.

Clara nods. "Did you kill him?"

I lift my head toward the sky, where the moon hangs heavy and white. "No, I think I would feel differently if I had. What happened?" My tongue is slow and sluggish in my mouth.

"I thought you were dead, is what happened," Clara says. "As soon as he wrapped you up in all that shadow, Rascal started whining, pawing at the stuff, but he couldn't get through it. And then all of a sudden, the smell in the woods changed from mold to spring flowers, and those vines were everywhere." She points to the remainder of a root system of little white blooms.

I drag myself over to it, not caring when my gown catches on twigs and tears. The petals are soft between my fingers, my touch bringing them back from gray.

"How can you do that?"

I look down at my shaking hands, trying to clear my mind. "I don't know."

My father is Death, a Reaper. As am I.

And my mother, her obsession with living turned to something else. Rotted into a desire to wear the skin of dead women and live forever. So, what does that make me?

I think of the rabbit, the rat, their hearts still and then pulsing at the touch of my finger. Of the flowers behind the vicarage, dead as Bram when he held them, but alive when I took them. And then Bram himself. Dear, good Bram who saw his heart wounds mirrored in my own. The woman whose own mother killed him when he saw too much and chose love anyway.

Gods below and above, *Bram*.

I choke on his name, look back at the wilting petals strewn about the red leaves. Snow against blood. One, a fool. Two, a thief. Three, a thing of contrasts. Death and life. Light and darkness. Brother-gods warring in my veins.

I want you to kill Vicar Thorn.

I have signed my name on too many lines, sold my soul to countless devils. And now Bram is gone, split open by a man I thought I knew and a mother I only wanted to love.

But I know nothing of love, not truly. Only what I have made of it. Only Bram. And whatever I am—monster or devil or demon—I must get him back. He is the only way for me to save my soul.

I turn back to Clara, Rascal beside her, but the look in her eyes stops my words.

"Clara, what's wrong?"

Her fingers sink into the damp earth, pulling brass shards from the dirt. She holds them up, lets them catch in the moonlight, and my heart thrums at the hollow of my throat.

"The bell," she whispers. "It's broken."

twenty-eight

My mother used to tell me stories of brave women. Women who were not afraid, who stared into the many faces of danger and laughed. But then she went wrong, stitching together skin that was not her own to make what, some paltry excuse for life? To rule a land stuck in between living and dying? A place where souls wander aimless, making deals, collecting on debts?

Esme Thorn is not the hero I thought she was, nor the mother I needed.

I look up at Clara, at the way she holds what is left of the bell, as if it were the last ticket home and the coach has already left the village. In a way, that is exactly what this is. My heart shudders, and I lift a finger to my throat, terrified of what I will find. All the stillness. But it rises to meet me, a single word thudding against my skin like a curse.

Fo-ol, fo-ol, fo-ol.

"I'm so sorry, Clara." My words are pale and empty things, and the look on her face tells me so.

She will never return home, never marry Liza, never move to the Queen's city and open a bakery with the one she loves. Will we die here? Cursed to stay in this unholy land until we turn to Haunts, our arms dragging long behind our bodies, sent by my mother to do her bidding?

And what of Ransom? My stomach clenches at the thought of him. The women he unburied from the churchyard, left their bodies to rot in the refuse around Blackbourne Castle. He deserves his fate here, to waste away until the skin sloughs off his face and all he is left with are bones and teeth.

And Bram. Something warm grows at my center and spreads, thins to ice when it reaches my fingers and toes. Perhaps he is already dead. *Fully* dead. I saw it happen. His own heart ripped from his ashen chest.

Can you die in the land of the dead? Father used to speak of two deaths: death of sin, death of bone. But can one die if one has no sin? Because why else would Ithrandril create a thing as beautiful as Bram Avery, if only to watch it become corrupt?

Clara's hand on my face pulls me from my darkening thoughts. "Whatever do you have to be sorry for?"

I stare at her as though she is a mirror, showing me all the shadowed parts of myself. A daughter of so much death.

"This is my fault. Whatever—whatever I did with the flowers, they must have broken it. Shredded the ribbon into nothing. And now—now—" It hits me like a tidal wave, the emotion. Tears break from my eyes, and what else is there to do?

Clara's arms wrap my shoulders, and Rascal paws my knee.

"We're all going to die here, you know?" Saliva strings my lips. There is silence, a breaking through the trees.

Clara stirs, lifts my gaze to meet hers. Eyes like stone.

"No. We are *not* going to die here, Adelaide Thorn. I have waited too long for this, too long for us to be friends again. I will not allow some trivial thing like Death stand in our way."

I blink stupidly. "Death is not a trivial thing. He's my bloody father!"

Clara brushes a sweaty strand of hair from my face. "The only things that hold any power in this world are things we give that power to. If your parents are Death, if a Reaper has been wearing a vicar's robe in Rixton all these years, it's because we gave him the power to do so. So, now, we take the power back."

"And how do we do that?" I ask.

Clara points to the remains of the bitterbloom flowers. "That, right there. That's where we start. Whatever you did there is how we take the it all back."

I stare down at the little blooms, each a reminder of what my mother did. How she plucked the plant by the light of the moon, when no one in Rixton could see and accuse her of being a witch. But Esme Thorn is no witch. She is something else. I close my eyes when pain eddies at the base of my skull, tiny pinpricks growing to dull, aching throbs.

"Addie."

I shake my head, tired of this. Tired of the monsters, the ghosts in the rowan wood, the way my heart grips my chest like an iron fist. My father was wrong about one thing, though. Whatever this is, this sickness, it does not make me weak.

If anything, it has made me stronger.

I snap my eyes open and take the pieces of the bell from Clara. In my hand, they thrum, the metal almost too cold to touch. It will never be truly whole, not after the brass has shattered, but neither will I. There will always be pieces missing. Things that should have been that weren't.

Years of love, parents who cared, friends who weren't lost. But that is anyone's life, is it not? A span of time with a few broken and missing pieces along the way. And though I am not whole, I decide which pieces are forever broken and which I will remake, reforge.

There is a flicker of something in the trees, a catch of white smoke.

The look in Clara's eyes tells me she cannot see the ghost, so I try not to smile when I catch its face. Frances Gordon, who gave me extra sweets at church, came for tea to the vicarage one too many times, and died with the taste of bitter lemon in her mouth.

Another one, Daphne Wates, hovers above the red leaves, a twinkle in her chocolate eyes. She was one of Ransom's, the girl before Lilith Corley.

And then Hester herself. I almost choke on a sob when she drifts down to me and places a hand on my cheek.

"Addie." Clara's voice shakes, and her eyes whip through the trees. "Something feels cold."

I do not take my eyes from Hester. "It's Hester, Clara. She's with us. All of them are."

They are like bees flocking to nectar. Young women I knew, those I didn't. They circle around us. The pain is gone, replaced by something like warmth. The same flames that ravaged my body when Bram tried so desperately to say those three little words.

Love.

Tears pool in my eyes, and the dead girls join hands. They are more solid now, colors and lines instead of bits of white smoke. Hester nods to me and the bell.

"We came to find you, Adelaide." Her voice brings fresh sobs from my throat. "We came to help you. Hold the bell, and we will give you what little we have left."

The words frighten me. Just another deal, or something worse?

"It won't kill you, will it?"

Hester laughs, a sound I know so well. Something like spring rain. "We have already passed on to the light, Adelaide, but we will not leave you to do this alone. This place is not our home, but there is an echo of home in you. Enough for miracles to be worked. And we want to help with that." A shadow crosses her face, and a tear slips down her cheek. "Please. Addie. It's the least I can do."

I do not understand a word of it, but I feel it. The warmth traveling through my body like cinnamon tea. Hester's hand goes to my shoulder, and the breath whooshes from my lungs. My bones turn to diamond. I am rigid, life and death passing through me like wind in a tunnel. For the light and for the shadow.

Golden rays shoot from my palm. White flowers, green leaves, a cascade of spring air. I open my mouth to cry out, but there is nothing more than breath. Rich, living breath. My palm burns, but it does not hurt. The light swirls, shoots up toward the sky, and the brass puddles in my hands.

One by one, the dead girls smile and drift away, evaporating like puffs until all that is left is Hester. Her black hair tumbles down her back, and for a moment, I remember her as she was. Living, running through the fields, dancing in the reeds of the River Thine.

"Take it, Addie," she says. "Take it and work miracles."

And then she, too, disappears into nothing but sweet-smelling vapor.

"Adelaide, what—what happened?"

Clara looks as though she has seen a hundred thousand ghosts. And perhaps she has. I smile, the warmth in me so deep and delicious it is like being drunk on wine.

"There is only one thing that can come from Death," I say, looking down at my hand. "Life."

And there, amongst the oh-so-familiar lines in my palm, is the bell and clapper bead, whole and good and mine.

"Let's go get Bram."

twenty-nine

Haunts circle the sky around Blackbourne Castle, their long arms flowing behind them like limp wings. The bitterbloom is thick, petals white as snow, wavering in the cold breeze that licks up from the forest. How many dead girls lie here, unburied from their graves in the churchyard, to be cut and sewn and pieced together like patches from an old quilt?

I still feel them, the last remaining life force threading through my veins. The bell thrums in my pocket and, with it, the power of life just there, shimmering beneath my fingertips.

Clara's breath is fog in the air beside me. Rascal is at our feet, teeth bared. My skin tenses when one Haunt swoops low, eyes sightless, slitted nostrils flaring for a scent.

I do not know if Bram is alive, if one already dead can die again. But I can picture his mouth, the shape it made when he tried so desperately to tell me he loved me. What I would give to have him say those words now.

"How do you know those monsters brought Bram here?" Clara's voice is a whisper at my shoulder.

"Because my mother and Ransom are working together." The truth is wormwood on my tongue. Bitter and sharp. "And she controls those things."

No matter what state his body is in, Bram is here. I feel it, a gentle tug in the center of my chest.

"Do you have a plan?" Clara asks.

I pull the bell from my pocket, letting it reflect the vibrant petals surrounding us. "Honestly, the only plan I have is to go in there and rescue Bram and get us all home."

Clara gives me an incredulous look. "Right, easy. So, we're just going to march into a castle filled with hundreds—maybe *thousands*—of living dead people under the control of your homicidal mother. Who knows where your father is hiding, who is Death incarnate, if you don't remember. And what am I missing? Oh, right, the fact that the skies are currently filled with beings that are sort of dead but also can definitely kill us."

I flash her a toothy grin. "See? Shouldn't be that difficult."

She returns the smile and buries one hand in Rascal's coarse fur. "I'll be honest. When I followed you through that door, I just wanted my friend back. I didn't think I'd get myself wrapped up in a demon battle."

I shrug. "There are worse things."

Red dotted lines, my name in places it never should have been, a deal to kill my own father.

I swallow the bile in my throat and tighten my grip on the bell. Whatever it was that grew the bitterbloom, I pray it is still there. The force not even my father could explain. My father, Vicar Thorn. My father, a Reaper, Death incarnate.

I suppose that will take some getting used to.

One of the Haunts swoops low to a courtyard, the same one I walked through only a few days past, when Ransom called me to his castle. If only I had seen the true reason for the rotting and mildew slipping down the walls. All the dead girls buried in the earth, trying to show me, to cry out and help them find peace.

I study the castle walls, nearly impregnable under the watchful Haunts. One finger grazes the curve of the bell. Without giving myself time to rethink my plan, I stand up from the bitterbloom.

"Adelaide," Clara hisses from behind me. "What are you doing?"

I stop, watch the shadows undulate around the blackened walls. Truth is,

I do not know. I have never *known*. But I have always felt. And that is what I have right now—a *feeling*.

"We're going inside, we're going to find Bram, and we're going to take him home."

Her brows draw in. "So, we're just going to walk in."

I turn back around, jaw set. "Yes, we're just going to walk in."

It is a task easier said than done. Thick brambles weave through the undergrowth. We make our way up the hill toward the castle.

"You know," Clara says, struggling over a twisted root pocked with thorns, "it would be so much simpler if the Haunts caught us and flew us in."

I stop and tilt my head back, watching the darkened forms whirl about us like poisoned mist. It is a wonder they haven't spotted us. I fidget with the bell, weighing my options. But there aren't any, not really.

I could be throwing everything away. Bram could be dead; Ransom is already a lost cause. Part of me screams to turn back, to run and run and run until we are safe, can ring the bell, and return to Rixton. We are both alive, no souls stolen, and do not need anything else.

And trapping Father here…would that be the same as killing him? I close my eyes, the memory of my name signed in wine and blood. The consequences if I do not carry through with my end of the bargain.

Bram's voice comes to mind. *He will hunt you down and take your soul.*

"Addie?" Clara's voice at my back steels my spine.

"Rascal." I call the dog to my side.

He looks up at me with those harvest moon eyes. It is like he knows what I am about to ask him to do, and he wants nothing to do with it. I kneel beside him, sinking fingers through his warm fur. He smells like apples, cedarwood, and soft wool. I bury my nose in his coat. Feel the comfort and courage that can only come from another creature.

"I need you to give us away, Rascal. I need you to let them know where we are."

He paws at the ground, his whine thin and low.

"We have to get Bram," I say. "We have to get Bram and go home. Please, Rascal."

There is something akin to pain in his eyes, a worry only he can feel. But

then he tips his head back, peels open pink gums, and sends a howl up into the ruddy mist. A chill cascades through my bones.

It doesn't take long for the Haunts to hear the sound. Three swoop down almost immediately, arms dragging long behind them. I recognize their faces—what is left of them. The three who took Bram, Rascal, and me from the church. They wear their broken-doll smiles, necks set at unnatural angles. A flock of downed swans.

"She has been looking for you," the one in the middle slurs through lips like rotting rose petals. "She will be so glad you've come back."

I hold my chin high, my jaw tight, even though every bone inside me is shaking. Even my marrow slips against me like it wants to run.

"Take me to her," I say.

The darkness envelopes me like water, lashing up in great folds when I am lifted from my feet. The scent of vinegar floods my nose, and I am drifting, drifting, drifting, nothing to carry me but these winds of darkness and the bell that thrums against my palm.

When I open my mouth, all I taste is the darkness. It hums against me like water, thick and cold. I blink heavy eyelids, searching for any light. My mouth is coated in film, and I struggle to my feet.

The bell. My fingers hurry for it, relief spreading through me when they wrap around the solid brass.

"Addie, are you in here?" Clara's voice materializes from the shadows.

I could almost cry from relief. Beneath me, the floor is cold, almost damp, and I crawl across it toward Clara.

"Yes, it's me. Do you have Rascal?"

There is a low groan and then a yelp when my hand brushes against something wet. Warm fur. Floppy ears. I throw my arms around his neck, burying my face in the hellhound's coat.

"Good boy," I whisper. "The best boy."

He answers with a swift lick of my cheek.

"Adelaide, I can't see anything."

It is funny, in thick darkness, what is seen and unseen. What is known and unknown. I try not to think what could be surrounding us.

"Reach out your hand," I say, brushing my fingers through the darkness. They land against something. Something cold, almost human.

I pull back, hand stinging, but when I lift it before my eyes, I can make out nothing. The blackness so dense it tastes of iron.

"Was that your hand?" The words are slow when they spill from my mouth.

Clara's answer is quick. "No."

My stomach flips.

"It's mine."

A scream curdles at the back of my throat, replaced by a single name. "Bram?"

I am answered with laughter so familiar it makes me ache.

"What's left." His voice is cracked and splintered, a dry husk. But it is still *him*.

I hear scuffling, Clara coming closer through the darkness. "Did you say *Bram*? Damnit, I can't see a bloody thing."

My fingers go to my pocket, where the bitterbloom blossoms and the bell and bead lie. Quickly, I fish them out and lay the little plant against my palm. If Mother could use it to do evil, I can use it for good. I close my eyes, search for the rapid beating of my heart, the reminder—

A-live, a-live, a-live.

Something like honey spills from my hand, a drip of light so gold it might be stolen from Ithrandril Himself. And maybe it is. Maybe that is what makes me different from both my parents. Touched by Ithrandril and Erybrus alike.

Clara gasps while the light grows, weaves itself around my hand and up my arm, until even the darkest corners of the room we lie in are alight with the glow leaking from the bell. I look up, my chest contracting.

Bram is slumped against the nearest wall, hands limp in his lap, head lolling to the side. His skin is so gray it might be made of paper, and the amber glow of his eyes is all but gone. His chest heaves, breath coming shallow and dry. I scramble across the stone and dirt, reaching toward him, and that's when I see it.

The place where Ransom's blade carved Bram like some hunter's prey.

His shirt lies open, ribs and flesh exposed beneath. Where healthy pink should be, all is dry and ashen. Tears prick the corners of my eyes. My fingers brush the fabric of his shirt. He sucks in air, putrid lungs pressing against skin.

"Don't," he rasped.

"Bram." I reach forward. "You have to let me help you."

I almost cry out when his hand wraps around my wrist. "I can't let you. Not now. You shouldn't have come. Ransom—"

"Stop being a noble idiot. I can help."

I study his face for any signs that might betray his words, but there are none. He is as set as stone. And in the end, that is what breaks me. That the man I love—*truly* love—would give himself up for me to breathe life again.

"Do you think really think so, Thorn?"

The voice lashes through the air like oak switches. I pull back, spinning on my knees.

Ransom leans against one wall, his fist full of Clara's dark curls, a hand wrapped tightly around her lips. Here, his illusion is fully in place. Honeyed hair, eyes like gunmetal, a cocked smile I still taste, as a kind of sickness on my tongue.

I am quick to my feet, the bell still glowing in my hand. His eyes flick greedily to it.

"Let Clara go."

Ransom's smile twists. A glint of sliver in the hand holding Clara's hair. "I wonder what would happen if I were to drag this knife across her throat. Would she die, you think? Or just bleed out on the castle floor for all eternity?"

Clara's eyes bulge, throat bobbing.

"You wouldn't dare." The words are barbs between my teeth.

Ransom's smile widens, and I notice the patched skin beneath, the black thread. "I have done so much worse, Thorn. Would you like to know about that too?"

Anger boils in my stomach. "That you murdered girls from Rixton, and when that wasn't enough, you dug up their bodies and pulled them apart to find the pieces you thought could save your own soul? Is that what you're so proud of, Ransom? That you used me to get to my mother, someone just as bad as you, just as rotten?"

His brow quirks. "You want to speak of someone *rotten*? I tried to use the bell. When my hand sunk into your pocket in the confessional—"

"So, you did take it." Bram's voice is dark fire.

Ransom's mouth parts, slippery and wet. "I did. But it would not work for me. You want to speak of things rotten, Thorn? Look in the mirror. Only Reapers can use the bell. Only Death. You think your sickness is *natural*? Of the earth? It's not. Your illness was never something that made you weak. It was your strength."

It is a truth I already know. Why I heard the sound of bells every time the souls came. My illness was never truly something wrong with me. It was so much more. *Is* so much more. The plunging of my heart in my chest, my breath coming quick, the pain, it was simply the truth trying to break free, to show me my strength lay with shadow and with light. That I contained multitudes.

Ransom's lips peel back, mold leaking from his gums. "We need you. You're just like us. And I did it all for you, Adelaide. Can't you see that?"

I recoil. "Take that back."

His smile widens, sludge seeping from between his teeth. "It's such a very strange thing, human life. No one really seems to see it for what it is."

"And what's that?" I spit.

"Something to take." Silver flashes in his hand, the knife pressed against Clara's throat.

Rascal's lips peel back.

I hold the bell out and watch the bitterbloom grow in my hand. The flowers shoot toward him, knocking the knife to the floor and pinning him against the wall. Clara scrambles up and runs toward me.

For a moment, Ransom doesn't react. He just stands there, motionless, sweating. And then his face cracks, every seam of skin stretching to show the rot beneath, the pulling black string, and laughter spills from his mouth like oil while he struggles against the vines.

I hear my heart in my ears, a cold feeling trickling down my back. "You're sick, Ransom. Please, let me take you home, find help."

His face contorts when the light from the bell brightens. It floods the

room, forcing me to shield my eyes. I feel the dead girls, their energy spinning through the bitterbloom, soaking into my skin.

"This *is* home, Thorn," he snarls. "I thought we could do this together, you and me. We could become stronger than either of your parents. Neither for the light nor for the shadow, but for ourselves." Something softens in his eyes. "I would have had you at my side."

A dark feeling spills through my bones, anger sharp and hot. "I am on no one's side, Ransom Black. Least of all yours."

He surges forward, mouth nothing but teeth and lashing tongue. Clara screams when Rascal launches himself at Ransom, flinging her out of the way. I peddle back.

Bram crosses in front of us, one hand slung against his peeling stomach. His eyes flash with danger. It takes him two strides to close the space between him and Ransom, and his free fist sinks into Ransom's stomach. Rot blooms, a stinking, sulfurous stench misting out.

"She doesn't need me to fight for her," Bram hisses between his teeth. "But I've been wanting to do that for a *very* long time."

Ransom spits something black from between his lips. "You aren't going to win this, Avery. Should I kill one of your sisters next? Polly, perhaps? Always with those sad, brown eyes, walking to the churchyard every day, just to lay flowers at your miserable grave. Or Isabel. Those lips would be delicious."

Anger is roiling off Bram like steam, ruddy dust spilling between the fingers clutching his stomach. He makes a move for Ransom, but I hold him back, hand soft.

"Bram, he isn't worth your time."

Something in the air shifts. A kind of warmth spreading out from between my fingers. It shakes me to my very core, and when I open my mouth to scream, all that comes out of me is a twisting vine. It grows from my lips, my viscera its soil.

Clara's eyes widen, and a sound like a sawn-off limb presses past her lips. The vine grows, the taste of it like honey in my mouth. It does not hurt. If anything, it feels like heaven. So warm, so welcoming.

So much like how home should feel.

The plant grows toward Bram, wrapping him up in golden light. I reach forward into his chest, feeling for the dry and sunken heart, then cradle it in my palm, dead and still. White flowers bloom along his skin, their centers yellow as bumblebees. And the lightest flutter in my hand—his heart restarting.

Ransom makes a sound like a gutted lamb, his lips curling. Bram is lifted off his feet, and I let go.

Between the shafts of light and green leaves, his skin knits back together, turns to something pink and healthy. Bones slip back into place, lungs inflating to fullness, and the flesh is pieced together and made whole. And then, he's gone. Every inch of him devoured by the golden mist.

The last of the vines leave my body. I surge forward, but the light is blinding. The air smells of autumn leaves, freshly cut fields, apples crisping on the branch. The room goes dark again.

I fumble for the bell, hurrying it to my pocket, while Ransom's voice echoes in the darkness.

"What have you bloody done?"

Tears sneak from my lashes and fall down my cheeks. The shadows are all-consuming.

"Bram?" My voice is light. I am half afraid to speak his name and not hear a reply. Never again.

Something scuffles, hands against stone. Clara moves in the dark beside me. Rascal's ears are piqued to the sound.

"She's become something stronger than you'll ever be, Lord Black."

My chest contracts. I push forward, swimming through the darkness. Bram. *Bram.* And then I feel him, solid, there, and…warm. So warm it is like he has been lying in the sun.

"Are you—gods below and above, Bram. Are you *alive*?"

An arm comes to circle my waist, a hand to my cheek. "As close to it as a dead person can get. What was that?"

I open my mouth to tell him, but it is Ransom's rasping voice that fills the space.

"You could have had it all, you know? Your mother promised me a spot at your side, magic beyond our wildest dreams. The power of Erybrus and Ithrandril combined. And you have traded that in for what? The petty ability to grow *flowers*?"

The bell glows once more in my pocket, feeding off the angry beating

of my heart. Ransom Black is fast against the wall, vines like ropes at his wrists. The poisoned shadows seep from him, every inch stinking like rot. I fist my hands, leaving Bram's side, until I am so close to Ransom the stench rolling off him sends my stomach roiling.

"Death can only take you so far. I am more than happy to let you stay here, molting in your own greed, but give me one answer, Ransom. *One.*"

He tips his chin at me, lips peeled back in a sneer.

"Why did you do it?"

Something in his eyes flickers, something akin to what little humanity he has left. He struggles against the vines, veins bulging blue in his neck.

"You'll never understand. Don't cry to me about being tied to a chair. At least your father was *yours*. At least for the brief years your mother held you, she did so with love. You want to know why the castle is rotting, Thorn? Want to know why my inheritance became nothing more than sludge and rubble? Because my father was all hate, down to his very bones. He knew from the day I was born I wasn't his. My mother had found love somewhere else. She couldn't take my father's purpling fists. But what were they to do?"

The revelation is a lightning strike to my guts. "So, you chose death?"

"I *was* death!" He rips against his bounds, skin shredding white between the vines. "I killed my father the day I came out of my mother. Not in blood and bones, but in knowledge. I was no Lord Black; I was not his trueborn son. I was the son of a stable hand! An embarrassment, a stain on Blackbourne's history. So, what choice did I have?" He glances at the shadows bleeding from his pale hands. "Those women, the power they gave me, it was all I had."

For a moment, I feel nothing but pity for Ransom Black. The lordling who never knew love. Only understood pain, loss, the slip of rot on his cheek. But anger replaces it.

The light from the bell pulsates. "You've been killing for so long."

He smiles at my realization. At the scent of blood on the air. Something creaks above us, and I feel Bram at my side. Ransom's eyes rove madly, laughter cracking out between his rotten teeth.

"He's coming, Adelaide. They both are. Your mother thought I might be able to sway you, but now your time is up."

Bram's hand is in mine, warm and solid. The fear rising in my throat tastes sour and sick. I hurry a hand to the bell, but it is still. Cold. Rascal whimpers, and Clara buries her nose in his neck.

Ransom's laughter echoes through the dim chamber.

The door is thrown aside, hinges ripped from the wall like splintered wood, and Death stands in the shadow. A Reaper and his Lady.

thirty

Shadows make quick work of Ransom's bindings. They slip from Father's fingers, wrap around the bitterbloom vines, and shred them to dust. There is nothing to be done for it. No quick fixes, no means of escape. They sweep inside—Father and Mother, Death and death alike. Just two more devils to sell my soul to.

It is Mother's hand I feel first, gentle on my neck, her fingers soft yet solid as iron.

"I knew you'd be back. Love does funny things to a person, does it not?"

I hardly recognize the woman who stands before me. Her hair, as waxen as ever, slips down around her shoulders, but where her skin and bone should be, the flesh is pale and half-eaten. An iridescent beetle climbs from beneath her exposed collarbone, its miniscule feet trailing up to rest at the hollow of her throat, where beats a black, bloody hole.

My fingers tighten in Bram's, and he holds me there, steady.

"What would *you* know of love?" I finally ask, screwing my courage to the sticking place, though the emotion itself feels soft and delicate. Like a single word or glance from this monster could send me to my knees, trembling like a sapling in winter wind.

There is a sneer to her lip, a peeling back, revealing sickly gums beneath. "All I have done, I have done for love, Addie. Can't you see that?"

"You killed women! You killed girls and unburied them to steal their faces, and when you couldn't any longer, Ransom followed." I fling a hand in his direction. "And for what?"

Black puddles in Mother's eyes like oil, slipping down her cheeks. Poison tears. I draw away when she lifts a hand to my face.

"Don't fucking touch me."

Pain blinks across her face. A shadow of something akin to betrayal. And then what is left of her twists, nothing behind her flesh but charred bone. I stare into the night-sky eyes of Death.

"I did it for you, Adelaide. I did it so that we could live together. I knew one day you would inherit the darkness that ran in your father's veins, and I could not bear the thought of leaving you or letting you go through it alone. Seeing the creatures of the rowan wood and not knowing what they were. Letting them drive you mad."

I raise a finger to my throat. Feel its beating. And in the moment—that brief and fleeting time—I realize it is not a sickness. It never has been. The way my heart leaps against my ribs, the way it feels like a fish on a broken string, a caged bird caught between bones, it is *not* weakness. It is a remembrance of life. That despite the evil in the world, the shadow and those who wear faces that do not belong to them, I am *alive.*

"You were sick," I tell her. "But it was not the sickness of your body that got you to kill Dinah Bo, Rosalyn Eckers, Frances Gordon. It was obsession and fear and everything you are made of." I back away from her, once more running into the warm wall of Bram's chest.

He puts a palm to my waist, steadies me. Mother's face puckers, the scent of brine filling the air.

Father—Death—comes to Mother's side. Ransom is now like a whipped hound at his heels. The pin on his cloak glitters in the golden light of the bell, his eyes trained on my hand. I tighten my fingers around it, and he looks at my face. Hunger breeds there beneath his brows.

"Join us, Adelaide. You belong here, with us. I was wrong. Your mother doesn't want the bell. She just wants us, together. A family."

The word cracks along my surface like glass. *Family*. All I have ever wanted. The three of us sitting before a fire, weaving stories of our days spent together and apart. Adventures had.

I look about the room. The shadows dancing in the corners, the rot spilling from Mother's face. There is greed there, hunger.

Something tells me she *does* want the bell, the power over death. I pull away from Bram and study his amber eyes, the way they already seem to hold so much of me in them. His hand trails my waist.

"What are you doing?" Concern knits his voice, thick and rasping.

I look down at the bell, feel the way it pulses against me. Clara and Rascal come beside Bram, Clara with tears in her eyes.

"Don't do it, Addie. Don't listen to them. Come home with us."

The woman who has only ever wanted to be my friend, share my sorrows, and bring me a basket of baked goods to warm my heart. I smile at her, a sad thing made from too many years spent hidden away. Kept apart.

"I'm so sorry," I say. "For everything."

Without a final glance back, without a second thought of stopping, I turn to my parents and hold out the bell.

thirty-one

There are monsters in the rowan wood, and I am one of them. I feel it in the way my skin burns the nearer I get to Death, the way it aches to become just like him. A Reaper of souls, a dealer of deals. Father's eyes glint while I close the gap between us, my heart thrumming wildly in my ears.

Let it. Let it beat like a wild, untethered thing. Let it set me free.

"Addie, stop." It is Bram's voice at my back, brimming with fear, confusion, the knowledge it is all slipping from his hands. Every spilled drop of blood will vanish.

I pause before Ransom. The skin of his face knits back together, the façade I thought I cared for, assumed I knew, drawing back, as it always should have been. Untouched by Mother's magic, the deadness of it all.

I ignore Bram and drink in the sight of Ransom, the man I once thought broken, hoped I could mend. The man I now realize has torn himself to pieces and sewn new ones over the old scars. To be kept hidden.

I reach forward and brush a pale curl from Ransom's face.

"I think there were parts of us that knew each other," I say, voice quiet. "I think there was something in me that knew something in you that first day we met out at the water. A kind of lodestone, two opposite ends of a terrible future. I even think you might have loved me—or, perhaps, the *idea* of me."

His face softens the more I speak, becoming every inch the man who kissed me in the confessional. The man I thought was home.

"And for all that, I am so sorry."

His face morphs like wind on a pond. I take no further time.

Squeezing the last remaining bitterbloom between my fingers, I allow the sap's warmth to course through my veins, then press my lips against his.

Something breaks in the room. A tension that weighs heavy. Sick air.

Ransom tastes of salt, the first bite of frost. Bile rises in my throat when Bram cries out, the betrayal in his voice a knife at my back. But I press the kiss deeper, willing the life coursing through me to leak from my mouth and slip into the chasm of Ransom's soul. He chokes, pulls away, sap dripping from his decaying lips. Ransom wipes at it, scowls at me through darkened brows.

"What…what have you done?" And then he is sent sprawling, shadows leaching from his skin, his screams like a tortured beast.

I don't waste time.

Turning to my father, I rip the pin from off his cloak. His darkness swirls, Mother's mouth opening in a shrill scream. But they are too late. I hold the clapper bead between two fingers, threading it with the slender strip of metal from the pin.

The warmth is still inside me, the power of so many lives. So many lives that were not mine yet were given to me freely. Heat floods my body, and when I turn to Bram, there is recognition on his face.

The metal clicks into place, the full power of the bell filling me up, like so much summer light. My father turns gray, skin like stone. He opens his mouth, teeth spindly and long, but his jaw freezes. There is pain in his eyes. Betrayal.

"What…what are you?" he struggles out between his hissing teeth.

Days ago, I would have said nothing. I am *nothing*. Nothing but wickedness and weakness. A woman with a heart that refuses to heed. And then I learned the truth, that I was a Reaper, a collector of souls. But now I know what I really am. *Who* I really am.

I turn to Bram, to Clara, to Rascal.

"I will never be like you, Father," I say, each word a cut across my wrist.

"I will never be like you or like Mother. Because I am *alive*, and I hold both shadow and light."

I lift the bell and listen while it rings pure and true and whole. Father's body seizes, shadows wisping, flinging out around us. He opens his mouth, bloody screams ripping from his throat.

Ransom is on his hands and knees, vomiting poison, but his face is breaking. The skin tears apart at the seams.

"Addie." His voice is weak, thin. On the floor, his body convulses, lines of darkness seeping from between the ripping black thread. The sound makes me queasy.

I take a few steps back from him, the bell still bright and warm in my palm. The wool of my dress sticks to my flesh.

"I'm so sorry, Ransom." Bram's hand is once more at my back, and I lean into it. "I'm so sorry I couldn't help you."

Father's shadows wheel around when he collapses to the floor. Mother is quick beside him, but already, he is nothing. Already, Death has found a new home.

It wriggles between my bones, pressing deep into the tissue of my chest, my throat, the gauzy space above my lashes. I thought it would be cold, this power, but it is like a sunburst growing inside me. Filling me up with so much warmth I could be a woman tied to a stake.

But no ropes encircle my skin. No longer am I tied down by men who wish to subdue me. Make me *better*. I am no monster, and I am no witch. Neither am I a god. I drag the honeyed air into my lungs while the thing that is no longer Mother cries out, kneads the shadows between bleeding knuckles.

I am the breath of life.

"Adelaide." Ransom's voice comes from the floor where he lies, nothing more now than a tangle of ratted clothing, jumbled bones, flesh melting waxy into puddles beside him. He is not dead. Ransom is something far, far worse. A tethered soul. "Please," he says, voice a puff of putrid smoke. "Finish it. Kill me."

The words draw pity from the darkest parts of me, but Mother's fists pound the ground. Her cries have turned to black bubbles on her lips, screams cracking from rotten teeth.

"This is you! Your destruction." It takes her three strides to cross the room, to tower over me with a tongue that smells of old blood.

I do not move or cower. Instead, I hold the bell tight in one hand, Bram's fingers in the other.

"We could have had everything, you know?" Her lips are pale and swollen, pustules ready to burst. "You held the power to keep your family together, and instead, you ruined it."

"You're wrong," I say, Bram so fiercely real behind me. "I do not need you. I never needed you or Father. We were never a family."

Her eyes go wide, the poison leaking into the glassy orbs. Clara's hand wraps around my arm, and Rascal growls. Mother stretches tall, gathering the darkness to her while Ransom groans on the floor.

"Addie." Bram's voice is hot in my ear. "Ring the bell."

The metal thrums in my hand, but when I look down at Ransom, writhing on the floor, my skin stills. I should never have brought him here, should never have followed my mother into the dark. And now, there are ghosts haunting me. My name spelled on too many lines.

My eyes flash to my mother, and I see the truth. Her lips form a sneer, a black line across pale flesh. Opening, opening, opening. The Haunts rise, two at each hand, stretching for me.

There is only one thing left to do.

I ring the bell.

The sound is clear and sharp as crystal. Snow against autumn leaves. Everything goes black. The moon and sky above go out. Clara gasps behind me. Mother's screams turn to hollow echoes. Bram's hand is tight around mine.

"Hold fast," he whispers, reaching through the darkness for Clara's hand.

It starts at my back. A wind like the first kisses of winter. Slowly, it turns, growing warmer, filling with the scents of rose hips, pumpkins harvested from the fields. The air begins to swirl, a wave of red light bursting forth around us. I am thrown back, head cracking against Bram's shoulder when we are flung to the ground.

The bell blinks in the blinding light of a ripped opening, the sudden warmth making me nauseous, and I fumble the brass. My fingers tense around the collar of Bram's shirt, and I turn into him. All swells to silence.

And then the screams.

My mother's screams.

She is bent over Ransom, his skin almost whole. Almost as though he is once more himself. Real. Alive. But he is anything but. Gray as a corpse in winter, lungs hardly moving.

Do not make deals with these people.

Mother's eyes flick to me, but they are not hers any longer. They glow bright red. As crimson as apples. She scrambles to her feet, claws outstretched.

"What have you done?"

I stare down at my hands, where the light from the bell is shining so bright my eyes cross, then look back up at her. My mother. Not Mother. A beast. A twist of wishful thinking turned obsession.

I struggle to my feet. Leaving Bram behind, Clara, Rascal. The bell vibrates in my palm, and I drop it to the far reaches of the pocket. The light from the door is blinding, beyond it, the scent of rye in the sunlight. I look to Mother. The way her hair sways like wheat about her face. Not her face. So many features that do not belong to her.

I feel them, the ghost women. Eddying at the back of my neck. But it is not pain, not really. For the first time, it is strength. I have found their bones where the bitterbloom grows, can feel each soul passing to peace while they give me the last of their power.

When I stop before Mother, I reach out a hand and run a finger down the crooked line of her jaw. The unevenness of all the sewn skin.

"Do you remember the flower beds, Mother? The dirt beneath your fingernails, the sun at your back?"

She does not speak at first. A quiver on her lips. Her mouth opens. A small hole at first. And then it grows. Wider and wider while the inky rot swallows her face. I wheel back, and Bram's hand is there to catch me.

"We must leave, Addie. The veil won't stay open for long."

I turn to the ragged red rip undulating before us, golden mist swirling around its edges. Beyond, wheat and rye fields, Farmer Whitley's orchards, the scent of harvest. Home. Not the vicarage. Never the vicarage. But Rixton. Where Bram belongs. Where I belong. Not here. Not trapped in a world cursed between death and life.

I turn back to Mother. To Ransom. A film covers his eyes, but he looks to the door, so much longing in him that it breaks me. Once more, he is the broken boy in the garden. Not the murderer my mother made him.

"Addie." It is Clara's voice now, tense.

The girl who followed me through the trees into Death, just to make sure I was all right. I breathe slowly until my muscles loosen. Brush a finger across Ransom's lips. He chokes on his own breath.

"Don't let this be your end."

I turn and take a hold of Bram's hand, Clara's in my other. A wind brushes through the opening—wet dirt, river water, leaves falling in the rowan wood. There are monsters there, but I am not one of them. There is nothing wrong with me. Nothing broken. In everything, I am whole. I have always been so.

Bram steps toward the rip, with Rascal at our heels. I watch Clara pass through, the weave of her plum skirt slipping through all the gold. Bram turns to me, his face soft.

"Are you coming?"

The question strikes me as odd, a sort of split happening inside. My name is still scrawled on lines. Lines that, if I leave this place, will still be owed. But Father is dead, is he not? The Vicar Thorn was never a true man.

One more glance to my mother, the sight of her breaking my bones. She leans against Ransom, the last bit of life leaking from between the stitched seams. Erybrus can decide what becomes of them.

I open my palm. A root wriggles from my skin, white petals blooming. I pluck it and let it fall to the ground.

"A remembrance of life," I say and follow Bram home.

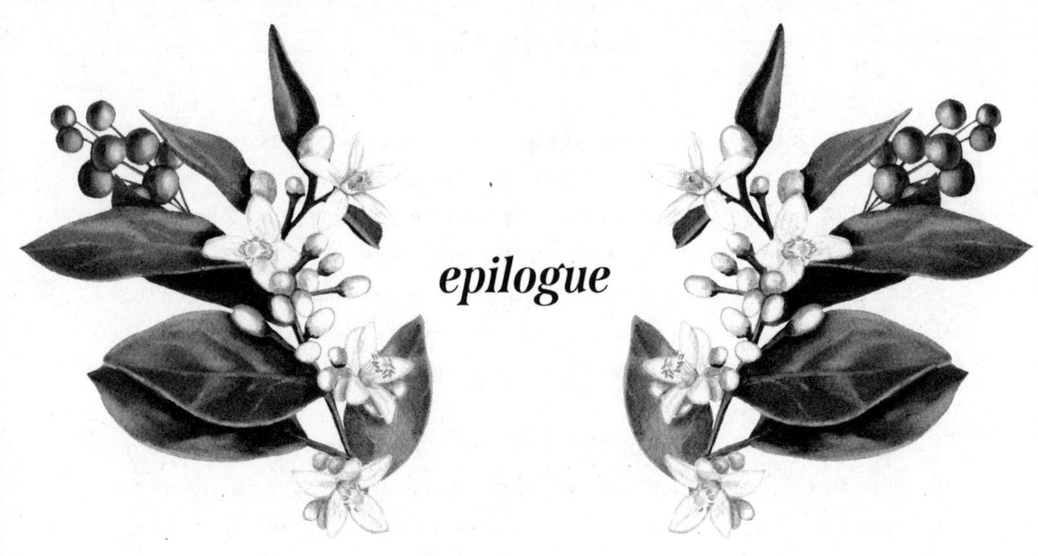

epilogue

There is a sense of peace when the world turns to spring. Daisies crop up along the banks of the river, their sunny faces a promise. Life returning. Ice melts, trees bud, and the air fills with the scent of thawing earth and brightening blooms. All around me, the stalks of last autumn's rye crop sway like a gentle, gold ocean.

I pluck a shaft, slicing away the remaining seed, and watch while they are caught up in the wind, carried toward the dip of the hill below. Avery Manor winks into existence through the branches of oaks and willows. Rascal runs a few paces ahead, nose to the ground, ears perked. He has taken a liking to hunting game, and I enjoy watching him run. Wild and untethered and free.

And he is not alone.

Since returning from the rowan wood, the slipping of my heart has not stopped. The pain still brushes the back of my neck some days. A remembrance of all I am, the power I could wield if I wanted.

Even the souls still come to me. Ghosts caught between living and dead. They cry out some nights, their voices whispers on the wind. Sometimes, I wonder if they are the voices of my mother or Ransom. So, I did the only thing I could think of to close the door to the rowan wood behind me.

The brass key rests against the tepid skin of my chest, tucked beneath the woolen bodice of my dress. I lift a tentative finger to trace its outline.

The bell was easy to melt down, forge into something new, to keep the door locked shut behind me. The magic sings through the metal, not the shape, and with this key I hold the power to come and go as I please. I have the power to leave Death and all it is in my past. But the key's weight around my neck is still a reminder of the things it could unleash. I close my fist around it.

No more devils. No more deals. The dead can make their own way.

I do not belong to either Ithrandril or Erybrus.

There are enough Reapers in this world. Let them carry the burden the gods gave them. If ever I need to pass back between the rowan trees, the key will see me through. But for now, for this moment of freedom, the dead can find other Reapers. Other doors.

A shout comes from below the hill, and Rascal's head perks up between the rye. Laughter lilts on my tongue when he bounds through the field, ears flopping like wet mops. At the crest, I spot a figure. It grows as it comes up the hill.

Bram. Holding something in his left hand. He swings it high over his head when our eyes meet, a grin on his face.

My guts twist. This man. My unmoving piece. Something to lean against. Something to hold and be held by in the storms. When he nears, I smell his ink-stained fingers, old coffee a film on his lips. He wraps an arm around my waist, pulls me flush against him.

"And how are you this fine morning, Ms. Thorn?"

I smile, study the curve of his jaw. "As fine as anyone could be, Mr. Avery." His face goes stern, a hard line, and I laugh. "Oh, excuse me. *Lord* Avery."

The title is new. Passed to the only remaining nobility left in Rixton. Blackbourne has been left to rot, the remaining staff carried over to attend to Avery Manor.

We found the bones there, buried where I knew they would be: in the castle gardens beneath the dead and dying plants. Bram and I dug them all up and laid them to rest, and the village blinked in shame. Apologies lay thick on their tongues, and I smiled, nodded, and heard them all. But my duty was not to them. My promise was not for them, to weave empty words to resolve them of their guilt. It was for Lilith. For Hester. For Dinah and

Rosalyn and Frances. I put their bones back beneath their graves.

Bram lifts the small box to my nose, and instantly, I am drawn in.

"Did Clara send marmalade cakes?" I lean toward him, greedy hands reaching for the box.

He pulls it back, a mischievous grin licking his lips. "Ah, ah, ah, there is a tax, Ms. Thorn. Delivery fees and all that."

I glare at him, but before I can speak a word, his lips are crushed against mine. All I can taste is the black coffee, the twist of orange, the catch of clove.

I pull back, swatting him on the shoulder.

"You already ate one!"

His smile widens, a thing so delicious I want it back between my lips. "Sorry, can't help myself. Here, you want one?" He pops open the lid of the box.

I rise on my tiptoes, catching the scents of citrus spice, vanilla, a hint of cardamom. Four pale brown cakes dusted in frosting sugar sit on lace cloth, tucked beside a brown bone that smells of only one thing: pumpkin.

Rascal sits eagerly at my feet, tail wagging, hunt forgotten. I wriggle my nose.

"You wouldn't happen to want one of Clara's pumpkin bones, now, would you?"

He scrambles forward in the grass, his tail a whip, lips peeled back, and he bays a desperate wail. I chuckle again, tossing my head to the yellowing sky.

It feels so good to laugh. So necessary. I wiggle my fingers between the treats and pick up the bone, holding it above Rascal's head.

"You ready?" I tease.

He jumps high, his wet nose slapping against my hand. I pull the bone back.

"Fetch, boy!" It soars from my hand, end over end, and Rascal becomes a black blur. Bram chuckles, and I turn, catching him taking another bite of marmalade cake. "You're going to eat them all before I have a chance!"

I launch myself at the box and trip when he pulls away, rolling into the rye, my belly tight with laughter. Bram collapses beside me, smothering my lips with his until I can no longer breathe. I sit up, wipe hair from my face, forcing my fingers into the box, and pull out a cake. After taking a bite, the crumb melts on my tongue.

Cinnamon, sugar, orange, the sweet sting of ginger.

Clara knows me so well.

"If she keeps sending us sweets in the post every week, we'll have to buy a whole new wardrobe come summer!"

Bram laughs and wipes his hands on his trousers. "I'm sure that can be arranged." He props his head on his hand, lying in the grass beside me.

In the spring light, he is beautiful. So new, so *alive*. The sunlight reflects in his amber eyes, and warmth blooms bright inside me.

The people of Rixton questioned us, of course, when he showed up breathing at the steps of Avery Manor, not a moment older than the day he died. Lady Avery would take none of their cynical words, though. A miracle, she called it. The resurrection work of Ithrandril.

When asked, Bram tells people he was sent back for a reason. The god of light knew Rixton would be without a leader once Ransom and my father were found out, and Ithrandril had breathed life back into Bram so he could lead the people away from this dark chapter.

They believe him. Or, at least, they don't ask for particulars. To question the judgment of Ithrandril is to doubt the very fabric of reality itself. And sometimes, people are more willing to walk through life in a fog than see with the truth and clarity that would shake their world apart.

I finger the key at the base of my collarbone. But maybe they are right. Perhaps it was all a work of the gods.

Or just a woman.

A woman who only wanted to live.

Bram stirs in the grass, closes the box. "I almost didn't see this come in with the post. Polly was hurrying them upstairs, and I just happened to catch her."

I roll my eyes.

Polly, Bram's youngest sister, was the most excited to see him return, and she hasn't left his side much in the past few months. Really, the only alone time we get together is either in the fields or in the small cottage, where I now live on the manor grounds.

After Bram and I returned, the village questioned the whereabouts of my father. We told them the truth. Or a version of it. That Vicar Thorn and Lord Ransom Black had been caught with the blood of village girls on their hands in the wood and, in their rage and fear of being discovered, turned on one another, slicing each other's throats.

Soon, the seat of the church in Lysdin will send another vicar to Rixton, another man to yell from a wooden box every Sunday. But Bram and I will not be there to hear. We find the fields to be more our church than any building could ever be.

Bram's finger sweeps my brow. "You deserve this, Addie. A soft ending to all the madness." He leans over, kisses me. A gentle brushing. "I love you."

He scrambles to his feet when Rascal comes whipping back, a stick between his teeth and pumpkin smeared on his upper lip. Rascal growls and drops the stick before Bram's feet.

"Meet you back at the manor?" Bram turns down to look at me.

I finish my cake and nod, the wind a gentle kiss at my cheek. He calls Rascal after him.

"Bram?"

He pivots back around, a grin so wide it might swallow the world.

"I love you too."

He smiles and jogs through the bramble. I watch him go. The key weighs heavy at my neck, a reminder of so many memories and lines my name is still signed to.

But what can dead things do against Death herself?

I stop, the wind whipping my hair into knots.

No.

I am *not* Death.

Death does not define me.

I lift a finger to my throat. Bram throws the stick for Rascal and grins back at me with a look that makes my bones ache. The wind shifts, a scent like apples and rye carried toward me, and I feel the gentle return of my heart. One sweet, beautiful true word.

A-live, a-live, a-live.

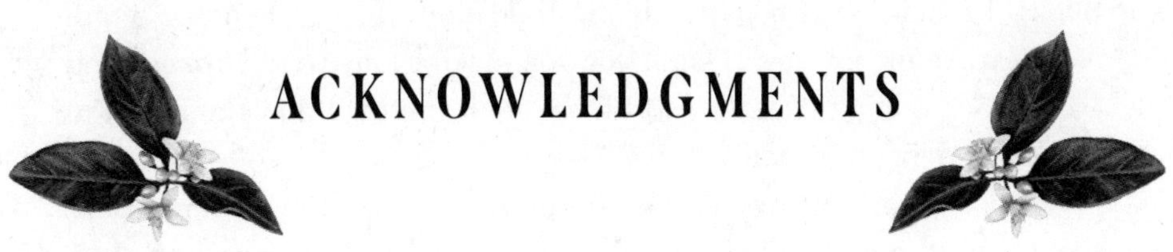

ACKNOWLEDGMENTS

In the spring of 2022, I started experiencing sensations in my chest I called my "flutters." That was a gentle term, dear reader. It felt like someone was piercing my chest with their fingers and ripping out my heart. My breath would catch, and I would have to grab ahold of something just to remind myself I was alive. I underwent multiple scans and tests and ultrasounds and even had to wear a monitor strapped to my ribcage for a few days just to figure what the hell was going on. I was eventually diagnosed with PVCs, or premature ventricular contractions.

It was terrifying. I had never felt so utterly helpless, and I was in place where I had absolutely no support. No one wanted to listen to me or help me through it. It made me feel like a burden, just another waste of space.

Until I found someone who did listen. I want to thank Dr. Amelia Sramek, who listened to me and heard my pain and anxiety and told me I wasn't crazy, and no, I wasn't going to die. Thank you for being a safe space and someone I felt like I could finally trust with my health. There's a reason I still drive three hours one way just to come see you!

I also want to thank my best friend, Amanda Havill Adgate, without whom this book would not exist. Thank you for texting me that one autumn morning and saying, "Did you know that bells used to be thought of as protection against the dead?" and not questioning when I said, "That's cool, but what if they SUMMONED the dead?" You are a true bosom friend, and I love you so much.

To my agent, Amy Giuffrida who never blinks at my wild ideas and supports me every step of the way. I truly could not think of a more perfect person to champion my work. To my editors, Amanda Chiu Krohn, Ashlyn Inman, and the entire team at Turner Publishing and Keylight Books: Kendal Cliburn, Jane Flautt, Todd Bottorff, and Lyndsey Smith of Horrorsmith Editing. Thank you for making this work stronger and asking each other, "Wait, should I be liking Ransom? I don't know if I'm supposed to like Ransom!"

To my A-Team siblings, thank you for your constant, unwavering support. You all are incredible, and I love that my agent sibling bookshelf is growing by leaps and bounds lately! To Jenny Adams, my publishing house sibling Amanda Linsmeier, and Isa Agajanian, thank you for all the encouragement, the commiserating, and the reminders that I can do hard things. I love you all.

To all my earlier readers—Annie Bayer, Zeyneb Holdridge, Ruth McKell—thank you for helping me dig the shards of this story out of the mud and fit them together!

To my Oma and Opa, for always cheering me on, always loving me, always being there to catch me when I fall. I don't think I will ever be able to put into words how much I love you both. Just know, it's *a lot*. My Mumsie—do not worry, Adelaide's mother is not based on you! I love you so much, thank you for being there to help heal my heart when I needed you most. To the baby sibs—Ty and Emma-Rebecca—thank you for letting me use you both as my guinea pigs when we were children and tell you all my creepy bedtime stories. Sorry not sorry for the nightmares!

To H—from the moment I met you, I knew you were a safe place, and I love you for it.

Lastly, to anyone with a chronic condition or illness—I see you and I understand what it is you're going through. It sometimes feels as though there is this shadow living inside us and we never know when it will rear its ugly head, never know when it will flare up and make us miserable. As a girl who also deals with a thyroid condition and diagnosed anxiety, I get it. You're not alone and I hope Addie's story reminds you how strong you are.

Remember. You are *a-live, a-live, a-live*, and isn't it beautiful?

ABOUT THE AUTHOR

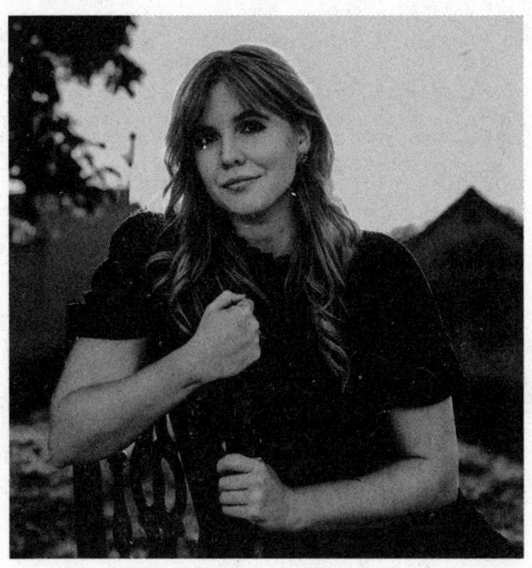

TEAGAN OLIVIA KING grew up in Michigan's wild Upper Peninsula but traded in the stormy shores of Lake Superior for the wind-beaten sandbars of Lake Huron. She holds a degree in Creative Writing from Northern Michigan University and is the author of several works of short horror fiction. She lives in an old farmhouse with her beloved, a rescue pup named Remus, a black cat named Chester, who may or may not harbor the soul of some long-dead deity, and probably some ghosts. She is the author of several works of adult horror and dark fantasy.

Turn the page to read the first chapter of

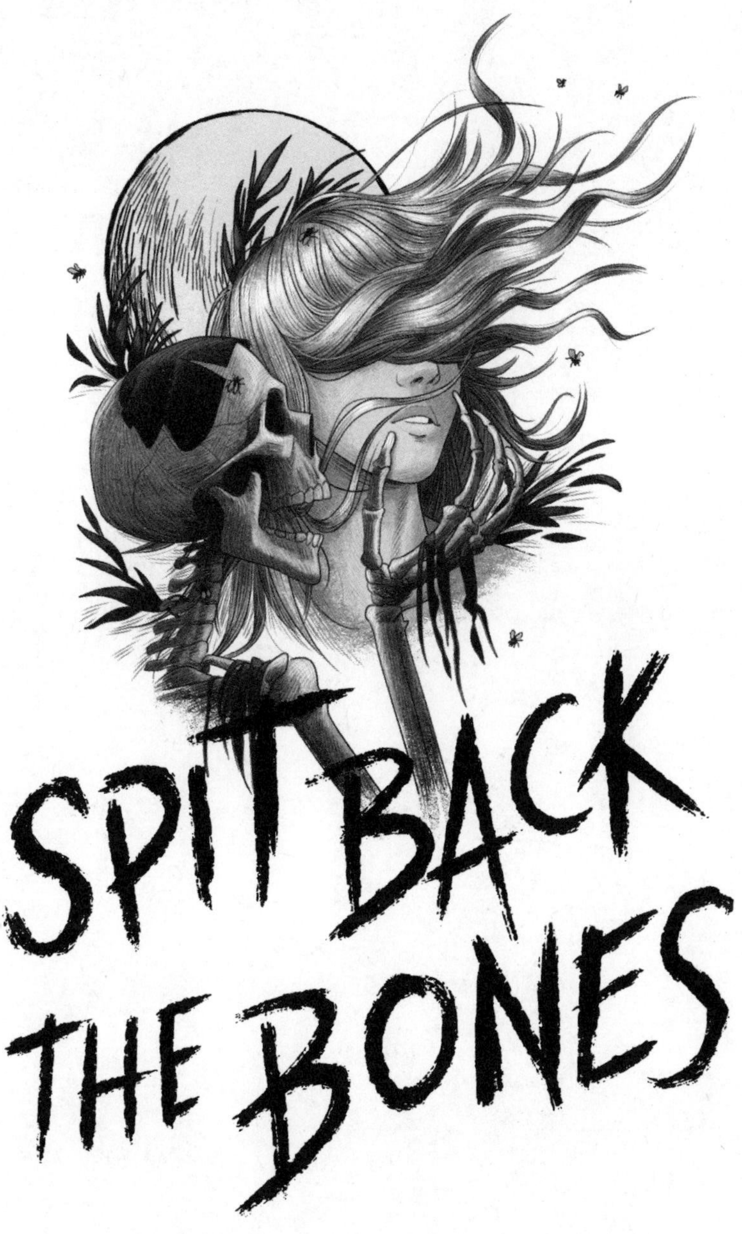

NOW AVAILABLE WHEREVER BOOKS ARE SOLD

1

THE LIAR

I wrap white knuckles around the worn leather of the old Ford's steering wheel and try to keep from looking out the window. Farther down the road, where the black tarmac chews itself into gravel, a cargo train bites along the rickety tracks, and red siren lights blare at me to stop. But I don't want to. The last thing I need is time to pause, to think, to have an opportunity to turn back, to glance over my shoulder and see the damned thing.

The bog.

The clock on the dashboard blinks 2:45 p.m. I'm late and the train isn't helping. Tires crunch when I bring the truck to a halt, and the bell rings in my ears. My neck throbs as invisible hands wrap around my throat, trying to pull my eyes toward the acidic water, but I can't. Not now. I still need time.

Dammit, you've had enough time, Mila, a voice whispers.

My voice—I'd know if it weren't. Would recognize dead prattles from the bog. I've spent most of my measly twenty years picking out the difference, separating my own voice from those of the mingling dead and fitting them into neat, straight lines. So, on occasion, when the two do cross, when they get mixed up in my brain and I can't decipher reality from those murky, gray depths, at least I have a page of scribbles to refer to. To pull me up and out of the water.

Metaphorically speaking.

Metal, I remind myself. The taste of death in my mouth is metal.

The one thing separating my words from those of the dead. My therapist thinks it has something to do with blood—the taste of metal. Blood from the body. She doesn't listen when I tell her the body was drained.

My fingers grip the wheel tighter, and I grind my teeth together. Fear catches up to me, turning sour in my stomach. The train takes for-fucking-ever and I sit here, like a goddamn idiot. No one should be afraid of something that isn't even *alive*. Not really. Sure, the voices talk, but they're dead. Just a bunch of bodies rotting in the tar-black water, bloodless, floating somewhere in the liminal spaces.

I take a steadying breath and look up at the clattering cars blurring past—rusty red and brown, stained by a hundred years of iron-ore dust. Even my own lungs are probably tainted with the stuff. Maybe that's what will kill me dead.

Or it will be the guilt.

It pulls on the left side of my neck again, the tendon greedily pressing against my skin, like a finger through nylon.

Don't look, I tell myself. *You can't look.*

But I don't have to face it to recall the bog's appearance from memory. It has been burned into my brain for the last year. Every inch of it. There are hundreds of bogs across Michigan's Upper Peninsula, but this one is different.

Angrier.

Deadfall pines sticking up like exposed spines. Stagnant water like stomach acid sparkling in the midday sun. Water snakes licking through the gray-green algae choking the shores and creeping through the reeds. Clumps of cattails and dry rushes luring you with the promise of sturdy ground, a foothold, only to give way beneath your weight when the bog opens gaping jaws to swallow you whole.

My body hums. No, I don't need to look to remember. To know the truth of what lies beneath that glittering surface.

All those bodies.

It isn't needed when I can still *feel* it. My skin swims and the lights on the track stop whirling. The gate lifts and I press the gas—gravel flying when the truck screeches over the tracks.

It's easy—*too* easy—remembering the way the body felt beneath my skin. The cold, the squelching wet, the dead and murky gaze despite the voice being very much alive.

He had no eyes.

I shove away the words—try to, anyway—but my mind has been playing them on repeat ever since last summer, and I haven't been able to stop. Four words, over and over and over, and I think they'll make me insane.

Maybe they already have. I reach over and flick the blue hair tie on my wrist. Once, twice. My skin stings.

He had no eyes.

Three, four, five.

I turn the truck onto another gravel road, this one marked by a simple black-iron sign: Thomas Road.

Fuck me, I think. *Fuck me.*

I've chosen the worst way home without even realizing it. Just a gut reaction. My body remembering how much I used to love this drive.

Before.

The white house appears first, a sign skewered into the perfectly manicured grass. The red and black letters are peeling away, but I've driven by them enough times to know what it says by heart.

Go to church, or the devil will get you.

No one knows who put it in Reverend Byron's yard all those years ago, but he has never bothered to take it down. His truck is missing from the driveway—he's probably out healing the town's sinners—but the space isn't empty. Simon, his oldest son, lies beneath the underside of a beaten-up, baby-blue Ford, brown leather boots sticking out. I slow my truck and roll down my window.

"Hey, asshole!" I holler over the sound of clinking wind chimes.

There is a crash of forehead against metal before he swings out from beneath the truck and starts spitting words that would curdle the stomachs of Credence Hollow's most devout. His eyes narrow in on me, and another string of expletives leaves his mouth.

"Hello to you too." I lean over the bench seat. Hot air billows in through the open window.

He is as tall, thick, and grotesque as I remember him. All muscle and reaching hands, lingering and hungry eyes. I do fast math in my head. At twenty-one, he is the typical all-American boy who has never had to fess up to anything in his whole life. Never had to take the blame or the responsibility.

The poster child for everything wrong in this world.

We love to see it, Simon Byron, you absolute shithead.

He reaches his fingers up to the crown of his head and they come away sticky with blood.

"Didn't know you were coming back to town, frog-face."

I roll my eyes. *Seriously?* The best thing he can come up with is the stupid nickname he gave me in grade school?

I shove aside thoughts of the bog and wiggle my eyebrows. "Surprise, surprise, motherfucker!" Then I flip him the bird and peel out of there.

I know not to stick around too long after Simon has had some blood spilled. The last time it happened was when his brother, Roe, punched him in the nose after Simon called me a word I will not be repeating, thank you very much. I had never seen anything like it—the look that came over Simon's face once he realized he was bleeding. Shadows gathered beneath his eyes, like ink-blotting paper, and I thought for sure Roe would be dead by morning.

I swear, Simon Byron is going to kill someone one day.

Gravel and dust sprays out behind my ripping tires. The trees turn into nothing short of tangled limbs, creating a dark canopy over the road. I crank the music louder, letting the iron rhythm steel my nerves. It is loud and screeching and fury-filled, and I settle into it. Because maybe those things are exactly what I have become. So very angry.

Maybe that's what happens to a girl who raises a body from the bog.

Maybe that's what happens when she's so scared, she puts the body back.

Three shrill beeps replace the rock and roll coming from the radio, and a staticky voice spills from the speakers.

"This is a special news bulletin. Police in Leo County today are still searching for local missing person, Owen Shelby, last seen the evening of June fifteenth by friends in a wooded area just outside Credence Hollow."

A sharp sliver of ice inches its way between my ribs.

"Sheriff Lowell is asking that if you have any information concerning this case to please call the offices…"

A phone number follows, but I'm not paying attention. Not to the voice coming from the radio, not on the way sweat is slicking my navel, the creases of my palms. No, I'm focused on my heart heaving in my chest. I count the quickening beats and pray I don't have a heart attack at the ripe old age of twenty and crash my dead grandmother's trusty, well-loved pickup truck.

I switch the radio off. Abandoned in my own wretchedness, I only stop when I spot the trailer. It is parked a way off the road, surrounded by year-old poplar growths, messy logging, and ruts in the mud. If I didn't know better, I would think it was abandoned.

But I do know better.

The curl of black smoke gives it away. It coils from behind the gray-brown aluminum, licking up against the clear blue sky. It doesn't take long for the scent to carry through the AC unit of the old truck—burning pine logs, ash, the sweet tang of weed. It is a welcoming smell, a comforting one, and for a moment, I let myself believe coming home for a few days won't be so bad. Maybe it can be like all the years before I left last summer.

But it's a lie. Everything spilling from between my lips these days seems to be. Lie after lie after lie. And deep down, it's stupid, *so stupid*. Nothing can be like what it was before.

Before the body.

Before I touched it and its eye sockets snapped open.

Before I killed it and sent it back to the bog.

The scent of smoke sours, and I press on the gas. I don't want to see him anyway—the boy in the trailer. Because the last time I saw Roe Byron, he was helping me put that body back in the bog. My nerves twitch and sharpen with the memory: the cool-like-butter surface of the still-ripe skin, the blackened lips, the cavernous hollows in its skull. And the voice. God, I remember the voices more than anything else.

He had no eyes.

They were all saying those words.

A chorus of the dead.

The voices are not strangers. I've been hearing them since I was a little girl with braids and a smile too big for this world. Since the day I almost drowned in the bog and Grandma Ruby fished me out. She wove strands of my hair together between her leathery fingers and said:

"It's a gift, Mila-May. One that takes a near-death experience to gain. The swamp is in us, and we are in the swamp. We must use our talents to help the poor souls trapped there. To give them peace."

I turned around, one hand on the floral cotton of her dress, angling my eyes to peer into hers. There was so much torment in the shadows above her sunken cheeks, pain masking the truth. The truth of what, I didn't know—still don't—but I think she understood what was coming.

She realized our family was cursed.

My older brother Jed admitted it first—the family curse. Saying the words, over and over, like the call of a loon on a midsummer night.

I'm a curse, Mila. There's something stuck inside me. Something I can't just pull out. And I'm scared one day it's gonna hurt somebody.

I'm a curse.

And I think, maybe I am too. Perhaps I can't help people. I can only do the opposite. Can only hurt them. Especially the ones I love. Isn't that why I'm coming home? To make up for all the hurt I have caused? To atone for running away when it all got too heavy, when I stared into the face of death and didn't like my reflection?

My sister's message beats like a tattoo in the back of my mind. *I'm leaving for college at the end of July. Would be nice to see you before I leave. Unless you're too busy…*

Something cold and miserable spreads across my chest, and a laugh bubbles in the back of my throat like bile. Right. *Too busy*. Too busy living a few towns over. Too busy working a dead-end job at a gas station, just to scrape enough money together to pay rent to a man who smells like cheap cigarettes and cat piss. Too busy pretending the past doesn't exist.

So now, here I am, forcing myself home to make amends.

Or, at least, to try.

Not that this is home. Nowhere feels like home anymore.

My insides churn like tar in the hot sun, and I crank up the AC. The cold blasts me in the face, waking me up. The trees stretch taller the farther I drive down the old dirt road. Outside grows chilly with air from the swamp. I smell it—the muddy tang, the spicy-sweet of cedar and black earth. When I roll my window down further, the breeze sweeps in and brushes yellow curls off my slick skin.

It's hot, even for June. A sort of thick, chewy atmosphere settling around the bones and warning of coming rain. I swallow and the sides of my throat turn to glass.

Jed disappeared on a day like this.

The wet heat hung in the air, like cobwebs threatening to choke me, while I watched him walk deeper into the cedars and never come out. He told me he was just going for a walk, but when he didn't return for Grandma Ruby's homemade ice cream and the chocolate birthday cake she promised, I knew he wasn't coming back. We searched the swamp for the next three days, my hands wrapped tightly around the wire handle of a Coleman lantern until my palms blistered. But there was no sign of him.

I caught our grandmother swirling her hands in the water on the last night, begging the bog to tell her where Jed was, but it gave nothing up, not even a voice. And she screamed things at it. Things that made no sense.

When I asked her what she had been doing down at the bank, she lied, told me she needed peace and quiet to figure out her thoughts.

Lying must be an inherited trait in this family.

When I was little and my mom would bring us to church, people used to whisper, saying my grandmother was a witch. Even the former Reverend Byron gossiped about her, bent over his pulpit like a frostbitten fern. He wished she would come to church and save her soul. And when I would tell Grandma Ruby this and wonder at why she didn't just come with us, she would scoop my sun-kissed hair up into her calloused palms and whisper:

"The bog is my church, Mila-May, the water my god."

And it was enough for her.

But it isn't for me. The bog took Grandma Ruby three weeks after Jed went missing, and I've despised it ever since. Hated the way it can crawl into my brain and whisper things to me. The way it takes and takes and only gives death.

Sometimes, I block them out—the voices—if I catch them quick enough. My therapist reminds me they aren't real and can't hurt me, but I think she says it more for her own benefit than for mine. To help her feel like maybe, just maybe, the world can fit into the explainable, scientific bubble she wants it to.

But they're real. I *feel* their pain.

A mailbox comes into view on the side of the road. If not for the rust and lichen clinging to the metal, it might have once been white. There is a single word scratched along it in peeling blue paint: *Thomas*. I take a deep breath, hold it for a few seconds, just like my therapist taught me, and remind myself of all the things I can control.

Literally nothing.

Literally, absolutely fucking nothing.

I turn into the driveway, pine cones crunching beneath my tires. The family cabin winks through the branches: dark-stained logs, bubbled-glass windows, the screen door with butter-yellow curtains swinging in the breeze, an ancient grapevine spinning serpentine from the porch rafters.

I should feel happy to see the house. It's where I grew up, where all my core memories took place. But it just sits there, staring at me with its dark-window eyes and whispers, *You don't belong here, Mila-May. You don't belong anywhere.*

Two bikes—one blue and one a rusted orange—lean against the uneven wooden stairs leading up to the door. Agatha, my sister, must be home; her girlfriend, Camille, with her. I let my nerves settle. Agatha will forgive me. She is the only person who hasn't totally written me off as a lost cause. But the truth is, she might know about the voices, but I never told her about the body.

The memory of that voice whispers in my ear.

He had no eyes.

I park my truck and try to wash away the image of the corpse I pulled from the bog. It wasn't just his eyes that were missing—it was his whole goddamn chest. I picture the open gash, the way the blood had coagulated black around its ripped flesh, turning to tar in the water. My palms dewy with sweat, and I wipe them on the worn denim of my shorts.

Roe trembled beside me in that moment, begging me to notify the cops, to tell anyone. *Please, we have to tell someone.* But I refused. I was scared of whatever my touch had done to reanimate the thing. Scared of who might have put that body in the bog and what the cops would do if they found them.

Terrified my brother was the one with blood on his hands. Worried his curse had made him a killer.

I swallow my guilt, the taste of it metallic on my tongue. Grandma Ruby used to say we were given the gift to help people, to bestow upon them peace and allow them to move on. That the gift wasn't meant for *us*. But then she died, and so I told myself her words were just lies too.

My fingernails sink into the worn fabric of the bench seat while I look at the cabin through blurry eyes. My coworker at the gas station, Denise, told me it was stupid coming here. That I didn't owe anyone shit. Her voice rings in my ears.

You don't have to go, honey. You know that, right? You have nothing to prove.

But she's wrong. I have everything to prove. I have to show my mind the lies I tell myself are true. That… The thought crumbles in my throat. Jed is alive, and he's not a murderer. He is not the one putting bodies in the bog, only for me to find and put them right back.

I lean my head on the steering wheel, staring at my palms. My vision swims and bleeds with salt water.

Everything is a lie here in the bog. We bury our secrets in the mud and the water, keeping them submerged until we can go down to join the rest of the dead things.

People used to call my grandmother a witch. But me?

Well, they just call me a liar.